His Soul to Keep

by

M. Flagg

The Champion Chronicles, Book 3

This is a work of fiction. Names, characters, places, and incidents are either the product of the author's imagination or are used fictitiously, and any resemblance to actual persons living or dead, business establishments, events, or locales, is entirely coincidental.

His Soul to Keep

COPYRIGHT © 2023 by M. Flagg

Cover Art by *Rae Monet, Inc.*

The Wild Rose Press, Inc.
PO Box 708
Adams Basin, NY 14410-0708
Visit us at www.thewildrosepress.com

Publishing History
First Edition, 2024
Trade Paperback ISBN 978-1-5092-5309-8
Digital ISBN 978-1-5092-5310-4
Previously Published - 2011 The Wild Rose Press

The Champion Chronicles, Book 3
Published in the United States of America

Michael's eyes flew open... The den spun wild as he tried to grip the carpet. It felt as if his lungs didn't work, and his nostrils flared as he tried to take in air. Crazy pressure built in his chest. Every muscle in his body jerked or cramped. Twisting around and clawing at the couch cushion, his skin crawled as if he were covered in spiders. He smelled dug-up earth and tasted terror before it slithered down his throat. Both feet felt numb as if nothing were beneath them when he finally stood. With his hands bracing his knees, his eyes went wide sensing something impossible. Call out to her! Save her! Save who, he thought before his legs buckled, landing on the carpet unable to move.

I am free... The new vessel staggered upright to see the world through ancient eyes...and it hungered... Torturous months of craving, thirst to fill eternity. Childlike hands, eerily small and smooth, placed a silver blade inside and closed the chest. They reached up high to place its former tomb atop a brick wall. Vengeance begins now...

Dark magic surged through Jillian's body as the demon bound itself to her... Even in midnight's darkness, vivid colors shimmered to stun them both. The beast-within leered as the innocent host vessel stared in awe. She would soon know all it knew—fully aware of 317 years of existence bound in the soul of a commanding vampire.

Dedication

This book is dedicated to those of us who stare at the crossroads in life, take one path instead of the other, and still manage to find our way back home.

Chapter 1

Son of my bloodline, more than a man, less than an angel...

Last night, Michael Malone heard these exact words spoken through the mystical healer. However, guilt far surpassed penitence while recalling all he'd done as a vampire for over 300 years.

Last night, there had been hours of merciless inquisition by the Georgian Sovereign Council. He absolutely admitted to profound remorse for two centuries of deadly acts committed without a conscience—before the angel Helena taught him how to dominate the beast-within and reclaim his moral soul. That happened over a century ago.

Last night, the weight of an undead existence brought him to his knees. The mystical healer's words were Helena's: *"Voice your most private desire."* Of course, he flatly refused. There had to be further consequences for all he had done as a powerful, arrogant vampire. Over a hundred years of protecting innocents could never make up for the death and destruction he had once caused as a creature of the night. Now he understood the meaning of love, which deepened his resolve to meet the finality of death.

Last night, he was prepared to forfeit this unprecedented mystically enhanced existence as a

Champion in the fight against evil. Then, instead of burning for eternity in Hell, Michael Malone was granted life.

But that was last night... This is much more than the start of a new day. I am truly, once again alive. That was his only thought as morning dawned. He needed to drink and eat. He needed to sleep. He needed to breathe.

Not to disturb the woman he would always love, he remained inhumanly still in Alana's embrace. Question after question kept his mind spinning out of control like a runaway rocket. *Son of my bloodline–I understand that part. But what does it mean to be more than a man, less than an angel? 317 years of undeath and I'm suddenly mortal again... Why?*

Afraid to move, his body cleaved to hers. Alana's palm stayed pressed against his bare chest. *His* Guardian's possessive embrace felt like Heaven, not like the Hell he deserved.

Last night. It had torn him apart. Sitting in front of the Georgian Council answering question after question about the volumes of death he had been ordered to write. Twenty volumes of the drink and drain, of hideous acts as a vampire without a soul. He deserved a silver blade to the neck, not deliverance.

He was prepared for an eternity in Hell. Instead, his heart began to beat. "Breathe in, breathe out... you need to do that now," the mystical healer had said. After the natural rhythms of life took hold, he had walked with her through the silent streets of Portofino to face Alana and Lukas, his human son after ten months of seclusion.

Very nervous and still unsure of it all, his lean, six-foot-three-inch frame had been unsteady. The drumming of a healthy heart, the need to breathe was a long forgotten, mere human necessity. Bewildered he had said, "Is this my road to redemption? The evil I battled in the passageway, being tortured by poison for eight days, destroying my sire... I simply did what had to be done." *For a child who shouldn't exist,* he thought, *because what was done to my son still fills me with rage.*

Instantly, the mystical healer had read him, and shaking her head slowly, gripped his arm tighter. "That is all behind you now. I know your soul. There is indeed a reason why you've been granted back an unfinished life. Fulfill your destiny, Champion."

"And what is my destiny to fulfill?"

Instead of an answer, she gave a tranquil smile before they entered the red brick building off the piazza. Stopping on the second floor, she simply said, "Patience, young man," and when she closed the apartment door, he studied the narrow staircase to Alana's home—his home.

Young man, he had thought full of misgivings. *I've walked this earth as a vampire since 1690.* He took the stairs completely lost. But upon seeing Lukas, a father's pride filled his soul. And when he took Alana in his arms, love filled his now beating heart.

No words... No explanations offered for what he himself didn't understand. *All I needed at that moment was the feel of my soulmate against me. And for the first time in centuries, I fell asleep as a mortal man in the fierce embrace of the unique woman I'll always love.* Last night, fear had paralyzed him at the foot of San Giorgio's altar. But this morning, the sensation of warm blood coursing through his veins held absolute terror.

****

Alana couldn't pull her hand away from the center of Michael's warm chest. Every incredible beat of his heart, every incredible rise and fall of his broad shoulders astounded her. *There's no denying how deeply I've loved him since the first time he spoke to me... when I was seventeen—and totally taken with a singular creature of the night.* No Guardian had ever been protected by a vampire. No vampire in recorded Georgian history had ever fought the beast-within to take back his own moral conscience, either. Only Michael.

Bright Amalfi sun teased her eyes open as it danced across the majestic sleigh bed. Safe and secure, the man she loved still tight in her arms. Each miraculous, even breath of sleep he took kept a euphoric grin on her face. His head of wavy brown hair molded to her breast. One strong cheekbone, a partial view of his intense profile... She feasted on every handsome feature she could see.

He's home. He's with me. Last May, I held his beaten body. I watched the effects of poison slither through his veins. And I watched his struggle to survive. Now, his skin is warm and his chest rises and falls. How unbelievable is this?

Brushing back his hair, she needed to glimpse more of her soulmate. When Michael walked into the bedroom last night, her stomach fluttered. Her soul quivered to the core. Devoted kisses had filled her heart. In a tentative tone he had whispered, "I don't understand any of this," and she had searched his dark espresso eyes, simply replying, "Neither do I."

4

Still full of questions, she felt certain he'd answer each one today. Her palm absorbed every mystifying beat of his heart. *How is he a living, breathing man again? Vampires don't change...Every Guardian of Souls knows that's a fact. Lesson 101...*

They had fought demons side by side. They had walked away from each other as well. She recalled the long lists created during ten years of loving him. Each one began with "but Michael can't ever..." *This morning, each breath he takes says otherwise.*

The feel of him against her called her body to life, and softly she sighed, "Forever and always." Those words had been her solemn vow to her immortal beloved last May. She didn't want to ever be apart from him again.

His thick lashes fluttered. She held her breath when his warm fingers threaded hers. He stirred. He sighed. The shift of his broad shoulders stoked her desire. With a moan, his hips settled in the bend of her body. Heat raced through her, head to toe like unfettered energy. He reached back, rested his wide hand upon her outer thigh. Instantly, her leg hooked his waist. *We'll make love. We'll talk. He'll explain.*

"Michael, my love," she whispered.

"Ah, my Guardian, if you hold me any tighter, you'll leave a bruise," he replied.

The throaty beginnings of a laugh began when he turned in her arms. Their eyes met, and another flash of heat swelled when he pinned her to the bed's soft, champagne-colored sheets. The urgency of his kisses, the weight of his toned body immediately stopped her question, and when his hand cupped her left breast, she gasped. She would draw the length of him deep inside to consummate their timeless love as never before.

His lips left hers with the whisper, "Your beauty could lure a man's mind into many sensual fantasies. I want to stay like this forever. I've missed you, darlin'."

That last word he reserved for her alone. Like thick sweet syrup it rolled off his tongue, and the most sensitive part of her throbbed in anticipation. After a jagged sigh, she moaned. For the first time, his heart would thunder like hers, and together, they'd enter that mysterious place where love is the bond and passion the instrument.

But Michael pulled away, slid to her side.

Her eyes eased open. Aware of his arousal, aware of hers, she kissed his chest and searched his pensive gaze. "Will you tell me how this happened? I want to hear every detail. Was it painful, I mean, to breathe again? Did it happen before or after the Council meeting? We were all so worried when Dad came back without you. Oh, I'll bet Lukas must have been thrilled with the sound of your heartbeat. He's missed you so much." He didn't answer her as his expression turned unreadable. And staring at the ceiling, those dark, dreamy eyes of his became distant.

"My son has grown four inches, and he needs a haircut."

After a quick kiss to her cheek, he left their bed. She watched his familiar, slow stride into the master bedroom's ensuite and then sank into the soft mattress, completely baffled.

****

Michael closed the bathroom door and twisted the lock. For the first time in his very long existence on this earth, he felt afraid to move, afraid to think. Leaning against the cool tiles on the wall, he took slow breaths. The continual throb in his loins was an entirely forgotten experience. An erection only a matter of will and want, the seed cold, dead. *Not any more...*

Tense minutes passed before moving to the white pedestal sink. Hesitant at first, his eyes finally locked on a clear reflection in the mirror. *How did this happen? More importantly...Why?* Inherited features— a strong brow, high cheekbones and square chin, the straight line of his nose all had a healthy glow. His lips were pink, not washed of all color. Unsteady fingertips eased across his neck where two small scars, the only tangible proof of his turning, of his sire, remained. He recalled how Cyril's venomous fangs had sunk into his jugular on a December night in 1690. In his twenty-seventh year of life, a young Englishman ceased to exist. Pulling away from the terrifying memory, there was no reason to check any other part of his body. He knew he was unscarred, untouched by time.

"How is no longer an issue," he whispered. "The why is all that matters now."

Stepping into the narrow shower, he twisted a knob. Cold water from the brass spout above trickled down his face. As he sucked in a quick breath, his skin tingled from the chill.

****

Lukas Malone hadn't slept last night. Enhanced abilities allowed him to hear his father's every breath in the bedroom next to his. Full of questions, one in particular had him anxious and edgy. And just before sunrise, while his father still slept in the next room, he wondered how it happened and *why* his father had a heartbeat. None of this made sense. As a vampire, his father was almost indestructible. *Not as a man... Demons exist in this world. No mortal can win against them.* To him, this was the only fact that mattered. Because if his father was truly mortal now, his father could die. In total darkness, he had pulled on a pair of jeans and a clean T-shirt before stepping silently into the bathroom off the hall.

At the black porcelain sink, Lukas stared into the mirror. They didn't look like father and son. Nope. Not at all. He had curly hair the color of sunlit sand and deep-blue eyes. A few months shy of sixteen, his features still remained what Alana called 'soft and sweet', not angular and strong like his dad's. And even though he'd grown some, he sensed he'd never reach his father's height or physical stature. As he brushed his teeth, more questions needled him.

Definitely—Lukas had a long list. They had only been together for one incredible week last May before his father was taken away to fulfill the requirements set forth by some kind of Document of Atonement. It hadn't been enough time for him. Raised by Helena, handed over to the sorcerers in the Second Realm, then brainwashed into trying to destroy his unnatural parent. But his dad had rescued him. Yeah, and at the age of thirteen all I wanted to do was stake him, he thought. One short year of not remembering the horrors of the Second Realm followed, until the night he turned fifteen. Then he recalled it all... It had been enough to make him puke. He spit out toothpaste and wiped his mouth with a soft towel as his mind raced.

The hall was dark, and he moved without sound to the master bedroom door. He stood as still as a statue listening through the wood to their soft breaths of deep sleep before he crept through the living room and out the front door.

Sitting on the top step, Lukas heard no movement downstairs—in a place where his father had healed ten months ago. The second-floor apartment was no longer empty, perhaps now more humming with life than ever before. And as day dawned, the woman he called "Gram" cracked the first egg into a ceramic bowl. He wanted to jump the stairs and run into her loving arms.

Instead, he didn't move. Swallowing hunger, not his worry, he mumbled, "Alive, dead, undead, immortal, and now alive again… friggin' complicated, Dad. Is it going to last? Will you grow old and die like any other man? Or will you forget to look both ways and cross some stupid street? Wow… this is unbelievable. I'll bet *she's* in shock and full of questions, too." For the first time in ten months, he felt so confused that he didn't think of Alana as "Mom." And she always smiled when he called her that.

Then he heard Alana's first whisper, and he fine-tuned his mystical ability to hear from a distance. His back stiffened when his father answered her. An uncomfortable ping started in his chest and sank like a rock to the bottom of his belly. As if he were in the room with them, he caught the entire hushed conversation. "Why would I be thrilled? Just say why you're alive. What if dark seers sense the change in you? What if something evil comes after me again? What if I can't fight it alone?" The intense desire to rage flashed through his mind. Fear and frustration did as well. Maybe he could get them to just send him back to school in England where he could talk this out with his friends. Or he could just run away… give his father and Alana some time to sort this out alone. He shook his head, knowing neither was an answer. He wanted his father to talk to him, explain what happened last night.

His stomach rumbled long and loud as rich aromas of a homemade breakfast wafted up the narrow stairwell. He suddenly didn't want to be found by his father until the question "why are you human again" was answered. "I'll bet someone downstairs knows the reason," he mumbled.

Silent footsteps met each stair. He entered the second-floor apartment and stood in the small living room. The simple surroundings brought to mind his hope for a secure life with his immortal father—that was ten months ago. He shook his head to clear it, and Gram's bright smile snapped him back to reality. "Morning, Gram," he mumbled.

She grabbed his chin and kissed his cheek, but he looked away. "Is something wrong?" She pushed some straggly blond curls off his forehead with a maternal touch that said unconditional love. Laura Bookman always looked elegant and statuesque, he thought, even in warn jeans and a loose blouse like today, always dressed comfortable and functional. With her auburn hair clipped high enough to create the illusion of a ponytail, he had never noticed the strands of gray in her hair. Until this morning. Undeniable warmth settled in her green eyes. Taking his hand, she led him to a chair in the cozy dining room. "Lukas Malone, you have not answered me," she softly chided.

"Is Gramps up?" He already knew the answer but asking was the polite thing to do. "What about Auntie Celia and Uncle T? Is the baby awake?" He knew those answers as well. They weren't exactly his family. Except for his father, he didn't have any. They were Alana's... her adopted Mom and Dad. Celia was her adopted sister. As for Uncle T, well, Thorn had been his father's trusted friend for years. They had all taken care of him these last ten months, and yeah, he thought, I've made them my family, too.

Gram's eyes narrowed in a serious squint. "Something is definitely amiss with my grandson, I surmise. Must we have a family meeting so early on a Saturday morn?"

"Yeah, I really think so," he replied, shifting foot-to-foot.

She gave an austere nod and walked into the bedroom that used to be his. Last night's endless wait for his father to come home had taken a toll on everyone. Lukas was sure of it when he heard her tell Grandpa he was urgently needed. Mystical hearing didn't allow for too many secrets, and with full concentration, he could almost sense a person's movements as they spoke.

Another spasm wormed through Lukas's gut, made him swallow hard. For ten months, life with the Bookmans at the Georgian Estate in Hampton Hill, England had been the epitome of happy-normal. Regular high-school classes at the Georgian Institute were fun, but challenging, and none of his new friends considered his unique abilities odd. Guardians of Souls, newbies and seasoned ones, accepted the human son of a mystically enhanced vampire without weird looks or strange whispers. Normal routines, like homework and chores, kept his mind off his father's forced absence. And while visiting Alana in Portofino every weekend, working the bookshop downstairs made him feel needed.

For a brief second, he couldn't wait to tell his father everything he had learned. How 'Gramps' and 'Gram' fit Miles and Laura Bookman. Perfectly. Months ago, 'Auntie' slipped out really easy for their daughter Celia and calling the empathic Thorn 'Uncle T' had made the huge man get all teary-eyed and confess, "I'm deeply honored, kid."

Celia's hug from behind pulled him out of those happy thoughts, and loudly, she smooched his cheek, which made him blush. Thorn didn't look at him, but sat next to Celia, and when Miles took a seat at the head of the table, Lukas thought he looked really tired.

Then he met Thorn's gentle eyes. "Did you tell anyone, Uncle T?"

The empath shook his head, saying in a soft baritone, "That pleasure belongs to you, kid."

Miles, the first person to gain Lukas's trust last May, studied him like a bug under a microscope. "What pleasure? Your father *did* come back last night, am I correct? I assumed Mother Anne wouldn't leave the church without him, Lukas. If anything had gone wrong I'd have been informed, and last night's peaceful sleep would never have been possible," he added with a typical dry expression on his face.

"Dad has a heartbeat," he stated in an indifferent tone.

Miles's back straightened. If one could see silence, they'd be in a total blackout. "I'm sorry… would …could you, please, say again?" His flowing British way of speaking had faltered, but Lukas caught the glance between Celia and Thorn.

"Dad has a heartbeat. I heard it. I felt it. So why is he human?"

As if he had said nothing unusual, Laura placed a plate of sausage biscuits and scrambled eggs on the table without missing a beat. But when Miles leaned forward, she moved behind her husband, and gripped his shoulders. Letting out a slow, even, "Good Lord," Miles seemed stunned.

Lukas imagined at least a thousand concise questions running through Gramps' brilliant mind. "You have to have an answer. You're like the best researcher for the Georgians, a-a Sovereign Council member even. I mean, explaining paranormal things has been your job, like forever."

"Thirty years," Laura said with a proud grin.

"So... why the heartbeat," he asked, staring down at the empty plate.

"Thorn," Miles stated in a sharp tone, rarely heard. "Did you sense this? Did you *not* think it important enough to wake me and *share* this information?" Laura placed a mug of coffee in Miles's hand, which he didn't seem to notice. Still glaring at Thorn, he added, "And you, young man, why *aren't* you thrilled to high heaven?"

An uncomfortable twelve seconds passed before Thorn said, "Monsignor Scarlatti already knows. He shares our gift of sight." The empath's huge arm came around Celia's thin shoulders. "Mother Anne left with the others for Villa Catherine already. I'm sure the change in him has to be documented by her before any formal conclave is called."

Lukas cringed at Miles's brusque nod. "Of *course*, there must be full documentation—of yet *another* unprecedented event! Good Lord!" He brought the coffee cup to his lips.

"I told Thorn not to wake you, Dad," Celia quickly chimed in. "You're on the edge of exhaustion. Michael's been your main focus since his first journal arrived over nine months ago. Okay, so you took two days off and returned to Hampton Hill in February when I had the baby. Then, it was right back to Portofino…to discuss, debate and qualify *twenty* volumes of a-a confession with other Council members!" Pure annoyance appeared on Miles's face, and Thorn tried hard to shush her. "Nope. This has to be said out loud—even though *you* think I should calm down! Chalk it up to postnatal hormones, sweetie, but it's true. And Lukas can handle it because we're his family." Her psychic abilities were unparalleled and because of what happened last May, he knew it firsthand. Then her beautiful green eyes widened. "It doesn't take a psychic to know you're stressed, Dad. We all see it. And Mom's been serving you decaf because she's worried, too."

Lukas scrunched his face staring at the sweet, light-brown liquid in his cup, muttering, "A no-buzz yuck for sure, Gram."

Celia gave a stubborn nod. "There. I've said it. Michael's always been unique. Well, so now, he's just-just… unique-er!"

With a smug smirk, Lukas leaned back. "It's more unique, right Gramps?"

Ready to go ballistic again, she huffed and shook a finger at him, but Thorn caught her hand. "Celia's right, Miles, she's a little over-the-top, but she's right."

After a gracious tilt of her head, Laura stated, "And

I agree. May through March, Michael has dominated all your waking thoughts, dear, even some nightmares."

"I won't argue the truth," Miles mumbled, quickly pushed the cup away, studying him again before saying in a usual bland tone, "I'll give you ten seconds to gather your thoughts before telling your grandfather what is really bothering you." Lukas looked away and the pause was a long one. "You know, the first time you called me Gramps my heart swelled with pride. And Gram suits my lovely wife as well. Come now, young man. Don't keep us waiting."

He rolled his eyes and played with a biscuit, quickly dropping it on the plate to shake his burning fingers. After blowing on it, he took a bite, chewed and swallowed, totally self-conscious of everyone's stares. "Last night he comes into my room. I didn't know what to believe when I heard his heartbeat. It's because he destroyed Cyril, his sire."

"Did your father say this?"

He picked at the eggs. "No, but because he's alive, I'll bet they make him go away again."

"Who do you mean by they and go away again, where?" a familiar voice questioned, how did I not hear Dad's footsteps, he thought, watching the long signature strides through the wide wooden arch. Oh boy, did his stomach clench this time.... Sitting close, his father wore ever-familiar black jeans and a black shirt with cuffs rolled to just below the elbow. Sniffing the biscuit on Lukas's plate added, "Now that's definitely a home-country aroma, Laura. My compliments," he added with a tinge of admiration. All eyes stayed on his father who draped an arm across the back of Lukas's chair. Many hearts beat faster around the table. "Push those curls away from your face and eat. I'd say it's time for a serious trim, little boy. Don't you agree—Gramps?"

Miles softly breathed out, "Good Lord."

"I won't disagree with you on that one, Researcher." His father's reply came with the hint of familiar grin.

Chapter 2

Michael took in every aspect of his growing son, the guarded look, his quickened heartbeat, but especially the sandy, straggly curls, which hid most of his sweet features. "Finish your breakfast," he said in a careful yet parental tone. He assumed Lukas had many questions, but they'd have to wait. Because he had many questions himself. And as much as he wanted to talk to the boy, he knew there were too many blanks he couldn't fill in.

His vampiric senses hadn't changed. Of that, he was certain. That his son had run down to talk to Miles instead of bursting in on him and Alana meant Lukas had grown close to the researcher and his family. A very good thing, he thought, because I really have no idea how long I'll be around now. *Life is unpredictable, fragile, and accidents happen...*

Laura handed him a cup of coffee, and instantly aware of the lifeless blend, he held up a hand. Looking only at Miles, he said, "I'm sure you'll need to speak with Mother Anne as soon as possible, Miles." The consummate observer's single nod came as expected.

"Dad wants a cup of real coffee, Mom," Celia whispered.

"Make it two cups of real coffee. I don't drink decaf." His gaze lit on Thorn and Celia, sitting close to one another. Her facial expression was an emotional cocktail. Although still petite with short, red hair like a pixie, she no longer looked bone-thin. "Wow, Celia B. Motherhood looks wonderful on you. Congratulations on the birth of your son. Where's the little one?"

Leaning back, Thorn crossed his thick arms scrutinizing him. "Sleeping in this morning… You ready to meet him?"

"Absolutely." He leaned into his son. "Finish your breakfast. I'll be right back."

Celia came around the table, and he stood to hold Alana's adopted sister in a tender embrace. Tears welled in her eyes. "I felt your first breath. Oh, Michael, how super wonderful is this? Ally must be—"

"You really look great. A son! You'll both be excellent parents, I'm sure."

She grinned with pride. "Go check him out. Thorn and I agree. He's beautiful."

He left her and crossed the small parlor alone, studying remembered nuances. Healing here. Loving Alana here. Seeing this living room first through the eyes of a seventeenth century Englishman whose life had been cut short by undeath. Then everything that happened here before he destroyed his sire to, once again, save his son. When Cyril flashed through his brain, so did every detail of that terrifying night in 1690 when he was turned into a vampire.

Thorn stood by his side. "You've come a long way, Champ."

They looked at each other, full of mutual respect. "Have I, now?" he whispered, following his loyal friend into the master bedroom.

****

The way Lukas's stomach cramped made him think

he'd puke. Plus, what he felt was all over the place. After the bedroom door closed, Lukas whispered, "Gramps, are you okay?"

"Remarkably fine if not a bit speechless... You must be thrilled beyond words, my daughter as well."

"She was real nervous last night." So was I, Lukas thought but didn't say.

"Give your father a bit of time to come to grips with this. Laura, I will have to stay in Portofino a while longer."

"No doubt," she replied. "I had better prepare a pot of 'real' coffee."

"I'll, uh, help with the plates, Gram," he offered.

"No. Stay and talk with your grandfather."

But Gramps looked deep in thought. "You're already cataloging everything about my dad, right? I-I mean, the human things."

"I won't lie to you, Lukas. This outcome is... most unexpected. Last night, I shook the chilly hand of a three-hundred-year-old being classified "Beyond Dead." That alone is remarkable, but to regain one's human life is mythically astounding. Mother Anne's description of this event will be carefully studied." Soon the aroma of strong coffee permeated the room, and when Gram came to the table, he added, "How much longer can you stay, honey?"

"One more day... I must be in London on Monday. Too many projects at critical stages await my attention." She placed Gramps' trusted laptop on the table. Handing Lukas the power cord, he plugged it in. "Why the sullen expression, Lu?"

"Gram, please work from here," he whispered, already seeing his world ripped apart like a piece of tissue paper.

"I'm needed in London. Besides," she added as she held his chin, "you'll be so involved with your father you won't even miss my sneaky kisses and hugs. But I will miss those deep dimpled smiles."

Gramps cleared his throat. "I'll speak with Monsignor Scarlatti, Laura, perhaps this can be done at the Georgian estate."

Her high ponytail waggled as her head shook. "You're a member of the Council. As Researcher for the European Continent, this falls under your jurisdiction. You must stay where the event occurs. Besides, the estate is full of people like Celia and Thorn who'll give me a play-by-play without even blinking an eye. And as for you, young man," she said with another comforting hug, "no matter how many kilometers separate us, you always have my love. Now you must excuse me. Alana most likely needs some company."

Her affectionate words, the quick pecks on his cheek were what he needed. What he craved. Plus, he liked them. With her gone and Gramps so preoccupied, happy-normal is dissolving altogether—for sure, he thought.

After she left, Miles touched his arm. "Shall we have a talk?"

"I don't feel like talking."

"Come now, tell me why?"

"Because it's not fair."

"Life is never predictable."

"Yeah. Tell me about it," he mumbled.

"Sit down and finish your breakfast."

"I'm not hungry. I... I've got things to do downstairs." He took the barely touched plate into the kitchen.

"Kayla can open the bookshop alone today."

"No. Mornings are mine. Dad can find me if he wants to." He left the apartment without another word. Instead of jumping the stairs to the ground floor as he normally did, he took them deliberate and slow. Ten months of good and now weird again... *What about his mystical strength? Am I stronger than he is? Will he even survive a vampire attack or heal instantly? Could he just die overnight? What if he wakes up tomorrow and his heartbeat is gone?* Then he'd never have answers to stuff in his head that hounded him night and day. "This fucking changes everything," he mumbled as he entered the shop through the hall door. And in Alana's office, his mind went to places not visited in ten months. Instead of happy, a different reality loomed. Mistrust came easy for him, reliable like a best friend.

****

Since the day Alana's parents died, Laura Bookman had been there for her. And when Alana saw her come in, she accepted the crushing hug. Her description of waiting for Michael last night came out in spurts before she finally sighed, "Oh, Mamma B." And no way on earth could she describe how she felt about this morning.

"You love him deeply. You're simply overjoyed, overwhelmed."

Over-curious, she thought as they sat on the couch in the spacious living room. "I... I never... I mean how could... This is something totally unexpected and no one... Did you see him? Did you see him breathe? Does Daddy B know? How about Celia and Thorn? And

Lu...he's with Michael, right?" Hearing Laura's distinctive laugh, she sank deeper into the soft leather.

"I haven't gotten the multiple-questions-without-coming-up-for-air in a long, long time. If I continue taking breaths to answer, I will hyperventilate. You could make one dizzy. But I do agree. Michael looks *tremendous*."

"As soon as he walked in... When I touched his chest, when I kissed him—"

Laura patted her hand, a gentle gesture that had her thinking she could get a grip on some of this anxiety. "Listen to me. Don't even try to put it into words. Let love fill your soul. You thought you had lost him forever just ten months ago."

She nodded and quietly settled into another motherly hug. Alana understood loss all too well. She had watched both her parents slip away after a freak car accident. The hospital room in Manhattan was filled with machines and antiseptic smells and terror. But in less than a minute, she was an orphan. Her mystical mission had begun five months before the tragedy, and Miles, a long-time close family friend of her parents, became her mentor. A new Guardian of Souls, a demon hunter imbued with mystical strength, needed emotional stability. The entire Bookman family had always been in her life and living with them tempered her loss. The Georgians pushed through the adoption process. Although they already shared in her joys and sorrows, as part of their family they taught her how to cope and how to face her destiny.

Laura, as if able to read her mind, said, "Stefania and Alfonso would be very happy for their beautiful daughter. I imagine them smiling down upon you to wish every happiness a heart can hold."

"Would they ever have understood my mystical mission as a Guardian, and then the deep attachment to a vampire on a mission of his own? Would they have welcomed Michael into my life?" Of course, Mamma B can't answer for them, she thought.

"Come," Laura said with a hand on her cheek. "Let's take a walk. Saturdays on the piazza, the warm spring sun, and good conversation always soothes the soul."

****

Michael studied the small miracle's wisps of auburn curls. In his arms, nine pounds eleven ounces—exactly. Every gurgle and coo brought awe to his heart. "Lukas weighed six pounds. I... I caught him in my arms right after—"

"Those were extremely different circumstances," Thorn quickly interrupted.

"I held my son for less than a minute before he was taken to a safe place...away from me." Celia's smooth hand came to his cheek in comfort, understanding. With the babe cradled protectively against his chest, Michael gave a distant nod. "The name... Is it heritage?"

"Nah," Thorn answered, "It's angelic. Came to both of us at the same time. Uriel is an archangel. A red-haired warrior called "The Fire of God." It's in the Bible. You *did* read the Good Book back in the day, didn't you?"

"Refresh my memory. It was the 1600s, and I didn't make a habit of memorizing the verses."

"The Book of Enoch says the archangel Uriel

watches over thunder, fire, and terror."

"How appropriate," he whispered, recalling that petrifying day last May.

Celia frowned. "Make that fire, lightning, thunder, and right after he was conceived, *total* terror."

He looked at her. "When I destroyed Cyril… *That* night? Are you sure?"

"One hundred percent positive," she replied. "Ally wasn't supposed to be at your side, and I wasn't supposed to know I had life inside me until Thorn and I left for England, with all the madness far behind us. I know you don't want to give him up, but believe me, it's feeding time." She took the baby from his arms and sat on the bed. The infant again had Michael's full attention until shyly, Celia whispered, "Uh, I'm nursing, sweetie."

Thorn gripped Michael's shoulder. "Let's have a heart-to-heart in the living room, Champ."

****

Michael sat on the living room couch's thick arm. Thorn eyed him from an armchair. "So you think we need a heart-to-heart?"

"The colloquialism fits, doesn't it? Restless and edgy—that about sums you up. So now that you're, let's see, I believe the correct term would be *mystically* human, will you be our son's Godfather? Celia insisted we wait to baptize him until after the Georgian Council released you. She's thinking an Easter christening bash at Vito's restaurant. You know, my empathic senses say my son will need your Champion skills for his future mission in life."

"Hopefully, that's many years away because I don't even know my place in the world of the living."

His eyes narrowed. "Godfather? Me? Can I be a Godfather? And what the hell does mystically human mean?"

"You meet all of the qualifications. Cleansed soul, pure heart, unprecedented existence…? And cool it with the unspoken questions. You're a touch skittish."

"Did you know this could happen? Has it ever happened before?"

"I don't think so."

"I mean, don't get me wrong, I'm eternally grateful, but human is throwing me way off."

"Someone far above the blue skies must have a very good reason. To ease all those irrational worries waltzing through your brain, I'd high tail it to Doc Chamberlain's office for a thorough physical."

Instantly, he grimaced. "I'll pencil it in somewhere after pertinent things on my To Do list."

"You know I read you like an open book; a somewhat familiar one after almost eight years. Take a deep breath because you need to… just like you need to eat, shave, and discover multiple uses for a bathroom. It's a humbling lesson." Thorn gave a quick chuckle. "I love to watch you bristle, Michael."

"Really funny, empath."

"Okay. You're overwhelmed, but here's what I sense. The kid's downstairs trying to concentrate on a customer, in other words, not too comfortable thinking about the new you. Miles is asking Monsignor Scarlatti so many questions that he's almost dizzy. Laura's having a field day with Alana's incomplete sentences. And you don't know what to do first." Thorn fixed his trouser cuff, a nervous habit Michael instantly noted. "No, Chamberlain already knows. Miles called him from San Giorgio's rectory. He's a first-class thinker, my Celia's father. The Medico Research facility in Florence has a full staff of doctors who treat humans. You've taken the good man away from his standard Saturday golf game, so be nice. You have to see him, Michael."

"No. Lukas and I need time together."

"Take him with you. Leave a note for Alana and go."

He studied his loyal friend. "Why did you play with your cuff before?"

"Wouldn't you like to know. Not everything that enters my mind is about you. Our son can't seem to get enough of his mother's milk. *You* try telling a new mother to supplement with formula. It's not a pretty discussion." Michael winced. "There. See how truth shuts you up? Just wait. Watch and learn is what I always say. I'm needed. It's time for round two."

The empath, broad and barrel-chested, had a gentle heart. Plus, he was a true friend. As Thorn walked away, Michael looked around the empty room. "Restless and edgy," he whispered. He took his friend's suggestion. After a few deep breaths, he ran upstairs for the key to the Mercedes sedan before taking his son away from his new Saturday morning routine.

****

On the drive to Florence, Michael expected non-stop questions from Lukas—not that he wanted to answer any, which he honestly didn't have an answer for. But instead, his son came off too quiet, too distant. And when he clearly heard the boy's stomach rumble, it dawned on him that his growing boy had, in fact, not finished his breakfast. Trying to ease into a conversation, he said, "So Alana doesn't wince when you call her, uh, Mom?"

"She's mega-cool with it."

Good to know, he thought. But her alluring hazel eyes, the curve of her womanly body, and the mystical strength of his Guardian just didn't evoke visions of motherhood.

"We're a family now. That's not gonna change, right?"

He glanced over with a thin smirk. "No, it won't. I just don't see 'Mom' when I look at Alana."

"I said its okay with her. Don't you believe me?" Then Lukas mumbled, "It figures."

The tone reminded him of the troubled child who had been at the mercy of three vicious sorcerers for four years. He'd been cruelly manipulated and at age thirteen, full of rage. Then I made a deal that altered his life for one short year, he thought, before I caused that mayhem in Manhattan, and all those terrifying memories came back. Last May, he had made a few mistakes, and it took a while for his boy to trust him. Why did he feel as if he'd have to climb that difficult mountain again?

Concentrating on the road and Lukas's mood at the same time raised his discomfort level as well as his misgivings about this new existence. And when almost clipping an Audi, his chest tightened—something truly new and just as shocking as the look on his son's face. Slowing down for once, the far-right lane seemed a much better choice.

"Are you okay?" he asked tentative and a little worried about his son's response.

"So what are you, still like twenty-seven?"

Well my son dodged that question like a pro, he thought. "I'm almost twenty-eight… But the centuries of experiences are—"

"Yeah, I remember, over three hundred years of knowledge in your head. When were you born, anyway?" Lukas sank deep into the leather seat.

"The fifth of May…1663," he awkwardly added, willing to deal with curiosity, not the sulk. "But I've always gauged my age by the night of my turning. I guess that's not happening anymore." He pushed *that* terrifying memory away again and glanced at Lukas. *I've seen my son—my not nervous son—open up to Miles, open up to me.* This guarded look meant trouble, and he hoped to lighten the mood. "Tell me all about the Georgian Institute."

"School is school. I've got cool friends."

Lukas grabbed his stomach, took measured breaths. The dead-pan look was bothersome, and Michael didn't know what to do. Would the boy clam up or explode if he pressed for details? Last May had been hard enough on both of them, and less confident, he asked again, "Are you okay?"

The mumbled, "Yeah. Sure," and nothing more confirmed his suspicion. Everything with his son was not "okay."

****

Arthur Chamberlain held the stethoscope to his patient's chest ordering, "Breathe again…and again," before taking the reverse route up his back. The blue gown resettled over Michael's broad shoulders as he questioned this new existence, the way any scientist would. "Lungs are clear," he informed as Johnny Baker, his assistant, noted Michael Malone's new chart.

28

The old one, several inches thick, had information on an undead existence. Last May, both scientists had worked on the mystically enhanced vampire's brutal injuries. They knew what devastation an unknown poison had done. But *this* patient was no immortal being. Although he could have given the case over to a humans-only doctor, whether the Georgian Council agreed or not, the man sitting before him would continue under his care. "Baker will take some blood for additional tests, and then we're done."

"Tell me about my boy," Michael asked again.

Writing on the chart, Chamberlain explained, "I've done monthly check-ups. Baker sees him every other week, even when Lukas is at school in England. Johnny makes sure he takes his vitamins and eats healthy. I've made him your son's personal physician. He takes care of any cuts or bruises even though Lukas self-heals."

"He's grown at least four inches."

"But he's physically underdeveloped for fifteen."

"My son's been through a lot."

"That's an understatement if I ever heard one. Kids grow at different rates and hormones kick in at different times, which might be a good thing in his case. He's got enough to handle without teenage mood-swings and chasing girls added to the mix."

"I did my best to get back to him, Arthur, as fast as I could."

"Of course you did, and the Bookmans, as well as Thorn and Alana have been great with him. He's not acting out. He's doing very well in school. Look. You've literally returned from the dead. Take some time alone to get readjusted to life. Agreed?" He studied a pensive nod. "After Baker finishes, come to my office."

Chamberlain didn't wait for a response, briskly exited the suite of examination rooms. As he entered his office for human patients, he thought about the other office, far below ground level at Medico Research Labs outside Florence. It was a heavily secured, sterile area where he studied victims of vampires as well as demons captured by Guardians of Souls.

Seated at his desk, his attention drew to Lukas, slouched in one of two chairs across from him. The boy wore a pout, rhythmically tapped silver orbs, which angrily swung back and forth to collide with each other along their paths.

"So is he like really human?" Lukas asked.

He answered without the usual, clinical coldness, "One-hundred percent healthy. How about you...stomach still cramping?"

"Shit. Did he say something?"

"No, but you're green around the edges. Can I examine you or should we talk?"

"Nope. Neither. I'm cool. Self-healing, mystical genes, you know the routine."

"It's okay to be nervous. Hell, it's even natural to be nauseous." Leaning forward, he tapped one temple. "What's happening up here?"

Focused on the swinging balls, Lukas mumbled, "It's personal."

He pressed a button on the desk phone, but didn't take his eyes off the teenager, saying into the speaker, "Baker, run another EKG on Michael." Lukas dropped his head back, muttering his favorite four-letter curse word, locking his arms across his chest. "I've raised four boys so I understand pissed off. Doctor-patient confidentiality works for minors, too," he said in a humorous way.

"My father wants you to talk to me."

"No. *I* want you to talk to me." A battle of wits would follow—he knew this kid. "Should I tell him I want to keep you overnight for observation? I'll use big medical terms and order a slew of tests that'll age him quick."

A flash of anger appeared in Lukas's wide eyes. "I have super-strength."

"I have big, burly assistants and drugs."

"You wouldn't," the teen said with a snicker.

"I would," he firmly replied without a smile.

"I still have all of *my* mystical abilities. What happens if he doesn't?"

He folded his hands and knew he heard the truth. He could just imagine how fast this kid's highly-intelligent mind was racing. At Miles's insistence, Baker had documented the many scars that crisscrossed Lukas's chest and back. His life had been living Hell until Michael rescued him from the Second Realm. No matter how well-adjusted he came off, ten months of 'normal' hadn't erased years of terror. The boy's guard went up like a wall of armor, and he tempered his tone. "Listen to me carefully. You can worry about 'what ifs' or *not* worry about 'what ifs.' I advise the *not* worry one, because what-ifs will drive you nuts. You've just come from nuts so try to be a typical kid—for once. Your dad's back. Give him some space but talk to him. His love for you hasn't changed."

"Yeah, but this human thing is way weird."

He paused before saying, "A *good* weird, though. Tell him what's on your mind and how you feel. Shut

31

down and he'll demand answers, which you obviously don't want to give." When Michael entered and sat next to Lukas, he studied father and son. Both looked uncomfortable as he met Michael's gaze. "I want to see you in two days, first thing Monday morning to go over the blood work. Don't find any excuse not to get here." He accepted the man's nod of agreement and moved to the window after they left his office.

Chamberlain studied them as they walked to the Mercedes, just as he had last May. Neither of them looked prepared for a human Michael Malone. He'd note this observation on the chart and discuss everything with Baker.

Chapter 3

After a stone cold, miserably silent ride back to
Portofino, Michael pulled the Mercedes into the empty
garage. "Where is Alana's car?"

"It's in the lot down the street. She keeps yours in
here." Lukas slammed the door, sprinted around the
corner, most likely into the bookstore.

Slumped in the plush seat, how to handle a teenage
brood consumed him. His son was capable of things a
normal person couldn't handle. The choices? Leave him
alone or trigger a reaction. Neither way do I win, he
realized. As the garage door closed, he welcomed total
darkness. After ten months of solitude, he could handle
a pitch-black void easier than his son.

Chamberlain's assessment of Lukas bothered him.
More child than man and small for his age... He
recalled his own lanky stature at fifteen as well as his
racing hormones. "Add it to your list of worries," he
muttered leaving the sedan.

Stepping into the private elevator, the door closed.
It was a slow climb to the foyer of his home on the third
floor. Patience, parenting, and getting comfortable with
being human again had him off-balance. When the
doors slid open, he studied the rose marble floor,
exceptionally proud of his good taste and detailed
renovations to the building. It had been his idea to gut
the third floor and create spacious, flowing rooms. All

had been authorized by him from Manhattan two years ago. He had already purchased the building from her great-aunt Rosa Bellini, and by the time Alana left the city *and* him behind, her new home was ready for occupancy. Expensive furniture, Florentine wallpaper, modern conveniences...nothing was too good for the woman he'd always love. *His* Guardian would live her new life in luxury.

Memories of Rosa caused an immediate twinge of guilt. She had helped to heal a poisoned vampire; she had cultivated trust and a sense of family in his troubled boy. He still felt responsible for the loving woman's tragic death.

He threw the Mercedes key on an antique peddler's bench. A new existence, he thought, but all of the guilt lives on. Stepping back into life after centuries of undeath wouldn't be easy. Not knowing why he was human again still rattled his confidence.

The ability to hear Alana's hushed conversation with Arthur Chamberlain on the phone in the living room slowed his stride. She was concerned about him, and he knew it. But as he came to the couch, she abruptly hung up the landline and ran into his arms. He slid her up his body and a sensual thrill shot through him automatically settling in his loins. The twinge of arousal was remarkable. Kissing her sweet lips blossomed into intense passion once again. The feel of her, the firmness of her breast in his hand under the lilac sweater she wore, elicited a sexy moan. When her fingers combed through his hair, a distinct pressure had him throbbing. The physical response was shocking, his rapid heartbeat and heat growing in his body as he put her down. Still locked in a hungry kiss, he sat on the wide arm of the leather couch, and leaning back, they toppled onto its soft cushions. His body raced toward pleasure while his head told him to hit the brakes and fast.

****

In a familiar way, Alana settled between his long legs. Pulling out of the steamy kiss, her head rested on his heart, and every thump filled her with wonder. No ordinary man could wear snug black jeans and a simple black shirt with its sleeves rolled up the way Michael did. Dark colors enhanced his singular, intense look. Even with her eyes closed, she could see only him. She could sense strength in his soul, in his muscular body. His embrace was a place of comfort as well as erotic joy.

Laura said give him time. Chamberlain had just said the same thing, but she hoped for an explanation. Years apart, and then realizing how much she loved him… What he had put himself through ten months ago had reshaped their destiny, and now, the possibility of a long life together had real meaning. She felt him deep in her soul. Being with him made her very core ache with a lover's need. In an intimate way, she studied his day-old beard, the width of his shoulders, the lines of his face. Her hands weren't willing to leave his chest. He shifted, and she drifted farther away to sit on her heels, to drown in the full vision of him. His eyes shimmered as his warm fingers threaded hers.

"How'd it go with Lu? Did you get a chance to talk?"

"Jeez, Mom, that's a tough one. Couldn't we start with something easier?"

She chuckled. "I think Mom sounds sweet. He lets

me call him Lu."

"If you're okay with it, so am I."

"Where is he?"

"Anywhere I'm not, apparently." He groaned in a frustrated way and pushed back to sit up against the padded arm. His hands slipped out of her hold, and he laced them to his chest. When he blew out a slow breath, shivers ran down her spine.

"Did something happen?"

"I expected non-stop questions, not a sudden shutdown."

"Do you have any idea how unbelievable *this* is? How unexpected—"

"No, *really*," he said with a touch of sarcasm. A distant look she'd never seen before settled on his face. "I asked for an end to my existence. I didn't ask for life."

His eyes dulled while hers blazed. Sucking in a breath, she held it. Maybe she'd misunderstood. "You wanted an end to your existence? Meaning... the forever kind of death?"

"Alana, I'm not about to lie."

"Nope, rewind and talk. Talk fast." The proverbial romantic, rose-tinted glasses had just ripped right off her eyes.

"What I did in undeath, unexpected questions fired at me by twelve individuals to explain or clarify... then sitting in the church after a *six-hour* inquisition—which took place a full month after I completed their Document of Atonement. I fucking came undone. Before I left you last May, I had no right to ask for your love." He looked at the wall, down the hall, at anything but her.

"Michael—"

"And whose idea was it to have my son here, waiting for my return?"

"We all thought—"

"I told him I'd come for him—when *I* was ready. That was the deal. He should have been forced to stay at school in England. I had no right believing I could teach him how to deal with life, either."

"Michael, stop," she managed to whisper. Illogical words came from a most rational man. She couldn't swallow, didn't recognize the chill in his tone.

"After I signed the Georgian document on the altar, I thought I was alone. But Mother Anne stayed, and I swear I heard Helena speak through her. How could I state my unspoken desire? I didn't. I couldn't. So, I asked for death." He looked away again, distant and detached. "What sane person could live with what I did without a soul? I begged for merciful oblivion, ready to face an eternity in Hell."

Her hand shot over her heart. "Just like that, you decided to leave the people who love you? Or had that been your decision all those months in seclusion?"

Shifting his long legs, he didn't reply. She clutched his sister's golden locket, felt the delicate ridges of its inscribed letter 'A'. Since the moment he had fastened the precious heirloom around her neck, she had never taken it off. The real reason behind his silence this morning suddenly knifed through her soul. "Before you left, we stood at San Giorgio's altar and vowed to love each other through eternity. It was our marriage, unique and true. Are you taking back your vow to me?"

He leaned forward. She didn't see surprise. She saw tension. "What?"

"You heard me. It's a simple question."

"I love you, Alana. I love my son."

"I thought you *requested* life so Lukas would have *two* caring parents. But you asked for death, to be gone from us forever without us ever even knowing why… No. That's not love. I don't know what it is, but it isn't love." Although dazed, she forced herself to stand. Holding back a river of tears took every ounce of strength. "Do me one favor. Don't tell Lukas what you really wanted. Hurt him like this and I swear to God, I'll walk out of your…life."

She left him. She didn't look back. Running downstairs, she wanted to burst in on Celia and cry on her shoulder. In a fog, she stood at the door across the hall. It immediately opened, and someone pulled her into what used to be *Zia* Rosa's home.

****

Gabriella led her to the dining room table saying in a whisper, "Just a warning…Your sister's eyes are drippy and her nose is bright red." The attractive ex-Guardian, also a healing sister like Mother Anne, was dressed in a denim blouse and blue jeans. The four women in the room had grown close while Michael was gone. "There's fresh coffee, but a bottle of wine could do both of you some good right now, Ally."

"A stiff drink might actually work," Celia said through a sniffle.

"To pull you up to speed," Gabby said, "we're discussing baby formula, which has totally ripped our sister psychic apart."

Alana sat at Celia's side. She couldn't help but stare at the other person present—Sister Magdalena, *Zia* Rosa's daughter, also a member of the mystical order of

Catherine who still practiced as a cardio surgeon at a local hospital. Maggie's smile, just like *Zia's,* was forever gentle and full of understanding.

"I know Maggie's right," Celia whispered. "I know Thorn's right. But why does it have to be so soon? He's not even two months old."

"Jeez, I'm catching real misery in both of you. Can't tell who's more upset," Gabby said in a feisty tone, one Alana often used herself.

"But you're nursing," she said, hoping to comfort her adopted sister.

Celia sobbed again. "I'm nothing but a…a new-mother failure."

Both healers looked concerned. A bond had grown even stronger between all four women. Gabby had fought at Michael's side with Guardian strength equal to hers. Both healers had walked his dream of survival. They also helped remove the nefarious beast-within from his soul. Things like that only served to make their bond tighter.

Celia blew out a long breath. "Oh, Ally, you look so sad."

"It can wait," she softly replied.

"No. It can't," Celia said with a hitch in her voice.

Gabby cracked a small smile. Her arms folded on the table and her soft-blue eyes narrowed. "I'm sensing the 'yes it can, no it can't' thing goes all the way back to kindergarten."

They both nodded, because, of course, Gabby was correct.

Celia blew out a sharp breath. "I swear that motherhood is wreaking havoc on my coping skills. Plus, my sixth sense is duller than ever… And Thorn gave our son formula because I'm not... not full enough."

"That can't be true," she whispered.

"Okay, Maggie, you're the doctor," Gabby stated. "Can't he have both?"

Magdalena nodded once. "*Mi dispiace*, Celia, but the baby *needs* both."

"Does that make you feel better, Celia B—at least a little," Gabby asked. "With parents like the two of you, I'm sure Uriel's destiny is already written."

Destiny, Alana thought, so what the hell is mine now? Celia had Thorn and Uri, Gabby and Maggy had their mystical mission as members of the Order of Catherine. Where was her assurance that Michael was her destiny? Maybe what she thought was forever had changed when he took his first breath, fully human again. Looking at Celia, she shook her head. "It'll be okay, sis, I know it will."

Celia nodded. Her lips quivered. "But he's my little boy. I should know best."

"Celia," Maggie whispered with compassion.

Her sister slowly shrugged and then studied Alana's face. "Michael still loves you, Ally."

Gabby met her teary gaze. "You are definitely hurting, Guardian."

She barely replied, "I know Michael still loves me."

****

"Christ, I'm starving." Lukas took the meatball sandwich from Kayla's hands, and he dove right in. The nineteen-year-old Guardian's huge olive eyes sparkled as she laughed. "Isn't it totally scrumptious? An entire loaf of Italian bread just smothered with meatballs and mozzarella and Vito's new sauce. I said I liked the first sauce, so Nico came back with another sandwich."

Sitting on the floor of the bookshop's back office, he swallowed, hardly chewing, and gulped a mouthful of water to wash it down. "Nico's sweet on you. You better watch out. There's that required, oh-so-sacred vow of virginity thing." He liked the pursed-lipped pout, the way Kayla dipped her chin. Her eyes shone like black onyx as he teased in a mischievous tone, "*Ay, que linda, Kaylita mia!* I think he wants to ask you out on a date."

She flicked the thick, long braid of shiny black hair over one shoulder and arched an eyebrow. "Cut it out, *muchachito*. I honor my mission *and* my vow. He's too full of himself and he likes to get into trouble. Vito's nephew can be sweet on me all he wants. That's as far as it goes. This is terrific, isn't it?"

He took another bite. "Heaven," he confirmed with his mouth full, still ravenous. "Call Vito. Tell him you have to taste the other sauce again. Nico will come running across the piazza just to hear you giggle like that."

"I didn't expect to see you down here today."

He shrugged. "I like being with you."

"How's your dad?"

"Human," he mumbled, quickly changing the subject. "Portofino's filling up for Easter already. Rich tourists like to throw Euros at the two of us. We're a main attraction in town."

Kayla rolled the tinfoil wrap into a ball and threw it. Lukas caught it mid-air as the tiny brass bell above

41

the door jingled to announce a customer. He watched the Guardian leave Alana's cramped office at the back of the shop with a full-on, deep-dimpled grin. Yeah, he knew how to turn on the charm and he heard her quickened heartbeat.

He sat at Alana's desk and propped his feet up on the papers strewn across it. Then he leaned far back in the chair. A second bottle of water went down in a few gulps before he crushed the plastic into a ball and made a slam-dunk into the garbage can by the door. His eyes slid to the calendar on the wall. "April first… Maybe Dad's turning human on April Fools is just a bad joke. Way fucking weird and just my fucking luck," he muttered with his hands locked behind his head.

****

Michael's first instinct had been to go after Alana, but he couldn't pull himself off the couch. With a groan, he kicked off the soft leather loafers and stretched his long legs out. What a mess, he thought. *In less than a day, I've managed to alienate the two people I love most.*

"Misery loves company," Thorn droned in a low tone as he came in through the apartment's original wooden door.

"Did you catch my crass stupidity? If you're here for the pep talk, you can save your breath. I screwed up big time."

"Hell, I'm a bit preoccupied with my own *faux pas*. They're both downstairs with Gabby and Maggie, and they're not talking about the latest action-romance movie with subtitles."

"You look as depressed as I feel."

"Well, thus the misery line."

He eyed Thorn sinking into an armchair. "What did you do to Celia?"

"I made the mistake of handing her a warm bottle of baby formula. My Celia's face clouded over, those sparkling-green eyes filled. She handed me the baby and slinked out the door."

"That was uncharacteristically harsh of you, Empath."

"I'm now aware, thank you. He's in Laura's arms, smiling and finally full." Thorn gave a low sigh. "Share *your* transgression, Champ. What did you do to Alana?"

"I told the truth."

"Uh-oh, not 'Dear God, I beg you, end this existence and send my soul to Hell...' Please tell me you didn't."

"Yep, you got it."

"That was uncharacteristically harsh of you."

"Twenty journals documenting death and destruction as a vampire felt like a two-hundred-year confession crammed into nine endless months. Not to mention another thirty days to think about it all and really want to stake myself... Maybe it was too much extra time in solitary confinement to think."

"Patience is a virtue."

"Patience has nothing to do with this. Every kill, every undead deed still haunts me like a ghost. I'm guessing the Council knew it would."

"And the first thing that popped into your brain was absolute atonement. Yeah... I caught the scene in the church, Champ—the weepiness as well as the bone-crushing guilt. Just in case you're interested, everyone who walked the dream of survival caught it, too."

"Well, that's embarrassing. You know a soul can

handle just so much. I absolutely broke down and then—"

"Destiny took you where no vampire's gone before. You've been given another unexpected chance."

"Which I've already screwed up." He laced his arms across his chest. Thorn stared directly into his eyes, and he knew better than to look away. Whether or not Michael let him into his mind, the empath would read every single thought.

"None of us, mystical, magical or human, gets to know why we are who we are. The future simply unfolds. Trust that destiny thing again."

"Yeah, and exactly what is mine? Everything's not all right in my head, with Lukas *or* Alana, either."

"Your son wants neat and normal. And try to imagine Alana's shock as she crosses heartbeat off her "Michael can't ever" list. So fall down, venture back up, and get your land legs. This mystical trip isn't over."

Full of irritation, he bristled. "I can't handle cryptic."

"Sorry. I'm not a visual empath. It's a feeling thing. Maybe you need a steak."

Michael's eyes narrowed. "A stake?"

"No, a steak—the slab of beef kind, smothered with garlic. Let's go. It's my treat."

****

From the bookshop's office, Lukas heard two sets of footsteps coming down the stairs. That his father hadn't come for him didn't bring relief. Instead, a more familiar mood surfaced. He slipped out the hallway door and sprinted up three flights. Grabbing a fistful of Mom's emergency stash, he shoved the euros into his pocket. He knew it was wrong—in a big way. So was palming the red car's key. Alana often let him drive it to a nearby lot on weekends, even though he wasn't old enough for a driver's license in Italy.

Lukas jumped each staircase and ran like the wind toward the lot. Minutes later, he drove around the parking lot to get the hang of smoother driving. On the two-lane highway, with the radio blasting and all windows down, the speedometer shot up fast, adding an incredible thrill. "I don't even rate a lame-ass reason why you're human. This whole thing friggin' sucks."

Careful to make sure the other lane was empty, he peeled past the other cars as if reality on the road were a video game.

****

The café Thorn chose was Alana's favorite on the piazza. Vito's nephew, Nico, introduced himself with true Italian flair, and sat them at an outside table. When Thorn called Celia on his cell phone, Michael heard every word of their tender apologies to each other. And when Nico took their order, Thorn asked, "Want to call Alana?"

He gave a terse, "No."

"Ever since Helena brought me back, the undead Michael Malone was my sole purpose on this earth."

"And I made sure the sorcerers didn't crack your brain open during the mayhem I caused in Manhattan."

"Yeah, well the Kendrick witches helped. Give credit where credit is due."

"A mystical Servant of Souls would have been a big score for evil."

"They've got to be shouting curse words from Hell tonight."

45

With a steady glare, Michael asked, "Why?"

The empath shook his head. "Just look at you now. I never expected to be sitting across from a living, breathing man on the piazza, and neither did those evil bastards."

They sat in silence, waiting for two thick, juicy steaks. Michael had never been talkative. Now, with incessant pangs of human hunger in an empty stomach, he felt more out of touch with reality than he'd ever been as an immortal creature of the night. He said very little during the meal, but after the waiter took their plates, the questions came in rapid succession. Thorn gave simple answers until Michael again asked, "Why am I here?"

"All I need to do tonight is lead you away from the gloom and doom filling your soul. This new part of your journey will take patience, which you're very short on."

Full of typical arrogance, he leaned back and crossed his long legs while draining the last of the dry red wine in his glass. He eyed the piazza packed with tourists. Didn't respond; didn't even nod. Two delicate glasses brimming with anisette liqueur appeared, compliments of Vito. Thorn pushed his away and ordered two cappuccinos.

Only then did Michael lean forward. "So, Empath, what do I do about this?"

"Meaning your inability to relax and enjoy being alive?"

He downed the sweet liquid and let out a sigh. "Life. Heartbeat. Screwing up… Take your pick."

"You still look morbidly miserable. Want to head back and get a jump on groveling or parenting?"

"Absolutely neither," he groaned with a tight jaw.

"What's the problem here—the moonlight, the tide, or the fear? Dragging your feet is so unlike the action-packed hero we all know and love."

"I lived action for three centuries. Perhaps I've had enough."

"Whoa, back up. Run that by me again and try to make it a little more convincing. This is *me* you're talking to, Michael. I've been in your brain. You won't last a day doing mundane. Listen with your heart."

"Every unexpected beat and every skip of one confuses me."

"Well, it confuses all of us. So you don't know if you *are* who you were. I'm not sensing any scary things happening *without*—so face the scary things within."

"I need time." He drained the second anisette, placing the glass down slowly.

"You need help and not the mystical kind. Call Chamberlain. He gives good advice."

"I'm not a tell-me-your-problems type of creature…uh, human." He shifted, stubbornly adding, "Well, I'm not."

"Let's step back to December 14, 1690," the empath stated.

"Let's not," he replied with dread in his tone. They stopped their conversation as Nico placed their coffee on the table.

Once alone again, Thorn asked, "What's the last thing you did before Cyril tore into your jugular?"

His locked arms tightened against his chest. "I cried to God."

Thorn added sugar to his cappuccino, stirring it while saying, "Why? I want the truth."

"You know why. My life was unfinished."

"So here you are, a healthy man once again. I don't care how old your brain is. This is a life-interrupted problem, not a new existence dilemma. You were a savvy businessman. You still are. That part's a given."

"I bedded many women," he said before drinking his coffee and then setting down the cup.

"That part's changed. You saw it when you opened your eyes last May. Alana's your soul mate. What else?"

"I have a son who shouldn't exist."

"Skip over the mystical part we don't have an explanation for, at the moment. Just remember, had it not been for the kid, you'd never have gone after three immortal sorcerers, or staked your sire. What else?"

"Lukas won't talk to me."

"The issue will resolve itself, sooner or later." Thorn leaned in, his broad body an intimidation without words. "Here's the thing. The life-interruption was three hundred years of incredible history—some good, some horrible. Go forward, Champ. Sing amazing grace how sweet the sound a couple of hundred times until you believe it."

He gave a slow smirk. "A hymn almost as old as I… What an interesting choice. Suppose I can't."

"Welcome to being human."

"What about Lukas?"

After finishing his coffee, a glaze seemed to sweep across Thorn's light-gray eyes. Slowly, his trusted friend shook his head. "Trust me when I say you've got your work cut out for you with the kid."

****

Without a word, Michael left Thorn on the second-floor landing and walked up the next narrow flight of stairs. The alcohol relaxed him. The conversation didn't. Unwilling to think about his friend's sound but cryptic advice, he entered his home and stared at his son's bedroom door. Hearing rapid taps on a laptop's keyboard, he ignored the nagging intuition to have a serious father-son chat, and Alana's warning came to mind. No. He wouldn't hurt his son the way he had hurt her. The chat could wait until he knew why he was back. His son's questions could wait as well.

More uneasiness gripped him while walking into the master bedroom. He sank into the patterned upholstered chair, slipped out of his shoes. Engrossed in a book, Alana sat in the middle of the sleigh bed wearing an old silk shirt of his. He imagined her supple body underneath. A full minute passed before he softly offered, "I'm sorry."

She placed the book on the nightstand, met his gaze. "I love you with all of my heart, Michael. I want to call a truce."

"I didn't mean to hurt you."

With a very hushed, "Don't," she turned on her side to face him.

Multiple sensations bombarded his senses, but his flinch was barely noticeable. He knew better than to shield his soul from her, and yet, what he felt, he pushed farther down. Unbuttoning his shirt, he stood. It hit the floor, and instead of telling her what he felt, he walked into their *ensuite*. He turned the knob in the shower, waited for the water to heat as he stripped off the rest of his clothes.

Standing in the tiled space, the tepid trickle of water didn't relieve one worry on his mind. He was stalling. He knew it. Nothing about this new existence felt right. Like an inexperienced lover, just a glimpse of Alana had him ready to lose control. He'd never had that particular problem—as a man *or* as an immortal. Pleasuring a woman, slow and sensual, had been his signature. He could go all night if he wanted to. With a groan, he yanked the valve closed and stepped out of the shower. He dried off with harsh towel strokes, avoiding his reflection in the mirror over the sink. And for the first time ever, he wished he'd had the foresight to bring a pair of pajamas into the bathroom with him.

Entering the master bedroom, he dropped the towel and slid under the covers in silence. Alana put down the book as she turned out the light next to the bed. Then she drew her body tight to his back. Through the silk shirt she wore, the heat of her radiated against him. And when she straightened the rose-colored quilt around him, he slid down to nestle the back of his head on her breasts. Her left hand found the center of his chest. Her leg hooked his thigh. My Guardian's love is a safe harbor, he thought, with an incredible woman steadfast and strong. When his eyes welled, he shut them tight.

****

A continent away, the sun set on a quiet New Jersey town. Leonard Gerhardt leaned back in a plush chair behind his desk. One hand slid over the Sire's leather-bound diary, a treasure he had found last May. Some would call it happenstance. This wizard called it serendipity.

The mystically enhanced vampire had destroyed his continent's sorcerers. Now, no North American wizard other than he could be called the most powerful practitioner of dark arts. No one in Valley Township knew he walked among them, and a string of large corporations would never be traced back to his ownership. There were many. An Austrian immigrant, who as a boy had suffered the perils of WWII, Gerhardt had aged well. He had wealth and prestige.

Of course, when he ascended to sorcerer status, he'd be ageless.

Tonight, something had changed in Portofino. Tucking Cyril's diary of spells in the side drawer of his desk and locking it, Gerhardt sensed the shift of opportunity. The phone rang and he lifted the receiver with a steady hand. "You have seen the vampire."

"In the piazza with the empath," his minion stated.

"The paintings are to be delivered to both locations by morning."

"Yes, master."

As he hung up the phone, Gerhardt reveled in such perfect timing. *Fortune is in my favor. The timing is perfect. Michael Malone will regret destroying my god.* Standing, he walked to the window. A grandfatherly grin appeared on his face. He stroked his snow-white beard, watched the busy street located precisely sixty-six feet from his secret domicile. A spell of the highest magnitude had been cast. For Gerhardt, it'd been mere child's play. From the outside, the place appeared deserted. And when strolling the grounds, he could glamour any neighbor, especially their pets. Disciplined study of Cyril's journal had shown him the way. Now, he'd put all he had learned to the ultimate test of destroying the vampire before restoring the Sire's legacy.

For ten months, the taste of revenge soured in his mouth, and he alone had the foresight to keep spies in

Portofino. Europe's Triumvirate of immortal sorcerers had not. Their oversight was his cue to trigger a paranormal event like none ever attempted. The idea began in May, when Zoltan, Cyril's last known progeny had the sorcerers' sniveling liaison at NWT tortured to death. Gerhardt knew better than to show himself. He stayed out of sight and schemed.

To this day, all of North America's portals to other dimensions remained closed. Except for one. Its location couldn't be discovered, which was an inconvenience. But Cyril's destruction had been the final outrage.

Gerhardt thought about how he found the ancient diary ensconced behind a loose stone along a charred wall of the Vermont estate. It had been the first omen, providing the script for this event. The Georgian Sovereign Council is ultimately responsible for the Sire's demise, he thought, but the traitor Michael Malone will be made to suffer.

Like a fierce, old lion, he strutted through the chalet's rooms. On the back veranda, he punched a set of numbers into an untraceable cell phone.

"I've missed you," a sleepy female voice said.

"You are ready to do what I ask, my dear?"

"Of course, Leonard… Are you in Siena already?"

"It's not your concern. We will meet in Florence when you deliver the host-vessel."

"The girl from Ohio is in place?"

"But of course, dear, she'll assist." He didn't say a tender goodbye, although she adored him as a lover, as a father. Her artistic talent would open the door, and he would take his rightful place as the first new sorcerer of the twenty-first century.

Meticulous research had also led him to the powerful vampire who sired Cyril in 1355. Leonard didn't procrastinate, cultivating trust in the princess. Veronique. Her brand of supremacy deserved loyalty, admiration and worship. He left the veranda, entered another room and sat where the web cam picked up perfect confidence on his face. With a flick of a wrist, the computer hummed and soon, the alluring creature in Florence appeared on screen.

"Leonard," Veronique sighed. "What brings this pleasure to me?"

"My dark goddess, it is time. In thirteen days, I shall deliver your legacy in an innocent vessel."

Her sapphire eyes glimmered with desire, her exquisite face tilted with the purr, "You will surpass every dark wizard this new millennium brings forth."

The screen went black.

Tomorrow was Sunday, a day set aside for his granddaughter. Serendipity had smiled on him not once, but twice. Gerhardt never suspected it would be this easy. To celebrate her good news and his good fortune, a congratulatory dinner would be in order. Then he'd gift to the innocent one a first-class plane ticket to Siena, Italy as well as a limitless credit card.

"Ah… family," Gerhardt whispered.

Leaving the room, all lights faded to darkness, but he hadn't raised a finger.

Chapter 4

On Monday morning, Jillian Gerhardt left her best friend after homeroom to chase the art teacher down Valley High's south corridor. Jocks cluttered her way like a tsunami destroying everything in its path. At least six big lugs copped a feel and more than a dozen "valley girls" scrunched their noses to show dislike for her. *You're a bunch of horsey divas who couldn't draw a straight line if they paid you,* the petite teenager thought with equal disdain.

"Miss De Rosa, Miss De Rosa," she shouted, now carelessly slammed into a locker. A paw of a hand crept up her inner thigh as a sloppy grin appeared on Arturo's face.

"You freak," she said with ripe disgust to one of the few boys specifically imported from an urban district to beef up Valley's football team.

"Hey, woo-man," he sang with a reggae slur, "you be my white sugar and I be your daddy." He snickered, pressed his groin to her ribs.

"Get off me, 'Ro, or I scream...like this." The high-pitched shriek got the attention of a Spanish teacher.

"Arturo!" He grabbed the hulk by the scuff of his neck. "*Escuchame, comprende, mi amigo...* no touch *la muchachita*—get it?"

'Ro cringed from the pressure applied to the base

of his neck and staggered back into the waiting arms of his sexually deviant buddies. No one trucked with the tattooed Vietnam veteran.

"We be cool, my man, we be cool." He adjusted himself through low-riding jeans with a hand on his crotch.

"Did he hurt you?" the teacher asked, "I know these guys, Jillian. When they see someone like you, they see 'mess with me' written across your forehead. You're all right?"

"Uh-huh," she replied in a small voice as her favorite teacher approached. When the in-crowd cleared, she said to her, "I…I wanted to tell you I got in."

"Oh Jillian, I'm *so* proud of you." Miss De Rosa turned to the Spanish teacher. "This young artist is the recipient of an impressive invitation to the University of Siena—one of six American students chosen to study art in Italy for the rest of the school year." After he congratulated her, he walked away, and Miss De Rosa asked, "Mom has your passport ready?"

Jillian nodded many times with an excited grin. "I leave this Thursday!"

"Congrats, Jilly!" Miss De Rosa offered an excited smile and a long hug.

****

Jillian's AP classes included a double period of portrait drawing, which whipped by. She shared no classes with her BFF—not even lunch, but after school, she bounced down busy McCoy Road with Paige Virelli. An up-scale commuter community, Valley Township had once been a patchwork of five lakes and huge, rural farms. Not anymore. It was suburbia at its finest. They got to the middle of her what-to-bring-to-Italy list when they neared the 'dork' pond.

"I still think it looks lame." Paige frowned as Jillian pulled her past it. "Who builds something so mega-weird smack in the middle of a suburban main street? It doesn't fit, Jilly, and even my mom says it's creepy."

"Yuck. The water smells like dead fish. We should've taken the shortcut and stopped for a donut and an iced latte. Do you ever wonder what lives in there?"

"All the time… Probably some weirdo," Paige said as they reached the end of the fenced property.

The intersection, as always, was treacherous. They waited for the light to change and stepped off the curb after looking both ways twice. As soon as they reached Washington Elementary, quick giggles and trip talk resumed.

"Omigod, do you believe this! I'm going to Italy! I'm *really* going to Italy—in a first-class seat with an unlimited credit card!"

"Oooh… Granddad strikes again."

"Do you believe this?"

"I'm like so excited! This is *so* cool. Are you going to learn Italian?"

"I don't think…maybe," she replied.

"Oooh! Oooh! You'll meet hot Italian boys on campus!"

"But the letter says we live in a house right in the middle of medieval Siena."

"Can we text across an ocean? You'll email right—like every hour?"

Shooting a bright smile at her best friend since

kindergarten, Jillian replied, "You betcha, girlfriend!" A white minivan pulled next to them and honked. They both squealed. "Ugh...we're caught." She waved to her mother, and then leaned into the open window. "Were you following us again? Omigod...wicked highlights, Mom."

The side door slid open. "Not too blonde?" her mom asked.

"Nah," she said as they climbed into the bench-seat.

"We've got company for dinner and then some. Paige's mom has an office full of taxpayers waiting to see if they owe or if they get a fat refund."

"I know," her best friend droned. "And April fifteenth is like two weeks away. I'm sleeping over tonight, right?"

Her mother's dark-brown eyes seemed captured in the rear-view mirror. "Naturally! So Miranda's or Toni's...which is it for dinner?"

Jillian leaned forward, between the two front bucket seats. "Can we get Chinese take-out? I bet they won't have shrimp toast and egg rolls in Siena."

"If you cut through the Y, it gets you to Hamilton Turnpike quicker."

"Girl with learner's permit doth not make an experienced driver, Paige. What if a cop sees me?"

Jillian gave a silly frown, which Paige countered with a sneaky smile saying, "I've got connections with a certain police Lieutenant."

"That might work for your mother, but—"

"You know you're like honorary members of the Virelli family. Uncle Den's mega cool."

Jillian agreed with rolling "uh-huhs" when her

mother chuckled. She sat back with a squeal as Alexa Gerhardt, mom extraordinaire, pulled into traffic. Already, Jillian felt homesick.

****

Johanna De Rosa drove down the chalet's unpaved driveway around midnight. No light came from the street on this section of McCoy Road and switching off the headlights made it more difficult. But she used her sixth sense to not disturb Leonard's neighbors on her left.

The small car Leonard had given her slipped into a huge garage beneath the stone structure. A heavy garage door came down the instant Johanna cut the engine. Her cell phone lit the walk to their worship room, located in a windowless interior section of the house. Joining many others, a thick circle formed around the center pentagram. Black candles blazed, and strategically placed red ceiling spots bathed them in melodramatic light. Through Johanna's imaginative eyes, the stout, silver-haired Gerhardt could double for Santa Claus.

Standing in the center of the star, the wizard waved a hand. A wall-mounted screen displayed the picture of a familiar girl. Thirteen minutes passed before Johanna's idol announced, "It is a devout privilege to offer mine own for our cause. The seed of the goddess shall rise again."

"The beast-within shall be freed to feed," they chanted as one.

He extended his sturdy arms, switching to an ancient language she had yet to master. The screen faded black with another sweep of his hand. Recessed spotlights glowed pale yellow, and Johanna's heart lurched as she heard in her mind, *"My sacrifice is a blood sacrifice, the most sacred kind. Mine is a pure lamb led to a sacred altar."*

Then he approached, silently ordered her to follow. She rose on command to leave the crowded room. When he took her elbow, deep loyalty swelled inside Johanna.

"Your part in this event is not unnoticed. You will join me in Siena and attend the birth."

Leonard's wise eyes held approval. Bowing her head, she whispered, "Your holiness, it is with great joy that I serve my master."

Chapter 5

Every night, they settled in bed the same way. Every morning, Alana awoke with Michael's head on her breast, his body wrapped snug in her arms. In sleep, he looked fierce, ready for action. Five days of this, she thought, and here we still are. No deep conversations, nothing more than a kiss goodnight. It didn't feel right, and Lu would agree—if he'd only talk to her. Lu's moodiness, Michael's distance, Celia's new mother woes, and now, both her father and Thorn spending long days at San Giorgio's rectory with Monsignor Scarlatti. *Palm Sunday's a few days away. The bookshop's busier than usual and all I care about is Michael.*

She couldn't let go of his truth-filled confession—five days ago, but she wouldn't hold back affection for the man she loved. Every touch, every look promised desire and held enough passion to make her soul tremble and her core dampen. He needed her near. But when awake, it was from a distance. "Maybe it's a start," she whispered.

He flinched. The fierce look faded and his expression became blank.

Thank God you didn't lie. I would've known. Please come back to me, Michael, my love. Her heart sank. Her hug tightened. One leg hooked his waist. Is holding him close more necessary than passion? She had to wonder…

Michael blinked several times to struggle out of the bizarre image trapped in his mind. Crucifixes filling his beloved sister's writing chest. On a high hill, the beast-within that once lived inside his undead body stares at the moon…

Not only foolish, he thought, it's impossible. The entity was safely entombed in consecrated earth at Villa Catherine in Siena. He wouldn't share this lunacy with anyone. Not Alana, not even the empath. He'd keep everyone at a distance until the macabre images ceased to haunt his dreams. His heart raced. His body tensed while forcing it out of mind, and when Alana shifted, he controlled his tone. "You're awake."

"Yes," she replied, not releasing him from the secure hold.

Her scent intoxicated him, caused a twitch below his waist. Her womanly figure molded against the width of his back like a predestined match. She was his, but he couldn't turn around and take her in his arms. A shiver ran down his spine as if the warmth of morning sun didn't exist. "Will you be downstairs all day?"

"I've got a huge stock delivery to catalog. And Lu is banned from helping because I got an email yesterday. The school hasn't received one homework assignment since the end of March. Dad knows the whole story. You should talk to him."

His shoulders stiffened. Miles's dry, probing questions weren't on his agenda, either. But his son's lack of responsibility, however, couldn't be avoided. "I'll call the headmaster. Steven Clarke, right? Where's his number?"

"I'll program it into your cell phone. Be understanding with Lu. Either he forgot to send it or he's doing typical teenage stuff, Michael. This isn't a call to war."

Lukas had a talent for hearing conversations, even through plaster walls. He replied at full volume, "I'll speak with Clarke and then I'll be quietly persuasive with my son." This should force him out of bed and into schoolwork, he thought. As he turned to Alana, she rolled her pretty, hazel eyes. "You don't agree?"

"Maybe Dad should talk to him."

"No. I'm his father."

"Has he been talking to you?"

"No."

"Have you been talking to *him*?" When he groaned, she added, "Tight-lipped isn't good, my love. It's worrisome in someone we care about."

He caught the dig, chose to ignore it by kissing her cheek before leaving their bed. Taking a tepid shower, he knew he had mastered stepping around every bothersome issue for days. Some mornings, he'd fall back asleep after Alana left the bedroom. It killed time. Some mornings, lost in thought, he'd lock the door and sit in the Queen Anne chair for hours. He still wondered how, and more importantly, *why* he was alive. And the unsettling mind-image, night after night, of crucifixes inside his sister's writing chest didn't occur in the daylight hours.

****

The towel hung low on Michael's hips when he came back into the bedroom.

"Your phone's on the dresser. Hit the number one to connect with Clarke's office," Alana said as she left their bed to shower.

He quickly pulled on a pair of black jeans and a dark shirt, slipped his feet into the comfortable leather loafers. He took the private elevator down. Walking out of the dark garage, he breathed a sigh of relief while standing in warm, Amalfi sun. Business didn't have troubling emotions attached. Patrick Christenson, his accountant, had relocated in Portofino to create The Malone Corporation in his absence. Hiking up the steep hill to Christenson's villa exercised both muscle and mind.

The footpath, not the paved road, was more his style. Memories of crawling up this mountain to rescue Lukas from Cyril flooded back. Seeing his son paralyzed with fear, driving a wooden pole through his Sire's chest, and then slicing off the demon's head. After his son had already turned Zoltan into dust and bone... Slowing his pace to study the dense trees, Michael spit out, "You got what you deserved, Cyril. You fucking made me a monster."

****

Not having to answer one probing question about his new existence was a welcomed break. And over coffee, giving an overview of what had been accomplished, Christenson had proved to be a financial genius. In ten short months, a highly reputable finance company to shore up sound businesses in need of assistance had been flourishing.

They moved from the kitchen to the dining room, which had been turned into an office. Michael skipped over the boring details, read through a stack of files, and tried to focus on pie charts and percentages during the Power Point presentation. "Your funds are secure and growing," Christenson finally stated.

Recalling the other vampire who had terrified his son, he asked, "You've dismantled the Hungarian's conglomerate?"

"It's all here. Zoltan's Vashkar Enterprises is fully dissected with every nuance legitimate, clean, and well-documented."

"Please spare me the rest of the details. Four hours is my limit." He eyed a second stack of binders, which seemed too many high hurdles for his mind to jump.

"Bottom line, Michael? You're a wealthy man with a solid portfolio and flourishing investments. And Ally's done terrific with the bookstore. It's so far in the black that I'm amazed at her business skills."

"You've done it all from here?"

Christenson nodded. "Are you ready to look for office space?"

"Not if I can help it," he replied with a scowl. After a tense nod, he stood. "I'll be in touch," he said before walking out the villa's door.

Making his way down the hill, as he'd done every hour previously, Michael pressed the preset number on his cell phone. This time, he spoke directly to Headmaster Clarke at the Georgian Institute in Hampton Hill and his irritation with Lukas hit new heights. No homework, unanswered emails from Clarke, and no explanation had his full attention as he hiked down the steep slope sure-footed and brisk.

His eyes quickly adjusted to the dark garage while he strode toward the elevator. When it opened, he entered and pressed the button with forced control. In a way, he didn't trust his reaction, not thrilled at all to jump into parenting. The ride up seemed endless, and after stepping into the marble foyer, silent long strides continued to his son's door. One hand gripped the knob as he heard, "Yeah, so come in. I don't lock it because, you know, you'd just break it down." The smug tone irked him more and walking in, he narrowed his eyes.

Closing some textbook about literature, his son leaned back from the desk, locked his arms across a dark-blue polo shirt that matched the color of his eyes. One glance at the open laptop's screensaver, he recognized the Georgian Estate in England. His focus drifted to the Internet icon at the bottom saying a curt, "Get up."

Muttering a curse, Lukas shot out of the chair and all but leaped in the opposite direction to the far wall.

"What's the matter? Afraid I'll get parental, and you'll be over my knee staring at the floor while sobbing?" Lukas eyed the door, and he cautioned, "Don't do it, because you won't get far." His son looked like he had stopped breathing when he slid a finger over the mouse-pad bringing up the Internet. A small box with a smiling yellow face appeared. "What is this?"

"An IM, which means—"

"I know what it means. Who are striderwolf02 and scribbles99? What the hell is a huggz3c and gamer111?"

"They're my friends at the estate. Why don't you send me back?"

While tempted, it'd be the easy way out. "Absolutely not," he stated in a clipped fashion. "Here with me is where you will stay. I spoke to Clarke. Get offline and finish all your homework assignments—by tonight." Lukas set his jaw, flashed a challenging glare.

Before completely losing it, Michael strode out of the room, slamming the door so hard that the window rattled.

"No fucking way," he heard mumbled through the thick wooden door.

How do I play this, he thought. Pacing the wide expanse of the living room, he didn't care for his son's game-plan. This defiance would push him into an unyielding corner. Then, when he pushed back everyone would come to Lukas's defense, no doubt, saying his son's backside shouldn't sting and *he* needed to exhibit more patience and understanding.

Christ, he thought, this is a setup and I'm as good as trapped. He walked out of his home, hurried down each set of stairs. Bypassed the bookshop and headed for the crowded piazza. The midday throng of chatty tourists annoyed him, and he veered in another direction. *Some Champion... Give me a God-damned vamp and let me see which one of us walks away because being human isn't all it's cracked up to be.*

By the time the simplistic beauty of San Giorgio Church came into view, his inner rant took a turn. Less than a week ago, Michael Malone, the mystically enhanced creature of the night, had ceased to exist. He readily recalled Monsignor Scarlatti's compassion, his ease dealing with a vampire, an unclean thing. Outside the rectory, he sensed the priest's acceptance once again. And although Miles left three messages a day on his cell phone insisting he come here, Michael had ignored each one. The spiritual leader of the Georgian Sovereign Council had given a young Englishman's soul absolution. But I have nothing to say, nothing to ask, he thought. *No. Don't lie to yourself... I just don't know where or how to start.*

His feet stayed glued to the ground in front of the screen door until Monsignor Scarlatti pushed it open. "It's been a long wait. *Va bene... Avanti.*"

Tall and impressive, the priest stepped aside, graciously motioned him in. Michael followed him down the rectory's corridor into the study, not knowing what to say to the other man in the room. He took a seat at the table across from the researcher.

Miles leaned back, scrutinizing him over rimless reading glasses. "It took you long enough. Seven days was the limit, and we had Thorn's word he'd get you here—one way or another."

The dry tone, the no-nonsense expression ramped up his uneasiness. Glancing at the monsignor standing behind Miles, he gave a thin grin.

"It's good to see you," Monsignor Scarlatti said in a friendly tone.

"Hello, Father," he replied, and then met the researcher's cold eyes. "I know what you think, Miles."

"I highly doubt it."

Monsignor said, "You are finding your way through life, *si*? It goes slowly."

"Slowly and blindly," he offered still glaring at Miles. "Want to take a swing, Researcher? I wouldn't stop you."

"I imagine you've taken enough swings at yourself since you've been back. It's obvious you've chosen to avoid me."

A truthful accusation, he realized, admitting, "I've kept to myself," before he closed his mouth. After a nervous shift, as both men looked behind him, he glanced over his shoulder. Then he stared as well. The stone bust resembled a knight. It stood next to a mural almost the size of the wall. Singed and discolored, the masterpiece depicted a scene of men either accepting a judgment or making a plea. They stood in golden ribbons of sunlight streaming through a stained-glass window. *XIII* was carved in the corner of the canvas. "Where did you get those?"

"They arrived yesterday by courier," the monsignor informed. "Why do you ask?"

He barely heard the question. "The painting has a distinct odor of scorched wood. Who sent them?"

"A Georgian from the Boston Museum, and Mother Anne received a similar painting."

"Is a number carved on it as well?"

"Yes, the Roman numeral twelve."

"Did you call Mary Kendrick in Manhattan? She's an art historian, a gallery owner."

"Monsignor is well aware of Mary Kendrick's skills," Miles interjected.

"Is that a sculpture of someone I know?" he asked.

"It appears to be medieval. The stamp reads 1355," Monsignor replied.

"Rutted and scarred," he whispered after a tight swallow. He honed in on the painting's once vibrant oils, hues of yellow and gray.

The priest sat down, leaned across the table. "What troubles you, *Signore*?"

Cyril's image swirled through his brain like a ghost in the mist. It made his heart race. Not giving an answer, he pulled out his cell phone. After minutes of fumbling, he aimed correctly to capture both art pieces in one frame.

"*Signore*," the priest repeated.

"I'm sorry, Father. What did you say?" he asked as he slipped his phone into the back pocket of his jeans. Something told him not to touch them as he ran his fingers through his hair.

Chapter 6

Alana glared at another pile of books to catalog between customers. Rarely were weekdays this busy. Had Lu been caught up with his homework, he'd be here to help.

"Not happening," she groaned, "One down, too many to go on another frustrating day." Her intuition clanged like a gong gone wild. If it continued, she'd have to stop this task altogether. And recalling the way Michael stormed down the street an hour ago had only heightened her anxiety.

Her sister rushed in and sat across from the cluttered desk. Celia craned her neck sideways with a frown, rubbing a wet spot off the pink, print blouse. "Thorn says we should start a clothing line for moms. It'll have a removable patch on the left shoulder. We can call it "Infant Spit-up Gear" and make a fortune, ya think?"

This visit was a good reason to put off the endless logging of stock. She leaned back with a chuckle. "So how did the formula go down yesterday?"

"I hate to admit it, but we've turned a corner. Uri slept through the night." Beaming proud, Celia moved a pile of books to the to-be-shelved table. "Um, did Gabby mention any weird vibes to you?"

"No, and I'm not feeling any demony things in Portofino. It's been quiet lately. I don't think I could handle mayhem right now, anyway. Wait. Did you have another nightmare?"

Celia read the back cover of a new paranormal romance. "The same box of crosses. Oooh...I like indigo blue."

"That's it—indigo-blue crosses?"

"What? No, they're silver and gold. I-I meant the cover of this book." She put it down. "I don't know, maybe it's the christening shindig that's got me jangled. But we had to wait until Michael came back, right?"

"My mystical nephew is already a child of God."

"I hear you, but maybe I shouldn't have insisted we baptize him on Easter. Then there's the party at Vito's restaurant, and did you hear? Momma B can stay for an entire week!"

"Lu needs her here, because if things don't change between him and his father, Grandma Laura will definitely speak up. I think Dad needs some TLC, too. What's been going on at the rectory every day?"

"Thorn says it's too sketchy to share. But I sense a new event brewing somewhere. And Dad booked a hotel room, which I think is smart. He's not sleeping well. Plus, Mom's bringing work."

"I don't know how she reads all that scientific gibberish and still has a brain at the end of the day. It'd drive me batty. I saw one medical text she edited. Doctor terms have too many syllables. Give me a good love story, and I'm happy." She stretched her arms wide with a long sigh. "So did you run the dream by Thorn?"

Celia's mouth turned down in an unnatural frown. "What is it about fatherhood? You know, Michael has good reason to be unhinged. My husband doesn't. Uh, have the two of you talked yet?"

"He's distant, and avoids talking like he's nowhere near dealing with life, love, *or* the pursuit of happiness. And Lu is behind big time on homework."

"No way! Jeez, I've been so wrapped up in milk issues that maybe I've neglected... Oh. This is about daddy issues."

She nodded once. "Lu's back to one-word mumbles. I found the red car in a different parking space yesterday. I swear I smelled cigarette smoke on his shirt."

"Did Michael?"

"If he did, he's acting oblivious." Her eyes narrowed. "Have you grabbed any strange vibes off Vito's nephew? Nico's a fast talker and I don't like him hanging around here so much."

"Sorry, Ally, the vibe thing isn't flowing the way it used to. What if I talk to Lu? There's a special place in my heart—"

"Normally, I'd say 'Oh please, Celia B,' but not this time. There's a great big knot in my gut saying Michael has to handle it."

"You know, maybe its motherhood or no sleep. I'm just not seeing things clearly."

"Hence, we have the reason why women like Gabby, Maggie, and Mother Anne exist. They have psychic clarity, which is never clouded by personal relationships, diapers *or* missing homework assignments. In spite of all the life snags, walking that solitary path is a huge price to pay for their mystical gifts."

"But the consequences of not fulfilling one's destiny are exorbitant."

Alana shook her head. "You're right on that one, Celia B."

****

An hour after Celia left, books were still piled high on Alana's desk. Studying an incorrect invoice, she looked up to see Michael watching her. With a helpless expression on his face, he tentatively handed her his cell phone.

"I need to send a picture to Mary Kendrick, quick. How do I do this?"

"What's the email address?" The blank stare said he didn't have a clue. "What's Mary's phone number?" Again, the same look. "Okay. I'm sure The Kendrick Gallery in Manhattan has a website. That email's the most direct way for her to see it." She turned to her computer. The Internet opened, and the homepage loaded while he paced the office. "What's the matter?"

"I've seen this painting. I can remember every detail from centuries ago, yet something about this one eludes me. Mary will know. I'm sure of it."

Pointing to the chair, she asked him to sit, but sinking down, he still appeared edgy. And as soon as the gallery site appeared, he shot back up. "Give me your phone. I'll send the picture to myself." She used both thumbs, typing in her email address. When the mail icon popped up on the screen, Alana opened it and the picture appeared. "Take a look."

He leaned across the desk with a soft, admirable "Wow."

"Now we forward this to her website and...*voila!*

Mary has it. Please sit again." Although he didn't appear calm, he complied. "I stored her personal number in your phone. See? Press this number and ... Hi, Mary...Oh, sorry. It's Martine."

He grabbed the phone away. "Martine, where's your mother? Okay. Stop talking... Yeah, I need to...Mary? It's—" With a wince, he held it a full foot away from his ear.

Alana could hear Martine's mother yelling at him from New York. "I told you to call—days ago," she whispered to him. Of course, he had refused, and so she called two days ago—without telling him. Martine emailed Celia regularly, and Martha Kendrick, Mary's mother, had kept in touch with Miles during Michael's ten-month absence. They were close family friends.

Glaring, he continued in short bursts, "Okay... I'm sorry... All right, I deserve... But Mare, I...I—" He handed her his phone. "She doesn't want to talk to me."

She heard the hurt in his voice, and calmly took the phone from his hand. After a brief exchange, she told him, "Mary will research the painting and email the info. Do you want to say good-bye?" Leaning forward, she snagged his guilty gaze. "I didn't think so."

In a friendly fashion, she said into the phone, "Thanks, Mare. And when Martine's ready to do the Tibetan bells thing, she should talk to Celia B. Give Martha our love? Great. Are you coming for the christening? Great again! See you for Easter. We'll talk soon," she said, ending the call.

Aware of his bristle as well as the brood sweeping across his face, she handed back his cell phone. He quickly snatched it, and in a typical pose, his long arms locked across his broad chest with his feet slightly apart. It was a vision of masculinity, rough and ready power. Not able to concentrate on work, she had to take a long, slow breath. "So, what else can I do for you? I've got tons of work tonight. There are leftovers in the fridge."

"I'd prefer to help you down here."

"Go up and eat something…please." That wasn't what she wanted to say but staring at his handsome face made her heart race. He looked so lost, so perturbed. Five more minutes alone with him, she'd bolt the office door, pin him down on the desk and after pulling off those tight black jeans, she would… The bell on the door tinkled which meant a customer had walked in. Thankfully, it pulled her back as she stood up. "How's Lu?"

"I didn't smack his ass if that's what you're asking. You'd have heard him wailing down here if I had. I took the considerate Miles Bookman route."

"Has he sent any of his homework yet?"

"There's only one way to find out." Michael took out his phone and hit the number one. His distinctive, wide strides around her and into the hall were a total distraction. Just his presence forced her to take another moment before going into the main section of the shop. Then she had a thought…

While the tourist browsed the shelves, she picked up the landline behind the counter to call Mary Kendrick again. Having all the necessary connections, I could pull this one request off immediately, she thought. And if she handled everything right, it just might help the man she loved—because nothing equaled her devotion to him. Nothing equaled the ache in her soul.

****

After Michael spoke to Clarke, he quickly headed up the two flights of stairs to their home. Reality stung as if he had been thrown into a tub of ice, and the necessary interaction with his son roiled him. Lukas wouldn't like what was coming next. He recalled the ripe scent of beer and cigarettes on his son's clothes. The odor of gasoline as if he'd been in someone's car. They were all issues, and he needed to plan, not procrastinate, even though he was definitely not in the mood for a confrontation.

He stood in the kitchen thinking, and Alana's aromatic pesto sauce, which smothered homemade tortellini, smelled heavenly. His mouth watered as his stomach growled, something he still wasn't used to. Piling the round pasta on a cake plate, he popped it in the microwave on the granite counter. Forget about the reheat setting. He pressed the number five and waited. After a ding, the pasta steamed and sizzled. One heaping forkful set his mouth on fire. Unable to swallow, he spit it out in the sink, continued coughing until he downed a glass of cold water. Not about to try a second time, he pushed the plate aside, once again deep in thought.

In that small office Alana's scent had called to him. Her body temperature had soared; so had his. And before he left, her arousal filled him with desire, so much so that he wanted to strip her and take her right on the desk. He studied the round mosaic table under the window in the kitchen, imagining her naked, lying across it. Before the next erotic thought had him hard, he forced Alana out of his brain and told himself to switch gears fast... *really* fast. It took a minute.

Then, staring straight ahead, he strode through the dining room and down the hall thinking, this time, I don't knock. When he wrenched open the door, Lukas jumped up from his desk with his fists curled tight at the ready. He eyed his son. Fear definitely stood in those narrow eyes.

"You're gonna smack my ass."

"Not yet." Very calmly, he walked over and closed the laptop's lid. "Pick up your school books. Come to the dining room—right now. Bring paper and pencil as well."

"This isn't the Seventeenth Century. I use a gel pen."

Not about to debate writing instruments, he replied, "A pencil."

As slow as a snail, his son searched the desk drawer. Every item dropped to the carpet creating more of a mess than it already was. At last, Lukas produced a pencil, which resembled a weapon in his hand.

"It has no point, and I don't own a sharpener."

"Get a move on. Let's go."

Lukas rolled his eyes, quickly stepped around him. Patience and calm, he told himself. Taking the pencil his son had tossed on the table into the kitchen, he pulled a knife off the rack and whittled a sharp point. Returning to the dining room, Michael sat at the head of the table. Without a word, he crossed his legs and folded his hands, simmering while his son squirmed and avoided his gaze.

"Headmaster Clarke wants pages 369 through 400 by midnight or the math teacher will lower your grade five points for each day it's been overdue."

"That's thirty-one pages!" Lukas shot up, started to

walk away.

"Where do you think you're going?"

"I do homework on my laptop, Dad."

"Nope, I want it longhand."

"No fucking way!"

"Watch your mouth. I hear another curse tonight and you'll find out if my mystical strength is still intact in a promised, parental way. Sit down."

Flopping into the chair, Lukas whined, "It'll take all *night* to write every equation out. Then what? I send this snail mail to England? I'll fail!"

"It will be faxed from the bookstore's office—after I review each page to make sure it's legible. Now start."

Lukas stared at the book. Both arms dangled at his sides as he whispered, "No... fu...way."

Keeping a cool expression, Michael knew he had him. He opened the math textbook, pointed to the first mathematical sentence. "Pick up the pencil. Use proper headings on every page. I assume you understand Clarke's request. First this assignment, and then three chapters on Romantic poets with essay questions answered and thirty pages of French translation—all overdue." After a pause, he said. "Look at me, little boy." Dark-blue, glistening eyes met his unyielding gaze. "All longhand, all legible... If you don't want to end up across my knee, I suggest you begin."

****

When he went down to fax the math homework, Alana showed him how to use that component on her printer. "How's he doing?"

"Well, at least he won't fail math," he replied as it sent. He offered little else, not willing to discuss the homework marathon or anything else.

He heard her come up after midnight, while his son was on the last essay question. She said nothing, going directly into their bedroom and shutting the door as his son struggled with metaphoric prose.

But two hours later, all assignments were complete. Although calm, he allowed more than a hint of a threat in his tone. "Learn the lesson, little boy. This will *never* happen again. Now go to your room."

His son's lips quivered, and those deep-blue eyes filled, but he got up without muttering a curse word and walked away.

****

Lukas knew he had brought this on himself. And he had punched the pillow repeatedly as tear after tear dripped. His head hurt like hell instead of his backside. They hadn't talked, well... actually, his father didn't look like he wanted to. With Alana and the bookstore so busy, he'd been eating dinner downstairs with Celia and Thorn to avoid his father.

He turned over in his bed, stared at the ceiling and swiped at his eyes. Everyone said he needed time. "Yeah, right," he muttered. "Maybe turning human isn't what he wanted." He rubbed his aching temples. "Shit... I'd rather my ass ache than my head."

****

Michael had waited until his son's bedroom door closed, and then went down to Alana's office. This was a bitter victory and faxing each subject assignment separately took time. Thankfully, not a single page had snagged. With the last page sending, he eyed the clock.

After a slow return to the third floor, he entered the master bedroom. Hoping not to disturb Alana, he undressed and crawled into bed. With an exhausted moan, he settled on his side. Her arm suddenly came over his; her warm hand covered his heart. The unconscious move had become a ritual, as if one of these nights he'd have no heartbeat.

"What time is it?" she whispered. Her voice sounded groggy and low, and stifling the uncomfortable ability to yawn, he replied, "Almost three-thirty."

"How's Lu?"

"Fast asleep, I'm sure. I'll wake him at seven to start the new assignments I had Clarke send."

"That's cruel."

"That's life," he replied, still miffed by his son's lack of responsibility.

She turned away. For the first time since his return, she made no new attempt to hold him close. It felt like a brutal punch. Subtle anger rumbled through his heart. And craving her touch, he ached for her. *Apologize, caress her and let your hand explore every supple curve. Feel her spring to life and take her. Satiate this natural, human need. Living seed will fill her now.* Like never before, he wanted release.

Taking shallow breaths, the inches between them seemed a chasm he just couldn't cross.

Chapter 7

Waiting for the coffee maker to stop dripping, Alana whispered, "Seven a.m. and all is not well." A drawn-out yawn caught her off guard—as did the feeling of Michael being lost to her forever. Not even the slightest chance of casual conversation this morning, and yet last night, she had sensed his need for her. Now, he sat quiet at the mosaic table in the kitchen, aloof and unapproachable. Whether or not the man she loved was ready, she wondered if what she'd done without his knowledge would end this stand-off between them. She placed two mugs of coffee down.

He took a sip and before he stood, she grabbed his hand, shook her head. "No. Let him sleep."

The cutting glower lasted a full thirty seconds. "Why? So we can sit here like this, darlin'?"

"You got it, buddy." His nostrils flared, his jaw tensed. He never liked that last word nor the tone her voice had when she said it— to him. "Lu's exhausted. He never *once* acted up while you were away."

"So what you're saying is it's me, my being back."

"You want to provoke him."

"No, I don't."

"Yes, you do."

"I sat here last night and *helped* him."

"My father would've—"

"Miles would've done exactly what I did. And my

81

son definitely deserved a more traditional punishment. I know Lukas well enough. He's in trouble."

"Then talk to him."

"He's not ready to listen."

"You don't know that! Call Clarke. Explain the extenuating circumstances in his life right now."

"No. Lukas will accept the consequences of his actions."

"You know how that feels, don't you." She braced for his reply, noticed an arrogant smirk instead of an irate glare.

"It seems I can't do anything right. Can't parent a teenager, send a picture from a phone or help in the bookshop. Last night you pulled away from me. What else do you want to add to the "He can't" list? Go ahead, darlin', jump in whenever you want."

"Get up and follow me because I'm not about to bicker this early in the morning." Standing at the door, she realized he hadn't budged, and walking back, met his intense gaze with one of her own. "Stand up and follow, Michael. I insist."

****

Annoyed beyond reason, Michael cursed under his breath, but followed Alana down to the first floor. She opened the basement door and took the stairs quickly. Frozen on the landing he relived the last time he'd seen these wooden steps—Celia's pitiful cries, Rosa's lifeless body, Miles's broken legs, Thorn bleeding to death, and Lukas taken to Cyril… Shutting his eyes, fear constricted his now healthy veins. His heart rate doubled and sweat coated his palms. Unpleasant, mortal feelings, which I haven't experienced in centuries, he thought as he leaned against the wooden doorframe.

"Michael, come down here," Alana called again.

He hesitated, took the narrow steps slowly. The smell of the earthen floor in a rarely used space assaulted him. Paused on the bottom step, a faint familiar scent poked through his haze.

Alana stood beneath the solitary light bulb. "I called Mary Kendrick back after you left. Her family held onto these for you."

"How did all of it get here?" he asked in disbelief.

"Medico had a transport plane coming to Florence via Newark Airport. Kayla's dad was more than happy to add everything to the manifest because it was for you. It arrived while you were preoccupied—with homework."

"All from my brownstone in Manhattan?"

"Everything you once treasured."

He scanned a dozen large, labeled boxes, easily ripped each one open. Clothes, boots, personal items— each held a distinct meaning. Some he had owned for centuries. Leather-bound books, priceless first editions signed by renowned authors. Reverently, he touched each book cover, recalled the precise minute when each one had come into his possession.

One specific item, apart from the boxes, had truly defined his mystical existence. The trunk was very old. His hand ran down and amazement replaced ambivalence as he stroked its oiled wood. Brass latches opened with ease, and both doors slid against the earth with minimal sound. Michael eyed every weapon…tools of his trade used to destroy evil entities that lurked during dark nights, always hungering for innocent prey and *his* Guardian's blood.

"Go ahead," she softly urged. "Look inside."

Without question, he complied. "Everything's here, stakes, swords of different lengths. Your scent is on all of them."

"*I* was preoccupied with polish and talc last night."

Then his eyes lit on an unexpected vision. The broadsword stood sheathed in carved black leather, wedged tight on a diagonal across the left side of the trunk. "My God…you found it."

"Not me, my love. Thank Martine Kendrick. It was left under a rusted dumpster in the passageway after your battle with Hell-beasts last May. Apparently, NWT only wanted your poisoned body. Martha went ballistic knowing they had captured you and she sent Martine to retrieve it."

"Never underestimate the power of a good witch. How'd she do it?"

"Mary pulled a strand of hair off your comb in the brownstone, Martha mixed it with a few unpronounceable ingredients, and Martine retrieved it."

"My Martha," he said with tenderness. "Decades ago, I rescued her from the claws of a hungry vampire. She was only five years old—and very brave. It was my first encounter with a mortal that didn't include the drink and drain."

"She has always loved you, Michael."

"I never thought I'd hold this again. Thank you."

"You're welcome. Now please get reacquainted with who you are," she said, already midway up the staircase.

Michael gripped the broadsword's hilt, pulled it clear from the carved sheath. The smell of oil and talc blended with Alana's scent, erasing all evidence of his battle with Hell-beasts. To examine it closer, he held it in his left hand, and then sliced the silver-coated blade through the musty air. Finding the nick near its pommel, he eyed three tiny letters—his initials. *The name's the same, but who am I now? What am I now?*

The last full moon of 1890 became a vivid recall. Bright stars lit the winter's Manhattan sky on the night he found the pristine blade on his brownstone's doorstep. The angel Helena's gift had never known an evil hand. It never would. *Helena allowed me to master the beast Cyril implanted within my soul. She knew I had made powerful enemies in the vampire world.* "I culled the damned creatures, and you were always in my hand after the Georgian's tagged me mystically enhanced," he whispered. He closed his eyes, sensed eternal enchantments engraved upon it.

Returned to its sheath, he leaned the sword against the trunk taking stock of other possessions the Kendricks had retrieved. A favorite long, wool coat, which hung from his shoulders in an intimidating way and comfortable boots, more suitable for fighting unearthly evil than the soft loafers on his feet. He set those aside, more eager to study his books. These treasures represented centuries of inquiry to keep his mind sharp, his manner of speech current through changing decades. *They were this vampire's daily walks in the sun, my private desires long before Technicolor dawns and the taste of Alana's sweet kisses.*

****

Not about to awaken Lukas, Alana dressed for the day and hurried down to get some work done before she opened for customers. *Thank God for the Kendricks. Those ladies always come through, especially for him.* Taking a slow breath, she had to stop worrying about

85

Michael and begin another busy day. She stopped on the second-floor landing hoping her sister would appear at the door. Disappointed when it didn't happen, she went down the next flight of stairs and entered her office from the hall door. An easy smile began. "How long have you been waiting?"

"Not long... He just needs a little time and space, Ally."

She sank into the chair behind her desk. Seeing a sympathetic smile, her eyes instantly filled. "I love him so much, Celia B."

"No one ever said love is easy."

"I'm not looking for easy. I'm looking for answers. He's slipping away, and I don't understand why. You and Thorn have a non-verbal line of communication going 24/7."

"Sweetie, Michael loves you."

"I don't know what to do for him. What if our destiny—"

"Destinies don't change, Ally."

"But he isn't a creature of the night now. He's a living man."

"Space and time... You'll know what to do and when to do it."

"You think? I love him too much to lose him again."

"You said it in his dream. You said it last May."

"Psychic wisdom spoken from a very wise soul," she whispered as a slight grin began.

"Nah... Maybe too many lifetimes of searching for my soulmate. In other lives, I often found peace, but never such incredible love."

****

Last night's homework session with his father had been torture. Today's list of assignments took most of the day to complete. Lukas knew the next time he slacked off his father wouldn't be forgiving. He eyed the IM when it appeared, typing back *"just sent to Clarke. No lie, Mom, all finished."*

"Good boy. Go to the basement and offer help. Be nice," was followed by *"no pouty face, capisce?"*

He cursed while typing *"help do what?"* Her next IM read, *"Don't argue either."*

"Yeah, right," he muttered and rubbed his aching temples. After hitting print, ten pages spit out next to his laptop. I could stall, he thought, but more than curious, he left his room and jumped one staircase, then the next. From the last landing he whispered, "Ready or not, here I come."

He took the basement steps slow— like a human. Eyeing his father on the floor amidst piles of books, he asked without attitude, "You want me to bring those up?" No answer came as he caught sight of an old trunk. Slowly approaching, he studied the weapons.

"Pretty neat, huh?"

He sounds normal, not crazy mad, he thought. "Cool stuff. Are they all yours?"

"Yes."

"You want the trunk upstairs?"

"No…only this."

He stared with admiration at the carved leather sheath. "This is the sword you used on the Hell-beasts. It's *wicked* cool. How'd you find it?"

"I didn't. Martine Kendrick did…"

Martine, he thought, recalling the crazy-wild girl with the bushy black bun. He'd often see his father talking, no, wait, arguing with her… during the year Lukas hunted him.

"Want to see how it fits your hand?" His father stood, slipped the spectacular weapon out of the sheath. When he handed it over, Lukas studied the worn leather where his father's unnatural grip had imprinted the hide. He ran a thumb up the sharp blade, knowing that if he sliced his skin, the wound would instantly close. Then his eyes narrowed. "Why three M's—not two?"

"I have a middle name, a baptismal name."

"Do I have one?" It was a question he couldn't ask last May.

"Lukas, I had you in my arms for less than a minute."

Securing the broadsword's tip in the earthen floor, full frustration surfaced. "Why won't you tell me how I was born? Auntie Celia read in the dream journal that *you* said I look like my mother. Who was she?"

"I don't know if you were ever christened. Helena never told me."

"But who was my mother?"

"Drop it."

"No! No birth certificate, no identity, nothing. I guess I don't exist!"

"I said drop it." His father grabbed a stack of old books, started to leave. "Bring the broadsword. I want it upstairs."

The cool order stunned like a slap. He bit back rage before *every* question spilled out. Slow and seething, he took the stairs.

****

Well aware of his son's temper, Michael wasn't about to calmly describe the dark seer, nor the "gift" of immortality she'd be given by three evil sorcerers. Had I waited a mere ten seconds longer, she would've ended your life before you were born, he thought, and one can't explain *that* to a boy who doesn't choose to listen. He brought up the rest of the books—by himself. And when he was done, the den looked like a disheveled library with no sense of order in sight.

Thirst suddenly surfaced, and not for blood. In the kitchen, he grabbed a cold bottle of water from the refrigerator and finished it in a few swallows. Accepting the necessity to eat, he pulled out a covered plate from the top shelf. At the counter, he waited for it to heat in the microwave, and then quickly devoured mouthfuls of lukewarm meatballs in a thick tomato sauce.

"Mom heats them up longer," his son quipped from the wide wooden arch.

"I'll remember to do that next time."

"You know, her cooking skills are radical. Sister Maggie taught her all of *Zia's* recipes."

Michael placed the plate in the sink, recognizing the emphasis on 'mom' and 'her,' aware of what worked on Lukas's mind. "Let me see your homework," he said in an even tone. He watched the reluctant shuffle out and waited at the kitchen table. Returning just as slowly, Lukas threw pages of paper down and then leaned against the side of the arch. Smart move, he thought, standing out of my reach. He studied sentences on the first page. "You're a very good writer, even in a somewhat complicated language."

"You read French?"

"I was in Paris for decades during the Romantic Era to enjoy parlor performances by Chopin." He tried to engage his son in a good way. "Have you picked up Italian?"

"*Certo, Pappa.* That means—"

"I know what it means. Have you begun Latin or Greek?"

"Next year... Gramps says educated men know these things. Mom agrees."

Another less subtle dig, he was certain. "He's right. Now please come here and sit down." As day faded into night, it was Michael's turn to take his time. Pages of homework were scrutinized, and he phrased every question with thought, having one distinct impression: his son couldn't wait to get away from him.

****

In the southwest area of Florence on *Piazza de Michelangelo*, Veronique stood on her balcony. From her boudoir, she always found the magnificent panorama stunning. The sensual lure of sunset over the Arno River, the distant Tuscan hills had drawn her to this particular estate on the piazza in the 1860s. She had feasted on the owner and his family for an entire month before ending their misery—after the property was legally "gifted" to her.

Raven-black hair like silky perfection fluttered in a slight spring breeze. Since the night of turning in 1282, black remained her preference. Stockings, corsets, suits or gowns, *this* vampire would never be 'caught dead' in gauche prints or muted hues. Her eighteen-inch waist and sensuous cleavage defied modern bone structure...an eternal medieval beauty. Anything she wore looked exquisite, even after so many centuries.

She had aged better than most Sires.

Gliding through the threshold, heat radiated from

soft lights, tinted bulbs found in wealthier Italian homes. Dreamlike shadows intrigued the mind, gave her ivory skin a hint of human color. After being bathed and dressed by minions, they provided her with sustenance of the most nutritious variety. With veins vibrant-blue and full, the dark goddess, as Veronique liked to be called, made her way to a secure internal room.

Feet barely touched cold marble—the etiquette of a schooled princess. Her presence remained undetectable when entering this space, more technologically advanced than the rest of her home. Only the trace of a favorite perfume hinted at her whereabouts. The ability to adapt to any century, any lifestyle sustained her throughout time. It had kept the vampire safe for hundreds of years while she roamed the earth.

With a regal flourish, Veronique settled at a polished ebony desk. Timing always exceptional, she sensed Leonard Gerhardt waiting in his own sanctuary thousands of miles away. The video link, projected on the far wall, shimmered to life. She whispered to the soon-to-be sorcerer, "*Ciao bene,* Leonard."

****

Veronique's digitalized image always took Leonard's breath away. Large sapphire eyes and soft crimson lips stirred his sexual senses. After lowering a gaze of adoration, he whispered, "Good evening, my dark goddess. All is ready. My sacrifice arrives in Siena tomorrow."

"You will be one of the finest new sorcerers in your century after this bold undertaking. My minions will assist as you see fit. Your granddaughter will be protected from discovery."

For a moment, the familial term shocked him. Yet he felt no tug to his heart. The prestige of pulling off what had never been tried remained his distinguished honor. Tasting triumph, Gerhardt replied, "The new host vessel will serve you well."

"Indeed," she sighed with a charming grin. "I have lost three offspring in this carnage, but I have missed only one's bloodlust so passionate, so sensual since 1890—since the meddling angel denied me the pleasure of his company."

"But in a virgin girl's body, my goddess, your progeny will stay close to you... this time."

Veronique leaned into the webcam. Her mesmerizing eyes filled the screen. "Will you join me for the maiden's turning? I do not grant this privilege to *any* living beings."

The lure of her voice, the sparkle of her white teeth that glistened like tiny white pearls... His groin tightened then swelled as if he were a young stud again. "I'd be honored, my goddess."

A feminine laugh teased his senses. "As Easter dawns, we shall mark a resurrection of our own." The video feed went dead.

****

Alana came up after another busy day, her mind anxious to switch gears. As an ex-Guardian, even after her ten-year mission, mystical strength had not diminished, and she liked mentoring Kayla Gonzalez. Their workouts kept her impressive skills honed and fresh.

The house seemed too quiet as she knocked on Lukas's door.

"It's open," was his reply.

She leaned in. "Homework?"

"Done."

"Dad?"

"Den."

"Thanks," she said, before walking down the hall.

She heard the CD playing, recognized a somber prelude, the illusion of raindrops on a windowpane coming from a piano. Michael sat on the floor next to neat piles of books. All familiar, all from his Manhattan brownstone... His living room had often reminded her of a library with custom-built dark wood shelves brimming with centuries of literature. He seemed relaxed, at home while focused on an oversized book with a glossy art piece on the page.

"Wednesday nights I train Kayla. I'll be home late." His brow stayed furrowed, his jaw tense. She wormed around the denim loveseat he leaned against and sat close to peer over his shoulder. "Will the shelves be floor to ceiling and mahogany?"

"Oak fits this décor. I'll contact the carpenter who tooled the arches."

"One wall or two, my love?"

"One will do for now."

Torn between forced conversation or just being together like this, she finally said, "Kayla has an early class on Thursdays. Instead of her coming here, we're working out at the Medico facility tonight. May I take the Mercedes? It's heaven to drive."

"There's no reason to ask, Alana," he replied before a sharp click of his tongue. "Of course... Mucha. Damn it."

She leaned closer to see over his broad shoulder. "What's a mucha?"

"Alphonse Mucha was a Moravian painter in the late 1800s. He created a series of murals called *The Slav Epic*. The one sent to the rectory is the thirteenth... Each one has a saying ascribed to it. Treaties are to be observed is attached to this one," he said in a hushed tone.

He seemed fascinated with it, and gently, she kissed his cheek. "I'll tell Kayla you said hello."

Instantly, he looked at her. "Be careful around Florence."

"I'm careful wherever I am."

"No. Be very careful around Florence."

Once again, he studied the picture in the book, but he sounded more like the Michael she knew. And leaving the den she thought, so maybe there's hope for us yet.

****

Hard-driving music throbbed through the headphones as Lukas pulled them off. The way his father had cut him short this morning still smarted. I'll never have answers, he thought, especially when he dies. He sat up in bed, leaned against the headboard shaking his head.

"Where the hell did 'when he dies' come from," he whispered. A scene like a shadow fluttered across the room, and he saw himself covered in blood. "Whoa," he whispered, shaking his head again with his eyes wide. "I'm definitely losing it," he groaned.

He left his room feeling strange and wondered if he should tell his father. Stopping at the door to the den, Lukas stared at him for a full minute. He doesn't even look up from some old book as if he's lost in time, he thought. "Night, Dad."

"Good night, Lukas," his father replied without interest.

Instead of going to his room, he swiped Alana's car key off the secretary in the living room and grabbed a rolled wad of Euros from a wide-mouthed Lenox vase on the hutch. Without a sound, he slipped out the front door. A speedy cruise along the Amalfi coast would clear his head, and he'd stop in the next town for a pack of cigarettes, maybe steal a bottle of beer.

****

Returning after midnight, Alana parked in the garage and took the elevator up to the back foyer. The light was still on in the den, and she approached with more than a little curiosity. Curled up on his side and moaning, Michael was asleep on the denim loveseat.

With little comfort in her soul, she pulled a forest-green crocheted blanket off the back and covered him. After tiptoeing down the hall, she entered their bedroom, closed the door. This is a first, another *unexpected* first, she thought as she stared at the empty sleigh bed.

Chapter 8

By Saturday morning, Lukas didn't want to think about the zombie sleeping in the den after reading worn books. He'd been out the past few nights, sometimes getting into mischief with Nico, sometimes just driving and smoking alone. He rolled out of bed, made it down the hall and took a quick shower. Today was Alana's day to sleep in.

Ten minutes later, dressed in jeans and a clean shirt, he ripped the heel off a loaf of Italian bread in the kitchen and jumped each staircase, confident with his mystical ability to land without injury. Entering from the hall, he walked through the office and into the bookshop. Kayla was dusting the shelves. The smell of lemon oil rubbed into rich-brown wood filled his nostrils.

"I know you're there," she said with a frown.

"What are you doing in Portofino already? I open. You close."

"Ally said you're banned from the shop until further notice." Instantly, he frowned. "Aw...where's the sweet smile with those deep dimples that makes all the girls blush?"

Sitting on the counter, he stared out the window. "I friggin' hate homework."

"Don't lie to a Guardian. You love school. It's all you talk about. Where's Michael?"

"Either sleeping or sitting on the den floor reading shit—hopefully, for the rest of the day… Can I hitchhike to England from Italy?"

She flicked a mantilla of waist-length, black hair off one shoulder and stared at him. "Guardians will find you and bring you back. You know, your father watched out for me and the other Guardians in Manhattan. Cut him a break."

"You're too nice."

"You're too sneaky. I'm not clueless, Lu. Nico is trouble. He's older than you and not known for thinking about what he's doing all the time. Cut it out, *muchachito*."

"Don't call me little boy. I can handle a couple of beers. Mystical genes, remember?"

She put down the rag soaked with oil and shook a finger at him. "Your father—"

"Won't find out."

"Well, you can't hide in here all day."

"Why not?"

"Because you have things to do," Alana said from the office door. "I want your room perfectly clean and straightened up. You have a book report due before Easter, so I suggest you finish reading the book and get that started. If you do, then there are mounds of invoices to be filed in my office. No dealing with customers today."

Jumping off the counter, he wondered how much of his conversation with Kayla she had heard. "I thought you were still asleep."

"Nope. I was downstairs with Celia and Thorn. I'll be out all day with her and the baby. She has a long list of things to get in Pisa for next Sunday's wing-ding.

We're having lots of company."

"Great," he mumbled. There'd be no buffer if his father started on him today.

"Thorn's left for the rectory already," she continued, oblivious to his pout. "Did you hear Gabby and Maggie leave for Villa Catherine this morning?"

"No... why? Did Mother Anne call a summit or something?"

"Tomorrow's Palm Sunday and they *are* real nuns. Oh, Gram brought your suit and a pressed white button-down from the Georgian Estate. You'll look great at the christening party."

"Is she upstairs?"

"No. She's off limits to you, just like the front of the bookstore is. Gramps booked a hotel room, and I'm not telling you which one it is, either. Oh, and your auntie insists on picking out a new tie for you to wear next Sunday."

He rolled his eyes as Kayla's giggle began. "Come on, Mom. It'll be purple or-or pink!"

Her arm came around his shoulder, but he pulled away when she brushed the curls away from his face. "I left a message at Mirella's salon. Make sure you get there for a haircut this morning. It's unkempt and too straggly. I called. She's expecting you."

When she kissed his cheek, he rolled his eyes again. No way would he sit with a bunch of old ladies in curlers today. Forget about cleaning his room, and the filing could wait until he was in the mood to sit still.

****

In a lovely hotel room off the seaport's piazza, Laura Bookman sat across from her husband to fix his morning coffee. Her usual Friday flight had been delayed, which left no time to talk with her daughters before retiring. She had coaxed Miles into bed at midnight, and affectionate moments had been plentiful. But today her intuitive nature positively hummed. His astute mind was somewhere else.

"There are new worry lines, dear. Would they have anything to do with Michael? My impression from both our daughters is he's not yet acclimated to the land of the living."

Miles sighed. "I tend to agree, but they're about something else."

"I know you'll have to be evasive if it's Council business."

"It's never been an issue before," he replied in a curt tone.

Leaning across the small table, her hand rested upon his unshaven cheek to cajole the man she loved. He gave a warm smile. "But we aren't getting younger." After a careful sip of hot tea, she added, "For months, you've not exhibited even the slightest sense of peace within. Salt-and-pepper is slowly fading to silvery white. I'm worried about you."

"I've aged this past year. I know. I'm fine, honey."

As he settled back with a cup of coffee, she pushed a bowl of cut melon toward him. "What has your attention, Miles?"

"Deepa contacted me last week."

Hearing the other researcher's name, she smiled. Deepa Chandra had a highly developed sixth-sense as well. "As much as I miss Manhattan, the city really is a hotbed of paranormal activity, an occultist's favorite place to play."

"This isn't happening in the city. There's a new

group of interest across the Hudson. Do you recall when a few years back, Martha Kendrick told us about a monstrosity under construction in Valley Township?"

Placing her cup down, she nodded. "Distinctly… Set on a major road with a pond in front of it. The property was vacant for years, she had said. Doesn't Mary's good friend live near it?"

"Yes. We met Patrice Virelli a few years back when Mary redesigned the art gallery. She's an accountant with her own business."

"Yes… A lovely woman with a young daughter."

Miles let out a frustrated sigh. "Here is another connection. I'm sorry. I'm getting ahead of myself. The property now has a chalet on it."

"In the middle of a commuter town—without ski slopes…That's rather odd, is it not?"

"It has a thirteen-car garage underneath."

Laura began to smirk. "Ah…a dark coven's favorite number."

"Precisely. But this group is more than a coven. It's some sort of congregation. Deepa did a little prudent digging. Leonard Gerhardt's name came up."

Laura pushed the cup aside. Her expression changed. "I haven't heard his name in years. I presumed he retired from certain *deviant* circles. What a nasty affair when the millennium turned, and the sorcerers chose someone other than his crazy son as their human liaison. After Gunter's suicide, I had thought Leonard slinked much farther away than Jersey to sever his allegiance to NWT."

"Apparently he started a group who worships legendary vampires. Deepa believes they've gone active…very active."

"Oh my," she whispered. Her superior sixth sense hummed as Miles told her about the art pieces.

After airing his thoughts, he added, "We've traced their postmarks to Vermont. The post office is precisely eighteen miles south of Cyril's burned-out estate."

"Cyril," she quickly said. "Three sixes equal eighteen, going south inverts them."

"Security video confirms that Gerhardt carried them into the facility for sending. To make matters more interesting, Patrice called Mary to say her daughter's best friend is now studying in Siena with a prestigious art program. Of course, Mary did some checking. The instructor turns out to be a member of the Order of Catherine."

"Does Monsignor Scarlatti know?"

"Martha called him yesterday."

"Too many oddities mean trouble. I take it there's more."

"Patrice's daughter's friend is Jillian Gerhardt."

"From Valley Township," she stated as her stomach sank.

"Deepa's investigation confirmed the girl's grandfather is—"

"Leonard," she said with a breathy sigh, too stunned to speak.

"Mother Anne has called the healers back to their motherhouse, all except one. She believes Sister Phyllis Verdi is meant to stay with Jillian and five other American students."

"Is Jillian part of Gerhardt's group?"

"No. The child's an innocent. Deepa's research indicates such."

"Is there a connection to Michael?"

"Only that Cyril was his sire. Something about these art pieces is odd, honey. Last year, Georgians combed the property three times. Everything burned, including his servant and his prized horses. Gerhardt's up to something. I have no idea what it is."

"But Deepa agrees."

"So does Monsignor. It's just puzzling...the timing, his grandchild in Siena, a Slovakian painter from Cyril's homeland."

"Perhaps Michael should know."

Miles gave a dry smile. "From what I see on Alana's face, he isn't capable of muddling through anything with clarity."

"By the way, he told Alana a truth she wasn't prepared for."

"I've heard."

"And Lukas is *not* happy with his active role in parenting, either. The few emails from him have a snippy tone as of late."

"Have you spoken to his friends?"

"Umm," she groaned, "Mick says Lu wants to go back to England."

Miles shook his head. "I'm sure Michael won't allow it."

"Can you do something?"

"If Michael asks, I'll happily offer advice."

Her husband's concern was visible. "May I try to help, at least?"

"I don't think it wise. We've repeatedly shown Lukas how to handle conflict. I didn't expect this behavior."

"Ten months cannot undo years of fear and mistrust."

"Lukas knows that's all in the past. He's safe with his father, and Michael proved to be exceptional with him last May."

"What if he's called to the mystical mission like Alana? He turns sixteen next month."

"Then Lukas will have a personal decision to make," he simply replied. Miles lifted the steamy cover of his breakfast plate, but Laura sensed that his appetite had vanished.

****

Leonard Gerhardt had booked several suites at separate locations, using different aliases. They'd be gathering places for his congregation on the night before Jillian's turning. This hotel, however, no one knew about, not even Veronique. Standing in the center of the room, he looked at the hill to the north of medieval Siena. With reverence, he pulled the ancient text out of the luggage's liner. Cyril's diary held the spell. He read it one more time. Then the faded pages closed, and it floated out of his hands. A thought made it invisible as it nestled in the room's hidden safe. The lock clicked without a touch, and he replaced a wooden floorboard.

Cloaked in dark magic, Leonard left unnoticed and ready to find the perfect prey in the surrounding hills. Rarely leaning on an Alpine walking stick, the climb invigorated him, much like the long hikes of his youth. The Tuscan countryside didn't resemble the Austrian mountains he had played in as a child. Nevertheless, the air was clean and cool for April.

In a patch of trees, he found the perfect spot. Calling forth dark powers, he set twigs around him and waited. It didn't take long. Out of its mother's view, a young fawn ambled into the center he had created. Charming the animal mind was a simple accomplishment, and as he intoned Cyril's incantation, he gutted it with a charmed knife.

Again, he waited. From the dense trees to the west, a lone wolf appeared, its coat silver-gray, its eyes bright with age and wisdom. Leonard used dark magic again—until its majestic will bent to his. A snip of hair, a trickle of blood... Both were placed in an antiquated vile. His thoughts merged with the animal. The wolf sniffed the fallen fawn, and then sank its teeth into the fawn's slender neck as Leonard squeezed the stilled heart. Precisely thirteen seconds later, their mind-link sealed. The wolf staggered briefly and disappeared through the trees.

Leonard added the fawn's innocent blood to the ancient vile. He fastened the amulet around his neck with a strip of leather, and tucked it into his crisp, white shirt. Sensing the wolf's position, he followed a path. Soon, more would heed his call. A snip of hair, a cut of the charmed knife... He'd have a collection of souls to decimate with demons.

And snarling and salivating, they'd shift into Hell-beasts on command.

When all was accomplished, he started down the mountain. For the rugged hike back, he leaned on the Alpine walking stick, a treasured family heirloom. *My bloodline comes to an end.* He cursed aloud. *Inheritance should pass from father to son, and mine foolishly took his own life.*

It made no difference now. His plan insured a thousand-year rule as sorcerer. The taste of success fed his ego like never before. Returning to the hotel room after sunset, he locked the door. This next spell from Cyril's diary was of great magnitude. He'd know the location of each creature he now controlled. No physical contact with animal or human would be necessary. "Six days of solitude," he whispered as if he were on vacation, not a life-altering quest.

****

Looking at Lukas behind the bookshop's counter, Alana's stomach knotted again. Defiance flashed across his sweet face, mostly hidden by stringy long curls. After pulling him firmly into her office, she closed the door. "Now we have *another* huge family issue! You were told not to be here today and you had the whole day to go for a haircut. Why didn't you listen, Lu?" She never raised her voice the way she did tonight. And when she pointed to the chair, Lukas plopped on her desk instead, haphazardly shoving unfiled paperwork aside. "It's time to open up," she said in a calmer tone. "I know what you're feeling. I'm feeling it, too."

"No, you aren't. He's all huggy kissy with you."

"What's really eating at you?" Touching his cheek, the tense pull-away brought to mind the first time she saw Lukas Malone. Dirty and frightened, a skinny, troubled boy huddled in a ransacked brownstone. Gaining his trust had taken months.

"I'm cool, Mom, really. I can handle it."

"Whatever you feel is okay, Lu." She paused before adding, "Things aren't all huggy kissy between us. He still loves both of us, but he's been through a lot."

"He reads old books and makes Clarke send more homework! I want to go back to England and be with my friends." He hopped off the desk, and before she could react, he sprinted through the store and out into the night.

Following him as far as the counter, Kayla looked at her. "Want me to track him?"

"No. Hopefully he won't do anything too radical. Let's close and call it a night."

"The piazza's still packed. I think we should stay open until nine, and I can close by myself. You can go up and... Oh, I've got a paper due Monday, so I'm heading home to Florence tonight."

"Not a problem," she said. Crossing to the window, her mind slipped into Guardian mode. "Everything's too quiet. Maybe evil finally got the message to stay away from Portofino."

"Is relocation in my future?"

"That's a total no, Guardian."

"There's been talk of fewer callings."

"Or is it not too many acceptances? Giving up ten years of your life isn't easy, especially at sixteen." She thought about her innocent world before accepting the mission. Then at seventeen, a mystically enhanced vampire saved her from certain death. "I had my doubts...didn't you?"

"Not really. My life plan is very clear to me."

She smiled. "I didn't have a life plan at your age. My parents' deaths coincided with demons and dimensional portals... The absence of silly pajama parties and normal fun I knew I couldn't have."

"I'm only three years in, but this life feels right. Does that make me weird or something?"

She turned to face the young woman. "No, It makes you better than most of us, someone to be admired. Get your things and leave now to get a jump on your paper. I'll keep the shop open a couple more hours by myself." Kayla started to protest, and she added, "That's an order from your mentor, Guardian."

After Kayla left, Alana stood at the bookshop's open door and squelched the desire to run through Portofino tracking Lukas's scent. After all, her Guardian skills were as sharp as ever.

****

Patrice Virelli rarely left her office during tax season. And until April fifteenth, she could run on empty and require very little sleep. Now she had to go to "Plan B" and quick. She threw her dead blackberry on the desk and picked up the landline to make the call. Reading over another 1040 EZ mess, she quickly closed her eyes and sighed when she heard her mother's voice. "Mom, I've got a huge favor to ask. Alexa just emailed me at work. That weird old coot of an ex-father-in-law actually sent her a plane ticket."

"To Italy?" her mother asked.

Looking at a picture of the two girls on her desk, Patrice replied, "She's probably already on her way to Siena to see Jilly. I need help with Paige. Do you think maybe Dennis would—"

"Don't bother your brother. He's on the night shift the whole month."

"He's not doing the patrol car thing again, is he?"

"Not that I know. Listen, I love having her, even though the phone never leaves her ear."

"I owe you. It's just until Easter. I'll work from home the week she's off. But this week, I just can't."

"Patrice," her mother said in that no nonsense way.

"Thanks," she replied with a tired grin. "I'll drive her over straight from baby-sitting." She hung up, let out a slow even breath. Being a single parent never gets easier, she realized.

****

"I swear, Paige, I feel like I'm living in a fairytale," Jillian squealed into the old princess phone in her assigned bedroom. "Siena's spectacular! I belong here! I know it!" The smells, the sights intrigued her artistic nature. The bed was bouncy, and lying on her stomach, both legs kicked the air. "You've got to see this house. From the outside, it's kind of regular with three floors of rooms. But inside it's got high tin ceilings."

"Meet any boys?"

"No. Just the three from the art program…and my study-buddy is Carol Reardon, who talks way too slow for me. I took the bed by the window 'cause Carol likes being close to the door. Some kind of phobia, I think."

"Come on… I want to hear about the art boys."

Jillian giggled. "They're totally dork-wads. But the other girl Betts is nice. I think she's nervous or something because she's been throwing up for hours. We spent the entire day walking *medieval* streets with Sister Phyllis. She's like our teacher-slash-den mother until the program finishes in June. She's a nun, but her portfolio…really great stuff; like she's an expert with charcoal. Miss De Rosa would love her art. I know I do." She rolled over to stare at the patterned tin above, so different from anything she'd ever seen. "I've never been around nuns before."

"What's she like? All mean and everything?"

"No. She's kind and full of neat info. It took me forever to stop gawking at her brassy brown hair with wicked red highlights. Did you know nuns wear artsy sweaters and jeans?"

"Get out! Send me a picture!"

"My phone doesn't work. I don't know what happened. It just crapped out in first-class."

"Oh no... Hey... Did you impress them all on Orientation Friday?"

"Betts thinks I'm like this rising star in the art world. The guys tore apart my portrait, like theirs are any better."

"Jilly, I'm jealous; I mean no going to school every day must be great."

"But we'll have tutors for *normal* subjects by Monday when we leave for the Amalfi coast. I can't wait," she said with a moan. "Sister Phyllis says the program only picks honor students. Hey, the grad student who babysits the dorks seems pretty hot." Paige let out a long, breathy 'Oooh' and Jillian giggled again. "He barely speaks English, though. Betts, Carol and I are assigned to an American artist. Lucy's like thirty, but she's fun. Tomorrow we sketch the city." Jillian looked at the alarm clock and suddenly stood. "Oops...gotta go."

"Nooo, I miss you."

"I miss you too, but an expensive restaurant on the piazza is throwing us a welcome to Siena dinner. The boys are with the Italian, and it's just Carol and me with Lucy. Sister Phyllis is staying home with Betts."

"Don't hang up! Doing Valley Mall isn't fun without you," Paige whined.

"I'll buy a new cell phone tomorrow, okay? Bye, BFF." She waited until the line went dead and replaced the princess phone on the nightstand between the beds. Earlier, talking to her mother made Jillian homesick, but hearing Paige's voice made her lonely.

The evening sky, so full of stars, drew her to the window. "I'm in Italy! Wow," she whispered, "This place *is* right out of a fairytale."

****

After talking to her daughter, Alexa Gerhardt had spent the rest of the day cleaning the house from top to bottom. Then she had a very early dinner and enjoyed a brimming glass of rich merlot. Since Jillian left, a full night's sleep hadn't come. Tired and lonely, it wasn't even dark yet, but she checked the doors and entered her bedroom. Curled on the bed, she studied her daughter's first art piece in a pewter frame, two little girls and their phone numbers in bright pink letters... Thinking how tomorrow night, she'd be in Siena with her daughter. Her eyes eventually closed.

From a strip of forest behind the house on Castles Road, a man studied the bedroom window. Through thick evergreens and wild foliage, he moved without a sound. He passed the pool and looked at the split-level's dining room window. The beveled glass shattered with an incantation, pieces falling like dead petals off a summer rose. He took a predetermined path to the rear door. Five carpeted stairs led to a kitchen, and taking an immediate left, he climbed another five stairs to an open bedroom door. One perfect stab through the heart produced no scream, only a quick inhale. The victim never saw her assailant; would never know why she'd met a premature death. It would look like rape, and the police wouldn't find a fingerprint to identify him on the pewter picture frame he turned upside down.

****

The unique piazza completely enchanted Jillian.

She imagined medieval knights on huge stallions racing around the oval. As the sun faded, the red brick buildings turned the color of her favorite crayon—burnt sienna. The changing tints and hues were something her artistic eye adored.

Dinner, a multi-course feast, took forever, and the ambiance of freedom filled her soul. She and Carol both begged Lucy to explore the narrow streets.

"I totally understand your yen for adventure, Jillian." Leading them away from the *Piazza del Campo,* Lucy laughed with delight. "You girls love to walk."

Carol gave a boisterous hoot. "I've never met anyone like *you* in Rosewood Ohio, Lucy. That's for sure."

Her roommate's interesting drawl sounded foreign to Jillian's New Jersey ear.

It took no effort at all for Lucy Novak to keep her persona cheery and charismatic tonight. She knew how to lay it on thick to intrigue the girl. Purple-tinted designer glasses added an exotic look. Dressed for drama in black from head to toe, Lucy's short blonde hair bounced when she sashayed, adding an aura of mischief.

"You're an actual American *living* in Italy," Carol drawled out with awe.

She eyed the girl who laid it on just as thick as she. "I came to see the art five years ago and never left. The entire city is a campus… law, medicine, music, art, literature—so beautiful and so much history." When they entered a smaller piazza, she watched Jillian's reaction.

"This is so gorgeous. I could sketch like

everything," Jillian said.

"You haven't seen the best part yet... My car's right by the bus depot. We could drive around, maybe up to the hill. There's a *fantabulous* view of Siena."

Carol stopped short, begged with excitement, "Ya think? Oooh... Please?"

Lucy pointed north as they walked. "Real artists go there. It's still Lent, but after Easter, fireworks over the *Duomo* are breathtaking."

"Should we tell Sister?" Jillian asked.

"You know, we'll get back in an hour." Both girls nodded yes, and she unlocked a small, black car. Jillian climbed into the backseat. Carol sat in the front.

****

Lukas sat on an outcrop of rugged rocks overlooking the Mediterranean Sea. His feet dangled high above the dark waters. Thinking about 'another family issue' fueled his anger. "What you were is *way* better than what you are now. You get hit by a car this time and you'll stay dead." He hissed out a sharp breath, thinking backward and forward simultaneously. He recalled his immortal father's raw power when destroying Cyril, the ancient Sire.

He also recalled the raw power of his immortal father's fierce embrace.

"Friggin' alive," he muttered. "No shit we've got another family issue. No way is this fair." He stood, pulled out his cell phone. After a quick text to Nico, he called his best friend at the Georgian Institute. Getting voicemail made his gloomy mood deepen. I can run away right now, tonight, he thought. *Yeah, right... not a chance. I've got super-power mom and formerly undead dad to answer to. Who am I kidding? Going back to England won't solve anything.* But he missed his Guardian friends. Above all, he missed Mick.

With inhuman speed, he made it to the outside entrance of the bookshop as Alana turned the 'open' sign around. Meeting her in the hall, they walked upstairs in silence. As they entered the living room, she touched his arm. "I'm really not happy with you right now." He shrugged, avoided her eyes and didn't answer. "Did you eat?"

"Not hungry."

"Lu, you're a growing boy. You have to eat—"

"So do you," he replied because she had lost weight. Her face was less full, her large hazel eyes dull. He gave a lukewarm grin. "I'm beat. See you in the morning."

She smiled with a nod. "Sunday Mass together? Just like always?"

"Yeah… sure." He watched her walk down the hall to the den before he sent a second text message to Nico. After a quick stop in the bathroom, he went into the den as well and kissed her cheek. "Thought I'd say good night," he whispered in an innocent tone.

Not looking up from some old book, his father asked, "Is all the homework done?"

"Finished and sent," he lied. After all, Clarke never checked for homework on Saturday. He saved warning letters for late Sunday night. Lukas saw no cutting look that said 'I know what you're up to' so he gave another hasty good night and left. He waited a whole half hour until he heard Alana walk by. Once the shower in her *ensuite* started, he changed into clean jeans before slipping out the apartment door.

Nico was waiting in the parking lot a block away.

They drove away from the seaport. Old and burning oil, his car had a new radio—always tuned to heavy metal. On a steep road that led to private villas up the coast, a driving guitar razzed hot rhythms and the constant crash of cymbals sent them both into mischief-mode. Nico offered a cigarette.

Lukas flicked his lighter a few times before a deep inhale. He choked—with continuous coughs. "Shit, these are strong," he said after a slower drag.

Nico lit his and blew out rings of smoke. He smirked before saying with a heavy Italian accent and a pretty good command of the English language, "Parisian... *Zio* imports from Turkey. I stole two packs."

"Cool," he said, took another inhale. They pulled off the road near a cliff. Out past the harbor, lights from the yachts illuminated the night sky. Nico reached into the back seat, and a dark bottle came into Lukas's hand. He grinned. "Shit. This isn't beer."

Pulling out both corks, his friend laughed. "I bring one for you, one for me. And we talk about the girl."

Resting his head back, Lukas took another drag. He exhaled and swigged the wine, which tasted sweet and bitter at the same time. "You mean Kayla?"

"*Si, si*. She like me, no? *Mamma mia... Che faccia bella!*"

With a sly grin, he held his hand over his heart. "I think she's all kinds of hot. But she really likes you, Nico. I feel it right here, and Kayla can kiss like a pro. Oh, *bella, bella carina*, and she's available... What else do you want to know?" He eyed Nico, took another hearty swig.

****

It didn't take long to finish off the wine. As Nico relieved himself in the bushes, Lukas threw one empty bottle so far that he didn't hear it land. Then his friend jumped in the car and revved the engine. He took the mountain turns fast, and the old car sped down the road along the coast. They almost made it into Portofino when flashing roof lights appeared out of nowhere.

Lukas sank down in the seat as high beams signaled a pullover. "Oh fuck," he hollered. Scrunched low, he spit out, "Get out! Go up to him."

Nico breathed hard and fast. "*Perche?*"

Thinking how much his ass would hurt this time, he hissed, "*Perche no? Per favore, ora vai da lui.* Go! Lie to him!"

"*Aspetteremo che sia—*"

"*No-no-no! Subito, per favore.*"

Cursing loudly, Nico staggered out, leaving the driver's side door open. With his hands high and splayed wide, he stood by the trunk yelling, "*Zio Vito, eh, ristorante? Sono Nico, si?*"

Lukas shimmied across the middle console as a light shone through the rear window. Then the cop yelled something about calling Vito and arresting Nico for drunk driving. While Nico begged and argued, he made his move. Out the driver side door he squirmed, and then rolled over the embankment. Gripping the stones with mystical strength, he estimated the drop to the narrow beach about ten feet. A bottle of wine had no effect on him, and after landing, he sprinted at the water's edge only to pick up the road a half mile away.

Racing up three flights of stairs without a sound, he sneaked in and made it to his bedroom. After pulling off his clothes, he threw them in the hamper by the closet and shoved his legs into pajama bottoms before peering up and down the hall. Alana's even breaths of sleep came from the master bedroom, but the light was still on in the den. Things *really* aren't huggy kissy between them anymore, he thought.

As the adrenaline rush ended, he felt woozy from the wine and really had to get to the bathroom fast. After peeing a river and flushing, he washed his hands, and just in case his father was standing in the hall, he swigged mouthfuls of mouthwash before mussing his sweaty curls to give the illusion of waking up groggy.

When he opened the door, the hall was empty. That bit of luck led to another brazen move, and walking into the den, he stopped short.

His very human father, sprawled half-on-half-off the short denim couch, snored loud and deep. No acute senses, no evidence of mystical abilities, and looking just like an ordinary man who could sleep through a train wreck. He rolled his eyes when walking back to his room and didn't care if he swayed a little or a lot.

****

From the high hill, Siena looked amazing. Jillian couldn't wait to get out of the back seat of Lucy's car. A few feet away, a ritzy limousine had its high beams aimed at them, and behind, a dozen tourists stared at Siena at night. Very excited, she followed Carol out of the car while Lucy cut the lights and walked around to meet them.

"Oooh," Carol squealed, "I can't wait to see, can you?"

Carol grabbed her hand; it felt like an electric current had just run up her arm. Jillian shivered, felt almost dizzy. "Are they all talking at the same time or something?" The whispers swelled as if she was running toward the tourists, but she hadn't moved. They approached, and as fast as danger entered her mind, it whipped away.

"Relax, be calm, my chosen vessel," sounded in her mind, the words spoken in a familiar voice. Her sandals slipped off; her dress peeled off her body. She thought she floated on air, but thirteen sets of wicked hands held her high off the ground. Thirteen sets of fangs punctured her veins. Her wrists and ankles were bound, her eyelids bathed with fragrant oil. Then like a weightless feather, she glided over a wall and landed on cool grass. The oil flooding her eyes made everything fractured, broken apart. In the moonlight of a starry sky, she saw three names engraved on a white cross... Anne, Pricilla, Rosalind Malone.

"You will know the last temple. He shall be your most desired victim. The blade will destroy him and the debt is paid," the voice said, and in her mind, she glimpsed the image of a man's penetrating dark eyes. His face bled into her memory.

"Grandfather," she thought she screamed.

"*My special one*," she thought he replied.

Howls broke the silence. A huge wolf appeared atop the wall. In its jaws, a thin silver blade glinted. With one graceful leap, it stood over her, licked her face clean with a velvet tongue. Then sharp teeth grazed her neck.

This time, she couldn't scream, couldn't move.

More wolves leapt from the wall. They dug up earth at the cross's base, and lashed by their claws, the hole deepened. Bindings tore from her wrists and ankles as terror blended with the handsome man's image in her mind. When his dark eyes turned bright amber, She felt paralyzed, disoriented.

The stately wolf sat, guarding her as if she belonged to him. The others slinked away as he nudged her arm and guided her hand into the deep hole. Her fingers bled as if the tomb's walls were lined with thorns. She touched cloth and fisted it, pulling with all her might.

Dragging the object up, a deep purple sash was tied around dirty, heavy linen that had once been white. She struggled to sit, and the wolf dropped the blade into her hand. She gripped its hilt, slashed the purple sash. The material fell away to reveal a wooden chest with a silver plaque caught in the moon's reflection. Only a foot wide and just as deep, it called to her. She found a crooked screw on its left side. Pressing hard, a small panel dropped and she pulled out a shiny key. It fit the lock. She heard a click and lifted a silver latch to open the chest.

Instantly, her body lurched.

What slithered through every open wound settled in Jillian's innocent soul.

Chapter 9

Michael's eyes flew open when he slid off the denim loveseat. The den spun wild as he clawed at the carpet. It felt as if his lungs didn't work and his nostrils flared as he struggled to take in air. Crazy pressure built in his chest. Every muscle in his body either jerked or cramped. Twisting around and clawing at the couch cushion, his skin crawled as if he were covered in spiders. He gagged on the smell of dug-up earth and tasted terror before it slithered down his throat. Both feet felt numb as if there was nothing beneath them when he finally stood. With his hands bracing his knees, his eyes went wide sensing something impossible. *Call out to her! Save her!* Save who, he thought before his legs buckled, landing on the carpet unable to move.

****

I am free, protected from those who captured me and assisted by those who know my power. The new vessel staggered upright to see the world through ancient eyes...and it hungered. It leered at its wooden sepulcher. Torturous months of craving, thirst to fill eternity. Childlike hands, eerily small and smooth, put a silver blade inside and closed the chest. They reached up high to place its former tomb atop a brick wall. *Vengeance begins now....*

Dark magic surged through Jillian's body as the

demon bound itself to her. She grabbed the wall's ledge to maneuver up and over, but inhuman hands lowered her to the ground. Even in midnight's darkness, vivid colors shimmered to stun them both. The beast-within leered as the innocent host vessel stared in awe. She would soon know all it knew—fully aware of 317 years of existence in the soul of a commanding vampire.

The nubile body was a new experience. Delicate and virginal, it wasn't *his* body. No surge of lust lived in this human. Weak from blood hunger, it allowed her the privilege of free movement while steering her mind insane.

Jillian recognized Lucy and Carol, but moving past them, she focused on a beautiful woman who stood apart from the gathering. Her raven hair loose and flowing, the low-cut gown of black chiffon billowed as she seemed to hover over the earth. Mesmerized by such large amber eyes, Jillian drew nearer still.

"You come to me, my legacy, and you hunger," the woman whispered sweetly. "But immortality is a gift to be earned."

A revelation occurred, and Jillian offered a wrist. This was its origin. The woman's pristine fangs appeared, sank into her tender flesh. The pain was pleasure and terror at the same time. The drink teased awake what her soul harbored, and a groan deepened in her throat. The origin ran a sharp canine across her own delicate finger, pressed it to Jillian's lips. Drops of ancient blood trickled to her tongue, and Jillian swallowed a taste of immortality.

"It is your birthright's primal need. Blood holds eternal wisdom for one who will know daylight. But humanity has limitations. I know all too well." An icy palm caressed Jillian's pulsing jugular vein. It made her swoon full of temptation, full of hunger. She bayed at the moon with a graceful howl. "When all is done, you shall never leave my side. You shall never be taken. Your grandfather promises to pave the way for rebirth."

"Grandfather," Jillian softly cried.

"Hush," she whispered. "Do not fear. My legacy will guide you." Another sob hitched as the beautiful vision stepped into the limousine.

Then Jillian's gaze turned to the magnificence of Siena at night. Part of her felt terrified, part of her anxious to explore the new ability to walk among the living. Her arms slipped into the sleeves of a dress. The flutter of material over her skin brought a shudder.

Lucy. Carol. They were her minions.

"The eyes are the windows to the soul," Jillian said, the demon in her daring either of them to look up. A blanket came over her shoulders and her sandals slipped back on her feet. She gave a sweet, "Thank you, Lucy," but the tall woman didn't take the bait and curtsied low while looking down.

Standing close like an equal, Carol hovered and stared right into her eyes. "Now *this* is *wickedly* exciting! Should I call you Jillian or the Chosen One? Oooh, I'll be your personal assistant after you're sired!"

Bloodlust swelled, keenly aware of little satisfaction since it had been harnessed within the mystically-enhanced vampire in 1890. Jillian smiled— like a cat seeing a mouse. She kissed the minion's cheek before sinking her teeth into her neck to take the life force. Clawing down Carol's face, the beast-within reveled in the screams until a vampire ripped her mouth away. The sight of him drinking deep and rough before tossing the lifeless body over the cliff stirred something akin to jealousy.

Not yet. Not ready, echoed through her twisting mind. She picked up its treasure chest and sauntered to the car. Licking warm blood off her lips, Jillian swallowed, then said to no one in particular, "I feel much better now."

****

Helpless moans. Rugged sobs. Unbearable, terrifying sounds filled Alana's dream. Memories of last May and Michael's screams slashed at her soul. Her arm shot out to hold him to her breast. Then her eyes flipped open, her mystical senses snapped awake. She jumped out of bed and ran.

In the den, Michael lay on the floor, his body jerking, his face full of terror. She reached down and as she said his name, he pushed hard. Her feet came off the floor. Crashing into a stack of books on the other side of the room, pain ripped through her ribs, and she hissed in a shallow breath.

He was clutching his chest, crouched and cowered by the denim couch, and she crawled back to him. Lukas ran in, hooked her waist, and it took every ounce of strength to break free from the teen's fierce grip. "No, Mom… He'll hurt you again."

"He didn't, he wouldn't… oh God, Michael, talk to me." Fear surfaced as her eyes filled. *What if his heartbeat disappears? What if his body is giving out?* "Michael, please, let me help you," she whispered. Before her hand got to his shoulder, he slapped it away and swayed as he stood. Lurching back, he edged around the couch to the wall avoiding his son. Sweat coated his face and his hands trembled. Then he staggered down the hall, holding the wall.

She followed as he shook his head and heaved in gulps of air. "Don't touch me. Not sure… The monsignor…I have to go." But she reached out again, and he jerked away. The fierce expression, the inferno building in his eyes didn't waver until she stepped out of his path. She followed him again—this time, at a distance. When he wrenched open the front door, bracing both wall and banister he lurched down the narrow staircase.

Then she sprinted to the phone in the living room, and Lukas came to her side. Too many odd smells came off him and his eyes were half-closed. "I'll track him."

"No. Go back to bed." Before he could argue, she added, "Don't question me right now!" She said into the phone, "Dad? Get to the rectory. It's Michael. Something's wrong, you have to help him, Daddy, please." Hanging up, her hand fully shook.

"Aren't you going after him?"

"Please just go back to bed!" The words came out sharp, but she didn't care. And Lukas shrugged before he walked away. When his bedroom door closed, she slid down the wall and let the tears come. The glower on Michael's face said it all. He didn't want her help.

The ache in her ribs was gone. The ache in her heart was not.

****

Dazed, yet driven, Michael saw the rectory's screen door open and the monsignor standing beside it. He staggered and swayed, about to drop as he reached it. The priest steadied him with a tight hold on his upper arm. Still, he stumbled all the way into the rectory's kitchen. Sinking down on an old vinyl chair, he gripped the table's metal edge. No words came as water ran in the sink and a porcelain kettle settled on the stove. The hiss of a gas flame began. Hunched over, his eyes filled, his mouth dried.

"What do you sense, *Signore*?"

Swiping his lips with the back of a hand, he felt drained of strength. Sweating and shivering at the same time. But guilt snagged him—a feeling he knew all too well. "It's free. Dear God. It's free and it has killed."

"I sense it, as well."

Steam burst through the teapot's spout the way culpability rushed through his conscience. The high, loud pitch pierced the silence as Miles came in. Soon, a cup of chamomile tea and a plate of square crackers were before him. He turned his face away, not sure he could stomach either.

"Drink slowly and chew them before swallowing," Miles ordered in a hushed tone.

As the room began to spin, he hung his head low while whispering "no."

"Put something in your system or you'll pass out."

The cracker tasted like paste. Swallowing hurt like hell, and the mug felt too heavy to hold steady. "I have to call her."

"She's beside herself with worry."

"I'll speak with Alana," the monsignor said with calm and control in his tone.

He couldn't get out a 'thank you,' afraid he'd break down and sob.

"I will not lie to you, *Signore*. This should not have occurred. Tell all you know to the researcher."

He didn't want to look at Miles. "I'm sorry I shoved her, but I swear… I felt it. I saw it happen."

"Did you hurt my daughter? I warned you—"

"I didn't, I wouldn't… I mean, what I sense… it-it can't be real. It's buried. How can it be free?"

"You're bloody well hallucinating," the researcher said with a glare.

"But she isn't dead and it's in her. Above Siena, I—*it* met Cyril's sire."

Shooting up, Miles's palms slapped the table. "It's an illusion! You weren't turned by Veronique! There is *no* link to another's sire. And no such entity exists—that inhabits a vampire's soul only to reanimate itself, deciding to take up residence in a *living* being!"

"I… I have to find her. Oh God… I have to kill her to take it back."

The cutting glare deepened. "What on earth are you going on about? It is a nightmare. Nothing more. Besides, you won't make it to the door. Start at the beginning—"

"I don't know where the beginning is! I … I don't know how… The girl's terrified, but—it's taken over her soul. She was an innocent. Didn't know—"

"You expect me to believe…" Miles leaned across the table. "I'm telling you it's impossible."

"And *I'm* telling you it's *free*," he yelled, running his shaky fingers through his damp hair. They stared each other down until Miles sat. "I swear on my life it's true! She opened my sister's writing chest. This thing that owned my soul for centuries settled in *hers* like it belongs there."

"And you expect me to believe the new host is *not* a vampire?"

"She's craving blood, death and destruction—just as I did when I didn't breathe. But it was buried in

125

consecrated ground, Miles, *supposedly* imprisoned for eternity."

"The Council has documentation from last May," Miles shot back.

"How can a vampire's beast-within take over someone who is still breathing?"

"I have no answer. But Cyril was unique. We both know he dabbled in dark magic."

The reply felt like a stone in the pit of his stomach. "Cyril was demented and twisted for the past century," he said in disgust.

"And I doubt Veronique would send us art pieces from his Slovakian homeland."

"I did *my* research, too. The mural in the other room is part of a series."

"Then you know *The Slav Epic* represents Cyril's people's journey."

"It's the thirteenth with the descriptive 'Treaties are to be observed.' Did the Georgians break a treaty, Miles? Did your Council overstep the boundaries between good *and* evil when they let mystical healers rip the beast-within from my soul?"

"There is no treaty between good and evil," Miles stated in a cool tone.

"Is the sanctimonious Georgian Sovereign Council answer something you've memorized for occasions such as this?"

Miles's next glare held no mercy. "I'll let that comment pass due to your current unhinged state. You should know Painting Twelve in the series was sent to Mother Anne. It's descriptive is 'Do not repay evil with evil'."

Full of bitterness, he asked, "What is this—a threat

or a warning?"

"Perhaps it's a clever ruse to throw us off the track of something truly evil. You should know the stone bust is also Slavic, as old as Cyril."

His eyes narrowed. "I destroyed my sire, damn it! He turned to dust and bone ten months ago."

"Your sire has worshippers."

Sitting back, Michael's right eyebrow rose as he took a breath. "Now it's your turn to start from the beginning."

****

Lucy Novak held open the door to a room in the basement of her apartment building, saying to Jillian, "I fixed this up just for you." She had promised to keep the girl safe and alive, keeping the thing within her soul content for seven dawns. That's what Leonard wanted, and she wouldn't let him down. Nothing occult interested her, but Leonard had said it was some form of preparation for eternity. Right after she agreed to help, thousands of dollars were deposited in her bank account, and she had followed Leonard's instructions perfectly. She used her charm on the landlord and gave him a full year's rent in advance—for the use of the basement. The old man cheered as if he'd just won the lottery looking the other way while she transformed the largest storage space. Paying cash for everything, she chose pricey antiques for the hideout and hung panels of curtains to make it look pretty. It was her desire to make Leonard's granddaughter as comfortable as a princess.

Watching Jillian pace her new room, Lucy placed sheets of plastic on the floor and continued with Leonard's instructions. She called the landlord down from the second floor with a contrived excuse. With a slash to his chest, Jillian marked her next victim. The girl yanked a crucifix off the gold chain around his thick neck and licked threads of blood off the silver blade. As if under a spell, he crept up the stairs and most probably into the arms of a waiting vampire with long, white fangs. Next, she got his chubby wife down. Jillian did her thing again and victim number three went missing. Their old-maid daughter came into the basement looking for her parents, and victim number four disappeared. An hour later, drunk as a skunk, their son staggered in. Victim number five didn't even know what hit him. Lucy watched from the door, unwilling to care about what happened to them after they left the building.

The thing inside Jillian is a pro, she thought, and no way am I getting on her bad side.

By two a.m., they were the only living beings in the building. Lucy pulled a map of the Tuscany Region from the nightstand's drawer and left it on the carpet by the wooden chest. Leonard told her what to circle in red—medieval Siena, two nearby towns, and the southwest corner of Florence. Why? She had no idea.

She locked Jillian in and went up to the first floor, confident about her promise to the only person who cared about her. Could she do this alone? How hard could it be without Carol, she wondered. *What a stupid move for someone who was supposed to be a wiz with magic skills, but at least the nun doesn't suspect anything.* Maybe Leonard had cast *that* spell.

She shrugged, never at all interested in worshiping vampires, yet knowing she owed Leonard Gerhardt loyalty. *He gave me a fancy education. Saved me from*

the foster care system nightmare all those years ago...
And trading sex for security had turned into love. After
Easter, she'd return to her only passion: recreating
spectacular masterpieces.

Eyeing the chilled champagne on the counter, she
had planned to drink a toast with Carol. She pulled the
bottle out of the ice bucket. She popped the cork, filled
an expensive flute glass and took the bottle to the
couch. "Just a dumb move on your part, Carol... You
told me not to look in her eyes. Too bad you didn't do it
as well. Eh... no worries... I'll bet your replacement is
on the way." She had one thing left to do before dawn.
The letter was written, ready to deliver. Licking her
lips, she refilled the glass. But what came to mind was
the way Jillian had fingered those bloody crucifixes
under the stunning Florentine lamp she had purchased
with Leonard's money.

Whenever sanity took hold, Jillian felt buried alive.
She couldn't even scream. Like a puppet on a string,
something inhuman controlled her every action. Total
terror raced through her, then a thrill. *Crosses do not
burn! And I breathe!* She laid four crucifixes on the
bottom of her treasure chest. *A gift, an offering to my
origin; each gem a reward for my release...* Jillian rose,
danced around its treasure chest. "Fifty-four imprisoned
me; fifty-four to pave my way."

When all energy drained, she collapsed onto the
elegant bed.

****

In the chapel of Villa Catherine, Mother Anne
watched the mystical healers file into wooden pews.
Dressed in blessed habits of black and white, fifty-three
pristine souls would quiet their minds and focus every

thought. Each sensed the impossible. Each was horrified by the sacrilegious occurrence. They didn't need to visit the convent's cemetery over the hill.

When all were seated, sadness took hold. "An empty hole lies beneath the marble cross inscribed with the names Anne, Priscilla, and Rosalind Malone, three of our sisters who walked this earth centuries ago. No explanation exists for such a brazen act of evil. Once again, a clean soul has been stolen for this entity to abuse."

"But the child isn't dead, and she's too young to turn," Gabriella said.

"You are trying to understand what even as a Guardian you had never experienced. No. The innocent is not dead."

"Phyllis is safe, Mother?" Magdalena asked.

"She won't be harmed. And although we fear for one of our own, she cannot return to the protection of the villa."

"The students," Magdalena said with a nod.

"Yes. If I summon her home, they would most likely be the entity's next naive victims."

"We extracted this demon from the Champion. Will it not come after us?"

"It doesn't want us," Anne replied.

"She's too young. She won't survive the turning without slipping into madness," Gabriella stated.

"Then it will be our task to insure she is never turned." Sensing the Order of Catherine's role, as well as the girl's waning humanity, Mother Anne braced herself for another unprecedented event.

Chapter 10

Sister Phyllis Verdi found Lucy's letter taped to the house's rear door in the kitchen. As she prepared breakfast for the art students, fear gripped her soul and sorrow filled her heart. Carol Reardon, the unsuspected deceiver, was already dead. But Jillian Gerhardt faced something far worse. Not needing to read Lucy's lies, she threw the letter in the trash. Above all, the safety of the other four teenagers in the art program was her sole purpose now. Local Guardians, already on alert, would be watching until Alana Ciminio and Michael Malone arrived.

As the students came in, she placed cut melon and fresh figs on the table. Loaves of Italian bread delivered by the baker's son created an aura of safety and warmth. The students sat, and Phyllis kept a sincere smile visible. "So guys, today is Palm Sunday. On our trip to the *Duomo,* we'll start the first portfolios."

"First portfolios," one boy asked.

"Uh-huh…one for each of you… as in assessment," she replied in a way that produced a group groan. "Hey, I do give you grades, you know. In the Chapel of St. John the Baptist, we'll sketch sculptures by Michelangelo. How's that for an intro to Renaissance art?"

She sliced warm bread, placing it in a basket. No alarm showed in manner or tone.

Betty, now the only female student, looked lost. "Where are Carol and Jillian, Sister?"

"Oooh, they might have food poisoning. Lucy took them to the university hospital last night. It's on the other side of the city," she lied. "It's a good thing you stayed here with me, Betts." Betty nodded, but the boys barely reacted. "I'm thinking they'll not be joining us for a few." She'd conceal the truth as long as possible, and should further questions come, Phyllis had other plausible explanations for their continued absence.

****

From the kitchen table, Alana watched a new day begin. Sleep had not been possible. Hours earlier, Michael had come home withdrawn and pale. He hadn't said a word. She had watched him walk into the den and close the door. Then she called her father. He offered little information and not wanting to jump to any erroneous conclusions, she did what relaxed her the most.

Without having to look at her great-aunt's recipe, she had mixed the necessary ingredients in a ceramic bowl; then kneaded the dough until it was smooth. And now, as full sun finally brightened the kitchen, she stared at two loaves of hot crusty bread. Dressed in a loose T-shirt and a pair of leggings, she nursed a third cup of coffee.

His distinctive footsteps sounded in the hall. She drew in a deep breath and waited.

Instead of coming to the kitchen, he went into their bedroom. The shower started in the *ensuite*. She set the table for breakfast… and worried, thinking about what she'd say to him… and worried some more. When he sat in silence at the kitchen table dressed for the day, she placed the fresh bread and sweet butter down. A slight smile came from her as he stared at it. "It's *Zia's* recipe."

After a small bite, wonder showed on his face. "You continue to amaze me, my love. It's delicious."

He sounded calm and in control, which eased her concern a bit. She poured fresh coffee into a familiar crystal mug, and when he took it from her, she noticed his unsteady grip. Avoiding her gaze, he didn't offer anything else. But there was much to be discussed.

"I spoke to Dad. Guardians are watching the student house in Siena. So who is this ancient vampire?"

"Veronique," he bit out.

"Dad thinks she's involved." She waited for him to say something. Anything... like give an explanation about what she saw in him last night. Instead, he turned and stared out the window. Bells and whistles instantly went off in her head. After what she had witnessed in the den, having to draw information out of him seemed a monumental task. Sitting down, she sipped her coffee before saying, "So tell me what I should know about this one."

His espresso eyes could pierce right through hers. "Veronique sired Cyril. She was his mistress for many centuries. I knew her as well, way back when."

She skipped over the 'I knew her' part. "How far is way back when, decades or centuries? Was she ever in New York? Maybe shipped her coffin over for a romantic rendezvous—or two?"

"Of course...Cyril lived in New York for hundreds of years."

"When did he move the estate to Vermont?"

"During World War One."

"And Veronique?"

"Before 1890, we often crossed the Atlantic, alone or together, to be with her. I said *before* 1890. She flitted off to wherever she wanted, but she preferred her estate in Florence."

Don't jump to conclusions, she told herself, and unable to ask the one question she needed him to answer, said with a flourish of her hand, "And?"

"We met the year I was turned, if that's what you're looking for."

"Just met or—" His glower cut her short, and she leaned back. "So what's she like?"

After an endless pause, he leaned back as well. "Veronique's pretty. Does that answer the question?"

It didn't. "Just how pretty is pretty? How old is she, anyway? If she sired Cyril, that makes her your grandsire. And there are other connections. I'm just guessing."

"Leave it alone, my Guardian. It's ancient history."

"I want answers, buddy."

His right eyebrow rose, a typical reaction to the term and the tone. "Ah, the green-eyed monster strikes again. Last May it was aimed at Gabby, a holy healing sister. Now it's a crotchety old vampire."

"I'm guessing Veronique doesn't have wiry gray hair and warts."

"You'd be right."

"How is it that Cyril looked like a bleached prune and *she* doesn't?"

"*She* feeds often. Probably uses every type of bewitched cream and magical mud bath to fight the aging process. Veronique is more than vain. Cyril was a recluse who avoided human pleasures the last century he walked the earth. This vampire continually craved passion."

"Just like you—before your re-acquaintance with conscience and soul."

"I never touched Veronique after I reclaimed my soul—*after* 1890, if it's any consolation, darlin'. In fact, I never touched any woman, alive or otherwise, after our first kiss."

Her foot kept time with the drum solo in her brain. "She's going down, *darlin'*, right home to Hell along with your old friend who has stolen yet another soul."

"The beast-within isn't my old friend, Alana," he angrily replied. "I contained its need to kill for the last hundred-plus years."

"This girl is an innocent. The Catherines will save her the same way they saved you."

"*I* didn't welcome the beast-within when it swallowed my soul in 1690."

"You actually believe she *welcomed* this thing?" She took her coffee cup to the sink. It clanged against the black porcelain. "Why didn't you ever tell me about Veronique?"

"Why didn't you read up on other vampires besides me?"

As she turned, her face flushed. Her glare intensified. "Just answer my question."

"Those two brutal centuries have nothing to do with us. Let it go. It was a different existence."

"Gee, I can't keep up. The brash 1690s Englishman looking for sex in all the wrong places, the gorgeous vamp with a virgin fetish, the mystically-enhanced creature of the night who fought for his soul, the immortal being who vowed to walk through the fires of Hell for me, and now, a living, breathing man telling me to let it go! There have been *so, so many* Michael Malones." She turned back to the sink, wishing it full of dirty dishes to scrub. "For *more* than a week, I've craved conversation, not a battle of wits. And you still haven't explained last night."

He came behind, locked her against the counter. "I don't want to bicker. None of it matters, Alana."

Warm lips pressed against her neck. Kisses traced her right shoulder. Just the slightest touch fueled a fire she couldn't control. She fought the peak of frustration telling her pulse not to race. "We need to talk," she said as both desire and her temperature soared. Straightening her shoulders, she turned to face him.

His lips crushed hers. His tongue pushed through her teeth like a battering ram. The rough pull to his chest, with one hand pressed to the nape of her neck, made her breath catch in her throat. His other hand slipped under the legging's waistband and his long fingers found the hottest part of her. Every question floated away while the slow, steady tease had her starved for more and she melted against him.

"I want you, darlin', right here…right now."

The gruff demand left her weak. Each feathery stroke fueled the heat within her. Her arms laced his neck, her fingers tangled in the thick waves of his dark hair. He moaned sensual, low. She whimpered, opened his jeans. Nothing mattered except this moment and Michael inside her. She ached for the first hard thrust of his erection. He walked her back and pinned her to the opposite wall as his fingers slipped into her. All she could do was pant and gasp.

"I want these off. I want you open and throbbing with one leg over my hip as I enter you." After tugging his jeans low, he pushed her leggings down with a groan before his fingers thrust into her again. "You're so wet and ready that I—"

Crashing cymbals stopped them cold. Some god-awful, raspy voice screamed unrecognizable words. The look of murder settled on Michael's face as they pulled apart, and he took short, sharp breaths as one hand slapped against the wall. He moved aside as she pulled up her leggings—still panting hard. He fixed himself with a tight hiss before zipping up, but he didn't tuck in the shirttails.

His slow strides took him through the dining room arch. An alarm began to beep at steady intervals joining in with the horrid cacophony. She closed her eyes and tried to breathe again.

****

Each uncomfortable step to his son's bedroom stoked Michael's irritation. He took one deep breath after the other before he cleared his throat, trying Lukas's door only to be met with resistance. Cursing, he placed an open palm against the doorknob and pushed once. The door swung open. And what rumbled through him while crossing the messy bedroom, glaring down at his son approached his own version of rage. He ripped the annoying alarm clock's cord clear out of the wall socket.

"It's Sunday, remember?"

Lazy lids fluttered before a grumbled, "Sorry. I forgot."

"No you didn't."

Stale odors filled the room. Moving to the closet,

he eyed the hamper before flinging its lid like a Frisbee. Sitting up with an endless yawn, his son finally looked at the shirt dangling between Michael's two pinched fingers. He flung it at Lukas as well, just as his son's feet found the floor. "You've sailed way past minor rebellion, little boy." As his son tripped and lurched out of the room, he muttered, "Son of a bitch... When it rains, it fucking pours."

No longer can I look the other way. Michael strode down the hall. When Lukas swayed coming out of the bathroom, he tempered his strength, grabbed one boney arm and brought him to the kitchen table. His son flopped into a chair as Alana placed a dish with slices of warm, buttered bread and a glass of orange juice down.

Leaning back against the black granite counter, Michael kept his arms safely locked across his chest. "Eat your breakfast."

"I'm... not hungry."

"I said, eat your breakfast."

Lukas stared at the plate, playing with the crusty edge of the bread. "You worried Mom last night."

"*Mom* and I have already had a conversation. Now you and I will have one."

"I don't feel good, caught the flu or something."

"You don't have the flu."

"I said or *something.*" Then his son bolted from the table.

Alana jumped up, but he touched her shoulder saying, "I'll handle it," and walked down the hall with amazing control. Sitting on the bathroom floor with his back against the tiled wall, Lukas's face was drained of color. Without saying a word, he wet the hand towel, crouched down, and wiped his son's sweaty face.

"I said I have the flu," Lukas moaned.

"Let's not add another lie to the trouble you're already in. Wine, beer, filtered and unfiltered cigarettes, not to mention sneaking out every night with stolen money in your pocket… This ends right now." He stood up and opened the medicine chest. Seeing an aspirin packet, he popped two pills out of the foil wrap. "Rinse out your mouth before you swallow these. Then go back to your room. Enjoy sitting, because after I deal with you, you'll need a pillow. Maybe two."

Lukas didn't look up. His lower lip quivered, and he palmed his eyes before taking the pills from his outstretched hand. Then Michael walked out, slammed the bathroom door and strode into the den. When he heard his son vomit, he slammed that door as well.

****

As Alana left the steps of San Giorgio, she missed having Lu beside her, using his newly acquired Italian on her neighbors. She also missed their Sunday discussions at Vito's restaurant afterward—about what it would be like when his father came back.

Now, nothing seemed right. With blessed palms in hand, she walked home alone. What they talked about this morning in the kitchen and no answers from Michael continued to work on her. What happened right after that would have her damp again just remembering his touch.

She couldn't go upstairs. She thought about what was sensed, about another ungodly event unfolding like a Venus flytrap waiting to ensnarl some unsuspecting insect. The quiet office and mounds of paperwork were easier to handle than thinking about Veronique or the innocent soul in peril—or Michael. Last week's invoices had just been filed when Celia entered from the hall.

"Something's going down, Ally, I feel it," she quickly whispered.

"You got that right. Holy Hell is about to break loose again…on many fronts."

"What happened upstairs with Lu this morning?"

She couldn't stop a long, disappointed sigh. "Where do I start," she softly replied. "If Lu wasn't as sick as a dog, I think Michael would have hauled him over his knee again. There's money missing from the hutch and I'm sure he's smoking and drinking. He didn't get a haircut, and he refuses to tell the truth."

"Uh-oh, that's never good."

"I get no words of wisdom from the gifted psychic?"

"Not about parenting," her sister mumbled.

"And this ugly event that's coming?"

"Thorn and I picked up on the fact that this innocent is protected by truck loads of evil."

"Where exactly is she, sis?"

"All I'm getting is somewhere in Siena. Maybe we should cancel the party? Have a quiet baptism today with just Mom and Dad here."

"Nothing like jumping from one thought to another." She gave a sympathetic grin. "You've been looking forward to this in a big way. So have I. It'll be great to see everyone again. Deepa as well as the Kendricks are planning to hop a flight. Don't cancel it, Celia."

"I don't know. This new evil feels weird. And you're not all right, Ally."

She blew out a long breath. "Home is not the peaceful abode I expected."

"How are, uh, certain things with Michael?"

"Stay clear of those vibes, too." She leaned back, shifting the conversation to what she could handle. "Give me a psychic update. What's everyone up to?"

"Monsignor and Mother Anne are playing the telepathic telephone game you're so uncomfortable with. Mom wants to get some work done while Dad's at the rectory. He called Deepa. Maybe there are clues where Jillian lived."

"And everyone at Villa Catherine is okay?"

"Totally… It's the ultra-safe place to be."

"Dad said the beast-within got out of consecrated ground."

"There are tons of spells a serious dark wizard can use to manipulate natural earth. The villa itself is different… Like an unconquerable castle, Ally. And either dark seer or good seer can sense if the girl gets near them. It's the normal humans you should be worried about."

"There are Guardians already on the student house, sis."

"But she isn't a vampire. Unless the Guardians have some ESP radar going, she can come right up to them. No silver cross is gonna make her snarl and slither away." Celia gave a sharp gasp. "That's it! I know what she's doing! She fills the writing chest with, with—"

Alana searched her shocked expression. "With *what*… don't stop now!"

"Crosses," Celia whispered, "crosses of silver and gold."

Chapter 11

Near quaint, different out-of-the-way churches bathed in bright sunshine, the beast-within used Jillian to find Palm Sunday observers who wore glistening icons of faith around their not so religious necks. Her sweet demeanor screamed "help this lost soul" to people on the outskirts of belief. Fresh off their knees, begging for absolution from a variety of sins made them pushovers. One swift slice of the enchanted knife, just deep enough to draw blood, and another crucifix was hers.

The earthly wizard's plan had its perks.

The beast-within soaked each stolen treasure in its victim's life force to let Jillian taste immortality. Bloodlust hit the stratosphere when it pawed the crosses. *No blistering pain! Human hands are different, scented with fragrant lotion, warm and alive…not like the vampire's icy palms.*

Lucy wrapped a long, black shawl around the girl's shivering body, leading her away from places known by the beast-within over a century ago. When they were in the protection of the dimly lit basement room, it whispered through Jillian, "Satisfying day." She drained two bottles of water, before grabbing Lucy's arm. "Well after sunset, we'll gather more…a perfect night to taint."

****

Standing at the dining room window, Michael sensed his son still asleep as he stared down at the busy street. After Alana's third insistence, he finally agreed to hear her out. Immediately afterward, horror swept across his face, asking in a low voice, "What did you just say?"

"Celia thinks it's collecting crucifixes of silver and gold," she repeated.

Both of his hands slammed the wooden window frame. "Damn it. I saw it night after night. This could have been avoided."

"I-I don't understand."

Brimming with fury, he faced her. She had given him every opportunity to open up and talk. But no. Like a fool, he flatly refused, time after time, day after day. What if it was too late? "I knew it, but *I* didn't understand. Where's Miles?"

"At the rectory, but why—?"

"Hurry… I'll explain everything to everyone." He grabbed her hand and pulled her out the door.

****

It took all afternoon, but Michael didn't leave any part out of his many nightmares, which now appeared to have been some sort of premonition, only in a roundabout way. There was no reaction from Miles who remained oddly silent, even while documenting Michael's absurd words. Still holding tight to Alana's hand, he didn't want to let go. She grounded him in a way he couldn't explain. She was his safe place, a woman of equal physical strength. And as *his* Guardian nodded in reassurance, he breathed a hell of a lot easier.

Then he met the monsignor's grave expression. "I'm so sorry. I should have told you everything days ago."

"Had you told us, do you think this event could have been prevented?"

"I'd like to think so, yes."

"That is erroneous logic. A finger in a dam doesn't impede the raging river destined to flood. You are but one instrument, not the symphony." He paused. "What course of action will you take?"

"I find it. I kill it."

Monsignor shook his head. "You are not a murderer, Michael. She is an innocent, just as you were when Cyril chose you for its vessel."

He swallowed his arrogance. "I find her, and I deliver her to Mother Anne."

"*Va bene*. This will be your aim."

"And I destroy Veronique," Alana stated.

Studying the perfect fit of their interlocked hands, he met her determined gaze and replied, "Sounds like a plan."

"You're not going to tell me it's too dangerous?" she whispered to him.

"No. Not this time," he whispered back.

She squeezed his hand but looked at her father. "What should be our time frame?"

"The Council will insist you gather all facts before taking any action as a Guardian, honey. Learn all you can about Leonard Gerhardt's part in this, study his sanctuary in Valley Township, understand all the connections."

"No," Michael interjected.

Miles glared at him. "*You* most certainly will not go off half-cocked to charge yet again into battle. There is a significant difference between the meaning of mortal and immortal."

"Yeah, tell me about it," he said in a dismissive way. "We move fast and put an end to this debacle. Alana's way is simple. It's perfect."

"This isn't a singular threat. It's an assault on all sides. Many unseen forces aid this demon. And how do you plan to find the girl?"

"I'll recognize the beast-within, Miles. I'll put an end to *any* undead thing that gets in my way. Then I give her to Mother Anne while Alana takes out Veronique. See? Neat, clean and over before—"

"Miles is right," Monsignor Scarlatti interrupted. "Move slow and exhibit caution. Discuss your strategy with the empath."

"I'll be sure to pick his brain as well as Celia's. By the way, your daughter had the same nightmare, Miles." The uneasy expression deepened on the researcher's face, and in a less aggressive tone, Michael said, "I'm sorry. I waited too long to tell you. I made a mistake. It won't happen again."

"This has been planned exceptionally well," Monsignor stated. "Comparing dreams with Cecelia, perhaps even telling the empath wouldn't have stopped this abomination."

"That's hard for me to accept, Father," he whispered before looking Miles in the eye. "Don't worry. I don't want Celia *or* Thorn near this thing. And the baby should be placed under mystical protection."

"Like at Villa Catherine," Alana said. Then she sat forward. "Is it possible, Monsignor? My mother too, just in case *anything* comes here while we're away."

"I shall ask Mother Anne."

"Philip should be brought here—for extra

protection against any vampires," Michael said. "I respect his talent with a silver sword."

"Arrangements will be made to utilize him in your absence, Champion."

Alana nodded once. "The strategy is sound, Dad."

Removing his reading glasses, worry lines etched Miles's face. "I'm not convinced. Veronique's powerful. You shouldn't go up against her alone."

"Take the time to plan this very carefully, Michael," the monsignor stated. "Speak to Thorn while I contact Council members. Then we'll discuss all we know once again." The wise priest clasped his shoulder. "Destiny calls each of us in a different voice. Nothing would have stopped this event. You must accept the fact."

"I'd feel better with Philip here in protection mode instead of being on his knees in prayer at San Marco's Abbey. No offense, Father."

"None taken." The monsignor smiled, held his gaze. "But now it is time, *si*? Put your house in order before this begins."

He wasn't about to argue.

****

In Thorn's arms and staring at Michael, the baby stopped sucking the bottle of infant formula. "Fatherhood changes a soul," Thorn said in a tender tone. "It's one awesome experience and yes... Throughout many lifetimes, this is my first shot at being a parent. So now I know what you must have felt when the angel took Lukas from your arms—right after he was born. I understand completely why you did *what* you did in Manhattan last year for the kid. This girl gets near my son, and I'll rip the demon right out of her with my own two hands."

Thorn's serious expression didn't soften when Celia took the baby. Michael saw a protective husband and father as Thorn studied his wife. Satisfied with two healthy burps, a fresh white spot appeared on her shoulder, and he handed her a tissue.

Celia grinned, saying, "Parent lesson number five: Natural fibers don't hold a stain."

Until Alana and Celia left the room with the baby, Michael waited in silence. And once they were alone, Thorn sank into an armchair and stared his way. This was one of many conversations that had to happen, and he leaned against the couch with his arms locked across his chest, not sure he wanted to listen.

"Go ahead… Stroll through my mind. It's easier than saying it all out loud." He eyed the burly man. "Stop playing with your trouser cuff and talk to me. I know you only do it when you're nervous. So…" He got a grunt and a frown.

"What I see in you worries me. Spare the details of what you're gonna do with the girl and let's get to the nitty-gritty. Put your house in order means deal with the kid." Thorn shrugged while he scoffed. "Considering what teenagers get into today, this is a cry for attention. Wine isn't Lagavulin and cigarettes aren't mind-altering drugs. As for telling lies and this stealing issue—I'd make sure he shakes in his shoes over that one."

"He'll shake all right," he replied.

"The living breathing you is *way* out of the kid's comfort zone. Just hear me out. If he helps you with the girl, he'll know you trust him and walk the straight and narrow, which will end the bad behavior."

"Absolutely not… No."

"Well if you think for a foolish minute he'll say 'Yes, Daddy' and stay put while you run around Siena, you're wrong."

"Not this time. Absolutely no… Lukas has a lot of growing up to do before I take him to a medieval city in search of a demon in disguise."

"Don't leave him out of this."

"No. You're a father now. You know what I feel."

"Rethink the 'no'," Thorn said as he stood. "I'll give Miles my two cents about a timeline while you hem and haw about what you know has to happen. We'll be expecting you."

Michael didn't reply, but staring at Thorn, he shook his head once before walking upstairs.

****

Pacing Celia and Thorn's bedroom, Alana breathed in wonderful baby scents, simply loving the feel of a sleeping infant against her breast. "Lu *not* being included spells disaster, Celia B."

"You've got your work cut out for you."

Suddenly sad, she barely said, "Don't I know it."

"Ally, you're miles away."

"There's a distance between me and Michael that I can't explain. It's all wrong."

"I'm not sensing wrong. I'm sensing way weird. Maybe the 'way weird' is stopping him from picking up where you left off last May. I don't know." Celia took the sleeping baby from her arms and gently laid him in an old-fashioned wicker basinet.

"Do you think Thorn convinced Michael to talk to him?"

"I hope so. But do you think the sweetie will

actually listen?"

She fully frowned. "Daddy issues are different than Mommy issues. He has to learn to listen and be truthful. I mean, suppose he's called to the mystical mission? A Guardian of Souls so fierce has to have his head screwed on straight. And he'll have to follow orders."

"His skills are already *far* beyond most Guardians' abilities."

"At least Michael and I agree to do this together."

"It's a big step in the right direction," her sister confirmed.

"Of course, Lu spilling his guts would be closer to a leap."

Chapter 12

He had slept; he had showered. Halfway through another huge homework assignment, Lukas suddenly lurched back. He sat on the bed and listened to bits and pieces of *both* conversations happening downstairs— simultaneously.

Breathing hard, he shivered at the thought of a beast-within... in a living, breathing girl. *Siena. An innocent with unspeakable evil inside...* He suddenly saw his father dying again and taking back the fucking thing to save her. And he'd be stuck here in this bedroom being forced to stay out of it and stay put! No average human would know there was a killer inside her. Not even Guardians would know. There could be many victims, faceless bodies. He couldn't shake the feeling that he had to be in this... until he heard his father cross the living room.

In the master bedroom, dresser drawers were opening and closing. Laying down, he locked his fingers behind his head. "If he says no, I can run after they leave. Yeah, that's doable. How hard could it be to get to Siena? Hell, Nico will drive me or I'll steal a car and drive myself. Sure... He'll be spitting mad, but Mom will talk him down." But it was a different tidbit he had heard that soured his stomach. *Put your house in order. Deal with the kid.*

"Fuck no. He won't smack my ass. He's human

and I'm faster than him now." Grabbing a pillow, he hugged it tight. "Take a hint, Dad. No fucking way I'm saying 'yes, Daddy' and stay put like some scared kid. You're not immortal anymore. You're gonna die."

****

Michael shoved his wallet into his back pocket. Hearing his son's whispers confirmed that Lukas had stepped too far over that unwritten line with eavesdropping. He sat in the Queen Anne chair and studied Alana as she came in. "Your clothes are ready. I figured you'd want to travel light."

"I want to travel light, not naked." She pushed the solitary sweater and a pair of jeans out of the way to sit on the bed, directly across from him. "Let's discuss this."

"Discuss or bicker... Which is it, my Guardian?" His elbows stayed on the chair's cushioned arms, his hands folded under his chin.

"It's three for including Lukas and one opposed."

"I'm his father, which overrules all."

"He'll do something dangerous...like try to find us. You'd put Lu in harm's way *again*?"

Close to furious, he stood. "That's hitting below the belt. He's not in this, Alana."

"You'll feel so guilty when he gets in over his head. Why are you shutting me out of this decision?"

"You have no idea what—"

"No, Michael, *you* have no idea. Give him a chance. Please."

"I'll talk with him when I'm ready."

"*We'll* talk with him—and right now. That's what you meant to say."

He strode to the door and turned to face her. There

was no delicate way to do this, but before he walked out, he said as calm as possible, "Why don't you ask him to join us for a chat. I'm sure he'll jump at the chance."

In the dining room, Michael remained at the window staring at the spring sky when they entered together. Showing nothing, he turned and walked through the wide arch into the living room as his son sat close to Alana on the beige leather couch. She took the lead explaining the new event. He studied his son's perfectly rehearsed reactions—didn't interrupt, nor tip his hand.

Her very direct description ended with, "This innocent is dangerous, Lu."

"She doesn't have demon strength like we do, Mom."

"But she's more dangerous than a vampire."

"I know I can take her down. How soon do we track her, Dad?"

And that was his cue. "*We* don't. You'll be at Villa Catherine," he casually answered. With her eyes wide, Alana looked about to speak, and he warned, "Do *not* say a word." He strode to the couch, leaned down eye-level with Lukas. "*Mom* may have forgotten about your super hearing. I haven't. Think you're in trouble? Just say 'Yes Daddy' and mean it."

Lukas's face began to flush. "You...you heard me."

"Every. Single. Word... Take a guess at what happens if you don't stay put. And no, Mom won't talk me down from being spitting mad." Irritation peppered his tone. "My order stands. You are not in this. Now go back to your room and think about why." He stepped back, and Lukas ran into his room slamming the door. Still fuming, he looked at Alana.

She whispered, "Please tell me he doesn't hear everything we say in here."

"Everything," he confirmed. "Who's Nico?"

"Vito's nephew."

"I thought so. Now, let's not keep the monsignor waiting. I can't do this without you and I wouldn't even want to try." He held out his hand. Alana took it.

****

Getting caught twice in one day stung like hell—reality did, too. Lukas stared at the books next to his laptop. Opening one up, he tried to read about Romantic Era poets, but couldn't concentrate. The thick book hit the wall with a thud. He flung his notebook, which landed by the closet and cleared his desk of all his homework with one swift swipe of an arm. When his senses hummed, he whispered, "It's not fair, Uncle T." He heard the door open and the man walk over to him.

"I warned you, kid. Honesty is the best policy."

"I hate platitudes."

"Yeah, well, it fits."

"He *knows* everything I said."

"You started out on the wrong foot and just keep tripping over all those pent-up feelings."

"I don't need a lecture."

"Yes, you do. A long one, which includes I told you so and actions speak louder than words. For the hundredth time, kid, you know better."

His uncle's massive hand rested on his shoulder; it only made him more miserable. "You see things. Why didn't you know he could come back breathing?"

153

"Don't change the subject. Here's one to grow on. Spill the beans, and no, Auntie Celia won't soften him up for you. Speak from your heart."

"He's gonna go ballistic. And he's gonna get parental on my ass."

"Those are two possibilities you have to accept."

When his uncle left, he picked up the books. And as every platitude replayed in his head, he fixed his bed and cleaned his room.

****

In the art studio of the student house, Phyllis Verdi studied today's sketches as shouts began. She ran into the living room. The grad student's hands flew wild, using his best broken English to translate the news-crawl under today's soccer match. Bodies found—chewed apart. Calmly she whispered, "Oh my, and six tourists are missing. Police caution everyone to be on the lookout for stray dogs or disoriented wolves. No going outside at night for any reason, guys." The students stared at her, not about to protest.

Betts asked, "What about Jillian and Carol?"

"I'm sure they're safe in the infirmary."

The girl looked close to tears, and everyone looked anxious. "Please call your parents immediately to say you're okay."

Wringing her hands, Betts blurted out, "Will you call home for Jillian and Carol?"

"I think I'll do it right now," she replied.

When Phyllis entered the art studio, she locked the door. With a heavy heart, she sat at the drawing table. Instinct told her Carol Reardon's phone numbers were false and Jillian's mother was already dead.

****

To the north of Siena on a hillside, the ancient citadel stood. "Pull over. I want to look," Jillian instructed Lucy. The sun had set on San Gimignano. The gloaming began—brief minutes between day and night when all appeared still and mysterious. Breathing in fresh, sweet air, the beast-within decided that in a few hours a new terror, merciless and brutal, would stun the tiny town. Carefully laying her treasure chest on the seat, Jillian stepped out of the small cat with a bright smile. "Dante called it the deepest abyss," she whispered. "Fourteen towers all in a ring; walls so high they touch the sky. "Heart of Hell" is such a lovely metaphor."

****

Lukas had to make this right. Hours had passed slower than a turtle crossing a road. Night had fallen, and more anxious by the minute, he stood behind his bedroom door. Using only 'human' ears, he heard the baby fuss, either wet or hungry. Dishes clattered on the dining room table, being set for Sunday dinner, a couple of hours too late tonight. He opened the door just a little and caught Alana's eye. After coming in, she closed it, flung the dishtowel over a shoulder and put her hands on her hips.

"Dad's not home yet?"

"No." As he relaxed, she added, "How *could* you, Lu?"

"Mom, I… I—Please don't be mad."

"I can't believe what you've done. I'm so let down that…"

"I'm *really* sorry. I didn't respect your privacy."

"I never thought you could be so rude. If your butt gets smacked, you totally deserve it." Then her face softened when she cupped his chin. And it truly felt like heaven when her hand slid across his cheek. "Dinner's almost ready. I've got to get out there, so... we'll talk later?"

"Yeah, sure," he replied. But when she opened the door, he saw his father—who didn't look forgiving. Not at all. And when he didn't hear Mom whisper, "Go easy on him" this time, he swallowed hard.

****

Lukas stepped back with his gut tied in knots as the door closed, and he thought he'd puke again. Inching further back, he glimpsed another intimidating look, which forced the decision to just stare at the rug.

"Did you apologize to," his father cleared his throat, "Mom?"

"Yes," he whispered.

"Good. But you're still in big trouble, little boy."

"I'm four inches taller and almost sixteen," slipped out before he could stop—like that made any difference. He could almost predict his father's answer.

"It wouldn't matter if you were six-foot and almost twenty-six. I'd haul you over my knee and smack your backside."

Both fists crammed into his jean's back pockets as his stomach rolled again. "Can't you just take a job where you sit at a desk somewhere?"

"That's not going to happen, and I'm not hearing what needs to be said." His father took a step forward, and he took a step back. "Start talking."

"I don't know what the hell you are."

"Try a very annoyed parent."

"I had an *immortal* father for less than a week! You're not him anymore. Change back again because people die, you know, without any warning. You go to Siena and I'll lose you." The next expression on his father's face *really* scared him. This time, his steps away were fast, and when his back hit the wall, shaking from head to toe, he quickly said, "I'm sorry. I'm sorry."

"You're not sorry!" The sharp, loud tone made him jump. "Listening to every word we say is beyond disrespectful! And I refuse to overlook the other unwise choices—the not so innocent mischief. It tells me I cannot trust your judgment in a life-or-death situation."

"Yes, you can! You have to!"

"Why?"

His mouth hung open, but he couldn't answer.

From the middle of the room, his father's eyes narrowed. "I know about last night. Nico didn't hold *one* detail back. Fifteen and in a car with a drunken smart-ass behind the wheel. Drinking, smoking, stealing... How much money did you take from the hutch?"

His palms stuck to the wall. Really shaking now, he yelled, "I didn't *count* it!"

"Do not dare to raise your voice with me. Not after all you've done. Self-healing didn't kick in the last time you got bratty with me, and it sure as hell won't kick in now, either. This is over. Do you understand?"

"Yes," he whispered.

"Come over here, right now." Everything blurred, but he complied, still shaking and unsteady on his feet. He glanced up, prepared to take his punishment, knowing he'd be sore for days. Once toe to toe with his father, waiting to be staring at the floor with tears in his eyes, he heard, "Talk to me, little boy," very calm and soft.

Lukas palmed his eyes as they filled again, and his nose began to run. "I'm going to lose you forever this time."

"That will absolutely not happen." He was instantly drawn into a fierce hug, the place of unconditional comfort he had missed for ten long months, and he held on tight. Maybe the weird feelings about blood and death were just his own fear gone wild.

A quick kiss met the top of his head as Lukas shut his eyes. "I'm not letting go of you, so talk to me. I'm prepared to listen for a lifetime."

****

At the dinner table, Michael kept Lukas next to him. They were both emotionally drained in a typically human way. His son had stayed in his hug for a long time. Then they sat on the bed and discussed every stubborn, wrong decision his son had made these past weeks. Misery was written across Lukas's face, and the way he shook said lesson learned. Then the fear that something would happen and he'd be fatherless had his son teary-eyed again. He addressed that irrational fear the best he could. But before they left the bedroom, he set strict parameters for Lukas's involvement in Siena with a very stern warning. He had sidestepped the questions about his heartbeat, simply admitting it was a mystery to him as well. Perhaps it was necessary to face the beast-within that authored his legacy of undeath, he had told his son. What he didn't say was that perhaps afterward, these heartbeats would indeed cease. Because if shoving that evil entity back into his soul saves an innocent girl, he'd take that chance.

They had talked for almost an hour and by the time

they came to the table, everyone had already started eating. The meal Alana prepared was delicious, reminiscent of Rosa's cooking. Engaging in conversation with those he loved and respected made it more of a pleasure. When supper ended, however, the light mood rapidly dissipated.

Celia gave a noticeable cringe as a brusque exchange began between her parents. "Great, here comes more tension," she whispered to Alana.

Laura's deep-green eyes blazed at Miles. No doubt, Michael thought, the researcher is stumped by this event—we all are. Rocking the baby, Laura again shook her head. "You can insist all you want, dear. I'm not leaving you."

Miles leaned forward. "You will be safe at the villa, Laura."

"That's the tenth time you've used the infernal *safe* in five minutes! You cannot shut a thriving business down because something is on the loose many kilometers away. I have enough know-how to keep Alana's customers happy. You're in Portofino. I am as well."

Celia protested, but Thorn interrupted with, "I know you don't want to hear it, Miles, but the lady has a point."

Miles uttered, "Read my mind," in an abrupt tone rarely heard.

At first, Michael chuckled and then said, "I agree with Thorn, who will stay here as well," spontaneously came out of his mouth. Somewhat confused, he looked at his friend. "I can't believe I just said that. But it makes perfect sense."

Celia's eyes were ready to pop and her hands flew

into the air. "Oh no… No, no, no! You *made* him say that, Theo Thornwell! I'm not going to Siena without you and Mom."

"Yes, you will go, just you and the babe," Michael firmly replied. Instantly, he softened his tone. "And please don't get so upset because I really do love you, Celia B. We both know this demon doesn't want an empath. And Thorn is always just a thought away, right? Out of all of us, Laura and Thorn are more than safe. I'm… sorry, Laura, I didn't mean to use the word again." Laura nodded graciously, but Celia sighed and looked away.

Miles said to Alana, "I expect continual updates from you, honey—you as well, Michael."

"Be confident in the fact that this time, I'll leave nothing out. Alana and I agree to wait until Tuesday morning to leave, Miles, and every precaution will be in place. Time-line, order of importance—we know what has to be done. So does Celia." Michael saw Thorn's satisfied grin. "Are you purposely putting words in my mouth, Empath?"

"Well, I figured since you were talking…" Thorn took Celia's hand. "The Catherines are down one healer. You have the skills they need."

"I… I know," she whispered, "I… I just realized."

Then Thorn's gaze landed on Michael's arm draped across Lukas's back, saying, "So it seems we have another issue out of the way, Champ. Well, kid, are you ready to put every mystical gift to the test?"

An easy, dimpled grin appeared on Lukas's face, and he gently prodded, "Tell Uncle T the truth, little boy."

****

Everyone left. Michael brought dinner dishes to Alana in the kitchen. "I want this event to go smooth and be over quick."

"So do I," she replied. "You seemed to enjoy talking to everyone at dinner."

"I did," he said looking through the arch at his son's open door.

"Maybe see how he's doing," she whispered.

"Not a bad idea, my Guardian," he answered before slow strides through the spacious rooms. He leaned against the doorframe. "Tuesday will come very fast. How's the homework situation?"

"I explained everything and apologized for, you know, the delays. Clarke answered my email. He only wants a debate outline on keeping the American colonies for taxation. I'm starting it now."

"Everything else is on hold?"

"Yeah... Until you call him."

Michael stood behind him reading the laptop's screen. "Not bad for someone who wasn't around in the 1700s, however, I'd need more persuasive facts to accept your position."

"Yeah, well, you're like a walking history book. I mean, you were in America when it still belonged to England."

"But I didn't follow politics, and I never paid taxes. Did you research Tom Paine? Now *he* could inspire a revolution. Go ahead. Google his name."

"Whoa...There are thousands of listings. *Common Sense, American Crisis...*"

"Your debate team can win this one, of course, being a colonial and all."

His son studied him and asked, "A what?"

161

"Don't send the outline until you research Paine. Either you'll get an A or be expelled. I distinctly remember one particularly heated rant. Paine kept going on about how an island couldn't rule a continent. The crowd loved it." Michael stretched out on the bed grateful for the one-on-one time with his son.

****

By the time he left Lukas, it was well after midnight. He walked through every room of his home listening for anything out of the ordinary. Satisfied that all was as it should be, he slipped soundlessly into the master bedroom. He had purposely kept his mind off Siena for hours. But deep within his soul, he sensed the beast-within seeking total domination over a young girl. Since 1890, only mystical strength had allowed him to keep such a powerful entity dormant. That somehow it could be resurrected fully horrified him.

From the foot of the sleigh bed, he watched Alana sleep. Her supple curves tempted to unleash uncontrollable passion, to take her without warning. Wanting only her was a fact, and yet, he had allowed distance to form a wedge between them. He stepped to the side of the bed, thinking no more curling in her arms like a lost boy. Aroused by the very sight of her, his erection throbbed to the point of pain.

Slipping off his shirt, shivers began. Suddenly unsteady, he sank down, into the Queen Anne chair. He reached for his soul mate, mere inches away, and as if gripped by an icy hand, his fingers recoiled. *New loss of life and an unknown battle gains momentum. I sense it. I feel it.* Outrage branded his heart, crippled the desire to touch her, to make love to her.

Drifting in and out of sleep throughout the

unsettled night, he didn't reach for her again.

****

Lucy found something she could use in a small storage space behind the basement steps. She rolled the metal foldaway bed into the room created for Jillian and hung a set of musty drapes from rusty nails in the crossbeams. Flopping onto the lumpy mattress, a shaky breath began. This is better than sleeping on the floor, she thought.

Fourteen crucifixes in the chest, and three dead bodies left out in the open for Monday's news. She didn't want to know where Leonard's people put the other eleven, but it would keep the police busy. *There is no pack of wolves, only vampires drinking up a feast.*

She had no idea why Leonard picked his granddaughter for something as wicked as this. Bruises marred Jillian's skin. *Maybe it has to do with swallowing blood or it doesn't get the human need for food, for rest. Without help, keeping her alive until Friday isn't going to be easy.*

A rattled cough punctured the quiet. "Lovely sparkling amulets gathered for my origin."

Then gurgling sounds forced her to sneak a peek. Lying in bed, Jillian licked dried blood off her fingers. Lucy grabbed a fresh bottle of water from the dresser and keeping her eyes glued to the carpet, placed it next to Jillian's hand.

"This'll help you swallow easier."

"Thank you, Lucy," Jillian chirped in a pleasant tone. "You can go."

I can go, she thought, I *have* to go! Instead of returning to the curtained cubicle, Lucy hurried to the door. She locked the basement room, crept up the stairs and fell onto her comfortable bed. "I fucking hope you burn in Hell for leaving me alone, Carol," she spit out.

Fear began to creep up Lucy Novak's spine.

Chapter 13

Monday moved like a blur, a glitch in time as everyone packed and prepared as best they could for the unexpected. As long as Michael kept his mind on Siena, he felt focused, ready to find and save another innocent no matter the cost to himself. He avoided Alana, not able to explain why he hadn't slept in their bed again last night.

While Alana familiarized Laura with the bookshop and what needed to be done to keep it going without her, Lukas seemed perfectly happy to help with the baby while Celia ran errands and packed for Villa Catherine. Michael met with Christensen to explain his precise instructions in the event things went off the rails. The woman he loved and his precious son would be taken care of financially—should he not survive Siena.

He also kept his appointment with Chamberlain at the Medico facility on the outskirts of Florence. To be on the safe side, he had the specialist run a stress test as well as a battery of tests on his blood. "I'll wait for the results," he told Chamberlain. Hours later, he paced in the office until the doctor came in and sat behind his desk. "Give it to me straight, Arthur."

"Have a seat."

"I prefer to stand."

"I prefer you don't."

Reluctant, he sat on the edge of the chair. "Did you find an abnormality in my blood?"

"You're as healthy as a stallion. Those tests were normal, too, by the way. Great cholesterol, excellent thyroid function, glucose levels perfect, and do I ever envy your blood pressure. There's no deviation from the original results. You're a healthy man."

"We leave for Siena tomorrow morning."

"This is a strange event, Michael. I've never seen anything like it."

"Neither have I." He paused, thinking about facing the beast-within—thinking why Lukas was so worried he might die. Those fears, he definitely wouldn't share with the specialist or anyone else. *Who am I kidding*, he thought when he left Chamberlain's office, *if any part of our plan goes sideways, these days are my last as a living, breathing man.*

****

Alana had a quiet dinner with her parents at their hotel. Walking home, she remained deep in thought. Laura was now all on her own with a business she had grown and come to love. It didn't take much for her mind to turn to Michael as she took the last set of stairs up to her home on the third floor. The fact that he obviously chose to spend yet another night out of her embrace really bothered her. *First the den, now the chair... not even a lingering kiss good morning today.*

The door was open. Three nylon duffle bags were on the couch. Leering at them, only two bulged at the seams, which brought to mind this morning's bickering match when Michael had quipped, "We're not going on a two-week vacation, darlin'," and she shot back with, "How about an extra pair of jeans, another clean shirt and shaving cream, just in case you aren't planning on growing a beard."

And tonight, seated at the dining room table, Michael came off relaxed in a white undershirt and a pair of black sweats. As if nothing out of the ordinary was on his mind. When his dark, espresso eyes captured hers, she could only muster a slight smile, thinking so who's the distant one now. "Polishing your trusted broadsword?"

"Bring me your short-sword. I'll make sure it's polished as well," he said, all business-like before looking away.

The hope of being crushed in his arms still filled her heart, but he didn't come to her. *No hello, how was your day. We're ending Monday on the same sour note it began with.* "My sword's just fine. What about Lu? Did he choose something from your trunk?"

"He did. I've already polished it."

"Is he in his room?"

"Yes. IM-ing or texting… Something like that."

She moved across the room, rapped a knuckle on Lukas's door before opening it.

"Hey Mom," he said with a sweet smile.

"Talking to your friend in England?"

"Yep. Want to say hi?"

"You do it for me. Night, Lu," she whispered, and then blew him a kiss.

Upon entering their bedroom, she placed her oversized handbag on the dresser. It often doubled as a briefcase. Miles had given her Veronique's file, firsthand accounts from the Guardian perspective. It had to be as heavy as a watermelon; at least eight inches thick! Closing the bedroom door, she decided to take a shower before reading the night away.

In the narrow, tiled space, she turned the knob and a trickle of water began. She gave a sharp sigh, longing for a huge tub where she could soak for hours in bubbles that smelled like lilacs and vanilla. After drying off, she tugged Michael's black silk shirt off the hook behind the door. Vivid memories of last May, making love to him all night, or talking 'til dawn... *I want him next to me, not in another room polishing a broadsword.* Call it a woman's intuition or just plain being able to read his mood... unless I do something drastic, she thought, he's going to avoid me again tonight. Grabbing Veronique's file, she curled on his side of the bed and turned on the lamp. It was difficult to concentrate as she opened the thick file and read the first page.

****

Hours ago, Michael had watched Alana come home, try to engage him in conversation and then close their bedroom door. Agreeing with Miles that she needed to know everything about Veronique before going after her, he was fully uncomfortable... on many levels. His on again-off again, sexually charged relationship with her spanned two centuries—right up until 1890. Before their erotic trysts, they had often hunted together, killed together. Veronique was crafty and creative, in a deceptive way more deadly than Cyril. I hope she's fast asleep before I enter that bedroom, he thought.

This event had him edgy, like a strange restlessness had taken hold. In many ways, it would have been better to just go it alone, leave tonight without telling her. There were many risks, no matter how well they had planned.

It was well-past midnight when he walked into the den to home in on the baby's heartbeat one floor below. He had to believe that the baby and Celia would be safe with the Catherines. Then he stretched out on the denim loveseat, but his feet hung over the arm. He couldn't get comfortable no matter how hard he tried. He studied the room full of piled books before slow strides down the hall to check on Lukas. Curled on his side, his son hugged a pillow. Siena would test Lukas's mystical abilities, his willingness to follow specific orders, but as for Florence, he thought, you won't be allowed anywhere near the cunning, ancient sire. Veronique was that deadly.

He left without a sound and began to pace the living room. Both hands raked through his hair as if the sweep-away motion could dispel each troublesome thought. And when he found himself staring at the master bedroom door, full of frustration he whispered, "I need you, my Guardian, I need to be near you." Then he paced the room again.

****

The master bedroom door closed behind him. The woman he would always love was asleep on his side of the bed with the thick file placed on the nightstand. He tugged off his undershirt and in his sweats, sank into the Queen Anne chair careful not to wake her. *Another day and night of killing... what was in my sister's writing chest should never have been removed from my soul. I kept it contained, but now, the beast-within is on the prowl—because of me.*

He thought about Alana, how she had risked her life in the city to fight vampires. He studied her soft curves, the outline of her inviting breasts draped in silk he had once worn. *I want her. I love her. I could devour this alluring woman and explode inside her. She owns my heart. She completes my soul.* In a starving state of full arousal, he moaned, shifted his hips in the chair.

"Come to bed," she whispered.

"You're awake."

"What's wrong?"

He didn't move, and unable to say what he thought, replied, "Nothing."

She sat up, pulled both knees to her chest. "You're letting this event consume you, and we aren't even in Siena yet. You know when it kills, and you purposely pull away from me."

"Yes," he softly said.

"Now admit you've only given me a crumb of truth."

Lust filled her eyes, and the sliver of moonlight turned his vision of her into a siren's sensual silhouette. He forced himself to look away. "I've never lied to you."

"You're so hell-bent on avoiding me, my love," came in a breathy voice, a sensual one.

After a pause, he offered a simple, "I'm sorry."

"That's it? That's all you can say to me. This thing's given you a new reason *not* to share our bed. I've trusted you with my life. And for ten years, you trusted me with your undead existence. Why can't we talk about what's *not* happening between us? How long do you think this distance thing is going to last?"

"I don't do avoidance, darlin'. That's your department. I truly despise cleverness, and coming from you, it's close to spiteful. I could ravage you right now." God, he wanted her, and tonight, she wore anger like a temptress. Crawling to the edge of the bed, she sat back on her heels. Her full breasts heaved when she glared cool enough to mask her desire and to raise his.

"Really? I'm not getting that. You're a lifetime away and not being open with me, which isn't smart because I have to be certain of you…one thousand percent. Do *not* doubt that I can take Veronique down without *you*. Her file reads like one long horror novel. And since the two of you were so… involved, maybe we should do this another way. I stake an old, cunning vamp who thinks she's a princess while you find an innocent girl. Then we avoid our whole sexual tension thing in Siena. How 'bout it, buddy?"

As soon as 'buddy' came off her lips, he stood. The snippy put-down made him seethe. Kneeling on the bed, she straightened her back. Fury as well as lust flickered in her hazel eyes, and he inhaled the scent of her arousal. It drove him insane, made his pulse race and his erection jerk. Boldly, her hands shot to his shoulders pulling him to her. Her kisses plundered his mouth. Every nip at his lips pulsated through him.

"I need you. I want you," she whispered as her hands ran up and down his chest.

He fought the desire to throw her down on the bed… to taste her and take her rough and urgent, to do what he'd thought about doing for days. Their eyes locked in a furious gaze when she ran her fingernails across his chest, when they slid lower pricking his skin. Her tongue forced through his drawn lips as she came off the bed and pressed her body to his. *Naked and underneath me, her quivering core against my tongue. Hearing her whimper from what I do to her like never before…* He gripped her wrists. "This won't happen, my Guardian. Not tonight."

"Why not?" Twisting free, she instantly had the length of him in hand. He groaned low, cinched her waist under the silk shirt. "Tell me, why not, my love," she sighed low and sexy.

"No, not now, not tonight," he managed to whisper.

Strategic nips slowly trailed down his chest, his waist, until his sweats were down and his arousal exposed. Then her lips found what she wanted. Swollen and stiff, he hissed in every breath ready to race toward release. Holding his hips, she left him. It was a merciless torture. Her long hair feathered against his burning thigh. The black silk shirt drifted off her shoulders and pooled around her like a sea of dark water. "I ache for only you, my love. Come into me."

The last rational thought left his mind as obsession pulsed through him, and he pulled her to her feet. The silky wetness at her core bathed his palm. His fingers teased her while the pressure of his thumb produced a soft cry, which melted into sighs of passion. Rough kisses assaulted her tender lips, called to the searing part of her, and the sudden buck against his hand sent his senses into overdrive with the blinding need to take her.

They fell onto the sleigh bed. He pinned her down, pounding into her thrust after thrust. Every guttural moan, every restless shift of her feverish body drove his urgency. Like a glove, she tightened around his erection greedily drawing him in deeper.

Nothing equaled this experience of total release. And as an orgasm shuddered through her, nothing equaled the sensation of filling her with hot, living seed. When her hold on him relaxed, sweat coated his chest, and he slid to her side breathing heavily.

Minutes passed, and after a dry swallow he whispered, "Did I hurt you?"

Her palm came over his heart. "Being ravaged by you is beyond description."

He closed his eyes, wondering who ravaged whom as he fell asleep.

****

Curious sounds startled Lucy in the middle of the night. She sat up, palmed her forehead. Tonight's earlier rampage through Monteriggioni had added many crosses to the wooden chest. It gave Lucy the creeps—the way victims shuffled away like drugged lambs to the slaughter. Another strangled growl started. Yawning, she crept over to look through a slit between the drapes.

Jillian had kicked off the covers, now writhing and rocking. *Knees bent, heels dug into the mattress... What the hell is this thing doing to her?* The pretty pink nightgown was streaked with blood; more bathed her inner thighs. Another curdling screech began, and Lucy's eyes opened even wider when Jillian gyrated and jerked her hips in an eclectic frenzy.

"The scent of lust unrestrained does he desire. *I* crave," Jillian growled, "*I* crave..."

Lucy jerked back. She tiptoed to the narrow bed. Sitting down carefully so as not to make a sound, she wondered if Leonard knew something like this would happen.

****

Their son let out a sharp cry. Celia bolted upright

173

in bed. Thorn sat up as well, quite a bit slower and much groggier. "There's a reason, dearest," he whispered.

"He didn't wake up, but maybe he's wet," she said, hoping with all her heart. When Thorn didn't reply, Celia's eyes instantly filled. "Oh God, that's why he didn't want to touch her. It knows, doesn't it?" Sad sobs helplessly escaped, and she rested her head against the father of her child, playing with soft tufts of auburn curls on his massive chest.

His kiss was reverent, whispering afterward, "Get everything you need. I'll drive."

"Let Dad come with us, please sweetie. I don't want you alone on the highway at four in the morning. Monsignor can baptize him tonight, just a simple blessing." Devotion flooded his soft-gray eyes, and when he started to leave their bed, Celia pulled him back. "Hold me one last time," she whispered as if out of breath. He kissed the tip of her nose, her glistening eyelids before a tight embrace. He was her loving soulmate—her completion.

****

Celia knew they'd both want to see her and the baby off to Villa Catherine and wasn't surprised that they were standing inside the small church. Her parents held their son over the marble basin. With hushed prayers and tepid water, Uriel Theodosius Thornwell was christened. He never awakened, never crinkled his tiny brow. Then Monsignor Scarlatti blessed her as well. "You must hurry. More will be revealed to you but remember that the Champion must hold your son while the demon is drawn out."

"Are you ready?" Laura asked with concern.

Thorn whispered, "We gotta go *now*," and hustled her out of the church and down the back streets to the parking lot with Miles and Laura following close.

Sensing her mother's question, she replied, "Because there's no trace of Michael in Ally's car. He-he only rode in it once last May."

"But it's quite small. Perhaps the monsignor's car is better suited for all of us?"

Miles quickly said, "Trust me. Only the red car is safe."

Walking with a quick step and Thorn holding her arm, Celia said, "Monsignor brought the beast-within to the villa's cemetery last May. We don't want to take a chance."

Thankfully, the car was unlocked, and Thorn pried tape off a spare key hidden in the glove compartment. "Forget about a baby seat. Forget about anything that might add to your stress," he said to her. "Mom and Dad will care for him in the back and hold on tight." The engine started, and the car took off as if it had Heavenly power under the hood.

She tried to calm the anxiety in her heart, but she wouldn't feel safe until she stood in the sacred walls of Villa Catherine.

****

Well after five a.m., Thorn walked into the second-floor apartment. His furrowed brow eased and he gave a weary grin. "You know it's me and I know it's you. What are you doing down here in the dark?"

"Where are they?" Lukas whispered.

"With Mother Anne," he said, turning on the lamp before he collapsed in an armchair.

"Why, Uncle T? Dad said we'd all leave together

175

later today."

"I have to ask. How did you know?"

Lukas shrugged. "I just woke up with the feeling that something happened and then I didn't hear any heartbeats down here. You didn't answer my question."

"Some things are not for your ears."

"But you're gonna tell my Dad why, right?"

"This is no time for secrets, but you were never here and we never had this conversation. Go back upstairs." He watched the kid walk out the door and leaning his head back, he closed his eyes. "Damn it, Michael. Why did you do what you did," he whispered full of so many emotions that he couldn't sort through any of them right now.

Chapter 14

For the first time since his return, Michael slept like a rock, not lucid until well after dawn. He stood under the tepid trickle of a shower and craved coffee...strong coffee. Trying not to think about last night's lusty interlude, he dressed in a hurry and left the room before Alana stirred. Like every day since his return, he walked into the den to sense a new life's safety one floor directly below. His eyes immediately narrowed and his relaxed expression changed. He raced down the hall, out of his home, and jumped the staircase ready to break down Thorn's door.

"Back away, unroll your fists and just breathe. Humans do that every now and again," came from the other side. When the door opened, he glared at the empath who looked as if he hadn't slept in days. "I was still prepared to take a fist in the face. Save the twenty questions."

He followed Thorn into the small dining room. "*Why*? Where did—"

"Quiet. Just sit down."

He sat, leaned forward. "Where are they?"

"Quiet!"

Not caring if Thorn read his thoughts, he straightened his back and waited while two mugs with hot coffee were on the table. "I took them to Villa Catherine—right after you did what you did. Our son let out one hell of a cry, which pulled both of us out of a deep sleep, thank you very much."

"What do you mean after what we did?" When Thorn's big fist thumped the table, both of his hands shot up with a quick, "Okay… Okay."

"My son is a mystical child…you do know that, don't you? Don't answer. It was rhetorical. You sailed *pretty far* over the top last night—in the very 'oh sweet mystery of life' way."

"I don't see what our sex life—"

"Well *we* did, and so did the demon in the girl—in vivid color." Slowly shifting, Michael stared at him in full disbelief. "Yeah, if you were standing both legs would buckle—or I'd kick them out from under you—just to watch you land hard on your ass. Maybe there was a damn good reason why you kept things cool with Alana. I guess three hundred years is one hell of a many-life-times bond to sever." Thorn's baritone voice rumbled lower. "It caught the x-rated show, Champ. It felt that zing of pleasure. Who knows what the demon will do now."

"Just tell me Celia and the baby are safe."

"You'll have no contact with them *whatsoever* until the holy healers remove this particular bastard from another innocent soul."

He didn't sip the much-needed caffeine. He chugged it down as his friend took a mouthful of coffee and then set down his mug. "Your thoughts are like a swollen waterfall. Forget about sailing straight to guilty. It's too familiar a place for you. No one knew that you're somehow still connected; that your steamy romp through erotic could transfer to the girl's uninvited guest-within."

He risked a soft, "I'm so sorry."

"Oh that's a given. Monsignor stated in a *knowing* way that after you deliver Jillian to the villa, you're to hold our son until this thing leaves her. Will you protect my son from this evil?"

"Like he's my own," he vowed.

After a decisive nod, Thorn looked away. "What time are you leaving for Siena? Soon, I hope."

"Very soon," he replied. Oh God, he thought as he stood, what have I done?

****

Holding the baby to her breast, Celia looked around Gabriella's room. Since the days when Catherine of Siena had walked these serene halls, the villa had been mystically protected. A constant congregation of fifty-four gifted women dwelled within this sacred space. She felt a deep attachment to all of them. "We'll be safe here—very safe," she whispered. "No one will find us, no evil, I promise. And if anyone comes near, they'll see a-a broken down place with weeds and dead vines until we know he's one of the good guys." Nervously, she rocked her son. "This should never have happened. What it's doing to her innocent soul is a total tragedy."

"Thinking out loud, sister psychic, or giving the little guy a heads up on the situation," Gabriella said as she came in holding a baby bottle.

"A little of both."

"Maggie told me to float it in a pot of warm water. I think I got it right."

"It's perfect, I'm sure. Your room's quaint and welcoming. I expected it to be, well, more you."

"I'm glad you like the decor. Just keep it to

yourself, okay? I prefer 'feisty ex-Guardian' stays in one's mind."

"My lips are sealed, but I really do like it, Gabby. Thanks for letting us stay with you."

"Can I feed him?"

"Sure." Celia settled the baby in her arms. Uriel kicked and cooed. Between mouthfuls of warm liquid, he made sweet gurgling sounds to thrill them both.

A pretty smile appeared on the healer's stunning face. "He's the most beautiful baby I've ever seen, Celia B. Don't worry. You can do this."

"Where is she, Gabby? How many more will die before Michael finds her? I mean, can he find her?"

"Malone will do what has to be done. He always does."

"Come clean. What have you seen that I've missed?"

"Not much. Jillian's a normal kid with a not-so-normal affliction. Thank God she isn't a commanding vampire—"

"Like Michael once was," she said, finishing Gabby's thought. "Let's hope he stops her before another cross goes into his sister's writing chest."

"I'm not sensing that. She's collecting crosses for a reason." The ex-Guardian paused. "Look, I feel your fears. But there isn't a devil in the desert that could penetrate the villa."

"Then why are you in your habit instead of a comfortable pair of jeans," she asked, although she already knew the answer. The Catherines sensed an unseen threat. This demon was unpredictable, which made the possessed girl highly unstable.

****

Laura put her fears aside and had opened the bookshop a half-hour early. Tourists wandered in admiring its charm and ready to buy. At nine a.m. on the dot, Thorn entered through Alana's office and walked over to her behind the counter. "The three of them are on their way to Siena." She breathed more relaxed as a group of tourists entered. "Ally said Easter Week would have a harbor crowded with yachts, a piazza full of tourists. She called it right."

"My daughter's turned into quite a savvy businesswoman." She caught a better glimpse of the empath as she handed a customer his package and began to ring up another order. "I take it you haven't slept, either. That makes three of us with dark circles beneath our eyes today."

"Have you talked to Miles?"

"He's at the rectory trying to access missing person reports."

"There's enough Georgian thought hovering over Italy to gain him quick entry into *any* database he needs today. God, I miss them already."

Flashing an easy smile at someone who didn't understand a word she said, she took the customer's credit card. "Can you wrap these books for me," she asked giving them to Thorn before he could respond. He cut patterned Florentine paper. She watched his desperate attempt at precise corners before sealing each with strips of tape. When he handed back the wrapped books, she put a solid hand over his massive one. "Stay for a bit. We could both use the company." As sweet as it sounded, it was an order. "You can man the register while I cajole Ally's clients… in English." He grinned, gave a nod as a new crop of customers entered the bookshop.

Although it took a few hours, by early afternoon they were a winning team. Laura decided to reset the polished mahogany shelves while Thorn rang up the latest sale.

The little brass bell above the door jingled as it opened again. She scrutinized four strange tourists. All wore ghoulish black eye-liner. Three sported blue, spiked hair; one was completely bald. The thin one, with a diamond pierced below his lower lip, gave a 'normal' customer a solitary, sneered smile. The lady eyed the sea of black leather with suspicion before hurrying out with unwrapped books tucked underneath an arm.

Taking in every inconsistency about these four travelers, Laura leaned into Thorn. "Oh my, my… Halloween Guardian Style, perhaps?"

"I guess word travels fast." Firmly, Thorn shook every outstretched hand.

The pierced one grinned. "Good to see you again, Empath. Cheers, Missus B."

"Good Lord, Nigel, have you no taste in clothes or hair color?" she said, trying not to laugh. "Since when do Guardians look like members of a new-age rock band from 1985? Petula, Mick, did you actually travel like this?" Then her gaze instantly swept up the tall Scot, whose stalwart frame actually dwarfed Thorn. "Neeb Gordon, are you on holiday from your senses? Does your saintly mum know about the shaved head?"

He dipped a square chin, saying in a soft bass tone, "Hallo, Missus B."

A hearty chuckle escaped. Quickly, she turned the sign to *chiuso*, leaned against the door. "What on earth made you dress like this. Are you all daft?'"

A mischievous grin crossed Nigel's very handsome face. His eyes sparkled with the worldly intelligence of a seasoned Guardian. "I thought you'd appreciate our disguise. We understand the researcher could use some help, as it stands."

Returning to the counter thoroughly amused, Laura's hand went over her heart. "Clarke has sent troops for back up?"

"We're more a front-line team," Neeb informed. In the ninth year of his mystical mission, Laura knew this Guardian to be unyielding. Never loquacious, tremendous strength remained his most admirable attribute.

"Lu is like a little brother to us," Nigel stated. "Clarke said we're to speak with Professor Bookman first. Can you take us to him, then?"

"I do love the smell of lemons, Missus B," Petula crooned in a dramatic way as the ringed fingers of her hand ran across a polished wood shelf. "So is this Lu's mum's place? We hear his daddy's back. Does the portrait at the Georgian Estate do Michael Malone justice—from a female point of view?"

"I hear the newbies drool over it, Pet."

"Commissioned in 1684 when the charmer turned twenty-one... Has living and breathing made him more than scrumptious eye-candy?"

She arched an eyebrow. "And since May, every impressionable, young psychic has probed the minds of Thorn and Celia to sketch the commanding creature. I understand it proves an interesting exercise. All I'll say is he's an entire cauldron of melted fudge and more."

Petula let loose a dreamy sigh, but Nigel gave a

sober glance, asking, "It is confirmed? The Champion has changed a bit, so to speak. Mick received numerous emails from Lu, which he shared."

"Sorry, Mum," the beefy seventeen-year-old whispered.

Only a year into the mystical mission, Mick called Lukas his best friend. Laura sensed her grandson felt the same. They were inseparable in England. "He'll be very glad to see you, young Guardian. But tell me, have you spoken about this with other newbies at the academy?"

With a quick shake of his head, Mick replied, "No, Mum, only these three."

"And that's the way it stays," Nigel said in a low tone. Shifting his stance, he peered into Alana's office just as Miles entered.

"Bad news travels fast, I take it. Glad you're here." Miles turned to Laura. "We'll speak upstairs."

"Of course, professor," she said with a gracious smile. "I'll reopen as soon as you leave." With footsteps like Alana's, silent and quick, the Guardians followed her husband through the small office.

Chapter 15

Michael walked down the narrow streets that led to the student house in silence. Alana stared straight ahead, but Lukas took in everything. Once at their destination, he gave a gentleman's nod to Sister Phyllis.

"I'm relieved you're here, Champion. To comply with your request, Alana, we've moved everyone to the third-floor bedrooms. And I'm happy to finally meet you, Lukas. Mother Anne always looks forward to your letters. Let's talk in the art studio. It's private." The healer led them through a large, sparse parlor. Next to a staircase, they took a quick left down a short hall. She closed the door behind them and ushered them to an old table speckled with every hue and tint of the spectrum's colors. Once seated, she met Michael's gaze. "You find the table intriguing?"

He gave a thin grin as his hand swept across its rutted wood. "It's not quite as old as I, yet it probably has just as much history."

"The University of Siena values authenticity. The house belonged to an artisan who worked with oils. Our administration wants to preserve this particular piece under glass, but the vote is squelched like a spider every time the request is reintroduced." She paused. "Sorry… Too much info? After so many years in the classroom, everything becomes a teaching moment. Don't be shy about reeling me in." Then in a friendly fashion, Phyllis met his son's inquisitive deep-blue eyes. "The students will love having someone around who speaks English. And you know all about Manhattan, my favorite place when I was your age— *many* years ago. I hopped a bus from East Stroudsburg with my girlfriends at least once a month, just to drool at all the art museums. My mother thought I was at the local library."

Lukas smiled as Michael stated, "My son will help insure the students' safety. That's a promise, Sister."

"Local Guardians have stayed low and out of your way?" Alana asked, adding as Phyllis nodded, "I'll meet with them tonight."

"We have a large cedar room in the basement. Feel free to hold the meeting there. Although there have been more victims in Siena, Veronique hasn't left her Florence estate since the night she came to the hills above the city to bite the innocent's wrist. I can't see into her estate. None of us can. There are dark forces protecting the sire as well as the girl."

"What about the woman who's with the girl?" Michael inquired.

"Lucy Novak's apartment is near the bus depot. We sense her holding the girl there. The landlord and his family are already dead, the beast-within's first victims. They have left Siena twice and it's paving the way for more kills. News programs tout the lie of diseased dogs attacking people at night. So far, the public believes the media." Phyllis paused. "I sense your questions, the outrage in your soul, Michael. Jillian uses a thin enchanted blade, like a scaling knife, full of dark magic. She marks her victims, tastes their blood, and steals their crosses. Vampires finish them off. This event's been planned with care, in a big way."

Alana said, "Those vamps will be dust and bone very soon—Veronique, as well."

"I sense a different pattern now. The beast-within has changed."

Michael saw Alana look down and swipe the corner of her eye. Knowing the reason, he didn't meet the healer's gaze, either and softly replied, "Thank you for the information, Sister."

Phyllis stood with a smile. "Come on, Lukas. I'll introduce you to the students and get you settled in."

When Lukas stood, Michael gave him a nod. "We'll talk later."

Once alone with Alana, he crossed his arms against his chest—and waited.

Alana swiped another bead of a tear and studied the moisture on her fingertip. On a day when she needed full focus, she couldn't find it. This morning, with clipped words and no emotion, Michael told her what Thorn and Celia had sensed last night. It still knifed through her soul, rattled her like never before, and now the day had turned more than tense, something she didn't expect.

She looked at him. "I'm asking you again. Did you know? Did you neglect to tell me how *very* connected you still are to this thing?" No response heightened the guilt growing in her heart. "We make love and something horrible happens again. I feel the same way I felt the night I turned twenty-one. Every Georgian knew then, and every Catherine knows now."

"Calm down."

"Why should I?" Pushing off the chair, she walked away.

"I am telling you to relax."

Turning, she glared at him. "Five years into my mystical mission, I broke the solemn vow of purity, and I pushed a mystically-enhanced vampire to the point of no return. When the beast- within resurfaced, how many did you drink and drain during those terrifying weeks in Manhattan? How many did you torture because we—"

"All right, you've vented. Now sit down and relax."

Stunned, she blew out a sharp breath. "Did you *know*!"

With swiftness that defied his new classification as 'mortal,' he came at her. "No. I swear before *God*." He strode to the door and had his hand on the knob. "Let it rest. We have a job to do, my Guardian."

"Before it starts, we need to talk."

"I said let it rest," he yelled, and left her standing there—somewhere between abject guilt and total embarrassment.

****

I am absolutely furious with Alana, furious with myself, he thought as he left the room. Raising his voice at her, to full volume like that, rarely occurred. What it was about her that makes self-control of *any* kind impossible when I'm in her presence, he wondered. He cooled off a bit as he took the stairs, and entering Lukas's room, stretched out on a bed. Still uptight, both hands locked behind his head as he stared at the ceiling.

Standing at the window, his son studied the busy, narrow street below.

"See anything evil?"

"Nope, but it's not sunset yet," his son replied.

"Jillian Gerhardt isn't an 'after sunset' kind of demon. She's as alive as you are, and very dangerous. Can we list dos and don'ts while Mom and I are in Florence?"

A bored roll of his son's eyes came before a shrug. "Stay put. Don't engage anything that isn't breathing without a seasoned Guardian at my side. The short-sword stays out of sight and far away from the art students. The stake, and only the stake, is on me at all times, tucked in my belt and under my shirttails. If anything looks fishy, get a Guardian."

A dry smirk began. "Wow, it's like you're reciting a dictionary, but keep going."

"Behave, be smart, 'cause if I don't, Guardians will report it and you get mega-parental."

Sitting up, his legs swung off the bed. "This isn't a training exercise, little boy. A vicious demon is steering Jillian's mind and actions."

"So why did Sister say things are changing?"

His jaw automatically tensed. "It's not important. Listen carefully. Should you sense this girl close, don't let her touch you." Lukas stared at him. Recognizing confusion, he added, "The beast-within will know you. The same way it knows me."

Lukas's eyes widened. "It *knows* you? Holy shit."

"That about sums it up," he replied with bitterness in his tone.

****

Miles removed his reading glasses after closing the new event's file and said, "That about sums it up." Petula seemed lost in the clouds. Young Mick grew pale while Neeb's wide brow knotted.

Nigel drummed the dining room table. "We need transport and a map of the region."

After writing down the address of the student house in Siena, Miles handed him the paper as well as the key to Alana's car. "You will leave immediately. Call Alana as soon as you're on the highway so she'll expect you." He looked directly at Mick. "I cannot impress upon you enough how dangerous the entity is. Use extreme caution."

"That's a wee bit hard without a description of the girl," Petula said.

"Alana will have one. I expect you to assist where you can but stay close to my grandson. The car's in a lot down the street. There's a map of the region in the glove compartment." To Nigel, he dryly suggested, "Use it."

They followed him to the private elevator. Petula's hand brushed down classic Florentine wallpaper. "Dusty-rose marble floors subtly highlight such intricate, patterned walls," she sighed. "The immortal hunk has *very* posh taste. How elegant, simply elegant." Neeb pulled her into the elevator, but praise for Michael's decorating decisions continued as the doors closed.

****

Lucy checked her designer wristwatch, another gift from Leonard Gerhardt. Already mid-day, Jillian still cried in her sleep. An odor of dried blood on the mattress filled the room. Dipping a cloth into a basin of warm water, she gently swabbed the angry marks that covered Jillian's emaciated body. Puncture wounds where thirteen vampires had bitten her were pungent, oozing pus. She wrung out the cloth, and as if humanity struggled to surface, a sorrowful whimper began.

Wherever Lucy washed, nasty red welts appeared. Not good, she thought. Loosely she draped the white sheet over Jillian. Then holding the basin of putrid water steady, she tiptoed out of the room and locked the basement door. The girl's in pain, she thought, not just in pain... she's dying. She had to do something. After dumping the foul mess down the kitchen sink, she threw a wad of Euros in her handbag and walked out onto the busy street.

****

Michael didn't want another bickering match with Alana. And cooped up in a house full of antsy teenagers wasn't where he wanted to be. He escaped through the kitchen door. Centuries ago, he had walked the same narrow streets. In the 1880s, he had feasted on many innocents in this region of Italy—after satisfying his need for lust with Veronique, his tour-guide, so to speak...

He made his way to the medieval oval. But last May, on the day he vowed eternal love for Alana, the two of them had walked this very same piazza. Seeing the quaint café they had visited that incredible day, he sat under the awning—at the same outdoor table. The waiter who had served them brought over a glass of the same red wine, which encouraged more frustrated thoughts.

The afternoon felt too warm for a Tuesday in April, and the oval teemed with noisy tourists. Italian folk melodies floated over meaningless chatter—simple harmonies accompanied by two accordions and a mandolin. In a minor key, a group of old men sang about lost love. Draining the wine, he uttered, "How poignant."

The waiter refilled his glass, said in broken English, "I remember you."

He inclined his head. *"Come stai, Signore?"*

"Sto bene, but no you, eh? Ah…it is *amore*, no? *La bella donna non e con voi?*

"No, she's not with me today." In more ways than one, he thought.

Patting Michael's shoulder, the waiter sighed, and left the bottle of wine. The second glass went down easy enough. He refilled the glass, uninterested in a blistering argument between two tourists. Shouts escalated, and he looked up just as a tall blonde swerved out of their path. Her ankle slammed into the empty chair beside him. He jumped up, and the bottle teetered before it shattered in front of her. Snagging her waist, he also picked up the small paper bag she dropped and held her steady against him. The attractive woman winced, sucked in a sharp breath. Her free hand gripped his forearm. He noted miniscule specks of blood under her unpolished fingernails, caught a rancid odor.

"Here, sit a moment. Your ankle is swelling," he said.

"No, I-I'm fine, thanks anyway."

"You're American?"

"Uh-huh." Her ankle gave way, and he held her tighter to prevent another fall.

"You do need help. I can walk you to your—"

"N-no, I'm fine. I-I h-have to go." Twisting free, she clutched the bag to her blouse and hobbled off at an uneven trot.

A watch full of diamonds on her wrist, dried blood

under her fingernails and full of fear... This held his attention for less than a minute before Alana filled his head again. More on edge, he paid the waiter, gave a hefty tip and left the loud piazza.

Alana's sharp words still hounded him while he continued to walk. The *Duomo* came into view. Always fascinated with art and history, he took in the cathedral's architecture, intrigued by the craft of Renaissance artisans who brought marble to life with unsophisticated tools and immeasurable skill.

Vampires couldn't walk this sacred space, so he had never been inside.

Entering through magnificently carved doors, tourists went one way; he went the other, aimlessly lost in thought. *I stood ready to enter Hell. I welcomed an end to my legacy of death last May. Now I'm in another nightmare.* In a quiet corner, he heard the dip of a fine horse-hair brush into a small glass bottle. A craftsman studying a chipped indigo tile caught his eye. Drawn to the scene imbedded in the floor, he asked, *"Scusi, Signore.* What is this called?" Clear eyes studied him. *"Ah... Per favore... Como si chiama?"*

The man came off his knees. *"Aspetta...aspetta... vieni con me, si?"* Then he pointed to a wall plaque.

Michael dipped his head, gave a soft, *"Grazie."* But as he read the English description, a sickening feeling took hold. *"Massacre of the Innocents"...how absolutely appropriate is the title.* Another study of the scene—another guilty thought. Not ready to face Alana, he sat on a marble bench and watched the artisan do his finest work.

Chapter 16

After dark, Michael arrived at the front entrance of the student house. The distinct odor of fear assaulted him once inside, enough to make him regret not sneaking in through the kitchen. Four panicked teenagers sat glued to the late news broadcast, which described strange deaths in Monteriggioni, a short distance away. None of them caught his swift move through the room.

He held the kitchen door as it swung closed. Sister Phyllis sat at the table with two cups of coffee as if expecting him. He joined her, and she nudged a cup forward, which he gratefully accepted. "Stories of ridiculous wolf attacks are on every TV channel, the web as well. The students don't understand Italian, but the massacre of innocents will mark a soul in any language, any medium."

He set the cup down, met her gaze. "I'm sorry, Sister, what did you say?"

"You're a commanding Champion, Mister Malone, but not too accomplished at shielding thought. I sense the full force of your uneasiness—it's enough to slam into the dullest mind like a head-on collision. I'd be careful with that if I were you. It's alarming." He followed her sightline to the basement door. Besides Alana's, he heard easily a dozen beating hearts coming from the cedar room. "You should make an

194

appearance," Phyllis stated.

He gave a nod before an unhurried descent to the basement. Standing behind the door he could hear Lukas translating Alana's orders into English. To whom...and why, he wondered as he entered. Snaring his son's attention, Lukas stopped mid sentence. Michael eyed four leather-clad misfits. The sound of Alana's Italian words, rapid and hushed, continued to hold every *other* Guardian's attention. However, when she stopped talking, all followed her eyes—to him.

Shock immediately replaced their serious expressions. Apprehension, uneasy silence lingered. *They are her colleagues; not mine. Signing the Document of Atonement placed a mystically-enhanced vampire above The Georgian Law of the Kill. But this impressive group expected an immortal creature, not a human being. Well, so did I.*

Just deal with it, he thought.

Refocusing the group, Alana said in Italian, "Michael Malone will handle the rescue of the innocent. We will only assist if necessary."

He bowed slightly to acknowledge *his* Guardian's comment, and then steadily pulled his son out of the room. The four oddballs followed. When he closed the door, Lukas began to resist. "They're Guardians. I get that. Now explain to me why the scent of my home is all over them. Do it quick."

"They came to help!"

"How did they know we *needed* help?" He leaned in, kept a stern tone. "You didn't do the blue hair thing in England, did you? Because you'd wail mighty loud if I *ever* caught you looking like them." Glaring pure ice at the tall Scot, he added, "including baldy. Talk fast, little boy." Climbing the steep stairs, he held Lukas's arm.

"I always text Mick, and remember the IMs on my laptop? Dad, please, they're my friends. Gramps sent them here."

"Stop," he ordered, studying each one. "Do any of you understand Italian?"

"No, Sir," they each replied.

"I didn't think so. We'll talk some place private."

The parlor was empty as they passed through. Once in the art studio, Michael closed the door and one by one, they told him their names. Nigel, who seemed a natural leader, gave a full explanation of why they'd been sent to Siena. Even though they looked odd, he sensed gutsy intelligence and experience—except in the young one. That worried him.

"You know about Florence?" he asked.

Petula stated, "I referenced some online Georgian documentation about Veronique while Nigel drove. You'd be amazed at what a cell phone can do, Sir."

"Good. You're prepared." He allowed a thin grin. "I apologize for the ruthless inquisition." With an expression closer to friendly, he shook their hands.

"Your son has fine form. Lu's quicker than most," Petula stated.

Nigel added, "He gave us a run for it during fight sessions."

"That's good to know. So both Clarke and Miles want you in this event?"

"That's a firm yes, Sir," Petula replied with a bright smile, her large brown eyes intense.

"And we'll be close to Lu at all times," Neeb assured.

"It will ease my mind. But check with Alana first. Your assignments are her department." He stood at the door aware of his son's eagerness, also the effortless interaction with his friends. Unmistakably, Lukas had formed solid relationships on his own terms in England, and all except Mick appeared close to the end of their mystical missions. To have survived countless encounters with demons proved these warriors a cut above most.

Then Michael heard Alana's footsteps and opened the art studio door. When she entered, the four stood in one sweeping show of respect.

Approaching them, she said, "Hi, guys. Let me bring you up to speed." In a tight huddle, all spoke softly. Michael stayed at the door, leaned against it in a casual pose. She glanced his way as they settled around the art table. "You have a right to hear our discussion, Michael. I met Lu's friends at the Georgian Estate when Celia had the baby. They are, without a doubt, the best of the best. Will you join us, my love?"

"Absolutely," he replied, coming to her side with long, confident strides.

****

While Jillian slept, Lucy tied a silk scarf across the girl's bruised eyelids. Something close to caring wormed its way into her heart. She had raided the landlord's fridge and found homemade chicken stock. Placing the warm bowl on the nightstand, she put three crushed aspirins in it and then shook her head. Sunken cheeks, cracked lips… Jillian needed care. *She's closer to death than just a few hours ago. Why hasn't Leonard sent someone?* She fixated on the man in the piazza. *Maybe I should have let that tall, gorgeous hunk walk me home. He had the widest shoulders I've ever seen. Drop-dead intense features... And the way he held me in his arms. Having him around would make caring for Jillian easier. I could stare into those dark eyes all day and whoa, Lucy!*

What if Leonard read her mind, or thought her disloyal?

Her ankle throbbed when she stood to pull Jillian up into a sitting position. A hand ran down the girl's bruised cheek. Weird growls began, but when Lucy pulled away, Jillian quieted. She picked up the bowl, brought the spoon to Jillian's lips. Then the girl's blistered fingers cuffed her wrist. Jillian seemed to sneer between mouthfuls of broth.

When her hand eased away, Jillian whispered, "Hard...to...swallow. I must fill the chest. It is my gift."

Her breath smelled like acid, and Lucy gently replied, "Sure, you will. But tonight you have to rest." The girl drew in a long sniff when Lucy spooned another mouthful into her. The way Jillian snarled made her cringe. It took courage, but she said, "This body can't die, demon. It's a chosen vessel, meant to please your, uh, dark goddess. Now let her rest."

The growling stopped. Pathetic whimpers began. *I have to find a doctor,* Lucy thought, *because if she doesn't make it to Florence, Leonard will kill me.*

****

After telling the Brits all she knew, Alana met Sister Phyllis in the second-floor hall. "I've never seen so many bedrooms in one little house."

'Isn't the architectural plan interesting? I've run this program for years, every April through June and when the students see it, they get a kick out of picking their roomies as well as their rooms."

"Who usually stays here?"

"University art majors—they have grandiose accommodations in a five-star hotel on the *Piazza del Campo* until we leave."

Then she switched to Guardian mode. "Everyone's upstairs for the night?"

"Yes. The second floor is all yours. Sleep well, Alana."

"Thanks. You too," she replied.

Like a den mother, she checked on Mick who happily roomed with Lukas. Closing their door, she stared at Pet, Neeb, and Nigel waiting in another bedroom. "Have you worked out a rotating night watch?"

"I'm first," Pet answered.

"Let's hope for a peaceful night," Alana said.

She left her colleagues to focus on the mission and entered the room she thought best suited for herself and Michael. Twin beds far apart would have to do. But when he appeared in the doorway, he stared at the beds.

"I'll take the one by the window," she said, pulling an old lilac nightgown from her bulging bag. "I picked this room because there's a small bath attached, in case you're wondering." He said nothing, and his annoyed expression didn't intimidate her. "Did you pack your PJs?"

"No." He threw his duffle bag down, sat on the bouncy bed closest to the door.

"Suit yourself, but it gets chilly at night."

"It's already fucking freezing in here. We need to talk."

She brushed out her hair. "Is this about the plan?"

"About us," he answered in an even tone.

"I don't think so."

"Excuse me?"

"If it's business, fine—we talk. If it's not, the answer is no."

Taking her nightgown into the bathroom, she closed the door. *No discussion. No bickering. This isn't the time. Stay focused on tomorrow and what has to be done.* The tub resembled a small, square box. She filled it with the hottest water she could stand. Stubborn stayed on her face, trying not to think about Michael.

Of course, that didn't happen.

Imagining his long lean frame scrunched into this tiny cavity Italians called a tub brought a gloomy grin. *An awful day after a complicated night, but no way in hell do we talk right now. He should have stayed here instead of disappearing for hours. There would have been enough time to switch gears from woman to Guardian. Not possible now…* Vulnerability and guilt couldn't be in her mind when facing a Sire like Veronique. And in this event, an army of Guardians was *her* sole responsibility. *Unnecessary emotions and lack of clarity puts everyone in danger. A sire can sense weakness. Veronique will kill every Guardian who stands with me. If Michael's unfocused, she'll sense it as well. That's a fact. No vampire has ever regained mortal life. No human has ever faced their own demon's origin.*

Miles confirmed it, and Georgian protocol for this event didn't exist.

When her skin pruned, she pulled out the rubber stopper. *I didn't think I could ever feel so unsure of him, of myself. And I'm to blame for not forcing a discussion of this mess before we left Portofino.* She needed a clear mind. A full night's sleep was necessary. Wrapped in a thin towel, she neatly folded her clothes and then slipped on the cotton nightgown. Certain that the man she loved had pushed the beds together, she came out of the bathroom.

Both beds were still apart; both were empty. No sign of Michael or his black duffle.

Too stunned to be devastated, she locked the door and crawled onto a springy bed.

****

After the coldest, quickest shower he ever experienced, Michael strode down the hall with a scratchy towel hung low on his hips. Every door was now closed—including the one to the room Alana had chosen for them. When the damn knob wouldn't turn, he shook his head, looked up and down the hall. Then he eyed what seemed a large closet. The bed and dresser took up all available space, leaving just enough room for the door to close and a slim patch of floor in front of a solitary window. Equally pissed off and hurt, he kicked the duffle into a corner. Before this went any further, first thing tomorrow he'd apologize to her for his insensitive words.

Looking out the window, the street was empty, the night dark. He couldn't fully focus on a possessed girl who, in more ways than one, felt too close for comfort. *Just as the Georgians once shielded me, now an unknown evil protects this child.* Retracing the disaster of a day, every new face flashed in his brain like an antiquated penny movie; a flip-book on a wheel—only his was in color. When the dizzying motion slowed, one stood out. The tall attractive woman, in such a hurry to get away from him, had stark fear on her face.

His mind jumped back to Alana. "Son of a bitch," he muttered. "You actually locked me out." The towel flew across the room. Lying on the mattress, his feet hung over its edge. After punching the pillow, one arm bent under his damp hair. *This is a fucking nightmare. Forget the apology. First thing tomorrow morning, we will have a long overdue conversation.*

****

Lucy had an idea. If it worked, no more people would disappear and the ugly thing inside Jillian would be appeased. The girl could sleep for a few days, maybe brought to Leonard in better shape. She ran up to the landlord's apartment, grabbed clean starched sheets, and a fresh nightgown for Jillian. Then she rummaged through every jewelry box and drawer, taking every cross they owned. Jamming them into the pocket of her jeans, she raced down to the basement.

Moving Jillian to the foldaway bed wasn't a problem. The girl had lost a lot of weight. Lucy held on tight, even as a low growl gurgled in Jillian's throat. She quickly changed the bedding. The same weird sounds came when Lucy helped her walk back to her clean bed. After getting the filthy nightgown off her, Lucy washed the sores, which had festered.

Jillian writhed and gasped as Lucy eased a fresh nightgown over her head. It smelled of lavender fabric softener. Liberally, she applied a thick white ointment the pharmacist had recommended. The girl's lower abdomen was swollen, bright red, but she piled on the blankets.

Ready to call it a day, she looked around the room.

The soft-pink bulb shaded by etched Florentine glass of many colors gave everything a homey, warm feel. But her imagination spun out of control. *What if she attacks me during the night? Three more days…that's all, Lucy, before you bring her to Leonard. He might still send help.*

Tomorrow she'd do something. Tonight, she had to think.

Wringing her hands, her eyes shifted from Jillian to the curtained off corner. Instead, she locked the basement door, and ran up the stairs. Hoping for sleep, she stripped off her clothes and sank into her own comfortable bed.

Chapter 17

Uncomfortable in every way, Alana had hardly slept. At dawn, no movement came from the student house. She wrote one sentence on a piece of paper, folded it without making a sound. Although she craved multiple cups of coffee, her mind was made up. She dressed and stood outside Michael's door listening to him snore. After wedging the note near the doorknob, she tiptoed away. If he woke up and tried to stop her, she had no idea what she'd do or say to the man she loved with all her heart.

With Guardian skill, she eased out her bedroom window on the second floor, silently landing on the street. As she ran, she picked up inhuman speed. The parking area by the bus depot wasn't far and the key to her red car was already in hand. Revving the engine once, she sped away without looking back. Flying past the yield sign by the highway's entrance, she left a message on Kayla's cell phone and then glanced at the map lying on the passenger side's seat. Thank God for the little things, she thought. She'd never driven to Florence—from Siena.

A quick strategy session at the Medico building would preclude ending the existence of a certain vampire. "You're going down, you lusty bitch. Dark goddess, my foot, I'll turn you into dust and bone just like any other vamp. And the stupid old man who's using his own granddaughter for God knows what? I'll hop the first flight to Jersey and send him to Hell, too. I don't care if he's human. No one with a heart could do this—no one!" She swerved into the center lane, cut off a blue jeep and barely missed a passenger van. Both horns blared and colorful Italian words came at her through the open window. Alana didn't care, her mind stayed stuck on one thing: an ancient vampire that had been intimate with Michael Malone.

"Ten months alone—after ten *years* of loving you...This is supposed to be *our* time, not demon time! Tossing and turning, turning and tossing all night! Forever and always didn't even get off the ground. No *way* does one decrepit sire stand in the way of our happiness."

Her foot eased off the gas pedal—just a little. Both hands gripped the wheel. Without signaling, she switched lanes. Miraculously, the road was clear. "You old bag of bones and skin. Magic creams, huh? It probably takes you half the night and a whole crate of ivory color-concealer sticks to hide *those* wrinkles and warts! How gorgeous can a undead demon be? I'll take you out before the next sunrise! Ready or not, here I come, you old witch."

Grumbling didn't help, but her persistence reached new heights.

She floored it. The small red car shot down the fast lane to Florence.

****

Michael didn't think he could be so furious with Alana. He held a five-word note in his left hand and paced the hall. "Oh, my Guardian, this time you really did it," he whispered. After folding it neatly and with a

205

great deal of self-control, he jumped the staircase just because he could. The smell of brewing coffee led him into the kitchen.

"With everyone arriving yesterday, I failed to give this to you," Sister Phyllis said as he entered. "The photograph came with Jillian's application. It looks like it was Christmas."

He took it from her. Smiling brown eyes, short shaggy hair framing a perfectly round face, and Leonard Gerhardt looked like a typical, doting grandfather. Who could do this to their own flesh and blood, he thought. "Rockefeller Center...I recognize it."

"I thought so, too. I have to tell you, I didn't sense any kills last night."

"That's strange." He continued to stare at the sweet, smiling face, sipped strong coffee she had poured into a delicate china cup. "Which room was hers, Sister?"

"Oh. You want a personal scent. I have something better." She left quickly, came back with a large brown portfolio. "I kept it hidden under the others in the studio. An artist's hands move all over a canvas. In this case, Lucy's have as well."

Sitting back, he released the coated elastic band. The first scent was unfamiliar; the second filled him with rage because he could already put a face to it. "The woman is American, blonde and tall."

"Lucy Novak's at least five-foot ten."

The unfinished portrait was of a fine-looking woman, perhaps in her forties. The words "Mom Extraordinaire" were printed in the corner. He gulped down the rest of the coffee, needing much, much more.

His voice filled with disgust. "I know why she didn't kill last night. Something's wrong with her. Do you have to prepare for the session with the art students?"

"Unfortunately, yes," she replied in a frustrated way, refilling his cup with the last drops in the pot.

"Please, go about your day. I insist." He'd brew more coffee, but he wouldn't be able to immediately discuss this new twist with Alana. That she went to Florence alone fully angered him.

****

Lucy dragged herself out of bed and dressed in a hurry. "Three days to go before life gets back to normal," she groaned, preparing peppermint tea for the girl. *I'll leave for Florence on Friday and check in early. Then I can wash my hands of this whole occult mess.*

She didn't want Jillian to die, but she didn't want to rile this demon, either.

The peace offerings, tokens of gratitude for not being killed during the night, came to mind. She counted the stolen crucifixes, some jeweled, some fashionable, some plain. Technically, *it* had killed their owners; technically, they already belong to *it*, she thought.

With the tea and her gifts, she made her way downstairs.

Opening the door, the smell was unbearable, worse near the bed. She tried not to gag, placed the crosses in Jillian's hands before folding the girl's burning fingers into fists. Something made her pull back the blankets, then the sheet. Sinking her teeth into her lip, she bit the gasp silent.

Bloated skin, festered pustules carved into the

lower part of Jillian's body... "Shit," she muttered, "I need a doctor. And the pharmacy opens at noon on Wednesdays."

****

Leaning against the kitchen counter, Michael heard the students come down the stairs. Great, he thought, now kids to deal with. He gulped down a third cup of coffee and locked both arms across his chest while crossing his ankles in a comfortable pose. A girl entered first, dropped her notebook and let out an ear-piercing shriek. She grabbed a skinny teenage boy's arm, and then they all stared at him. Michael stared back, in an arrogant way with a hint of a grin.

"Relax," he said in a calm tone, "I'm here to help."

One boy acted brave. "You're ...like, American?"

"Yep," he replied, but the girl started to sink, and he rushed over, guided her into a kitchen chair. She appeared awestruck as he asked, "What's your name?"

"Betty, uh, B-Betts," she sputtered.

"You're not about to faint, are you?"

"No, um, no... but... are you an undercover operative?"

His grin grew wider, saying, "I'm here to see to your safety," before moving back to the kitchen counter.

Still staring, she eyed him while whispering to another teenage boy, "Is he on TV? I swear I've seen him on TV or maybe in a magazine. Uh, are you gonna take us home?"

"No. I'm afraid the four of you must stay put a while longer."

"So dude, like, who are you?" the teenage boy asked in a nervous way.

"I told you to relax, didn't I?" He pointed to the empty chairs. Betty's wide eyes stayed on him as they huddled together. "Are you ready to listen?" The group nod bordered on comedic, but he had their undivided attention. Directing a thin grin at Betty again, he heard her heart skip a beat. "You truly wouldn't faint on me, would you? Please take a breath, young lady."

Lukas bounded through the swinging door and went directly to the fridge. "Morning, Dad. Hi guys… Hey, Betts, are you okay?"

Her wide eyes went wider. "You've *got* to be kidding. He's your *father*?"

"Yep. Don't worry. He's way cool. Right, Dad?"

Clearing his throat and thinking blue heads of hair and all that leather, he asked, "Where are your friends? Your *friends,* Lukas—"

"Uh-huh, got it, Dad, I'll go check."

Michael instantly blocked his path. "Not so fast."

"I still get to go with them to the museum, me and my *friends,* right?"

He nodded once as Lukas sat next to Betty, who continued to stare at him. "Is there something you want?"

Giving Betts a sweet dimpled grin, his son said, "How about cinnamon toast this morning. I like the way you make it. My dad's great in the kitchen, Betts. Trust me. He's been cooking for like, a really long time."

The intended implication made him smirk. "I didn't mean breakfast."

"Did we hear cinnamon toast? How fabulous! Morning, Sir," Petula said. Mick followed her in and echoed the greeting.

He narrowed his eyes. No blue hair, and no hint of

black leather or Goth eyeliner on either of them. Nigel and Neeb entered, also looking normal in casual yet functional clothes. Nigel's white-blonde hair didn't have one blue-spiked tip. The two men offered a respectful "Morning, Sir," and joined everyone at the table. Seated next to Lukas, Petula smiled, daintily pushing brunette bangs off her forehead.

"Dad's making cinnamon toast, Mick," Lukas said to his friend.

In a shy way, the newbie said, "Me dad cooks breakfast all the time, Sir."

"Does he now," Michael replied. British heritage crept into his words as if it were 1690 again, the draw of an accent that belonged to another existence.

Grinning wide, Lukas announced, "Cool—cinnamon toast for everyone."

A room full of hungry people stared at him again. "Nice move, little boy," he whispered.

Betts jumped up. "I know where Sister Phyllis keeps everything. I can help! I always help in the kitchen!" She opened the breadbox and handed him half a loaf of bread.

"I don't think this is going to do it."

"There's a bakery down the street," she said.

Michael pulled out his wallet, handed Lukas a large bill. "Mick and Neeb will go with you. Stay alert." After they left, he said to the wide-eyed girl, "So, young lady, where does Sister keep the cinnamon and sugar?" She blushed and pointed to the cabinet next to the stove.

****

Considering Alana's many mystical skills, the coordination of driving and talking on a cell phone wasn't one of her talents. Into her cell, she said, "Kayla, I'm totally lost. Did I take the wrong exit? I swear I'm turned around here. I know Medico's not anywhere near the main part of the city, and I've passed the same post office three times."

"Is there a shoe store next to it?"

"Yeah, and a clothes boutique with a flashy sign on the other side. So where am I?"

"Not far, so find a parking spot, a legal one. I'll look for the Mercedes, and you can follow me."

"Wait. I have the red car."

"Okay. Red car it is. Be there in about ten minutes, depending on traffic."

She dropped the phone on the seat, pulled a tight U-turn to a chorus of beeping horns. Finding a legal parking spot wasn't for the faint of heart, but she managed to get one—after some gutsy moves.

Turning off the ignition, she leaned her head back and called Celia's number. It went to voice mail. "Sis, I really need to talk to you. I'm in Florence—without him. Just call back. I'll leave my phone on." She saw no sign of Kayla's car, and in a moment of complete weakness, she made another call. Dishes clanged in the background.

"You shouldn't have done this, my Guardian."

Cool anger came at her. "You changed the rules when you decided to sleep in another room."

"I didn't… oh, forget it. Alana, come back to Siena. This is not the way we do this."

"I'm taking her out at sunset."

"No. You're changing course right now and coming back to Siena because—"

She hit the off button, threw the phone down

dismissing his curt words. Defiant and still pissed off, she threw up her hands and let out a long, sharp breath.

Ready to explode, Michael walked out of the kitchen and stared at his cell phone. Now away from teen-talk and excited chatter, he craved the quiet parlor. When his phone chirped again, he choked down his initial response and quickly said, "I'm sorry. Please accept my apology."

"What did you do now? Alana tried to talk to Celia. That's a no-no. I'm getting trouble in paradise and some way-off vibes emanating from Siena. Something has changed."

Thrown by Thorn's grumpy tone, he asked, "What do you mean?"

"What did you do?"

"I've no idea what you're talking about."

"Don't dodge the 'come clean' question. I'm worried about my wife and my son, so the zeroing in on you thing is a little murky at the moment. What the hell did you do?"

His irritation spiraled. "That's between us."

"So where is she?"

"In Florence. Without me."

"You are clueless, aren't you? Something's screwy and you muck up the mind-waves. Damn it, why'd you let her leave? No. Never mind. I don't want to know." After a tense pause, Thorn added, "The girl's dying. This is not a good thing."

"It's a *very* good thing," he barked. "The way I see it, the demon dies *with* her, and I get to Alana's side before Veronique has a field day on her neck. Then the holy healers can wash their hands of this twisted event."

"Is there anyone there who can kick your rear?" Thorn shouted.

"Why kick my ear?"

The next groan exploded like a growl. "Wake up, Michael! It'll jump to another innocent soul if this girl dies."

"It can jump from soul to soul!? What the hell is *that*, damn it! "

"Find her fast. Jeez, you picked a great time to become a fool."

The line went dead. He stared at his cell phone. Furious, he punched in Alana's number.

****

Lucy tended to the sores on Jillian in a gentle way. The girl slept peacefully most of the morning. After another bowl of thin chicken broth with crushed aspirins, Jillian said, "Count them, Lucy."

"There are so many."

A lost sob escaped.

Lucy's fingers shook as she touched the crosses, but her voice remained sweet. "You have forty-five." A burning hand closed around her wrist.

"Fifty-four must pave my way." Jillian slumped back, her eyes closed.

Swallowing fear, she replied, "You're close. Really close." Lucy inched off the bed, crept to the door. Then she locked it, anxious to get out of the building.

****

Rushing into the pharmacy, little bells above the antiquated door tinkled like angelic chimes. "And how is the art student today," the owner asked.

In fluent Italian, Lucy replied, "The salve isn't working. She doesn't want to go to a foreign hospital.

213

She needs a doctor… who'll do a house call? Please find me someone I can trust." Her eyes misted, and after a demure swipe, Lucy rested a hand just above full, pushed up breasts. Her fingers feathered down where the low-cut, lacey blouse ended.

He leered before writing a phone number on a small brown bag. "Call before six."

She gave a coy smirk, shelled out crisp Euros for sterile gauze pads, vitamin bottles, and cotton balls. "Find a way for me to thank you…when she's better," she said before leaving.

A favorite outdoor market was next on the schedule. True, it was a tourist trap with street vendors peddling knockoffs of fancy designer *everything*. She often sold exquisite replicas of famous art works there as well. Like the murals she'd painted for Leonard, only an art historian would know her works weren't original. She had lived in Siena long enough to make many acquaintances, very few friends—but no one would recognize her today.

On a side street, she pulled from her shopping tote a wide-brimmed hat with a long brown wig sewn into it. Tucking away stray blonde hairs, she became someone else. Dazzling red sunglasses perched on the bridge of her nose as she sashayed down the medieval bricks like a thrilled yet inexperienced visitor. Today, she chose a gauche outfit that screamed cheap, and blended in perfectly, snapping picture after picture with a disposable camera. She stopped for a coffee at a little trattoria, watching groups of tourists hurrying by, talking in an array of different languages. Continuing with her care-free stroll, the best produce stand in the old part of Siena was at the other end of the crowded market. She sashayed down the street looking at this and that thinking how fresh fruits and vegetables would do Jillian a world of good. It might even prolong her life. Confident in her ditzy demeanor, she suddenly had a yen for ripe, soft peaches. Standing at the bin she heard a boy say to someone, "Shit. I told you to just pick any postcard." After a glance, she thought, shit is right! *What the hell are the art students doing way over here?*

"Look, dude, chill, okay?" the teen replied as if still riding mean waves in California. "I promised my parents a pretty postcard every week. My mom's gonna nag me like forever if I don't send one."

The boy quickly shook his mop of sandy curls. "You got what you came for. Pay for it and let's go. We aren't supposed to be so far away from my friends."

As they argued, she kept her back to them and grabbed a particular peach. The cutie-pie's hand suddenly shot over hers, his grip stronger than expected.

"Oh, *mi dispiace! Scussa, Signorina, scussa,*" he offered in proper Italian. Instead of pulling away, his hand stayed over hers.

Lucy gave a genuine smile, mesmerized by such deep dimples and royal-blue eyes on a face that could only belong to an angel. The art students beside him continued comparing depicted scenes of Siena—so close that she wanted to run.

"Stealing note cards and a juicy snack, Lu?" The attractive man's yummy British accent drew her in. "Your father would bloody well have my hide if he thought I let you stray as much as a reach away. Not a bright move, young Master Malone."

"I swear, Nigel, they friggin' wanted these," he insisted, finally letting go of her hand.

"I'm not having it, mate, and Michael won't take kindly to this, either," he scolded, "Pinching the lovely lady's hand, palming a peach, and getting cheeky." Leaning down, the hottie tried to catch her eye. "So very, very sorry, miss. He meant no harm."

Nodding many times, she whispered, "*Va bene,*" and headed straight inside the store for a quick getaway. She grabbed what she thought she needed in a fluster, paid in cash and didn't wait for change. Two words came together that made her want to scream: Michael and Malone. The vampire was in Siena!

****

Michael leaned over Sister Phyllis's shoulder in the museum's sketching room. With charcoal pencil in hand, she said, "Lucy must have had help getting assigned to me. I have no idea how she managed it. Here. It's finished."

He took the sketch and stared at the woman from the piazza, wondering if perhaps the 'chance' meeting hadn't been so chance. "Tell me about her, Sister."

"She's working on a doctorate in art history, and she's exceptional at replications."

"Where in the states is she from?"

"Valley Township, New Jersey."

"Why am I not surprised? What else."

She handed him a piece of paper. "This is her address."

He didn't look at it as he walked to the door. "Thank you. Your students are back."

Once in the hall, he heard Nigel say to Lukas, "Try something like that again, and I rat on you."

Lukas narrowed his eyes, muttering, "That's cold, Nigel. I didn't do anything!"

"Keeping a lark from Professor Bookman is one thing. I'm not about to tangle with your father," Nigel replied.

Michael sensed tension in the experienced Guardian and noted his son's immediate pout. He'd get to the reason why later, but right now, he had to check in with Miles. Pulling out his cell phone, he asked Petula, "Who's on the shift?"

"Mick and I, Sir, Neeb and Nigel are off a spell."

He shook his head. "I want all of you here. No one leaves." He pressed a programmed number on his phone. Striding away as Nigel started to speak, he held up a hand.

Lukas ran up to him. "Are you calling Mom?"

"Gramps," he answered.

"Can I say hi?"

"Did you give Nigel trouble?"

"No, we're cool."

He heard the researcher's voice. "Miles? Let Deepa know Lucy Novak lived in Valley Township. Find her link to Gerhardt and keep me posted? Thanks." His son gave a hounding look. "Lukas wants to talk to you...hang on."

His son reached for the phone, and Michael's senses went wild. Roughly grabbing his son's arm, he yanked the phone back with a free hand. "Sorry, Gramps, maybe later; I need to talk to my son...right now." Slipping the phone into his pocket, he pulled Lukas down the hall.

"I'm sorry! I don't know why I did it! I put it right back!"

"Put what back?"

"The peach… And I apologized to the lady. I swear!"

"*What* lady? Describe her."

"She was tall. Had long black hair, red sunglasses, a-and a big straw hat."

Nigel came toward them. "It's my fault. Sir, please, not to interfere, but Lu shouldn't suffer my mistake. He's telling the truth. Nothing happened."

Fear snaked up his spine. "Go stand by Neeb, Lukas." He watched his son go, and then walked Nigel to the other end of the hall, saying low, "No one leaves. Two of you are to stay with my son at all times. The woman who touched him has the girl. Unless she scrubs her hand with bleach, the beast-within will know his scent. You do not let him out of sight for a second." Nigel nodded in full compliance, and pushing open the door, Michael strode out of the museum. On his cell phone, he hit another preset number and waited. After the recorded message, he whispered in an unsteady voice, "The demon has Lukas's scent. I cannot do this without you. Please come back to me, my Guardian."

****

Lucy dropped the tote on the kitchen table, flung the hat down as well. Creeping down to the basement room, she unlocked the door and moved toward the sleeping girl. When she placed her hand on Jillian's burning forehead, the girl growled and bared her teeth. She backed away quickly, ran upstairs.

Stories about a wild-child came to mind—some mystical mistake that had rocked Leonard's world at the time. "No," she whispered, "Can't be. He said the kid was crazy!" In a panic, she checked the answering machine, her cell phone as well. No warning—no nothing from Leonard. Why would the vampire's semi-human son be in Siena? She poured a glass of wine, too frightened to even taste it, then poured another and leaned against the counter.

"I'll bet the thing inside her smells him on me! Think, Lucy! How the hell are you going to do this alone now?" Lucy spun around so fast that she had to grab the counter to steady herself. The wine soured in her gut and came back up her throat.

Chapter 18

"Spectacular doesn't describe this night," Veronique whispered at the open balcony doors. An exquisite scarlet robe slid off her ivory shoulders. One slender arm rose as she snapped manicured fingers with a slow, sensual flourish. "What did Leonard send me tonight?"

"They are beautiful. Come see, goddess, in the sauna," the minion replied in admiration. It bowed, held the door.

Sauntering down the hall, Veronique's elegant steps down black marble stairs were full of flawless grace. One by one, the human servants offered their pulsing wrists. Some she took; some she refused. Her silken hair barely moved as the vampire glided across the foyer. More wrists to taste, more to reject, she mused.

If the presents appeared as beautiful as her servant said, two thirsts would be sated by morning. A lover of classic bone structure, she had often watched Florentine masters sculpt men from stone…and she had tasted many of those unsuspecting models. Her sultry entrance into the sauna dripped of languid eroticism. Tall, muscular Scandinavians stood naked, their skin coated in fragrant oil. Her gaze shamelessly lingered on what gave the most pleasure—after their necks. "They are altered."

"As you prefer, goddess," the minion replied.

Her purr slid into a passionate growl. "Send Leonard a case of my finest Champagne from the winery. No, wait," she suddenly said. "Let me taste one first. Sometimes the most perfect fruit of the vine is not the sweetest." She walked up to the closest twin, kissed his mouth. The other stood behind, kissing her shoulder blade. A ring of soft laughter erupted. "Tell me truthfully, are you both equally sweet? Prove who is the sweeter." The man before her offered his neck. His lusty, sea-foam eyes held no fear. Veronique's pupils faded to smoky amber. Ruby lips parted to expose sharp, pearly canines. "Do I scare you?"

"No, goddess, you do not." The steady vein throbbed, called to her. He leaned down, his arousal heightening two different lusts. The arrogance of his manner reminded her of another's passion—before soul and conscience drove a most commanding lover away, never to return. The way this one slid her up his body brought back more memories. Her leg hooked his waist as he held her bottom. When he thrust his erection into her, her canines sank into the vein on his thick neck— for a quick taste.

****

The short, round doctor's English was worse than her Italian. Lucy caught some Middle Eastern country's name, along with refugee and gynecologist. But she wasn't a doctor here in Italy, and now served as a nurse's aid at a hospice run by a well-known charity.

Steady antibiotics from a plastic medical bag now dripped into Jillian's vein, and she hadn't stirred during the exam. "No uterus bleed, no rape is good." The next mismatched nouns and verbs didn't make sense until the woman added, "Infection, so not live. You take to hospital."

Lucy panicked. "No. Here! She can't leave. You *make* her live."

"You feed, yes?" Lucy nodded. "Protein, meat, soup?"

"Yes."

"Good, good, good," the woman replied, patting Lucy's arm. Crossing herself, she added, "I pray."

"You aren't Muslim?"

She removed the needle from Jillian's vein and disposed of the drained bag before pulling off white rubber gloves. Then she dug into her blouse and produced a plain, gold crucifix.

Tears came into Lucy's eyes—big, sorrowful tears. "Please, you give to her? I have money. Wait." Running upstairs, she rummaged through a dresser drawer and returning, she shoved a wad of Euros into the woman's hand with a dramatic sob—swiping drippy eyes that brimmed with despair.

Hesitant, the woman took the money, and then, almost reverently handed Lucy her crucifix with the gentle whisper, "For sick child... I make prayers." After rummaging around in the satchel, packets of antibiotic tablets were in Lucy's hand. "You call *domani*?"

"Tomorrow. *Grazie, grazie!*"

After seeing her out, Lucy went back to Jillian, threw the cross into the chest, recalling the eerie words, "Many more I need..."

****

Alana had enough of Florence's tight band of Guardians who resisted her logic. She had met them in small groups all afternoon. In all the months that she'd come here to work out with them, she never thought to discuss philosophy. The Law of the Kill was universal, unchanging: If it was demon, then it was dead. In the late afternoon sun, she had gone over her plan with Kayla and her father, Cesar, also an ex-Guardian. He didn't agree with tonight's strategy and then filled her in on *more* stories about Veronique with caution in his words.

Alana's frustration deepened as she stood in the conference room at Medico Research Labs. It was soundproof and private—perfect for the meeting, which should've led to the destruction of Veronique Durant. But not one Florentine Guardian would agree with her. Not one would commit to a deliberate strike tonight.

Her cell phone vibrated as Michael's name flashed across its screen—again. This time, she turned it off and studied sixteen warriors, eight mentors, Kayla and Cesar. She blew out a long, slow breath. After a full minute, she cleared her throat, very uneasy to admit, "I am definitely not feeling the love. Why?"

"We do not approach her," a mentor stated for the fifth time. "The Council itself orders us to stand clear of this Sire. Throughout Florentine history, too many Guardians have met torture and death."

"And scores of her minions have been staked. Veronique's existence must end."

Blank stares and no responses came this time around.

"We reach a point of impasse," he stated with a stiff bow.

"Why aren't you eager to stop this thing's unholy reign of terror?" she asked. But Cesar shook his head.

About to give it one more try, she noticed Arthur Chamberlain through a window motioning her over. Without excusing herself, she left the conference room and followed him down the deserted corridor.

"Send them home, Alana."

She stared at the specialist, worked up the courage to say, "I'm sure you've already heard about what happened between us two nights ago. Everyone *else* has."

"Without breaking confidentiality, I'll confirm that Michael couldn't have known this entity is linked to him. Miles is on the phone for you." He peered down at her before leaving his office.

Fully embarrassed, she picked up the receiver from his desk. "Dad? What's wrong?"

"Have you spoken to Michael?"

"No, I—"

"Go back to Siena. Your timing is wrong. Veronique will still be there tomorrow."

"I'm taking her out. It's time."

"No, Alana, I insist it is *not*. Stand down immediately, Guardian, or I will order you held and brought back to face the Council in Portofino. Is that understood? And you *will* drive with extreme caution. That travel corridor is treacherous after dark." The line went dead as the flush raced up her face.

Her father rarely pulled 'mentor' rank. Nor had he used a sharp tone in many years. Very uneasy, she hung up the receiver and pulled out her cell. Finally listening to Michael's messages before her inbox was full, fear as well as anger took hold. She ran down the corridor, took the stairs instead of waiting for the elevator. Minutes later, she jumped int the red car and headed for the highway.

****

After cooking fruits and vegetables, skins and all, Lucy had thrown them into a blender. She had crushed packets of vitamins, stirred them into what now looked like baby food. Slowly, she fed the nutritious concoction, spoonful by spoonful, to Jillian. A fresh silk bandana covered the girl's eyes. "Tomorrow night you'll feel much better. Oh... I-I have something for you."

Jillian fingered the simple cross with a whispered, "More I need..."

When Lucy dabbed her mouth, Jillian took a deep sniff of Lucy's hands. Impossible, she thought. *I touched the vampire's son hours ago. I scrubbed my hands raw!* Then like the strike of a match, she recalled the tall gorgeous hunk from the piazza. Jillian's previous growls came back in an enlightened flash. *He helped me stand. I leaned against his chest.* Sitting on the bed, Lucy slid a full foot back. *No-no... No fucking way!! Broad daylight, but he stayed under the awning in the shade.* Nervously, she bit her lip, tried to relax.

Then, very sweetly, she said, "Jillian? Tomorrow I'll bathe you. I'll wash your hair and fix it so you look very pretty. We'll leave on Friday morning, okay? There's this lovely dress I bought. It will fit you perfectly, and you'll be as beautiful as a princess. It's white cotton with eyelet lace like little tiny flowers...so, so perfect." Softly, she said Jillian's name again. The girl's lips quivered as if she were about to cry.

****

From across the table in the kitchen, Michael

225

studied Sister Phyllis. Engrossed in the students' daily journal assignment, she said, "They're all in the living room playing a card game."

He leaned back in the chair. "They are loud, aren't they?"

"Kids are supposed to be loud. Not sad, not moping around, and not possessed by a vampire's former beast-within."

"You love what you do. It's evident."

"I'm a teacher, and you're a Champion. I deeply appreciate your being here…as well as those four colorful characters and your very polite son."

He returned a warm smile. "I had nothing to do with that, Sister. He hasn't been with me long."

"I know your son's history, Michael. Whether direct or indirect, success as a father is yours."

He looked away to change the subject, not convinced. "It's quiet tonight."

"No more missing citizens or crazy wolves were on the evening news. We're back to the region's typical tragedies."

"This isn't close to over," he warned, hesitant to admit, "I'm concerned my son's in danger."

"There you go, projecting worry for the twelfth time in six minutes. At least this time you voiced it." Phyllis shook her head. "You know, children often surprise us."

"I don't like surprises."

"You don't like to show how deeply you care, but it's there. You nurture him in many ways. And he loves you in return, almost to the point of adoration. Your directness teaches him more than you realize. He's lucky to have a father with a well-developed feminine side."

A slow grin began. "A *what*?"

"There's an abundance of tenderness in your heart. Lukas forces it out of you with innocent love. You're a terrific role model. Don't think otherwise. With that said, I have sketches to grade in the studio."

They both stood. "Is it time to break up the party out there?"

"The museum opens early for us tomorrow." The healer grinned, obviously reading his thoughts. "Yeah, I could order them upstairs, but you'll get quicker results. Use the look that makes Lukas jump. Believe me, it'll work. Sleep well, Michael."

Michael watched her leave. After hitting the light switch, he stayed in the darkness trying to figure out his next move. He had to get to the girl. But the only person he wanted to run strategy by was miles away and not speaking to him. "God, how I need you," he whispered before entering the parlor.

At the foot of the stairs, he gave the order, "Everyone to your rooms, right now." There were no challenges, but he stopped Lukas. "You're up by five a.m."

"I know. Night, Dad," his son replied going upstairs.

Michael walked to the window. Neeb met him there, saying, "I'll take first watch."

He nodded. "I was about to suggest it."

Nigel joined them. "There's talk. Things have changed. We still want in, Sir."

"You're already in. Grab some sleep. We need to be sharp, ready for anything."

Slowly taking the stairs, Alana in Florence without

him reclaimed his thoughts, and seeing Lukas in the hall, he asked, "Want to talk a bit?" They entered the small room, and his son's mouth dropped open.

"You slept here last night? Is this why Mom's pissed?"

The blunt truth made him groan as he sat with his back against the wall and his legs stretched out on the rickety bed. Lukas sat cross-legged by his knees. "She's really mad at me."

"Did you call her at least?"

"Too many times… She won't return my calls."

"What did you do?"

He recalled Thorn's same words. "I kept it all too tight-lipped for my own good, which I now regret. Listen, I was rough with you at the museum. I didn't mean to grab your arm so hard, but I need to tell you the reason." Studying his son, he said, "The woman who reached for the peach, I recognized her scent on you. Yesterday in the piazza, she tripped over absolutely nothing right in front of me. How she managed to be in the same place as you is another mystery. She has the girl, Lukas." He hoped to see caution, even a healthy dose of fear, not blatant curiosity.

"It isn't a coincidence that both of us touched her."

"Not by a long shot. I'm assuming we have a bit of out-of-this-world help now. But I'm worried because the demon knows you're here."

"So do it tonight, Dad. We can find her together."

"I know exactly where she is," he stated in a bitter tone.

His son's expression changed. "Yeah, I get it. You don't want me near this thing, and until you're absolutely sure I'm safe, you'll let it keep killing."

"Don't put words in my mouth, little boy. I believe Jillian is ill. Think it through and say what you sense."

"If she's sick in a *human* way, it can't kill."

"What else?"

"We have the advantage."

"Keep going."

"There's got to be something they don't know."

"Why?"

"Because Siena would be crawling with vampires trying to help her kill... but it's not."

"Very good."

"Let it weaken for another day and tomorrow night we—"

"Wrong. Go back." Changing position, Michael mirrored his son's pose.

"It's not wrong. It's perfect."

"It's *wrong*. This isn't a homework assignment. Lives are at stake, yours included. Think logically. Why is it wrong?" He watched with pride as his son's eyes swept the tiny room, eventually lighting on the open window.

A slow but mischievous grin started. "Daylight insures no vampires will interfere. But what if this girl dies, Dad?"

"I need Mom. I really need Mom."

Holding up his own phone, that grin spread across Lukas's face. Michael narrowed his eyes. "You wouldn't, would you?"

"No problem. She sees *my* number and I guarantee she'll pick up. But it'll cost you." Two thumbs flew across the keypad entering each digit of her number.

Shocked by the sound of familiar footsteps,

Michael whispered, "Stop. End the call."

"No way! Come on, Dad. It's a cool plan. Shit. The ring sounds strange. Maybe my battery's dying."

He eyed the door. He eyed Alana, whose hands clipped her hips.

"I'm just surprised you didn't think of it sooner, Lu," she said.

Instantly, a syrupy soft "Sorry," rolled out of his son.

"Save the charm, buddy, I want to speak to Dad. Alone."

Michael watched his son leave and close the door. Then he leaned back casually against the headboard. It was truth time.

****

Minutes passed—in deafening silence. There Alana sat, straight-shouldered and unyielding on the bed, a short reach away. He gave no hint that the very sight of her brought blessed relief. But running off to Florence with the intention of destroying Veronique without him to watch her back didn't sit well—not at all. "You not only hung up on me. You ignored my calls. Shall we only talk business or can we get to the root of the problem now, darlin'?"

"I'm a little leery of being alone with you in here."

"Why?"

"We should talk downstairs."

"I'm sorry?" he asked, very aware of where this was leading.

"Or I should open the door so no one thinks I'm, we're…"

"What occurred between us the night before we left for Siena isn't the issue, Alana. And, as uncomfortable as you feel about everyone knowing we had sex, the girl hasn't killed since. It was a brilliant strategy on your part. I congratulate you, my Guardian."

"You're gloating. I came back. So you got your way and more."

"You ignored me. You trashed the safer method of using me as a decoy...*as planned*."

"I didn't come back here for a fight."

"You could've fooled me. Just be prepared. This isn't about business. It's about us. I tried to talk to you last night. You locked the door."

"You did the walking."

"You gave me no choice."

"See? We can't even talk about this without bickering."

"I'm not bickering. I'm discussing," he sharply replied.

She glared at him. "Oh *please*, just say what you really feel."

"I'm not the one with the problem." An arrogant smirk crossed his face, and then her hand flew through the air, grazing his cheek as if she planned it. In less than a second, he had her arms pinned tight and her tense body pulled close.

She struggled. He held on.

"I... I didn't mean to—"

"Oh yes you did, my Guardian. Now that you've got it out of your system, let's have the talk. You want business? We'll start there. How do you think Veronique has escaped decapitation for hundreds of years? She's a monster, worse than Cyril. Has the Georgian Council lifted their centuries-old Do Not Approach order? Because as long as I've been around,

Guardians have been told to stand down. How foolish to run off to Florence without me to entertain Veronique! I know what distracts the sire and you are *not* it."

She tried to break free as he angrily ordered, "Don't. I'm just getting started. I came back to you. Whether or not romantic notions steered my suddenly living brain, I did come back...to *you*. Someday I'll share what shattered my soul and stayed in my unbeating heart for ten months, for three centuries, but now's not the time for true confessions."

He sensed a Guardian's mystical strength building within her, which further fueled his fury. He held her tighter. Her glare didn't stop him. Neither did, "Let. Go."

"Absolutely not. I have this overwhelming need to talk. The night I came back, I wanted to make love to you. But all I could do was hold onto you for dear life. Changing existences—man to vampire to immortal being to man—let's just say I couldn't switch gears. Am I now *fully* human? I'd say the other night confirms it. Doesn't it, my Guardian?"

"Yes," she answered, but her warm hazel eyes blazed like a tiger's.

His mouth dried as his heart raced. Never loquacious, he couldn't stop himself now. "How was I to know the nightly vision in my head of crosses piling up was a warning? I thought I was losing my mind. You sensed my avoidance and *assumed* arrogant indifference. Try absolute terror—given the chance to finish a life stolen from me centuries ago. Let's skip over the angst with my son. Jumping into parenting felt like walking a tightrope without a net beneath. But we'll have that conversation at a later date...*if* we survive this event. I wasn't open with you. Now you're angry, and I'm very aware. But let's fast forward to Monday night, and don't cringe, darlin'. It's truth time, remember?"

Releasing her, he paused to rein in his emotions. Like a vapor-swollen cloud, one feeling he kept hidden took fury's place. She hadn't interrupted once and voicing everything in his heart hurt more than expected. His tone softened and his eyes grew moist. "When did I ever *not* want to make love to you? I can't control what I've always felt—when my heart didn't beat."

"How could this demon sense what we did? Tell me, Michael."

"I honestly don't know. But it triggered some kind of sensory overload because it hasn't killed since. You walked out on me, my Guardian. It wasn't the other way around." The last six words came out a strangled blur of syllables. Willing his eyes to clear, he had to look away.

Alana leaned in, kissed his brow. "I love you. I always have. I always will."

Her hands held his face, and he wanted her more than ever. She unleashed what was in his soul—the passion, the desire to love and be loved in return. Like a precious gem, this bond to her had many facets cut deep and fine.

He watched her stand. The light switch clicked. The room went silent and dark. She came to him, rested at his side. He took her in his arms, and her head settled under his chin. Kissing her hair, then her lips, when she turned in his embrace, her body molded to his as it always had. His kisses turned urgent and he tugged off her blouse as she unhooked her bra. Then she went to work on his shirt as their tongues teased each other. Her breasts were in his hands and he wanted out of his jeans immediately.

As if she knew, his belt came undone along with his jeans and his zipper came down. "God, I want you," he hissed as he twisted her beneath him on the narrow bed. She tugged at his jeans and he stood for a second, slipping out of his shoes as well.

In the next instant she was standing. "No. I want you on that bed." And guiding her down he knelt between her knees. His mouth captured a breast and teased her nipple. He licked down to her waist, and as she arched off the bed, he unbuttoned her jeans, easing them off inch by inch as she panted. Kneeling back he pulled off her shoes and flung them to the floor before he pulled off her jeans. The scent of her arousal had him throbbing and hard. He reached down and lowered her panties with a groan and a growl. And then she was naked and writhing on the bed.

He grabbed her bottom and bending down he tasted her, greedily, erotically loving the way her hips rocked, roughly licking to counter her motions. He pushed her thighs further apart listening to her swallowed whimpers as she tried to make no sound. He felt her orgasm and that drove him wild.

He came up her body and kissed her with enormous need. She responded with the same urgency. "I've wanted to do that for days," he whispered as she panted. When he guided his erection into her, she drew in a long breath. "You're tight and wet," he whispered in her ear. She moaned a soft "yesss" and he thrust deeper, rougher.

The bed creaked and they both stopped and held their breath. Then he eased out of her and drew back. Her arms reached up for him, but he stood and pulled her up. "We won't rock the floorboards like this," he whispered, sliding her up his body.

Her arms flew around his neck and her legs hooked his hips. "Oh God, you are such a vixen," he whispered. Then once again, he guided himself into her, pumping hard as he held her bottom as her hips rode the rhythm. He slipped his thumb down and touched the tip of her. And then they orgasmed together as he filled her, feeling every burst of seed.

The way she moaned and whimpered and gasped... It was beyond sensual. The feel of her supple body boneless in his arms brought immense satisfaction. The heat rising from his body on this warm night was something he hadn't experienced in hundreds of years.

And she clung to him. It felt beyond real. He pulled her hips off his waist, patted her luscious bottom as he kissed her, full of devotion. Then he eased them both back down to the narrow bed and just held her to his chest.

Minutes later, she whispered, "Talk to me, Michael. Tell me what happened the night you came home to me."

He spoke softly, answered every question. With his eternal love in a possessive embrace, they talked for hours. Sweet affection filled the night. Over ten years of loving each other brought their devotion to a higher level.

When he entered her again, there were no aggressive moves. No rough kisses. Their lovemaking was gentle and tender, quiet and subdued. This time, the hot spill of life filled her as if this climax were a new beginning.

****

Lucy had laced sweet wine with a sedative and then sat with Jillian as she drank it down and fell asleep. Leaving the basement, she threw the soiled bed linens from yesterday in a trashcan behind the building. Once her tub filled with hot water and orange peels, she scrubbed every inch of her skin until it hurt. "Many more I need" worked on her again.

Drying off, she chose a tight black dress that hugged all the right places. The teased, short bob looked like she'd spent the day at a hair salon. Shimmering lipstick and pricey perfume topped off a sultry charade.

Close to midnight, she slipped out the rear door and shimmied through a crack in the fence that led to another tiny yard. Hurrying between two similar buildings, she came out on a different street. In her favorite late-night haunt, her favorite bartender handed her an apple martini, then another. Salvatore liked her.

Flirty and talkative, Lucy conned him into giving up the silver crucifix around his neck.

"You're trouble tonight, *Lucia mia*," he said with an easy smile, handing it to her.

"You don't know the half of it," she answered. She noted the glint in his eye, always thought him a kind, attractive man.

After he moved to another customer, she caught the conversation of three tipsy tourists. When the men walked out the door, she winked at Sal, followed them out.

After all, four gleaming crosses were better than one.

Chapter 19

The next morning, Lukas and the Guardians escorted four art students into the museum's café. They feasted on fruit, juice, and fresh baked croissants. Sitting alone with Mick across the room, he studied Betty's sad face, and listened with piqued curiosity.

"What's wrong, Betts," Pet was asking.

"He didn't come down this morning."

Pet sighed and patted Betty's hand. "A day without seeing such perfection will simply have to suffice. Perhaps we can compare adjectives."

"I can add a few," Sister Phyllis whispered.

Lukas continued listening with a dimpled grin while the other students grumbled about the early hour, today's assignment, or missing the States. Nothing new there, he thought. Off at a corner table, Nigel and Neeb weren't talkative, just peacefully sipping tea.

Mick nudged his shoulder. "Any thoughts on today, Lu?"

He gave a loose shrug. "Mom's back. Dad's happy. Everything's cool."

****

Thorn joined the Bookmans in the study of San Giorgio Rectory. "You aren't sleeping much these days, empath," Laura said to him.

Miles glanced up from the computer. "Mary Kendrick confirms the original murals are safely under guard in a Czech museum. This tells us Leonard has been planning the event for some time."

"Like ten months, maybe," Thorn grumbled. "What about the piece of rock over there? Is it a fake as well?"

The monsignor stated, "I sense it authentic."

Miles said, "Perhaps we should move it out of the rectory."

Monsignor shook his head. "No. It is to remain in this study."

"At least let it face the wall," Thorn suggested. "Personally, it looks just like the old sire, if you ask me."

"Cyril was a knight," Monsignor Scarlatti informed, "A nobleman who fought heathens off his native land. It has been suggested by Georgian researchers that Veronique authored the decimation of Cyril's family to make his corruption from innocence complete."

"But no researcher is able to prove it." Miles said, "The writings of Cyril's colleagues were studied for centuries. Any knight courageous enough to inscribe his name on parchment as testimony to the changes in the nobleman met a horrible fate...presumably at his command."

"So where are we?" Laura asked candidly. "I'm sorry, but a medieval history lesson is not what's on my mind at the moment. I miss our daughters and our grandsons."

Thorn leaned back. "No activity in Siena again last night. Alana's back with Michael, and he has a plan."

Laura smiled. "Celia sent that to you?"

"It's straight from Michael's head. Celia and son send love to all."

Amused, she looked at Miles. "Alana's turnaround is your doing, no doubt."

"This must be perfectly timed, honey. Deepa's been formally brought in on this event and the Kendrick witches have offered to assist," her husband replied.

Laura sensed immense worry in him, grew more concerned about both her daughters.

"All factors are now in place," the monsignor stated. "Deepa will locate Leonard's cult. The Champion and the Guardian must stand together to defeat Veronique. But first, the girl must be saved."

"I'm curious." she asked, "Where is Philip?"

"He'll join us when needed. Portofino is safe, which brings me to another point." He said to Miles, "I suggest you and your lovely wife enjoy the lovely spring day together. Holy Thursday's service must be prepared. In other words, Researcher, I'm kicking you out."

Laura squeezed Miles's hand. "Are you my husband? Do I remember you?" A charming smile began. "I've so missed you, my dear."

****

At her desk in the Manhattan penthouse, Deepa Chandra studied the letter that just arrived by courier. She slid a finger under the seal, a silver dragon embossed in an indigo blue circle. This letter was the Georgian Council's official call to action. It gave full control of all and any methods she would use to unearth Leonard Gerhardt's followers.

Deepa's sharp mind and primed sixth sense served North America's mystical warriors since arriving last May. With ease she had settled into the Bookman's previous residence. All but one of this continent's portals had been closed by Michael Malone. And the task of documenting the death of demons trapped in this dimension had gone smoothly. Until last week, she thought. In an unofficial way, she acquired photographs of suspected vampire worshippers. Now, in the middle of the night, they remained spread out on her desk, her official mission. "What am I not seeing, and where are you, Leonard," she whispered. *Seven vampire worshipers spotted in Florence...* A look of sheer disgust clouded her usually tranquil expression. The researcher leaned forward to scrutinize the image of a most dangerous wizard and knew she needed help.

****

Jillian tugged at the silk scarf and blinked through darkness. Her hand brushed the bedspread. She inhaled deeply and a brutal smile appeared. The beast-within recognized two scents...one a bonus. Stiffly, she sat up. Her feet curled against the floor. A command came from deep within and she stood, clutching the wooden chest as she crept out the open basement door.

The first-floor dwelling was empty. Standing in Lucy's bathroom, a sliver of humanity guided Jillian through necessary functions. After sponging her face and arms, she raided the closet. A long black skirt and sweater fit the demon's monotone sense of sight. Many bruises were now unseen. A paisley scarf cinched her shriveled waist, and although her feet were smaller than Lucy's, slip-on sandals would protect the bottoms of her tender feet. Like a true expert, she used makeup underneath the dresser's mirror to conceal purple blotches on her face. A little blush didn't hurt, applying it so she wouldn't look suspicious. The chest fit perfectly into a tote left on the kitchen chair, and a wide-brimmed hat with long brown hair sewn into it would serve to disguise her appearance.

Stepping out into bright sun, she kept repeating, "Fifty-four, fifty-four—"

****

Michael and Alana had slept soundly locked in each other's arms. By mid morning, they were together in the empty kitchen of the student house. Today would be a long one. They both sensed it. He made the coffee as Alana rushed to answer the phone on the wall.

"Hello," she said in a cautious tone as Michael came to her side. Alana froze, met his quizzical gaze. "Yes, can I help you, Paige? No, Jillian's not here right now. Can I take a message? Yes, the art students have been very busy. Sure. I'll tell her. Oooh... Sorry. We... a bad connection...not to...worry..." She hung up quick. "Did we just dodge a bullet?"

Michael unplugged the landline and called Portofino on his cell phone. Monsignor Scarlatti answered, and he handed his phone to Alana, listened to her repeat Paige's message. Then she said, "Thorn wants to talk to you."

"This event is over today." He took his phone back, welcoming her nod of agreement.

"All's right with your world. Good. Now focus because it's gonna get bumpy," Thorn said in a serious tone.

"Yeah, hello to you, too... How's Celia?"

"Ready when you are. It's the quiet before the storm again."

"Then let's shake things up."

"Don't be so eager. There are many variables— even in daylight."

"What could go wrong?" Calm, confident, and in control, Michael leaned against the counter.

"Keep your head clear, that's all I'm saying. Just look before you leap."

The line went dead, and staring at his phone with irritation, whispered, "Well that's cryptic."

Alana handed him a cup of coffee. Her smile lit his heart. "What is?"

"The quiet before the storm, variables, and the ever-popular look before you leap. Damn it."

"You're very handsome when you brood, my love. Wait another day, maybe?"

"No. Not another day. She's dying." He drained the cup, placed it in the sink. Both arms laced his chest. "Call in local Guardians to watch the students. We do this today."

"Thorn doesn't do clichés unless he senses something. I mean, I don't doubt you, but maybe—"

"It's now or never, darlin', that's my take."

Pulling out her cell phone, Alana scrolled through numbers programmed two nights ago. "What time do you want them?"

"Noon," he answered. "Fifteen minutes later, Jillian's in the arms of Mother Anne."

****

Outside Lucy Novak's apartment near the bus depot, Michael addressed the individuals that would make this happen the right way. "Nothing gets in. Nothing gets out. Nigel and Neeb take the front, Lukas and Mick the back. Petula, you're inside the hall."

Only he and Alana would handle Jillian Gerhardt.

They entered in silence. He sniffed the air, sensed something off. The first-floor apartment door yawned open, but Michael jumped the basement steps with Alana following. Two sets of trained eyes focused through darkness on an empty antique bed. Alana held up a musty drape. With a murderous scowl, he strode over and grabbed the sleeping woman by the throat, watching her choke as he pulled her up and off the bed. Terrified crashes of her heart didn't stop his glare into her bulging blue eyes. Alana touched his arm, and he released Lucy Novack, catching her before she crumbled to the floor. His arm banded her lower abdomen in a crushing way.

"You're scared. That's good. Where is she?" Coughs, sputters... Her wide eyes darted to the bed. After a violent shake, he listened to more squeals without mercy. "What did you do with Jillian?"

"I'd answer fast if I were you. He gets highly irrational in situations like this." Alana handed her the bed sheet. Lucy clutched the cotton to her bobbing breasts, but Michael ripped it away, dangled it just out of reach.

"No. Not until I get an answer. Talk fast."

She flailed against him. "I-I d-don't know."

With her feet searching for ground and more useless yelps, he hauled Lucy up the stairs, careful to not crack her ribs. Striding into the apartment, he threw her down on the couch.

Petula came over. "Bloody hell, Ally, he's more than fierce. He's positively frightening."

"Wait, Pet, he's just warming up," Alana answered.

Whether or not it was for Lucy's benefit, their banter did the trick. Lucy clamped her knees together, hugged her shivering body. He leaned down, snagging her chin with a knuckle. "You don't move. And no clothes," he said to Alana.

He had to see the room again and went directly to Jillian's bed. What he inhaled turned his stomach. *Infection, blood, vampire venom, foul body fluids… she won't last the day.* "Son of a bitch, where are you," he whispered, aware of what had to be done next. Going to the base of the stairs, he shouted, "Pet, you and the others are on the kids. Send Lukas down here." It didn't take long. His son met him by the bed as Michael stated, "Take in Jillian's scent. Memorize it. See her in your mind." Lukas did so with his eyes closed in a relaxed fashion. "Good." Then he added sharp and stern, "If you pick up her scent anywhere, run away as fast as you can. Do you hear me?"

"Yeah, I hear you."

Grabbing the sheet off the floor, Michael stomped up the stairs. His son followed, and when they entered Lucy's living room, he saw Lukas gawk with curiosity at the naked woman cowered on the couch.

"Fear heightens her scent," his son whispered.

"*Now* you understand one particularly important conversation we had."

He threw Lucy the sheet. "Cover up in front of my son."

She wrapped it around, left a good portion of her breasts revealed. "Stop leering at me, vampire." Then she gave Lukas a flirtatious grin. "Beautiful bone structure like a Renaissance angel… I'd love to sketch you. You don't look at all like your father. But I've seen a picture of the dark seer. Leonard knew your mother well."

The comment turned Michael's tone to ice. "You don't speak to my child. Don't look at him and don't touch him…ever again. Got that, Miss Lucy?" He gave an unexpected charming smirk and sensed her body's very sexual reaction. "My Guardian will watch you dress. Pick something nice because we have a date." Then he lost the grin. "My sister's writing chest, where is it?"

Her gaze flickered for an instant. "By Jillian's bed."

"Try again, and this time I want the truth."

"It's right *there* on the floor!"

"You're lying. I don't like liars."

In a satisfied way, her mouth quirked. "Why would I lie?"

Leaning close, he eased a palm down her face; let his lips brush her ear. "You will never again hold a paintbrush after I get through with your fingers. Do you understand me?" She jerked back. "That's right. Not too chilly anymore, and definitely not what you expected. The vampire thing was getting old. Go with my Guardian. Remember. Pick out something nice." Although Lucy's head bobbed, he scented fear. And at the student house, he'd frighten her even more.

Alana helped her stand. "Do we have another houseguest?"

"Absolutely," he stated cool and aloof.

****

Michael waited until everyone left, and then ripped through the building. Lucy had been on the second floor recently. Vampires had walked this hall on the night the beast-within invaded Jillian's innocent body. Close to crazed, he tore the basement room apart. Nailed boards flew off revealing two small windows. He scented everything to form a mental picture he'd never forget.

The infection began with diseased claws and vampire bites. The ingestion of human blood brought it to her internal organs. His lusty tryst with Alana in Portofino forced more bacteria into an innocent body. Only a year older than Lukas, this child would soon be dead. Then he froze, picking up another scent and the sharp smell of antiseptics.

"Who helped you, Lucy," he said to himself.

Medicines on the nightstand hit the wall after a swipe of his hand. Eyeing Lucy's phone on the floor, he pocketed it. Alana would know how to retrieve all the numbers called. He stared at the carpet where his sister's writing chest had been, and then dropped to his knees. Michael drew in a deep sniff. The blood of many innocent victims filled his keen senses.

He walked to where Lucy had slept and inhaled deeply. "Three different men in one night... You were a busy little helper." He'd make her talk. It wouldn't take long. After resealing each window, Michael left the room. "You're coming back, demon, and I'll be waiting," he vowed.

****

Sister Phyllis saw Petula come into the sketching studio at the museum. She read the Guardian, sensing eight mystical warriors to protect four American teenagers. Betts waved to her new best friend, and Petula smiled with a hearty wave back. Casually, Phyllis met the woman on the far side of the large room. "You don't have to say it. I caught it all."

"He sent us all back, Sister."

"To assist the Italians, yes, I know. But Michael has Lucy."

"A lot of good she'll do us now."

"It's a variable removed. Jillian's mind is struggling for release; however, the demon's planning like a demented person, not immortal evil anymore. God help the poor souls this thing attacks."

****

Michael ducked under the red rope that cordoned off this section of the museum. Guardian's lined the hall at attention. His pace slowed when approaching the art students on a break. Betty smiled wide with adoration. He gave a thin grin, and a spellbound smile lit her face.

Petula held open the door. "Sister is waiting for you, Sir."

With a detached "Thanks," he entered and noted the healer's grave expression. "Where is she, Sister?"

"Far from this part of Siena, but the girl's unable to control it. Perhaps the Guardians—"

"No. They won't see her coming before she kills them." He sat heavily on a tall wooden stool, his shoulders hunched and both hands gripping his knees.

"It needs Lucy, Michael. She will return. When she has fifty-four crucifixes."

"Why fifty-four…Oh, God," he said as the answer came to him. "But only six healing Sisters removed the beast from my soul."

"Our entire congregation had to become one unstoppable force in order to remove the demon from a vampire's soul. I'm sorry. You couldn't have known." She paused, reading his thoughts. "You're not a murderer; nor Lucy's Ultimate Judge. Please don't let this mind-set continue. And yes, our Order will aid this child because she didn't choose to be a satanic instrument. You didn't either—in 1690." Serenity appeared in her eyes, the same compassion he'd seen in Mother Anne. "Everything happens for a reason. I'm not the first one to tell you this."

"How was she able to walk out without Lucy's help?"

"The demon grows desperate. It's driving her mind now. Prioritize and you'll have clarity."

First Lucy talks, he thought, and above all, these Guardians keep the students safe. He stood, softly saying, "I don't speak Italian very well."

"Let's see... Stay alert, people; don't let Jillian near the students if they see her. I can translate for you." She held his gaze, adding, "Do what must be done."

Chapter 20

As a vampire there had never been a time when Michael Malone didn't enjoy the process of intimidation. He entered the kitchen as Alana stared down Lucy who shook in a chair. "Do you believe she tried to run? And I offered her a chocolate croissant." His Guardian gripped the woman's shoulder and Lucy winced. "I told you before, I'm different. One shove and you fly across the room. And did you know Michael still has a dark side?" He tried not to smirk when a smile crossed Alana's lips. "He is so *very* strong. And when he manhandles me—" He pulled Lucy up. "Hey, I wasn't finished with her yet!"

"You don't feed the hostage, my dear, and you don't share our passionate bedroom romps with a wannabe sorcerer's love muffin, either." He kept Lucy in hand while Alana leaned into his left side. As Lucy stared with disbelief, he kissed Alana's cheek, and then moaned with a devilish look he had perfected. "She and I need some personal time."

Alana's fingers immediately raked through his loose brown waves—a blatant tease, which prompted a suggestive whimper. "Do what you have to do, my love. It's for a good cause." Her steamy expression met Lucy's curious one. "My sweet nature evaporates when I'm jealous."

Grabbing Alana's round bottom, he gave a sensual

groan. "Be nice, dear."

She peeled off his chest with a dreamy sigh. "I totally love it when he gets this way. Tingles reach my toes."

He sized up the tall woman before pulling her by the arm. "Come on, Miss Lucy. I know the perfect spot for us to get better acquainted."

Alana closed the basement door behind them, let out a trembling breath. Then, pushing open the swinging door, she came face to face with Lukas. "No. Don't tell me. You *didn't* close the ears!"

"What's Dad gonna do? I mean, he's not a vampire anymore. He can't, you know, bite her?"

"I should ground you for eavesdropping again! Your father's dangerous without fangs, as *you* already know. Close the ears!" Her right eyebrow arched before she let the door swing closed—and melted against the kitchen wall with a grin, wondering if Michael had felt her temperature zoom straight up when he touched her.

****

Kicking the cedar door shut, Michael knew exactly how to handle Lucy Novak. The clean aroma was, at first, overpowering. Then the scent of fear came off the curvy blonde standing in the center of the room. He leaned against the door, his arms lashed to his chest in a way that hinted just try and leave.

"Lucy, Lucy, Lucy... What *shall* I do with you? I don't bite anymore. There's that," he said, giving a look that would sizzle down her skin. She stepped back. Her hand shot to her neck. "I'll bet Leonard's got his chest all puffed out, expecting a soulful vampire, which I've spoiled by having a heartbeat. What a pity. What a party we're gonna have. So when will it be?"

Her body reacted as if he asked for a kiss instead of information and keeping his strides menacing, said in a low voice, "Talk to me."

"Leonard told me about you."

"Did his description do me justice?"

"No... Definitely not."

He enjoyed the intended effect and stepped in closer. "Give me what I want. Give me the where, as a bonus, and I let you walk."

"Don't touch me," she warned...in a half-hearted way.

"That's not what you desire. You'd like me to rip off your blouse and pull down those jeans, which just happen to hug your hips in a most provocative way. Getting what I want from a woman has been legendary for over three centuries. Aren't you the slightest bit curious about the how? Let that naughty imagination run wild. It still won't equal what I can make you feel." Her heart fluttered and her face flushed. He gave a charming grin. She took in a long, shaky breath. Then he turned, took a slow stroll to the other side of the room. As he sat on a barrel, she eyed the door. "I'd have you on the floor and beneath me in mere seconds. Tell me what I want to know."

"You're teasing, fishing for information."

"I like natural blondes, love the hairstyle. It suits your face in a cutesy kind of way. Maybe I purposely kept you naked in my arms at your place."

"You did it to scare me, not because you're hot for me. I wasn't born yesterday."

"Neither was I." Still grinning as if this were pleasant conversation, he switched tactics. It was time to turn up the heat. "Join me over here, Lucy. Come stand close enough to kiss and tell me whether I did it to terrorize you or because I want you. When I pulled you off the bed like an obsessed lover, my hand stayed low. I'll admit it. Perhaps a finger strayed even lower. You'll never know if I did it on purpose or not." She seemed to shiver as if his liquid tone caressed her. Her arms hugged her breasts as she scrutinized his face, and then shook her head.

Michael hopped off the barrel in one slow, easy move, straightening his shoulders to trigger another erotic thought. The way she shifted from foot to foot said she was almost there. "Trying to get those x-rated images of steamy sex with the enemy off your mind? If I reach my limit, I might get rough, so you don't want me to come... to you. I get extremely hands-on when I'm angry."

Lucy ran. In a split second, he had her up against the door. Her fingernails scraped down the fragrant cedar as he pressed against her back. Tracing a slow path up her outer thigh, up her ribs, he heard the gasp, felt her shiver. Turning her to face him, his hips glued to hers, sensing another thrilling jolt thunder through her. One hand pinned her wrists high up the door. His eyes brimmed with fire. "To be naked the way I found you...squirming in my hand—you'd like that."

"You're all man," she sighed.

"Oh, I'm much, much more." His lips hovered over hers. "I'll bet I could ring out the skimpy thong you're wearing. Now there's a fantasy you'd love." She squirmed when he unsnapped her tight hip-huggers. His knee grazed that swollen part of her, and she sucked in a jagged breath. "Give me what I want or you'll never get what comes next."

"No… I-I can't," she whimpered.

"You're so ready." One finger slid across her belly. "Do I stop?"

"N-no, don't stop."

"Maybe a little persuasion will help you experience that one moment of uncontrollable pleasure." Her back arched. He let go of her wrists, instantly gripped her hips and ground into her. "When and where."

"Saturday… Florence."

He stepped a full foot back and let her slide down the door. Crouched low to meet her moist eyes, her flushed face, he said without emotion. "Thank you. Now get up."

"You bastard! They'll kill me!"

"What a misguided little bitch you are." He watched her shake, ignored the tears in her eyes. When he stood, she cowered, fumbled with the brass snap on her jeans. Reaching down, he gruffly hauled her over one shoulder.

He couldn't get out of the room fast enough. Storming up the stairs, one furious push splintered the lock. He slammed her down in a chair, fully glared into her drippy eyes before walking away. "Put our guest in the small bedroom," he said to Alana. "Keep her quiet. She doesn't move, understand?"

"I certainly do," Alana answered without emotion. "What's next on your agenda?"

Michael yanked the spigot hard, lathering his hands at the kitchen sink with a large amount of dish soap and the hottest water his skin could stand. Only looking at the woman he loved, he stated, "I save a girl."

****

Michael left the student house with his phone and the Mercedes' key. Outrage was his choice of weapons, not his trusted broadsword. Overpowering an emaciated child didn't require a fight to the death.

With just enough of Lucy's scent to disguise his presence, he entered the building through the back door. No heartbeats. No fresh scent of Jillian. He walked downstairs, and choking down fury, he clicked on the table lamp and stood in the shadows.

Ten minutes or ten hours—he didn't care how long he'd have to wait. Time didn't matter. Sooner or later, a dying girl will walk in, he thought, and this will be over.

Chapter 21

Lukas didn't need to see Alana pulling Lucy up the stairs. Staring out the window of his room, his expression stayed blank and his eyes wide. He'd heard every word of the interrogation and he gripped the windowsill. His father's outrage. Lucy's whimpers and whispers.

He shook his head to clear it, but in the tiny bedroom his father had slept in, Alana was shredding a towel. Long strips ripped to tie Lucy to the bed and then the lock on the window clicked and the whoosh of curtains closing. "Holy shit," he said as he ran. From the doorway, he saw Alana secure a strip of towel across Lucy's lips.

Her panic felt like an electrical spark. "No, just breathe through your nose. You won't choke. I promise," he whispered. Lucy didn't look at him, but Alana did—in a questioning way as she powered down from Guardian strength. He added, "Need help with something, Mom?" A small cell phone sailed across the room, which Lukas caught in his left hand.

"Find the last number called."

He maneuvered through the menu. "Only one number…called yesterday. Just press—"

"Yeah, I know." Alana came over and took it. After hitting the send icon, she frowned. Lukas heard a voicemail message, and she waited exactly ten seconds, didn't say a word before ending the call. "Let's see who calls back. Why aren't you on the front door?"

"Oh. Sorry."

"I'll be in here watching Lucy sleep off the muscle relaxer. Ugh! Thank God for drugs."

"How long will Dad be gone?"

"However long it takes. Why?"

"He's alone, Mom."

"Your father knows what he's doing. He'll be fine."

He couldn't shake a creepy feeling, but nodding once, he left the room. Lukas didn't see 'fine.' He saw blood. Oh God, he thought, this is how he's gonna die!

****

Leonard Gerhardt's eyes flicked open. He couldn't hold the trance. *An intrusion, an aberration!* Clutching the amulet around his neck, he staggered up from the floor and stumbled to the window of the hotel room. *Who stands in my way—a Georgian or a mystically-enhanced vampire? Why can I not see the host vessel? Why can I not sense Lucy?*

"Impossible! I missed nothing." Full of fury, he snapped his fingers. Cyril's diary appeared before him. Carelessly he grabbed it, leafed through the brittle pages like a madman.

****

In a rundown apartment, the enchanted knife plunged into the drunken man's chest. Jillian pulled it out with a jagged jerk. The thing within her watched his paralyzed body sink down—his eyes wide, his mouth open. He'd forget to breathe within the minute.

This had been a disciplined assault after a long bus ride to the not-so-popular immigrant district on the outskirts of Siena. The beast-within needed no help to finish its victims. The thin blade felt powerful in hand, but licking it clean would infect this body, weaken it again. It steered Jillian to the sink to wash off the blood. Then it leaned down, ripped another treasure off a thick neck and put it in the wooden chest before she left.

She knocked on the door across the narrow hall. An elderly woman appeared, and before she could speak, the knife plunged into her stomach. Jillian closed the door and stole another crucifix after the human sank speechless to the floor. She followed the scent of impending death, found an old man in a bed. He stared directly into her eyes and saw what lived inside her. Gasping, *"Diavolo! Diavolo!"* he took his last breath. She tilted her head, stared into lifeless eyes, and then ripped the crucifix off beads clasped around his hands.

Walking away, the necessity of human nourishment surfaced. She found a pan on the stove. It was still warm. Bitter greens soaked in oil and garlic... the meat salty, chewy. She ate slowly and then reached for a bottle of yellow juice instead of the wine bottle on the counter. Standing at the table, she opened the chest and pulled out her treasures.

The crosses were placed in glistening lines. "Six rows of nine. Six healers surrounded him as I entered my tomb. Only one I need and fifty-four..." The inner walls of Anne Malone's writing chest were stained scarlet as if Jillian had decorated its former sarcophagus with primeval paintings. Replacing her treasures, she laid the enchanted knife inside before closing it.

A new thought began. Jillian lit a candle, placed it by the stove. She turned every knob and pulled on a brass lever. The hiss of gas sent a thrill through the beast-within, but the girl lurched back. She shoved the chest into the canvas tote and as close to a run as possible, hurried out of the wooden structure. Her steps didn't slow until she crossed the street.

In a narrow alley, drained of energy she slid down the rough bricks. Then an explosion deafened her. Screams, shouts for help. People running in every direction. Fire licked the sky and jumped to another wooden house. Thick smoke seemed to find her. Jillian gagged, pulled her body inward. The demon inside craved chaos, but the deafening cacophony of sirens and horn blasts hammered her chest, enough to allow a human thought. *Scream and run. Someone will help me. Plead release, even death to end this nightmare.*

The demon roared within, forced her to stand. It led her away. Clutching the tote, she searched for Lucy in unfamiliar streets.

****

On the opposite side of Siena, the immigrant worked another busy twelve-hour shift. Outside the hospice, she checked cell phone messages for an update on a very sick teenager. A number lit its screen, and about to call, she startled when the daytime supervisor tapped her wristwatch and yelled. Turning off her phone, the doctor softly replied, "*Si, si, si, subito!*" and followed the prissy nurse back into a place of death.

Just before the shift ended, she took another IV bag of antibiotic fluids and medical supplies for her patient. In her mind, she tallied the cost to pay back as a donation to the charity that ran the hospice. Praying forgiveness for the sin of stealing, everything fit snuggly in the small satchel, a proud reminder of a physician's status in the country of her birth.

****

Soon we will be tested, Sister Phyllis thought as she cleared the dinner plates. Now dressed in religious garb, she'd deal with the students and then enter deep meditation. Turning around, she forced a friendly smile. "One more day at the museum and after Easter, we travel."

"Why only one more day," Betty asked.

"Italy's a *really* religious country. Churches will be packed tomorrow, but museums will be closed. Good Friday's very holy in the liturgical calendar."

"Are you going to be in a church? You're a nun, right?"

"Gee, Betts, you noticed? Did the black and white penguin suit give it away or something?"

"Why *are* you dressed like that? I almost didn't recognize you," she said in a serious way.

"Some habits are hard to kick." Even the Guardians laughed. "I've got special prayers to say tonight, but I'm with you guys all day tomorrow. Maybe I'll roll up my cuffs and bake Easter bread with colored eggs wrapped in sweet dough. That's what my mother always did on Good Friday." She noted worry on Alana's face but smiled again. "Dinner was excellent, a classic Italian feast. Thanks for cooking tonight."

"My *Zia* made the best gnocchi," Alana replied with her hand over Lukas's. "Pet, would you like to take Neeb some supper?"

"Sounds perfect, Ally, and I'll sit with him a bit if you don't mind."

Caution had replaced calm in the mystical warriors. When Petula left, she studied her students. "It's time to get back to work. We'll critique and discuss in the studio tonight. Will you be with us, Alana?"

"Not tonight, Sister. Nigel will."

Nigel began a slow smirk. "I'm a bit of an artist, you know… with somewhat eclectic tastes." He stood and said to Alana, "This puts the little newbie with Lu on the front door."

"I'm by no means little," Mick replied with a scowl.

"No antics," Nigel said as he left.

Alana booted up her laptop on the table. "I've heard stories from Daddy B. Keep a sharp eye on the street. Any funny stuff, and I'll defer to your father. That goes for you *and* Mick."

The boys stood. Lu appeared preoccupied as if listening with only one ear, which made Alana shake her head. But it was well after sunset, and she had a full contingent of Guardians to coordinate. Plus, she hadn't heard from Michael, which worried her even more.

****

Jillian had walked many crowded blocks before she found a deserted bus stop. Keeping her eyes cast down and the hat pulled low, she whispered with a sob to the driver, "So lost… Medieval Siena… Bus depot, please… Please…"

He let her on without paying. Only one other person was on the bus. She held the canvas tote firmly in her arms as the bus crawled along the clogged streets. The beast-within didn't want either of these humans to be its last victim. It wanted the vampire—or his son.

****

The bus stop was right outside the hospice, and from a change purse, the doctor pulled out the correct coins to drop into an old-fashioned slot. Only one seat was empty. She took it. *Tonight, spend extra time with the sick child.* The tall blonde woman's concern for the girl touched her heart. *The cash she so generously filled my hand with is a blessing.* Pulling out worn, wooden beads, she kissed the crucifix, offering these evening prayers for the sick young girl.

****

In Gabriella's room, Celia stood at the window staring toward Siena. Magdalena lay on the bed, singing a soft Italian lullaby to her son. When Uriel closed his eyes, Celia saw the gentle nun's face turn serious. So has Gabby's, she thought as she glanced at the dark sky. The ex-Guardian came to her side. Celia's hands clenched. "It's tonight. I feel it."

"Looks that way."

"Oh, God."

"You'll be fine, Celia. This thing will leave the girl."

"What if it comes at me, Gabby? What if it senses I'm different, that I have a child?"

"We'll make sure it doesn't. Please don't worry. No one other than a Catherine has the kind of power you pack."

"It's an awesome gift to have this ability to see, to heal, to be blessed with the birth of a child, the love of a soulmate. Something could go wrong tonight."

Gabriella gave a warm smile. "Moments of doubt... They're killers."

"Amen to that," Celia replied. Edginess wormed through her. She tried to think positive, but there were too many possibilities. None but one was comforting.

****

Lukas glared at Mick who was shuffling cards for another game of solitaire. "It's been too long. I'm going after him."

"Him who," Mick asked.

"My dad," Lukas said as his fists flexed.

"Bloody hell, Lu, you told me what he'll do if you don't follow orders!"

"I swear something's off."

"Nothing's off! What's giving you the jitters?"

"If I knew, I'd share, okay? Shit. I'm going."

The cards flew out of Mick's hand as he stood. "No, you're not."

"This girl is dangerous."

"He's strong and she isn't. He'll get her to the healers."

"That's it!"

"What's it?"

"He's not gonna trudge up the mountain with her on his back. Come on. Neeb will let me into the room."

Mick caught his arm. "What room? Lu, we were told to stay put and—"

"You just had to use those two words. Shit. I'm doing this." He ran up the stairs. Seeing Petula lean against Neeb on the floor he thought, wow, they're, like, in love with each other. Then Neeb stood and eyeballed him with suspicion. Lukas pointed into the tiny room. "I need something from Dad's bag. Can I check? Wow, Lucy's *still* out."

Petula's bright eyes lit on Mick. "Now what could the two of you possibly be up to?"

Lukas forced an easy smile. "Not a single thing, I swear. I just want to check for my earphones, I swear, that's all." Neeb moved aside. "Thanks. I owe you." He tiptoed over to the black duffle. Crouched down, he palmed what he needed like a pro. "Shit," he muttered, "I'll bet I left them home." He walked out saying, "Thanks, Neeb. Come on, Mick. We better get back to the door."

Mick seemed to breathe easier when they entered the living room. Then Lukas jangled the key to the Mercedes in his face. "No way," Mick mouthed.

"Yes, way...come on."

"We're disobeying orders! We can't leave!"

"You're gonna let me go it alone?" Lukas ran out. His best friend followed at Guardian speed.

****

Deepa Chandra stood at the penthouse window in Manhattan. Ready to give up, she studied the budding tops of trees across the street. *No paper trail, no credit cards, no airline tickets purchased. Every Guardian is combing the tri-state area for Gerhardt. I'm missing something.* At least she had identified a dozen cult members, had Guardian's watching them. But a continent away, the event was ready to rocket into the unknown. She sensed it.

Miles had confirmed the revised Order of Procedure. First, Michael would get the child to Villa Catherine. Second, Gerhardt would be found. Third, an ancient Sire would be destroyed. Her responsibility: expose everyone involved on this continent. Gerhardt's location was the key. Walking to her desk, Deepa decided to work backwards. She might discover the glitch, where he seemed to disappear off the face of the earth. *Why can't I find a gray-haired old man? Why do I sense there's more here than I see?*

****

Philip Segallo's driving skills came in handy tonight. The monk from San Marco Abbey weaved in and out of heavy traffic in Monsignor Scarlatti's old sedan. The Bookmans and Thorn fit comfortably in the wide back seat. They were quiet. Philip understood why. They each had emotional connections to the important players in this paranormal event.

Monsignor sat in front with him. "You are prepared, should your Guardian skills be needed?"

"As always, Monsignor," he softly replied.

"Michael trusts you. You were integral to his rescue in Manhattan. You were integral to his seclusion at the Abbey."

"And I'll be right there if he needs me."

"You will drop everyone off at the bus depot before we go to the villa. Guardians will escort them to the student house. We are almost there?"

"We're more than half-way. There's heavy traffic."

"Many attended Holy Thursday services, I'm sure."

Philip nodded once, more than ready to protect the Spiritual Leader of the Georgian Sovereign Council—with his life if necessary.

"When we reach our destination, there is an item in the trunk you will carry in."

"Not a problem," he answered as he approached Siena.

****

Alana rubbed stiffness from her neck. She'd been hunched over the laptop reading endless updates from Guardians in Siena and Florence. Phyllis had given her a large sheet of heavy drawing paper and a set of colored pencils. Angled words, all different sizes, made it look like a series of spider webs, but it was no disorganized spreadsheet. The navigational chart held the whereabouts of all involved in this event tonight. It bothered her, no sightings of Jillian Gerhardt. She glanced at the earlier entry about an explosion a good distance away. Guardians had gone to check it out.

Like her adopted father, Alana's mind stayed alert and her fingers worked the keyboard, demanding constant information. *Thank God for cell phone technology and instant info. Thank God I read Italian faster than I speak it.* Two tones announced a new message. Her jaw dropped and her eyes narrowed as she read *"urgente - figlio con Michael?"*

She shot up out of the chair and ran into the living room. It was empty.

Chapter 22

Recognizing both scents, sheer rage thundered through Michael. He opened the door and grabbed both boys by their shirt collars with such speed that they felt his hands before they saw them. The young Guardian froze on the spot while he glared at his son.

"This is definitely not one of your smarter moves." Clamping his son's upper arms, he lifted him up a full foot, with his feet dangling in the air, looking straight into his eyes.

"I...I brought your car key."

"That's the spare," he barked while lowering him. The snatch of the key was a blur.

"Aren't you gonna answer it?"

"Answer what," Michael bit out as the phone vibrated in his pocket. He pulled it out while Lukas rubbed his arms, backed away. Angrily he hissed, "I've got them. No. No sign of her. Finish what needs to be done and then come, just you, while the others protect the students." He shoved both phone and spare key into the back pocket of his jeans. "I'm furious enough to get parental right here, right now. Do I even have to tell you how much it'll hurt to sit, little boy?" The next merciless glare settled on Mick. "You disobeyed direct orders, young Guardian. I'll discipline you as well."

Mick stammered, "No, Sir, I mean yes, Sir...I'm sorry, Sir," and looked down.

"Alana will take both of you back to—" Mid-sentence, Michael's senses went wild. His gaze locked on the door. "Get behind the drape. Stay perfectly still. Do it now!" Silent against the wall, Michael watched Jillian walk in, cross the room. What he scented on her was chilling. So much so that he couldn't move. She tossed the wide-brimmed hat on the floor, and a canvas bag landed softly on the bed. Pulling out his sister's writing chest, she opened it, rifled through its contents. Bathed in the table lamp's pinkish glow, the girl slowly turned. Her cracked lips formed an insane smile between hollow cheeks. By the second, it was harder to see only the innocent victim in front of him.

Eternal evil stood in her eyes as he whispered, "Oh my God." What steered her every action weighed nothing, yet just its presence felt like a thousand-pound bolder crushing his chest. It suffocated, yet at the same time, drew him in.

A throaty growl erupted from the depths of her. "Michael, my traitorous tomb for three centuries… You have come to me. This vessel does not have the strength of your body nor the passion of your persona— which I crave." Like a twisted dancer, her hips rocked, her hands hidden in the gathered skirt. "Your lust revived me in ways a nubile host cannot perceive."

Gaining some semblance of control, he said, "You're a garrulous bastard."

"At last I see you. How striking a man we were…" Sweeping up his frame, unabashed hunger filled her bloodshot eyes. "We were unstoppable together. Now your heart beats while your mind recalls undeath."

He had to take the chance that the girl was still reachable. "Jillian, I won't let it hurt you anymore.

Come to me, honey, slow and steady. A picture, your mother's portrait… it isn't finished. Do you remember her face, what she looks like?"

She moaned, swooned unsteady. One foot lifted off the floor in a tentative step. "No. Yes. Help me…save me."

Her words triggered unexpected memories. *1690… Pleading for life when Cyril stole my humanity… 1890… Harnessing the mystical ability to reclaim my soul from this evil… and last May, wanting the finality of death…* Then he realized he no longer stood next to the door, approaching her, drawn to her…

"So much guilt—you can't live with it, Michael."

He tried to stop, shook his head. "No… Jillian… You are Jillian. Look inside. See past it."

Tears pooled in her eyes, forming an abyss of distress; perhaps aware of what dominated her soul. "You can't save me. No one can." One sob sounded and he took another step.

With an ungodly shriek, she lunged. A blade plunged into his left shoulder. White hot, human pain forced a quick inhale and then a sharp yelp. She clawed down his chest and wrenched the knife out, causing him to yelp again. "Take me back," she shrieked, "You are where I belong!" And as his blood dripped from the blade, she licked it. "So powerful, so unique is the bloodline."

Michael's heart rate skyrocketed; his breathing went erratic. With a hand covering the seeping wound, he yelled, "Get out of the girl, you bastard!"

The knife dangled at her side as she walked to the bed and sneered. "Come take me out, Michael. I dare you."

Numbness shot down his legs, and clutching his shoulder, he staggered back, slid down the wall. The blood oozing out… the evil legacy of this thing within her…

Suddenly he watched the drape rip down. The wound, the girl, the beast-within, and his son's foolish move. Pains shot through his chest, yet all he could do was shout, "No! Don't touch her, Lukas! Get back!"

"Not a chance in hell, Dad."

She snapped her head up leering at something glistening around his son's neck. "The product of our demon seed—you will be the most precious offering."

"Move and I kill you," Lukas threatened.

"Is that what you think? It is what I need. The last crucifix."

Michael whispered, "What is she talking about, Lukas?"

"It was a gift from Mother Anne. I wore it here on purpose."

His palm pressed harder into the shoulder wound. With little time left, he yelled, "Run! Do you hear me? Get away from her!"

"What does she mean, a precious offering?"

He grit his teeth, staggered to his feet. "It's the fifty-fourth."

"The fifty-fourth what?"

And that's not going to happen, Michael thought. The vow to never let anyone or anything take his son from him again forced his resolve. *More than a man, less than an angel* shot through his mind. Muscle and skin knit together instantly as his heart rate soared. Sweat dotted his forehead and ran between his shoulder blades, but he stood steady on his feet.

Then, like a bad dream gone wild, Mick was at Lukas's side—with one hand in the air holding a silver crucifix.

Michael yelled, "Guardian, stand down immediately. That's an order!"

But Jillian's dull eyes had already lit on Mick as if mesmerized by the cross.

"Sorry, Sir, but I say give the girl what she wants. Is this all you need, then?"

"You're nuts," Lukas bit out, "Quit talking to her. I've got this."

Ignoring both of them, Mick took a step forward. "Don't worry, luv, I'll get it out of you. Here, demon... Put the magic blade through me arm and jump into a body that can handle you." The young Guardian shifted his weight and shoved Lukas hard. Michael watched his son careen across the room and then, his forehead slamming into the nightstand before losing his footing. Acting on pure instinct, he leapt to grab his son just as Jillian grabbed Mick's crucifix and sank the blade into the young Guardian's stomach.

Fully furious, Michael shouted "No!" Lunging, he swatted the cross from her hand. And as Mick crumbled to the carpet, the final offering landed in his sister's desecrated writing chest.

The lamp on the nightstand flickered. Jillian let out an inhuman growl and reached for the chest. Evil was about to be unleashed.

Michael grabbed for it, flung it to the floor. Blood stained crosses flew out landing like tainted raindrops on the carpet. Wild and crazed, she pulled at her hair and screamed. He yanked off the bedspread, held her arms down and wrapped it around her. Now, she wouldn't touch anyone. Then, seeing his son crawl to Mick, he yelled, "No! Don't touch the knife."

But Lukas was kneeling at his friend's side whispering, "Why, Why did you do that? Dad, he's gonna die. I shouldn't have brought him—"

"I'll take care of Mick." With Jillian pinned to one side, Michael pulled Lukas off the floor. "Guardians heal the same way you do." And as raw hate stood in those teary deep-blue eyes, he softly added, "It's not her fault, son, it's truly not her fault."

While his son swiped at his eyes and stared down at his friend, Michal placed Jillian on the bed, tore into the top sheet and bound her tight. Then he went back to Mick. The blade was buried deep with only half its hilt visible. This would hurt like a bitch, but it would be quick. He yanked it out as painful cries began, the teenager sucking in gasps of air. "Good. Your lungs work. Lukas, reach for my phone to call—"

"There's no need, and I brought help," Alana said as she entered.

Someone was kneeling beside Mick. An older woman who inspected the wound before opening a doctor's satchel. He stood, looked at Alana. "He pushed Lukas aside and I—"

"Mick did what a Guardian's trained to do... to save the innocent." Her eyes narrowed. "She stabbed you?"

"I don't know why... I didn't sense the blade."

"You healed, just as you've healed before." He gave a slow nod. "But she got to you."

"The beast-within got to me." Michael picked up the cherished heirloom that had been his salvation last May... now desecrated with innocent blood.

Alana took it from his hands. "I'll bring it with us."

He nodded, hushed an unsteady "Thanks."

"You have to get her to the villa, Michael. But I've got to warn you, Siena is suddenly crawling with vampires. They want her, too." She kissed Lukas's damp cheek and took his hand in hers. "Mick will be fine, but Dad can't do this alone."

Still weepy, Lukas met her gaze. "Promise you'll stay with him. Promise."

"I won't leave his side," she replied.

Michael lifted the moaning girl, held her against his chest softly saying, "Fight, Jillian. Peace is only minutes away."

"You have to hurry," Alana said. "There's little time left."

Before he could ask, Lukas took the car key from his back pocket.

****

The bus depot's parking lot looked like a war zone out of a scripted horror fantasy. Guardians flanked father and son. Like a swarm of angry wasps, vampires lunged left and right only to meet pointy stakes and silver broadswords. They snaked their way to the car, and near it, one undead thing broke through. It slashed the key out of Lukas's hand. Like a seasoned warrior, his son pulled out a stake and turned the creature into dust and bits of bone. A silver-tipped arrow whizzed past Michael's head, and another vampire burst apart next to a blue minivan.

Lukas stopped, searched the ground. "I can't find the key!"

"Let it go. Reach into my other back pocket," which his son did. "Now let's get the hell out of here.

Open the back door."

"Do you want me to hold her?"

"Absolutely not," he replied as Jillian began to twitch and jerk. Foam bubbled from her mouth. Lukas lurched back with a look of shock. "Which means you have to drive. I mean, can you?"

"Yeah, I, uh, have…experience."

Folded in the back seat, Michael gave a narrow-eyed frown. "Experience?"

"Just add it to the long list of things I shouldn't have done." After starting the car, Lukas tried every button until the seat slid forward. "Man, you have long legs. So, like, where do I go?"

"Open your senses and drive north. Trust me. Just do it."

With a smooth turn of the wheel, he backed the car out of the space as if he'd been doing it for years., which made Michael wonder just how much experience a fifteen-year-old could have.

"What if we don't make it there in time?"

As they headed north, he eyed his son's slender frame behind the wheel, sensing pure instinct in him. "She's moving toward life now, not a tragic, meaningless death."

****

As soon as Alana entered the student house, Neeb carried Mick upstairs. Laura and Miles followed close behind the doctor who, out of nowhere, had shown up on Lucy's doorstep. Knowing the young warrior was in good hands, she let out a slow breath and looked at Thorn. He stood, he sat, and then he stood again, which made her nerves jangle as well.

Eying the empath, Nigel whispered, "He's been

like this since he arrived."

With a warm smile, she went over to him. "I don't see a shred of your usual calmness." Thorn sank to the sofa, started to play with his trouser cuff. "Wanna tell me what's wrong?"

"Dear God, I love Celia with all my soul and he's my son! There's trouble at the villa. I sense it."

"Say no more. I'll take Pet and Neeb, but Nigel will stay, okay?"

"Oh God… It's all around them. It's all wrong! I-I have no clarity. What the *hell* is out there?"

As if Alana had shouted their names, the two Guardians entered with Miles. "What is it?" her father asked.

"Something's not right. Get Lucy to open up, maybe help us find Gerhardt. There are too many lives at stake. We're going to the villa."

Thorn stood suddenly. "You'll be doing this blind. Only *inside* the villa is safe. Everywhere else is fair game for anything evil. You have to be careful."

Gripping her short-sword, Alana replied, "I always am."

****

In the upstairs hall, a muscular Italian Guardian moved aside as Miles entered. Laura had Lucy sitting up. The gag was off, and his wife held a glass of water.

"I've got hammers in my head," the woman moaned.

Miles checked the binding around her wrists and feet. "These intricate knots are surely Alana's work. My daughter could've been a boy scout."

"You can't hold me against my will, mister," Lucy quipped.

275

"I'll not suffer insolence, Miss Novak," he dryly stated. "Your part in this is unconscionable, and by law, considered kidnapping. As for following Leonard's orders without question, that stupid decision is on your soul."

"You're a Georgian," she muttered with a sneer. "Don't deny it."

"Why would I? Should we wash our hands of you, it will mean certain death. You are aware of that, are you not?"

"You're his wife."

"You aren't entirely evil, I sense, helping a dying child, even if it was for the wrong reasons," Laura said. "What a brazen undertaking for only one person."

Lucy's eyes shifted. "That's none of your business."

"It is entirely *my* business," Miles curtly informed. "Would you leave us, honey?"

"I'll close the door on my way out." Laura stopped in the threshold. "Listen to my husband, Miss Novak. The next step decides your destiny."

When alone, Miles studied Lucy. A pretty woman, he thought, very nervous, very much alone. Deepa Chandra's research paid off. Creating a viable psychological profile with such thorough information took no effort.

"You'll be released shortly. If we sense cooperation, Jillian's disappearance will remain out of the local authority's jurisdiction. Should you refuse the Council's assistance, we will, however, turn our backs on you. It's only a matter of time before we locate Gerhardt. Who killed Carol Reardon?" Lucy's lack of reaction heightened Miles's worry. "Answer my question, please."

"She was Jillian's first victim," Lucy huffed in a snippy fashion, "Jillian's a murderer in the eyes of the law."

"The law *per se* will never substantiate that tale. And we both know the beast-within is the killer—not an innocent girl. Can you imagine desecrating your own grandchild's soul to win favor from a thirteenth century vampire?" He added coldly, "You were Jillian's age when you met Leonard."

"What are you, a fucking mind reader?"

"What happens to Jillian after your rendezvous with Gerhardt in Florence?"

"You seem to know everything. Why don't you tell me?"

"What will he do when he realizes she isn't with you?"

"Leonard loves me."

"Leonard doesn't love you. He'll kill you faster than he chose to kill his granddaughter. Tell us about this event and we'll protect you, Miss Novak."

"You're a bastard, just like Michael Malone."

The accusation came off bitter, but tears stood in her eyes. "Think on my offer. I will pull it off the table very shortly." He left the room. Only then did all-consuming fear for his family grip Miles's chest like a vice.

****

Mother Anne stood in what had once been a medieval ballroom, a place of music and laughter. Now, it was stark, a consecrated sanctuary. Bleached white linens, starched and crisp, graced a simple wooden cot. Tonight's exorcism came into focus for her as Philip placed a steel box next to the sole piece of furniture. She sensed impervious walls around this new eternal prison for the entity within the innocent Jillian.

When the ex-Guardian left, she inclined her head to Monsignor Scarlatti, a gesture that was both warm and personal. Throughout fifty years of friendship, she had never seen such outrage in his caring eyes. "They're almost here. My sisters and I are ready. Are you, Sebastiano?"

"As I always am, Annie," he answered in a weary way.

****

Gabby carried a habit folded over an arm as she rushed in. "It's time. Put this on."

Full of queasiness, Celia swallowed her nerves. "Why?"

"It's blessed—and not as uncomfortable as it looks. The demon won't single you out by scent or sight in case anything goes loopy. Here. I'll help."

She quickly wiggled out of her dress, and Gabby slid the holy garb over her head. Latin prayers recited by every Catherine at the same moment in time came from both women's lips; words Celia didn't expect to know. The cincture tied around her waist, and over her short auburn hair, Gabby fitted the white cap, which fastened to a bib. More devout prayers began as a long black veil settled over the stiff wimple. Then the healer tied a heavy cotton smock over the habit.

"Why, Gabby," she asked.

"No baby scent allowed. Let's get him to the chapel. I'll take it off after the little guy's in Michael's arms." Celia trembled as she wrapped her son in a crocheted blanket and brought him to her breast. "Don't kiss him, Celia. Don't touch his skin."

"Of-of course, but I can hold him as tight as possible, right?"

"Squish him like a cuddle bear. We're taking the back way down. Just follow, okay? Everything's good."

With confident steps they hurried through the villa. Stone stairs, thick walls... The floor was smooth rock, yet their sandals fell silent. A heavy wooden door with an ancient iron latch led into a small sacristy. As if she stepped back in time, to the era when Catherine of Siena lived, goose bumps prickled her skin. Dozens of candles lit the chapel.

"There's no electricity in here, but you already know that," Gabby whispered.

Sweet incense filled Celia's lungs. Rejoicing at the tiny miracle so peaceful at her breast, she cradled her sleeping son as she took it all in. Each woodcarving, each marble statue looked familiar, and now she knew why. A sense of belonging swelled in her very old soul. *I've spent many lifetimes here. Sacred memories of a contemplative life, and each one welcomes me home.*

****

Lukas squinted, shifted behind the steering wheel. "I can't do this. It's like a maze and dark as hell!"

"You're fine."

To his left, a faint light glowed. He straightened his back. "What is that, a shack?"

"Look harder. Trust your senses."

Pride and love resonated in his father's calm voice. *Trust is easier said than done. How I wish I could...* Sitting up added inches to improve his sightline, but more apprehensive, his eyes blurred and burned as the Mercedes hit every pothole and bobbed like a boat in storm-driven waters. "I…I'm sorry, Dad. I can't."

"You're fine."

"I'm not fine."

"Yes, you are. I have tremendous faith in you, little boy."

He wanted to believe he could do this. Concentrating hard, he knew the girl was near death and he had to help her. Then, that decrepit shack he saw through the wrought iron gates seemed to transform into a hidden castle. "Whoa," he breathed out.

"Pull up close."

Skidding to a stop next to a huge old car, he jumped out to open the back door. His father's long frame unfolded out with Jillian secure against his chest. Then the front door opened, and a blond monk nodded to his father. Once inside, Lukas sensed he shouldn't follow, and stared directly into the ex-Guardian's eyes.

"Neat robe," he said with a weary grin, "I like the hood."

"You've grown at least half a foot since that crazy night in Manhattan. How've you been?" With a hand on his shoulder, Philip led him into an old-fashioned parlor.

"I'm good," Lukas replied, craning his neck back toward the foyer.

"Give him a sec, and hand over the key."

He let out a whiny, drawn out "Why?"

From behind, a familiar arm instantly had him locked in a hug. "Because I love you, and I'm proud of you, and you don't have a driver's license." His father shook Philip's hand but didn't let him go.

"You look good, Michael, and it's only been two weeks."

"Trust me, it feels like two years. I'll call Alana when this is over. Take the Mercedes back to Siena. It's a sweet ride, Phil. The two of you can compare driving experiences," he added with a frown. Kissing the top of his head, his father added, "The monk drives. And this time, you stay put in the student house until I return."

Even though it sounded parental, Lukas couldn't help the wide grin.

****

From the villa's door, Michael watched his son leave. He closed it and twisted the key in the lock knowing Lukas was in the very best of hands with an ex-Guardian who was a peaceful man—and deadly with a silver blade. Then, as if expected, he turned to face someone coming down the center staircase.

The Sister dipped her head in recognition. Dark, beautiful eyes held his gaze as he gave a slight bow of humble respect. He had seen her in his dream of survival. Tall and stately, the healer's tranquility made him feel as though he stood in the presence of a saint.

"*Buona sera, Campione,*" she whispered.

"*Buona sera, Sorella Rosalinda,*" he replied with a deeper bow. He followed many steps behind as she led him through the parlor and into the villa's chapel.

Once there, he didn't know where to look first. An art connoisseur's dream, the history of this sacred room piqued his interest, captured his imagination as well. Images of angels lined the wall, Seraphim, Cherubim, and the fiercest defenders of Heaven. Each icon, each stone knave... Twelve carved pews leading to a stone altar were individual masterpieces. Still in awe, standing at the entrance to the chapel, he studied the petite nun by the tabernacle. She faced a magnificent crucifix with her head aimed high. As Gabby motioned him forward, he realized the baby was in the tiny nun's arms. "Where is Celia, Gabby," he asked with deep concern as his long strides brought him to her.

"See," Gabby said to the nun, "I told you. No recognizable scent."

When the sister turned to face him, Celia's green eyes were full of tears. "You...you won't let go—no matter what happens?"

Affection for her filled his heart and it took a moment to find his voice. "Before God, I swear I will not let him go." He'd never seen the gentle psychic so distraught as when she placed her baby in his arms.

"Talk to him, okay? He likes it when you talk to him."

He nodded, swallowed hard as Gabby removed the heavy smock Celia wore. As the new mother used the habit's broad, black cuffs to dry her eyes, he sensed more than distress and left the altar with Uriel cradled in his arms.

Michael sat in the front pew as the babe's wide eyes shot to his. The silence of the stone chapel felt like a cocoon. "Will you be a formidable warrior in our mystical army," he whispered. So precious, so small, he thought, with a destiny already written by the angels. His gaze shifted to the high, stained-glass windows bathed in candlelight. "We're surrounded by Champions, little one. Each archangel had a significant role in the war against eternal evil."

Then a lone wolf's howl penetrated the walls, and the babe startled.

Chapter 23

Leonard wanted his sacrifice back. He knew the villa wasn't a shack, sensed mystical protection of its grounds. A grove of gnarled trees became his parlor-trick of an enchanted shield. The talisman on his chest would summon forth his creations, demonic minions to retrieve the host vessel.

A spell, written in Cyril's hand, could reshape matter, and animal blood magic held inimitable power when used by such a gifted wizard as himself. Thirteen demons would multiply on *his* command. With a wave of a hand, the villa was revealed. *Whatever these so-called holy healers think they'll do to my sacrifice will not work.* Because fifty-four crucifixes had been gathered. Dead or alive, Jillian would come to him.

And elevating his status to the echelon of sorcerer was right on schedule.

****

Philip drove slowly over the rutted road, the villa no longer visible in his rear-view mirror. "Are you sure they'll be safe?" Lukas asked.

"I walked around the villa twice before we left; didn't sense anything in the shadows." Less than a minute later, they heard it... a chorus of unnatural howls. "Oh no. Good Lord... And now the dreaded gray mist descends. Close your window."

Lukas hit the button, watched it ascend. "So where

are they?"

"My guess is all around us." An enormous wolf appeared, and Philip hit the brakes. Stretching out of its skin to stand upright, bones shifted, creating an unnatural thing with a long snout and longer fangs. With another sinister snort, its front paws morphed into clawed weapons. "Uh-oh, it's Hell-beast time, but don't worry. This car is like a German tank."

"No way is that a Hell-beast. It doesn't look like the ones my dad fought last May."

"Because it's a wizard's pitiful attempt to alter body mass… So where are the swords?"

"In the trunk."

"Then we've got a problem."

"No! Just friggin' run it over!"

"Don't get annoyed and learn to cooperate," he said in an even tone.

More appeared through the murky mist. "Oh, shit," Lukas mumbled.

"I'd lay odds that we've got wolves infected with demon. Help would be nice."

"How far away from Siena are we?"

"A couple of miles, but they're not straight ones by any means."

"Why are these things here?"

"To stop an exorcism, which isn't on my agenda tonight." The huge mutant sprang, and Philip floored the Mercedes. It slid up the windshield and clear off the trunk, landing on its feet. He executed a tight veer between gnarled trees. Fast and accurate, they neared a clearing and he pulled over. Headlights appeared, and he grinned. "Take a look. We've got company." Gunning it, all four tires screeched as they made a quick U-turn and raced after the other car.

"Awesome! Uh, is it who I think it is?"

"*His* Guardian to the rescue… I hope Ally's a better driver now than she was in Manhattan."

"Hey, you miss every pothole. I almost hit the trees before."

"Years of dodging some serious craters in New Jersey. Watch and learn. In a week, I'd have you driving like a pro. But isn't fifteen too young for a legal license in Italy?"

"Yeah, well, I got curious," Lukas replied as they sped along.

"Curiosity, huh." He veered hard to the left clipping a loping Hell-beast with a hard thud to the headlight.

"That thing looked way weird. Think it's like, full demon?"

"Maybe yes, maybe no." The car skidded on loose dirt to a sideways stop, right where it had been parked before.

"That was cool."

"That was luck." Blowing out a long breath, he faced his passenger. "Where did you say the swords are?" Lukas aimed a thumb over his shoulder, and Philip popped the trunk from inside. With one strong tug, the ex-Guardian's brown robe tore to reveal a black T-shirt and trousers. "Stay in the car. Michael wouldn't want you in this."

"You don't know that! I'm fighting."

He jumped out before Philip could stop him. "Inhuman speed," he said, "now let's pray he's got inhuman strength." A familiar weapon was already in Lukas's hand by the time he stood at the trunk. "Isn't that your father's broadsword?"

"Yeah. Now it's mine," Lukas answered as he turned and skewered a lunging Hell-beast directly through the heart. And crouching, the teen looked ready for another.

Philip grabbed a much lighter broadsword from the trunk. Springing out of the small red car, Neeb shouted a warning, and Lukas nicked another attacker. Wounded and howling it lurched away as he shouted to Alana, "Are we killing them or taking them out of commission?"

Over snapping and snarling, she hollered, "That depends. Some aren't fully shifted."

"Does it make a difference?" Lukas asked him.

"If they aren't fully shifted, there's hope for their souls. I'd let them live." Philip glanced to his right. Some crazed, clawed creature was trying to climb the wall by a stained-glass window. With silver swords drawn, Neeb and Petula were heading its way.

Sizing up another snarling attacker, Alana shouted, "Use those mystical senses, Lu. Become one with the animal mind. Ow," she whined, grabbing her arm. "It clawed me! The nerve of that demon thing..." After rolling her right shoulder, she chased it down.

A wild-eyed, half-changed creature salivated, ready to leap. With a wild roar, Lukas charged. It shifted direction in retreat. "Okay. Now I got it," he shouted. When the next mutant lunged with speed, he skewered it through the heart. As the Hell-beast sank, a black mist rose. Its features morphed and a gutted wolf lay at Lukas's feet.

Philip patted his shoulder. "Good move. Keep it up." Then he heard Alana yell, "Where are you

Leonard? An unsuspecting child, an unsuspecting animal… Nothing's sacred to you!"

****

As soon as Michael heard the first ungodly howl, he knew that Philip had turned the car around and that his son was in this battle. So was Alana and two other ex-Guardians. He fumbled with a blue ribbon clipped to the pacifier. When Uri sucked it into his tiny mouth, he thought a sweet "thank you" had sounded in his ear. And when hellish howls reclaimed his concentration, the baby spit the thing out again. "So much for peace and tranquil meditation," he whispered.

This time, he held it to the infant's lips, but kicking and cranking, Uri turned his head away. With the babe tight to his chest, he walked over to the chapel's side aisle closest to the outer wall. "I know he's strong, but I'm his father. I'm allowed to worry." Squirming in his arms, the babe studied the smooth stones as if he also knew what was happening right outside. A chubby hand stretched out when the howling swelled again.

"I know. Conjured Hell-beasts," he whispered. His gaze swept up colored glass that formed the archangel's weapon, similar to his own trusted broadsword. Lucifer in the form of a snake lay at the archangel's feet. "You won't get her. Not as long as I live and breathe. Unnatural forces at work, demons and the mystical warriors who slay them… We'll send you all home to Hell."

When the mystical healers' demanding prayers began, Michael walked down the side aisle, leaned against the chapel door with a groan. Restless, worried, and unable to stay in one place, long, smooth strides took him to the first alcove's mural. An eerie feeling began—seeing that the saint's face was the spitting image of Celia's.

When a new chant rose from the great hall, full attention turned back to Jillian. Sickened and sad, it was death rattling in her chest. Even at this distance, he heard it. He sensed it. He stared at the distant altar in the chapel. "It's on my soul. I could have stopped this long before it got this bad. Please don't let her die," he prayed as he rocked Celia's son. "Come on, Jillian, fight like hell."

****

The howling didn't sway Monsignor Scarlatti's resolve. Holy water had been sprinkled around the great room and on all its inhabitants. A man of purpose, he was forever cautious and mystically strong of soul. With his straight shoulders draped in a purple stole, he repeatedly summoned the entity forth. *This child purposely brought herself to seizure, which mercifully shut down her dying body. But death will not end this demon. It will jump to any wavering soul to desecrate another life.* Just as she had last May, Gabriella stood at his side with silver broadsword in hand. When the final disruption began, the healers guided Jillian's mind to sanctuary. "Lead her not into temptation," he intoned.

"Deliver her from evil," they replied.

Jillian's eyes opened, but it was the beast-within leering at him. "You will have no victory. You cannot take root." Her heartbeat sputtered as his oiled thumb marked her forehead.

The cold-forged iron box rested at his feet. Inside the sarcophagus, ancient glyphs had been pounded through the petals of lilies on all six sides. This tomb could not be opened, nor was it necessary. And when the beast-within gasped mouthfuls of incensed air, Jillian's battered body arched off the bed as if it were the entity's last effort to escape.

It was drawn into its new tomb. Mystical words inscribed on its walls paralyzed it. And when the Sire, its origin was destroyed, immortal oblivion awaited. As he draped his purple sash over its sarcophagus, he said to Celia, "Now you may take your son from the Champion's arms."

****

Celia followed Sister Rosalinda with anticipation in her heart. Exhausted as she was, to get to her baby her steps were quick. Many lifetimes spent in prayer and meditation had perhaps prepared her for tonight, but Thorn's urgent concern pierced her soul with such speed that her heart ached. *Tortured animals are howling in madness, and a girl is still very close to death. We're safe*, she said to him in her mind, *but there's so much more to do.*

Rosalinda opened the chapel door, and Celia ran to her son. When Michael placed him in her arms, she breathed a sigh of love, of blessed relief, and she could barely whisper "Thank you."

Unable to form a word, Michael inclined his head to her. Then he followed Sister Rosalinda through the chapel doors. Always three feet ahead, her spry step allowed his long strides. They came through the parlor, crossed the stone foyer into the great room. A narrow path to Jillian cleared, and his approach slowed.

Nestled in white linen, her face was as pale as humanly possible. Erratic heartbeats meant life slipping away. Glaring down at the iron box with murder in his eyes, cold hatred filled his soul.

"You feel it. The entity seeks an end to its suffering. Only the sire's death will return it to the eternal fires of Hell. Our part is done, Champion. Touch the child and sense her soul," Mother Anne whispered.

Kneeling next to Jillian, he saw a young girl his son's age. When he took her cold hand in his, he sensed her very essence as if they were still connected. "Mother, she's dying. I didn't succeed."

"Is the beast within her?"

"No. But a child is not meant to die so young."

The healers formed an unbroken circle around the three of them. In a rare moment of acceptance, he became aware of some very familiar faces. The six sisters who had removed the beast-within from his own tortured soul came into focus. The ancient Labbiel who had saved Thorn's life stood with Rosalinda. Another individual from his dream of survival, disfigured from a brutal fire that had killed her mother—over fifty years ago. The one called Aurea, who in his dream had led him to the tranquil oasis of his sisters' grave beneath the lilacs. So much had been revealed in my complex fantasy of salvation, he thought, and now they have all shown themselves to me as they save Jillian.

Mother Anne called his name. He blinked, came out of his memories to meet her gaze. "When she awakens, we will not be present. That's why you were summoned."

"I'm sorry. I don't understand."

"We have freed her soul. The doctor who cares for the injured Guardian will take over to heal her physical wounds. But be aware. The evil man still wants her, Michael, dead or alive."

And that will not happen, he thought, holding on to Jillian's cold hand. The fragile nature of human life, the finality of human death had become crystal clear. Mother Anne placed her hand over theirs, and as her grip tightened, so did his chest.

"Another life is unfinished," he whispered.

"A child with a God-given talent, typical insecurities and wonderful dreams," she replied.

He closed his eyes and absorbed it all.

Chapter 24

Standing ready with the others, Alana and Lukas both saw Leonard at the same time. She whispered, "I hold him while you rip that thing off his neck."

Lukas gave a quick nod. "I can do that." He bent down, grabbed another mutant creature by the scruff of its neck and hurled it to Petula. When the Guardian put the suffering animal out of its misery with a sword through its heart, he shouted, "Many thanks, Pet."

"Don't mention it, Lu," she called back.

Crouched like a cat about to pounce, Alana stopped under the last stained-glass window. "The others will keep the Hell-beasts busy so we can get to him."

At her side, Lukas muttered, "I can't wait to take him down."

About to move, they heard the faraway whisper, "*Lucy allowed this to happen. Johanna should have taken the dead fool's place.*"

"Who the hell's Johanna?"

"Probably another one of his flunkies... Not something to worry about," Alana replied.

Then Leonard added, "*You took my inheritance, vampire, and now I will take yours.*"

"What did he just say?"

"More loony rants because I think he's losing it." She was ready for action. Suddenly, Leonard's narrow eyes seemed to glow through the darkness with his hand around something on his chest. Every creature howled in a maddening, choral frenzy. "I can't wait to see what you're holding, Leonard," she bit out.

"Mom, look at that huge one over there. Phil hit it with the car, but it just slid off." The creature snapped back its head as if listening to something. "What's it doing?"

"I don't know, Lu."

Then it snorted in their direction. Its eyes glowed evil with saliva dripping off long fangs, and picking up speed, it avoided the tip of Neeb's sword in full retreat. An uneasy feeling crept up Alana's spine. Her hand automatically shot out across Lukas's chest. "Stay perfectly still."

Petula suddenly shouted, "Bloody hell! Where did it go," while Neeb cursed loud and long.

Alana watched the remaining mutant Hell-beasts close in around the three Guardians. Philip gripped his sword and shook his head. "How did they know to do this?" Phil asked.

"I don't like it. Not one bloody bit," Neeb muttered.

"That makes two of us," Petula said.

Phil whispered, "I know animals, Pet. These things are being controlled. He's near."

"So... Our wannabe-sorcerer came for the show. What could possibly be on their little, devious minds?"

"To keep us occupied?"

"Ya think?" Petula smirked, and then said in a sing-song way, "Very bad little doggies."

Neeb snuck a sideway's glance. "Don't talk to them, luv."

"Why?"

"They're full of demon—not dog."

"I'll wager a coordinated effort brings them tumbling down," Petula replied.

Alana thought the strategy brilliant as they made a choreographed lunge. She turned to Lukas. "When I call out, run fast and yank that silly piece of jewelry off Leonard's neck."

"Shouldn't we help them first?"

"They've tangled with Hell-beasts before, and they know what to do. Just remember. *Not* until I call out to you." As black mist rose from shriveling carcasses, she sprinted to the grove of trees. The vision of tainted souls streaming out of innocent animals filled her with rage. Watching with pride, she saw Lukas hug the wall, ready for her order. Then she crept up behind Leonard.

Gerhardt spun around, facing her with a sneer.

"You crazy son of a bitch," she hissed.

In the blink of an eye, he seemed to disappear, only to reappear out of reach. Then, Gerhardt twisted the object in his hand and grinned.

A piercing scream shifted her focus. Snarling jaws of the huge Hell-beast clamped Lukas's right leg, dragging him to Leonard. On the gravel, Lukas twisted with another scream, and bones crunched in its jaws as the creature shook him like a rag doll. Each terrified cry heightened her desire to forget about Leonard and run to Lukas. Then the rancid stench of an impenetrable mist descended, as if to snag Alana in an unexpected maelstrom of inertia.

She heard a snicker. "It won't let go. Not until I have what is mine."

Pure panic propelled her forward. With a perfectly aimed, paralyzing jab to the old man's chest, the glass amulet shattered. The air began to vibrate as the mist lifted. The huge Hell-beast holding on to Lukas morphed into a once majestic wolf before collapsing—on top of him. As the dying animal howled in pain, she shoved the wannabe sorcerer with uncontrolled fierceness. He flew through the air, and at the wolf's final yelp, Leonard Gerhardt landed next to Michael's son. She sprinted forward. Her boot pinned his chest to the ground.

"I have marked him for death," the wannabe wizard shrieked.

With no mercy left in her, she yelled, "Shut up! Or I swear, I'll kill you."

Neeb ran over, and with one heave, he sent the dead wolf crashing into the chapel wall. Then the Guardian knelt next to Lukas, who was writhing in pain and crying, holding his bleeding leg.

But hatred had swelled within Alana as never before, and the tip of her short-sword was aimed at the center of Leonard Gerhardt's chest, poised to run through his evil heart.

****

Some feet away, Petula swiped blood off her cheek. "I count thirteen dead wolves in all." Then her eyes shot to the tree line. Animals appeared, but not the tainted kind. Timid and submissive, deer and wolves approached. An impressive buck with a huge rack of antlers came last, giving the dead carcasses a wide berth. "What is this? Bloody reinforcements?"

"I don't think so. Read their stance," Philip replied, swiping his brow.

"I'll wager they need a bit of Heavenly action to let them know we understand. Don't you agree, Father?"

"I'm a monk, not a priest, Pet," he replied with a grin.

"But you can give a blessing, can't you?"

He fully smiled. "I certainly can."

"This is a Francis of Assisi moment, enough to melt my animal loving heart." The tip of Petula's sword met the ground as she hummed an old hymn.

In a bloodied black undershirt and ripped trousers, Philip blessed each animal with one hand resting on the soft, silky patch of fur between peaked ears. Then pointing to the prone old man, he shouted, "Guard!" After cantering to their assignment, the canines among them snapped and snarled at Leonard. The fierce buck stood poised over Lukas as if it were guarding him.

****

When Michael opened his eyes, he was alone with Jillian in the great room. Jillian's fingers twitched and her hands warmed as her heart pumped steady. He heard someone humming the hymn Thorn had alluded to before this event began. He also heard cries and hitched sobs coming from his son.

Suddenly, she took a labored breath, and before she could speak, he whispered, "Don't be afraid. You've been in a terrible car accident, but I've got you now." With care, he scooped her up into his arms and hurried to the open door of the villa.

The scent of his son's blood, the sight of Neeb lifting him off the ground with Petula at his side all came at him at once. Looking past the buck, he saw his son's bloody leg—and then the rage on Alana's face. It matched what he felt as he walked over and glared down at the wizard, saying full of bitterness, "Miserable bastard—you took mine now I'll take yours? What kind of hocus-pocus shit is that?"

Leonard's lips began to move, and Alana yelled, "What are you gonna do now? Put a whammy on him, you fool?" Her weapon at Leonard's throat drew a trickle of blood. "I told you before to shut up. You should have listened. Say another word and 1 will slit your throat wide open."

Michael had never seen Alana so over the top, and calmly whispered, "We have more to do, my Guardian, and we need him alive." Her nod came too slow for his liking, and when he whispered her name, she threw down her short-sword and ran to his son.

As Leonard's hand shot to his throat, Michael warned, "Do not dare to move because I *will* kill you. Look at your granddaughter in my arms. Look at what you did to *your* inheritance."

He heard Alana ordering, "Pet, get the maniac back to the student house. Tie him up and knock his teeth out if he tries anything." Looking over, she shouted, "Did you hear that, Leonard? Do something stupid and she'll have a field day on your ugly face."

Grateful for these seasoned warriors, Michael met Neeb carrying his son to the Mercedes, and continued to hold Jillian tight to his chest. Standing at the red car, Alana was talking to Phil. Then the ex-Guardian nodded once and gave a loud, two-fingered whistle. When Petula gunned the engine, the wolves formed an escort at the sides of the red car as it drove down the rutted road away from the villa. No vampire would impede the lone Guardian's path to Siena. Next to Phil at the villa's door, only the buck remained a proud, stately guard.

Disgust was etched on her face before she turned

away. At her side, he said in a calm tone, "It's all right. He'll self-heal."

"I should have locked Lu in the car. I misjudged this part, Michael. Three teenagers took the brunt of this man's lunacy, Jillian, Mick, and our son." Slowly, her gaze rested on Jillian, tight in his arms. "Nightmares will haunt her life forever," she whispered.

"We'll make sure that doesn't happen." To tenderly kiss every fear from Alana's heart, to see Lukas and Mick instantly healed, to send Jillian back in time before such madness began—every wish burned inside his heart.

She palmed her eyes. "How is she?"

"Light as a feather and fast asleep, thank God. She cannot stay here."

"I'm getting that. I'll drive...very carefully."

His grin could've been a loving embrace. As she settled behind the wheel, Michael leaned against the car as Phil approached. "There's a huge buck watching you."

"I know."

"Made new friends, I see."

"I love animals. They respond to me. So I assume we'll join you in Siena as soon as the monsignor is ready to leave?"

"Bring Celia and son with you...and my broadsword."

"You got it. In case you're wondering, Lukas was amazing. You'd better go."

Michael sat next to Neeb, and Philip closed the car door. Then he studied the fresh tears in his son's eyes, and said to Neeb, "I'll trade one little girl for one little boy."

"Not a problem, Sir."

It took a bit of maneuvering, but they made the switch. As Alana drove away from Villa Catherine, Lukas buried his face against Michael's neck. Pride and panic simultaneously surfaced. Rubbing his son's narrow back, he hugged him tight and eyed the bald man scrunched low with Jillian in his arms. "You're very tall."

"Six-six, Sir," Neeb replied in a soft voice.

"After what just went down, lose the sir and call me Michael."

****

Goodbyes had been said, and dressed in jeans and a pink sweater, Celia felt more herself. After Phil loaded the iron box into the huge trunk, he took the diaper bag from her saying, "Mother and child in the back." She smiled, kissed his cheek after he took the baby from her. "Celia B, I've missed you. You look great."

"This thing is a boat."

"I learned to drive on a Caddy way back when."

"Oooh, yeah... I liked our visits to your uncle's ranch. Every summer in Ulster County... Jeez, to be fifteen again and clueless about demons or twisted humans who would kill their kin for sorcerer-status..."

He settled her in the back seat as Monsignor Scarlatti sat in the front. Lifeless animals that Gerhardt sacrificed sickened both of them. Guardians would come and burn their misshapen bodies. As he started the car, she whispered, "He destroyed their souls, too."

"Evil tampering with innocents," the monsignor said.

"You got that right," Celia whispered with her son cradled to her breast.

Chapter 25

Veronique tore into the vein of tonight's second victim. The twin was already dead weight in her slender arms. Then she drained and dropped him on the floor of her exquisite boudoir. A scream of rage welled in her throat. The back of an ivory wrist swiped her crimson lips. "Bitter. Not like the other. Twins should taste the same."

But tonight, no mere mortal quenched her thirst. The sire eased off the bed. Fisting the other body's head of blond hair, she flung the muscular man out into the quiet hall. Naked and free, she began to pace between an ornate dresser and heavily draped balcony doors.

"I smell you—daring to watch my window, daring to study *this* immortal being. I should drain you all one by one." Guardians everywhere…More than she had ever sensed before. Not fully rattled, she was confident that after tomorrow's sunset, a special child of the night would be created. *A bold siring with a beast already ensconced in her soul. Her journey to undeath will be cause for celebration.* She whispered, "A formal ball… I may just do that."

With a slow sashay into the video room, the Sire stretched and preened in front of a pre-set camera. Her digital image filled the entire wall, and she studied her eternal beauty, her femininity, and captivating features.

"Truly, I'm the vampire queen of the new

millennium. To have survived The Dark Ages only to rule in The Era of Technology brings such intense pleasure. Cyril was a fool to not embrace contemporary life." She strolled away. "The son destroys the father. The origin mourns her loss only to retrieve what is rightfully hers." Bright amber eyes shone with devious joy as she sighed, "Ah, Michael."

Donning a red silk robe that clung to her snowy skin, she glided down the marble staircase. A cunning smile crossed her ruby lips when she reached the indoor pool. Her robe fluttered to the marble; a solitary toe scraped the steaming waters. She craved heat to make the blood warm in her veins as if she still lived. And warmth always led to other naughty pleasures.

****

Lucy's wrists hadn't been bound tight, but the melodrama of rubbing them with a pained expression on her face while the Georgian and a handsome Guardian watched thrilled her to no end.

"You may choose to refresh yourself, and then proceed downstairs. There is a contingent waiting to take you to Portofino," Miles Bookman informed.

Purposely, she aimed a sarcastic grin. "You can't hold me against my will. You're not the soul police." Shaking her short blonde hair, she primped in a fashion-conscious way.

He untied her ankles. "I highly doubt that either Leonard or Veronique will allow you to live. The liability issue should weigh heavily on your mind at this moment. Don't walk away, Miss Novak. No ordinary human can protect you."

She met his stare with annoyance. "Instead of being all gloom and doom, why don't you save the lecture for someone who believes in innocence and guilt? You don't scare me, old man."

"I most certainly do." In Italian, he told the Guardian, "Let her pass when she's ready. She has free will. It is not our intention to persuade otherwise." The hunk gave a stoic nod, stepped back with a casual lean against the threshold.

"You heard the man. Stay away from me." Lucy stretched when she stood. Her legs felt weak, and she shot him an angry pout before strutting down the hall. She liked intense features on a man, but after the demoralizing encounter with Michael Malone, she left opportunity behind and slammed shut the bathroom door.

Cool water splashing her face felt good. A shower would be nice, she thought while looking in the mirror. But what Bookman said made her shudder. *And being held by these people makes me a big-ass liability.* Would Leonard's vampire friends smell the Georgians on her? "Shit. I hope not," she mumbled. The possibility that Leonard had used her brought disappointed tears. She bit back a sob. Rubbing her eyes, her hands shook. This time, she scooped up the cold water to drench her face, and then rubbed her skin raw when she dried it.

Walking out, she sauntered past the Guardian, held her head high. She came down the stairs the same way. Going for the front door, she avoided the stare from a huge hulk of a man with a head of curly red hair at the living room window. Her hand clenched the knob, already tasting freedom.

"I'd rethink your decision. Taking proper care of the girl won't save your soul, but it does carry a few brownie points."

An eyebrow rose. "What are you, another mind reader or something? Go to hell."

"Been there, done that," he sadly replied. "You're only secure with a blank canvas and a picture to copy. At a tender age, he seduced you, replaced the father who beat you and your mother for years. That's how she died. What an intriguing offer—to study in Siena with all expenses paid. You picked up Italian like you'd been born here. You'll be dead before sunrise."

"Stop it, you freak!" As hard as she tried, she couldn't turn the glass knob. She shut her eyes tight. Michael Malone and the embarrassing near-seduction filled her head.

"He wouldn't have touched you, certainly not in that way. And trust me, Lucy, he will protect you."

Leaning against the door, she stared at the carpet. It felt as if the beefy man's eyes drilled clear through to her soul. She wanted to run upstairs and crawl in a bed that smelled like Michael Malone, but her feet didn't budge.

"Lucy, follow your heart," he gently whispered.

She set her jaw and replied, "That's what got me into this mess in the first place." After a sharp tug, the knob twisted. She walked out. Three Guardians were waiting. With a bitter glare, she walked the other way. Somewhere inside there were tears, but they didn't surface.

Three streets over, she entered her favorite bar. Sitting in the dark back booth, Lucy ordered a bottle of vodka. Someone she considered a friend brought over a glass with two cubes of ice. In fluent Italian, she whispered, "You know I'm good for it. I'll be fine,

Sal."

"Those men last night were trouble. Why do you lower yourself? Ah, *Lucia mia*," he sang in a resonant tenor voice, "I care about you."

"Don't bother," she replied, trying to forget that last conversation as a hostage.

Glass after glass went down easy. After five shots on an empty stomach, her head dropped to the table. The bar was a blur. So was Salvatore as he walked over and took the bottle from her hand. "You're in big trouble, *Lucia mia*. I'm no dummy. I know I'm right." Her head bobbed up and the dull-eyed look confirmed how soon she'd be on the floor. "Call me a fool, but I like you too much to let you go," he softly crooned like a Venetian gondolier. "I gave you my crucifix last night, didn't I?"

With an arm around her waist, Salvatore pulled her out of the booth. She recognized the stockroom and knew they were taking the back door out. "*Madonna mia*, it doesn't take a genius to see something's wrong, eh?" At the end of the street, he steered her through a doorway and up a narrow flight of stairs. Then she sank down onto a worn sofa. "A pot of coffee instead of a beer would do us both some good."

Lucy blinked her eyes and narrowed them to focus. He stood far, far away by a kitchen counter, holding an electric pot and a long black cord. In her current state, it resembled a snake—a slithering snake that'd turn into a vampire and kill her right in Salvatore's home! She shook her woozy head and caught Sal's groan as he pulled something out of his pocket.

"How come I get voice mail," she heard him say with a laugh. "I know you're up, *cugino mio*, you have pep up your ass at midnight and you won't get punchy until dawn. Where are you when I need you, eh? Bring me a milk before you go home." He left the phone on the counter, sat on a green kitchen chair. "*Lucia mia*, are you still with me, *bella*?"

Her eyes closed and her face met the sofa cushion.

****

Alana drove the Mercedes through Siena's narrow streets, stopping at the closest point where the back door of the sedan could open to let them out. A local Guardian took the wheel as others flanked Michael and Neeb racing toward the student house's front entrance. If any nosy neighbors peeked out a window, they wouldn't recall what they saw, anyway.

Mystical events were like that; never seen by the innocent's eye.

After Neeb ran up the stairs holding Jillian, Michael followed with Lukas in his arms. Petula met her in the living room. "Nigel's got old Lenny tied up right proper in the basement, Ally. Oh, and I indulged in a bit of pick-pocketing. Looks like a room key. Shall we venture a guess and say the rusty old battle-axe has been under our noses the whole time? Imagine the nerve of that cheeky fox."

Alana gave a slight grin, hiding the onslaught of emotions ready to surface. "Evil has balls. We'll check it out later." In perfect Italian, she updated the group of Guardians waiting in the kitchen.

****

In Manhattan's Georgian penthouse, Deepa Chandra led Mary Kendrick into her study. "Miles just called with the news."

"The girl is safe?" Mary asked.

"Gerhardt's plans are curtailed and the death of an age-old Sire is imminent."

"That's why I called."

"You are a woman of distinct talents," Deepa said as they sat.

"From a long line of witches who understand how forces in the universe can be manipulated either for good or evil. I've come to help."

"Your mother Martha is well known to the Georgians."

"Wait till you see what my daughter can do."

Deepa smiled. "We are all thankful you've chosen good over evil."

Mary returned an open grin. "My family goes way back with Michael, Miss Chandra."

"Please call me Deepa. I've read about Martha's connection to him."

Mary gave a graceful nod. "Mother met him as a child in great-granny's arms some thirty-odd years after he didn't bite necks anymore. She still adores him."

"He can be quite charming."

The Council knew of the Kendrick Witches' allegiance to the Champion. These three women had kept Thorn safe for eight days while Michael was NWT's poisoned prisoner. She met Mary's gaze. "I look forward to working with you. My frustration with finding every last member of Gerhardt's cult is growing."

"A few nights ago, Mother decided to get... involved, should I say? We aren't joiners, Deepa, we're doers." Mystical ability radiated from the impeccably dressed art dealer. Crossing her legs in an elegant manner, Mary appeared at ease, her large olive eyes astute. "We did some research of our own. This is out of loyalty to Michael—not because I'm about to get religion." The wry smile was also sincere.

"I have no trouble with a difference of belief. Miles has high regard for your family."

"Mother likes him, too. I think it's an ageless attraction to tall men with accents. So let's talk Gerhardt. He moved in many circles, all bad and unrealistically grandiose. The phony artwork gave this whole mess a nice twist and made the Georgians chase their tails. That marble knight, well, it's a different story."

Deepa leaned forward with a quiet, "How so?"

"In the 1300s, Slovakian Knights had busts carved by Christian monks. Set in the legendary mythic circle, they grouped into twelve, like the original apostles. After Cyril was sired by Veronique, he absconded with his marker, leaving the circle broken. Leonard must have found it at the sire's estate. Mother believes he got his paws on an ancient diary with some serious voodoo attached. I think the stone bust was sent to the monsignor on purpose, and as long as it and this diary are out there, pieces of the event remain hidden, like Leonard's personal 'up-yours' to your Georgian Council."

"I'll inform the monsignor. I'm sure the grave marker will be returned if the burial site is found. But as for a diary, I highly doubt such a tome exists. His hotel room will be taken apart." Deepa settled back in the chair. "This twisted worship of vampires is another outrage."

"The way I see it, the event is like a reversal within a reversal, a conundrum that didn't make sense—until

Mother had a look-see at Gerhardt's chalet. She found this." Mary handed over a rolled print. "It looks like M. C. Escher's *Heaven and Hell* but check out the edges of the wings. I decode faster than any Georgian, Deepa."

"It's a fractal."

"More like pay dirt, exposing everyone in Gerhardt's little dark world. Whoever sketched this is talented, but I'm better. Take out the magnifying glass in your top drawer and look closer."

Deepa didn't appear shocked. This good witch had the ability to see thought like the empath. She studied the print. "My God, around each wing miniscule letters, but pull away and they become shadows."

"You have to hold it up to a mirror to get the full effect. Local politicians, movers and shakers in DC, performers, businessmen… You name it. All networked worshipers in the name of Cyril. I'd like to get the goods on each one, but a sudden burst of mass exposure will ruin our economy. Together, we can make sure it's done the right way, slow and without loopholes."

"Finding this is much appreciated. We'll proceed with caution."

"I believe the Georgians have a huge task now, however, giving the Devil his due just got a hell of a lot easier." She stood, stately and unassuming. "What do you say we forget the late hour and usher in this Good Friday a little early? Give me a table and place to plug in my laptop. You make a pot of coffee, and I'll make a list that'll keep Guardians busy for the next year. Even though Celia's party won't be happening, we'll still take a trip to Portofino and hand Miles an Easter basket chock full of dirty bunnies."

"Yes, of-of course. I'm still in awe. Thank you."

"Okay. I'll confess. That trip part is Mother's suggestion. You'd figure after seventy-two years the woman would get over her thing for Michael Malone."

Chapter 26

The Medico Labs helicopter touched down in an empty corner of the bus depot's parking lot. "Vampires appearing out of nowhere… That's never a good sign," Arthur Chamberlain said to Johnny Baker, his senior assistant. "Stay ready for my call. These creatures don't want innocents tonight. They want Georgians and Guardians of Souls." Baker nodded as four mystical warriors flanked the doctor. They hustled him to the student house. Chamberlain knew the injured Guardian would heal. But Miles's call confirmed the girl was in bad shape. So was Michael's son.

****

Breathing a sigh of relief, Phyllis Verdi kissed her blessed habit and changed into jeans and an old black sweater. Her sisters would keep the students asleep until the house was quiet again. Now she could focus on Mick's wound, which would heal quicker if she touched the incision.

Walking into the young Guardian's room, she smiled at the older woman, placed a gentle hand on her shoulder. The healer sent a silent message. No harm would come to the teenager. Phyllis knew she'd hear the words in her native tongue. Backing away, the woman's eyes misted as she blessed herself.

Touching torn skin, muscle and tissue began to seal, and his eyes fluttered open. "Stay relaxed,

Guardian. No more heroics for at least a week. You'll be in Doc Chamberlain's care shortly."

With a glassy stare, he whispered, "Thank you, Mum."

Phyllis turned to the woman. *"Very good work, doctor, now please follow me."*

As they walked down the hall, the doctor's perceptive gaze lit on Neeb's bloody arm. *"Animale,"* she said, then with a click of her tongue added, *"Lupo!"*

They entered the small room as Phyllis answered, *"Yes, you understand these are unnatural wounds, but please hurry. Go to the child. I cannot help her the way you can. I'm not a doctor."* Further explanation wasn't necessary, and Phyllis watched the doctor assess Jillian's condition.

Seconds later, Chamberlain dropped his medical backpack on the mattress and grinned. "Is this a bedroom or a closet?"

She smiled. "Hello, Arthur. Her name in English is Juniper."

"Thanks, Sister, we'll take it from here."

Medical terms began to fly between the two physicians, which didn't need translation.

****

Lukas's eyes glazed. He twisted, clenching his teeth as Michael turned to Miles. "I don't like the pasty gray look. Why isn't he self-healing?"

"I have no idea," Miles replied in an anxious voice.

Michael held Lukas down on the bed, but bloody fingers clawed at his immovable arm. Gently, he whispered, "No. Hold still."

"Dad, my leg...Is it there?"

"Of course it's there."

"I can't feel it!"

He leaned down, blocking Lukas's view as strip by strip, Laura cut off his bloody jeans. Standing close, Alana appeared panic-stricken so he caught Laura's eye.

"Go talk to the Guardians, dear," Laura stated. "Do what you do best and leave Lu to us."

Swiping her face with the back of a hand, Alana mumbled with disgust, "Oh God, I'm covered in animal blood."

He looked at the woman he loved. "Your mother's right. We're fine here."

"Fine? None of this is fine," she protested.

Laura said, "Take a moment and wash it all off before you go downstairs."

Michael whispered, "You need to plan the next move. Will you do that for me?"

"He's right, dear. Please do as he asks."

Alana looked dazed before turning away. As the last strip of material came off, Miles covered his son with the bedspread. But Lukas continued to fight, and Michael couldn't keep him still. "No! Let me see my leg! Please," his son got out between hitched breaths and sniffles.

Not one wound had closed, and smoothing his son's matted blond curls, Michael hid such deep worry that it shook him. "Shhh... I swear it's there. Doc Chamberlain's on his way."

"No, no doctor! I can heal myself!"

"You need a little help this time."

With bloody clothes in hand, Laura shushed his son, kissed Lukas's cheek. "Be good and listen to your father." When she turned to Michael, her eyes were full and fear definitely claimed her face.

****

Alana stood at the bathroom sink scrubbing her face, arms, and hands. Although never squeamish at the sight of blood, Lukas's shredded leg made her want to faint. And there were other emotions she couldn't get beyond. Losing control of such sudden rage in front of Michael, making poor decisions, insisting Lukas come *with* them to Siena, *not* killing Leonard the instant she had him in reach... The mystical mission must come first, she had always told herself.

Rubbing a towel down her cheek, she realized *his* Guardian isn't as secure as he thinks she is. Her shoulders ached with weariness. *This isn't close to over, and I'm exhausted. Veronique isn't some run-of-the-mill vampire. She's evil incarnate and taking her down warrants full-throttle alertness. The innocent fighting for her life, an injured newbie stabbed in the gut, Lu's leg in such a state... Think strength, Ally, be one thousand percent in control.* "Because I'll be the one driving a wooden stake straight through your heart, bitch."

When she came out of the room, Michael and her father were huddled over Lukas. Although her heart absorbed every uneven sob, she didn't waver. There were reports to hear and information to analyze. Get a grip, she told herself, because there's so much more to do.

****

A black backpack dropped on the bed. Michael gave a nod as Chamberlain said into his cell phone, "We'll need land transport to get to you, Baker. Have three ambulances lined up as close to the house as possible. That's right. Three patients and another doctor will travel with us. Call now. I want three separate teams on alert at Medico." He clipped the phone to his belt and examined Lukas.

Michael caught his eye. "How bad is this? Phil said mutant Hell-beasts."

"Looks like one gnawed through his bone. I'll straighten it out and brace the leg before we move him." Chamberlain manipulated his son's ankle. Arching off the bed, Lukas screamed and screamed. "You just made your father wince and your grandfather jump. Cool, huh." He looked over at Michael. "I'm not worried about the scrapes or cracked ribs; however, the right shoulder is dislocated. And the leg—this is too extensive, even for someone with self-healing skills. I'd like to sedate him."

Miles whispered, "It will help."

Again, Michael nodded once to Chamberlain. He wasn't taking any chances and brushed a hand down his son's cheek. As Miles rolled his son's hip, Chamberlain sank a syringe into Lukas's flesh ignoring his screams.

"I'll also give him a shot of gamma globulin. It's a necessary precaution against rabies." More resistant, Lukas lurched and cursed. They held him steady as Chamberlain administered a second syringe. A whiny "ow" accompanied a quick jerk, but the full dose emptied. "You've got about a minute before he's too woozy to wiggle, Michael."

As his son fought the sedative, he sat close. "You're one gutsy kid, I'll give you that. Don't fight it, son." He soothed with "I love you, little boy, you know I love you," and repeated it until his son's sobs stopped and his eyes closed. Then he stood, swallowed his worst fear, and gave a worried sigh before saying to Chamberlain, "You'll take good care, I already know."

"Miles will help me prep him for travel. Maybe you need to sit down for a minute."

The researcher looked just as worried. A cold scowl settled on Michael's face. With murder in mind, he stared at his son's bloody leg one last time, ready to put an end to anyone that had a hand in this.

****

As Michael reached the bottom stair, Celia snagged his hand. "He needs medical attention, the human kind, sweetie. You have to accept it."

He stared into her tired eyes. "You can't do anything, can you?"

"Not right now, but Lu won't walk with a limp, that's a fact. Let the doctors do their thing. The old goat knew exactly what he wanted when he made that Hell-beast attack. His sick-o mind runs rings around Clayton's," she stated with anger in her usually sweet voice.

Thorn had Uriel in his arms. "You can't rip Leonard limb from limb, Champ. Think of a fitting end to his screwed-up vision of sorcerer-ship success. Get vengeance out of your heart because it never sits well with you."

"Get out of my mind, Thorn," he replied as Alana placed a key in his hand. "What do I want with this?" She took the baby from Thorn, didn't answer. About to ask again, red lights flashed in the front windows. Thorn grabbed his arm when the Guardians walked in. Michael stared at two stretchers and then glared at Thorn. "That hurts... let go."

"I figure pain will get your mind off killing. Is it

working?"

"No." More annoyed, he repeated, "What do I want with this?"

Coming over, Alana stated, "Thorn won't let go until you calm down, and you should know better than to fight him."

Jillian was the first casualty of evil brought down. Chamberlain and the woman from Lucy's apartment followed. Then they brought Lukas down, and he fought to get to the stretcher.

Thorn yanked him back. "Get a grip, Michael."

When Mick hobbled over, supported by a Guardian, Michael's demeanor changed.

"See? Right as rain I am, Sir."

He said with respect, "What you did took more than courage."

"It was an honor to assist, Sir."

"The honor is mine, Guardian."

"I'll watch out for Lu. I swear on my soul."

"I trust you will…absolutely." The door closed. Michael took a deep breath, and Thorn let go.

Alana caught his gaze. "So now we have Leo's room key. Want to take a look?"

Thinking, once more, murder… Michael studied the key as Thorn leaned in. "Head downstairs for the wizard, and I'll jump you. Let it roll off those broad shoulders and save it for another time. Every dog has its day, and every fool gets what he deserves."

"Are we going the cliché route? My son told me how much you love to use them."

"They work for me, and don't insult an empath. Look at the situation with clear eyes. You saved the girl. Your boy's out of the picture for round two. Did you catch that, thickhead? You're pretty good at taking out evil creatures. Three immortal sorcerers, Cyril, other vampires we won't name… And you've neutralized crotchety old Mister Wizard. Veronique isn't going anywhere. Relax a bit. Check out the hotel."

Alana took his hand. "I heard a Guardian say it's one of the classiest around, my love. Five stars… What do you think Leo's got in there?"

"I'm curious, not convinced." He still wanted to get his hands on Gerhardt.

Thorn groaned low. "I hate it when I have to spell it out for you but let me simplify…just this once. As soon as you leave to take apart his hiding place, *we* leave as well. Phil has a lead foot, so before you know it, that thing in the iron box will have a place of dishonor cemented into an alcove in San Giorgio's basement, and we all get to sleep in tomorrow. Are you getting the mental picture now?"

"And snuggled next to Celia, you'll be a focused thought away. Am I on the right track?"

"There you go," Thorn confirmed with pride. "But I'd wait 'til just before dawn to visit Veronique. That gives you hours to—"

"Thank you. I get it." Michael kissed Alana's cheek. "Say your goodbyes while I wash up and change my shirt."

Chapter 27

The swanky hotel was nestled in the hills, very close to a high hill that looked down on Siena. Driving past an eager uniformed valet, Michael pulled the Mercedes into a close spot.

They both smiled, showing no trace of what they were thinking or what they had just gone through. As Michael helped Alana out of the car, she raked her fingers through her long brown hair, smiling bright as the valet ogled. To accommodate her casual steps, Michael narrowed his stride; put an arm around her waist to draw her close. They looked like a couple who had spent an adventurous evening in the medieval city, perhaps taking in Siena at night—unaware of the curfew because of rabid wolves. Alana gave a sweet grin of familiarity to the concierge before they took the gilded staircase to the third floor.

The room key dangled from his hand, an added benefit for the chambermaid. A passionate kiss to Alana's full lips produced a sigh from the starry-eyed girl. Slipping the brass key into its slot, he twisted the crystal knob to Leonard's room. Then they disappeared through the threshold and locked the door.

Alana let out a breathy "Oooh, would you look at this," when a high chandelier glowed to life in the room's marble foyer. "Evil loves opulence. The suite has a masterpiece for a ceiling."

He left her to open wide the balcony doors. Hand-carved woodwork screamed exquisite and the period pieces added to the richness of the room's décor.

"Leo has classy taste, I'll give him that."

Michael stared at the distant hills. "And a perfect view of Villa Catherine's cemetery. What a bastard."

Alana called his name. He followed her voice through luxurious adjoining rooms. "Look at the open shower in the corner. Are those water jets in the ceiling? And *this* is the biggest bathtub I have *ever* seen. Oooh…Wide, shiny black porcelain, brass handles around a pristine oval. Too bad he sat in it."

"I've memorized his scent, darlin'. It isn't on the tub. Come, let's have a look around." Only one drawer in the armoire held clothing. Five suits neatly hung by color…and one tuxedo. Michael rifled through each pocket, found nothing odd.

From the dresser, Alana said, "He's a neat freak. Look at the socks. They're like egg rolls. Wait… The drawer's different." She dug a fingernail down. The bottom popped up. "Well would you look at that. I found his laptop." She set it on the desk, opened it and pressed the space bar. It hummed—at super-speed. "What I wouldn't give for Celia's talent with passwords right now."

For once, Michael wished the irritating, non-verbal connection to Thorn's mental skills could work both ways.

"Okay. I've tried Jillian, granddaughter, Veronique. What else?"

"Try inheritance," he suddenly said.

She typed it in and leaned back with a gasp. "How did you know that?"

"I have absolutely no idea."

"*Really*?" Her gaze narrowed, and she grinned as he shrugged. "You never were a very good liar. You played the telepathic telephone game with Thorn."

"It worked, didn't it?" They studied the screen— interlocking angels and demons.

She opened a desktop folder labeled "Layout." "What *is* this? Floor plans to old Leo's church for evil worshipers?"

"It's Veronique's villa, or rather her idea of a Renaissance fortress." He pointed to different parts of the blueprint. "Secret entrances, underground passageways at seven points... I'll bet the Georgians have always wondered how she managed to disappear before any talented Guardian could get a silver sword to her skinny neck. She could give anyone the slip at any time."

"Not now she can't."

The Internet opened. "Are you sending it to your laptop?"

Not looking up, she chuckled. "Boy, you really lack computer skills, don't you? I'm sending it to every Guardian in Florence."

"Did I tell you how much I love you lately?" he whispered with a sensual smirk.

"Later," she said as she typed at maximum speed. "So what time do we do this?"

"As Thorn suggested, just before dawn, and make sure there are enough of them—with sharp silver swords and pointy wooden stakes for all her minions."

As Michael walked away, Alana said, "Gotcha."

****

Alana's strategy began to take shape. The

attachment going to the Guardians had a simple message, but then she sent specific instructions to Cesar Gonzales in Florence. Another brilliant suggestion entered her mind, and with cunning ease, she attached Gerhardt's document files to emails, sending them to a certain person in Manhattan. In the event that something went wrong and the Georgians were compromised, the Kendrick Witches would have a field day with this.

Proud of her accomplishment, Alana leaned into the screen. "Veronique, I hope you enjoyed your last sunset because you are history." Just thinking about the sire brought calculated coldness. In work mode, a Guardian's concentration never wavered. But as soon as she relaxed, she heard water running and Michael calling her name. Then she followed his soft, low voice.

With a scrunched expression, he sat in the black porcelain tub, bubbles up to his neck. He grinned—in a mischievous way.

"That's Leo's evil tub."

"I told you. His evil ass never touched this."

One long finger crooked, beckoned her closer. She took a step. "You used a whole bottle of bubble bath?"

"Two."

She took another step. "You look like a floating head."

"But I can assure you, darlin', I'm all here."

That sexy, low tone stirred some very erotic fantasies. Neither shy nor hesitant, she stripped off her clothes, which trailed from that exact spot to the tub's side. He seemed totally engrossed in the way she moved, the intensity of his gaze raking heat down her body. Was he planning what he'd do to her? Just the thought flooded her with desire.

Suddenly sinking under the bubbles with a sexy smirk, Michael reappeared quickly—coughing up water.

"Forgot to do something?" she teased.

"I'm new at this human necessity to hold one's breath."

Wet waves of his dark brown hair looked as if they'd been painted on his high cheekbones. He took her hand, easing her into the tub, into his arms. She sighed, rested against his chest.

He answered with a moan.

The water's warmth felt perfect. Hot enough to excite, cool enough to be a silky, soft blanket. The scent of lavender relaxed her, but his slow touch evoked passion. Her arms reached back to encircle his neck. Every breath he took still filled her with wonder, and when his hands disappeared under the scented foam, the sensation of brushing waves thrilled her beyond imagination. Amidst weightless bubbles and the exotic scent, she nibbled his earlobe whispering, "I...I don't think—"

"This isn't the time to think, darlin'...just feel."

His Guardian could only sigh.

Chapter 28

As Michael and Alana entered the kitchen of the student house, Neeb informed, "Four a.m. and all's well. A local wants to speak with you privately."

"Get Leonard up and walking," Alana ordered.

Michael nodded as the woman he loved left his side, all business and no longer playfully sensual. He had also switched gears. A large mug of coffee came to his hand, and he said to Sister Phyllis, "Thanks. I need this."

"There's breakfast if you're hungry. I know the next few hours will be treacherous." She sat across from him at the table with a serious expression. "I called Arthur. Mick is resting, Jillian's condition is grave. You know Lukas will be fine."

"I'm grateful for the update, and I appreciate your concern."

"Please eat something, Champion. The human body needs fuel." He accepted the warm plate of cheese and bread she offered. "I'll keep you both in my prayers," she said as she left.

Once alone, he pushed the plate away and listened to the Guardian's rapid Italian. *Vampires all over Siena, Florence crawling with them as well...* When Alana came over, he pointed to the plate. "Put something in your stomach. It's a long night." She took a hesitant bite of bread and leaned back lost in thought. "The strategy will work, my Guardian. Veronique won't know what hit her."

She nodded agreement just as Leonard appeared with Nigel and Neeb at his sides. Petula came through the swinging door and Michael handed her the Mercedes key. "The back entrance, Pet, and get it as close as possible. I don't care if we have to shove him through the window. Be quick. Be careful. I want an army of Guardians to flank you, by the way."

He stood, sneered at Leonard. "It's show time and you have a front row seat. Not a hair on your miserable head will be out of place when you meet Veronique." Flicking dry dirt off the old man's shoulders still had him thinking murder. "We should have brought your tux. It completely slipped our minds." The wizard appeared shocked, and with arrogance, Michael leaned down. "I'm sure it won't make a difference how you enter Hell. You don't remotely resemble a kindly old clockmaker now. You are truly a sadistic bastard."

Fool that he was, Gerhardt scoffed. "At her side, my power will return."

"Bring it on," he coldly replied. "Give the Hell-beasts my regards while you roast for eternity." He gave a decisive nod. Neeb led the man to the waiting car. There was just enough room for the doors to open, for the five of them to cram inside.

****

Lucy woke with a start. Someone was running up the stairs. Convinced a vampire had found her, she stumbled into the kitchen as far away from the door as possible. The knob twisted. She held her breath and shook.

"Damn it, Salvatore," a man's voice boomed, "No

sleep for twenty-four hours and you need milk? It's five a.m., cousin. You had better be up and the coffee had better be…"

Totally shocked, she stared at the man who had been positioned outside her room at the student house. He looked exhausted, frazzled, and his voice came off cranky.

As he entered the kitchen, Sal let out a yawn, unaware of the face-off between them. He plugged in the electric pot on the counter next to her. "*Lucia mia*, this is my cousin, Geri."

The Guardian approached, took the milk bottle out of the bag, and sat in an arrogant fashion, glaring right at her with contempt. She spit through clenched teeth, "Bastard! You guarded that door like a pit bull! You're one of *them*!" She collapsed into a kitchen chair sick to her stomach.

As the minutes passed, Sal still looked confused when he poured three cups of coffee in silence. Finally, the Guardian blew on the hot brew. "I'd take the Council's offer. These streets are full of vampires. I know you can't process the word, Salvatore, but *she* can."

Lucy planted both elbows on the table, looked away. Aware of the dark sky outside the window, her fingers trembled as she rubbed her forehead.

He pulled a pen and a pad from his jacket pocket. "This is the address of someone who will protect her, Salvatore. Call it Divine Providence that you needed milk; that this woman isn't dead in some alley already."

Sal shot to his feet. "*Madonna mia*, what the *hell* is wrong with you? Who is this council you speak of? Using words like vampires, last chance, and glaring at

Lucia like she is garbage? Why do you do this? Why is she in trouble, eh? What did she mean you guard like a pit bull?"

Holding up both hands, he shook his head. "Just trust me, *si*? The least you know, the better. *She* knows what I mean."

Her face showed nothing. How do you tell someone that death awaits you, probably tonight, most definitely right on his doorstep? Still ready to argue Sal opened his mouth. Before he could speak, Lucy whispered, "Please, Sal, stop." She met Geri's intense gaze and gave in. "I know what he means."

Sal's eyes stayed on his cousin as the man stood and placed the cup in the sink. Their eyes met. "Trust me and ask no questions, cousin. You must stay here until the sun is fully up. Then when you go, don't dawdle or stop along the way, and don't tell *Zia* Angelina where you are when you get there, *capisce*?" He left the paper with an address on the counter and walked out with a steady gait. Lucy knew she couldn't go back to her apartment. She'd leave Siena with the clothes on her back and nothing more.

****

The entrance Alana chose fit her plan to perfection. Guardians would penetrate Veronique's stronghold from different ports, and the coordinated attack would catch her minions off guard while Michael created a specific diversion with the sire.

"Only fifteen minutes till dawn," she said. Michael instantly frowned. "What's wrong?"

"Well over a century ago, I spent a lot of time here. I knew about the tunnels, but I didn't know about this particular way in."

She arched an eyebrow, not saying what she thought about his previous sex escapades with the deadly creature. But that connection was the crux of her strategy. Nine Florentine Guardians, each one handpicked, confirmed this entry as the most obscure; perfect for this mission. Gagged tight with his hands bound, Leonard slumped to the ground. Two more stood over him. Staring directly into Michael's eyes, she again asked, "Are you sure you want to do it this way? I could have them flood her room first."

His thin-lipped smirk came off confident. "It will work. I know this creature."

They entered a narrow break in the stone wall, immediately descending rocky steps. Narrow twists and turns resembled a medieval labyrinth. Alana's senses stayed in high-gear as mystical warriors followed her choice of earthen corridors, turning left or right in chilly darkness. Only Leonard needed help. Neeb was assigned to him, and for the tedious walk, rarely would the old man's feet actually touch the ground beneath him.

****

Thorn held Celia close in a never-ending I've-missed-you cuddle. Her head rested on ginger tufts of hair that covered his ample chest. Both had awakened, even before the baby's insistent gurgles. The baby immediately fell back to sleep while Thorn became tense and concerned.

"Ally's a great strategist," Celia whispered with a yawn.

"I know."

"There are no more variables."

"I'm not convinced. I mean, I lived in Michael's

mind for eight grueling days during his dream of survival. I thought after his unprecedented journey to mystical man things might be different. No such luck. He's too sure of himself."

Celia checked the basinet. "Our son has our gift."

"He does," Thorn confirmed.

"So what do you see?"

"They're already in. Why am I in his head again? This vision's in Three-D, dearest. Marble statues everywhere, probably original masterpieces by da Vinci and Michelangelo... This demon's lair could be featured on 'Homes of the Long Undead and Infamous' if one existed. Ugh... he's too intrigued by the art. He had better focus." Full of uneasiness, the small hairs at the back of Thorn's neck itched something fierce.

"I think I'll send a little sixth sense fine-tuning Ally's way." Celia kissed his chin, resting her head on his chest again.

His massive arm devoured her and concealing fear, he asked, "Do you sense the final outcome?"

"I'm seeing dust and bone...and human death."

****

In the chapel, Mother Anne also sensed the Champion's loss of focus, his eagerness to end this event. Gabriella and Magdalena came in, took the pew directly behind her. Soon, all fifty-three heaven-sent souls made their presence known to each other. Mother Anne sensed Phyllis's mind now linked to theirs as well.

One stained-glass window caught her attention in the ending night and just before the bright light of dawn. Tooled with reverence so very long ago, the Archangel Michael cast Lucifer out of Heaven. Tied on his belt were the keys to Heaven and Hell. Chains leashed his stalwart left hand; his broadsword pointed the way. She realized that over three centuries ago, Martin Malone had chosen the correct name for his son.

Anne prayed for the Champion as well as his Guardian. She implored protection for everyone involved. As Good Friday dawned, the mystical congregation entered into deep meditation as one entity. They could not alter destiny, but the ancient sire, whose beast-within was born of Satan himself, would not win.

****

Doing something for eight hundred years could become a habit. Veronique rarely engaged in them. This one, she had to admit, had merit. Gliding through her estate with grace in the minutes before undead rest, she recalled how sweet the young Guardian's blood had been. The conceited crusader smashed through an expensive window and took out her minion with a crossbow, nearly grazing Veronique's cheek. The steamy pool kept his hypnotizing blood at just the right temperature before she put the boy out of his misery.

Guardian blood made her alabaster skin glow. Her long hair glistened from essences imported from Egypt. A fresh black silk robe made the slightest rustle on buffed steps before the first inkling of dawn. Standing at a carved curio in the hall, Veronique rubbed oil of lavender into her hands and kept them under her nose to inhale the tranquil aroma. It filled her with peace before dreamless somnolence.

Tonight, it reminded her of life in the palace with her father and her mother. *A potent vampire turns a virginal princess into a demon. The Sire has an ageless beast-within. Unbeknownst to anyone, his new child receives endless knowledge in the first moments of undeath. Why do I recall you, my Sire? Is it because I stand on the eve of true immortality? The first kiss is always most memorable. How my eyes blazed like polished amber the first time these pristine canines lengthened.*

Instead of a requested kiss, her fangs sank into his cold throat, fully acclimated to an altered existence after less than one full night of death-sleep. *This nubile body shuddered with sexual bliss as I consumed my very origin, doubling my strength. Then I staked you. Every vampire I have sired remained under my control except one. Cyril was a mistake... purely a sexual whim.* She sighed. A satisfied smirk began. *One more sunset before being reunited in a timeless bond...*

"My world changes and very soon," Veronique cooed, entering her softly lit boudoir. "This is my turn to reign, a new era. It's time to recapture my roots, so to speak." As she pulled her fragrant, scented hands away from her nose, the door closed. From the center of the room, she turned, feasted her eyes on the most handsome lover she had ever bedded.

"I don't think so," her intruder said in a casual way.

For a brief moment, a sensual shockwave ran through her before full composure settled over her dainty features. She gave a wanton sigh. "As I live and don't breathe. Michael Malone."

****

"Hello, Veronique." Michael's charming smile had its intended effect. The sire's curtsy confirmed the grace of a refined lady. Alluring eyes lingered on his chest before sliding down to fixate on her favorite part

331

of his anatomy.

"What's this I hear? There's a rumor going around. Have you found a cure for undeath?" An iota of pure jealousy flickered, and the English words rolled off her tongue like melting chocolate. "You know I need my beauty sleep. Couldn't you have called on me earlier? It's been well over a century since our last rendezvous," she purred before a well-rehearsed pout appeared.

Mesmerizing, bright blue eyes flashed desire of a different nature. Michael didn't even blink. Recalling her craving for idle chatter, he inclined his head in a gentlemanly fashion. He'd let her talk herself into a tired state, as she had always done.

"You've turned into a modern-day crusader these last hundred-plus years. First, finding a way to tame my progeny within you, and now, a *heartbeat* accompanies a cleansed soul. Whatever has gotten into you?" She shook her head slowly, her raven hair fluttering like soft silk in a spring breeze. "And destroying Cyril, my most successful creation, my last remaining progeny... Such an outrageous act took many innocents to lessen this burden of unending grief. Zoltan, that *other* one you destroyed last May," she said with a flip of her hand, "He was too pushy—achieving a throbbing erection with every thought of torture. Not like you, quick to harden and oh so slow to enter—enough to make me beg. But Cyril's destruction—one might consider me in mourning still."

"You always wore black, Veronique," he stated, blasé and unaffected. Long strides brought him closer to the vixen. "Don't go putting that fashion faux-pas on me. Black or red, red or black...a fox is a fox is a fox," he added, mixing sex appeal with insult.

Ever so slightly, her head tilted. "Cyril loved your banter. I thought you too *punny,* never caring for it myself. Were you mine I might have whipped such a tendency out of you...after a full night of punishment in my bed, in my bath, on the dining hall table. Zoltan liked it when I whipped him. He worshipped me." Her tone turned cold. "He knew his place."

"He and I had a conversation just before my son lopped off his head. I found him sadistic, pretentious...and stupid." Off-balance and entertained is where she'd stay until Alana makes an entrance, he thought. Sure of his strategy, he stood his ground, and sensuous sways brought her to him. Her large but deadly eyes danced. Her hand brushed down his chest and her icy fingers drew circles on his black shirt.

"Did you know that right after Cyril turned him, I took Zoltan as my lover?"

Michael gave a devilish grin, and in spite of the lavender, her unique scent filtered through to prickle his senses. "He didn't mention it."

"Umm," she sighed, more interested in unbuttoning each button and pulling the shirttails *very* slowly out of his jeans. He shuddered, her touch like flint striking stone. "You *are* warm. Do you remember those endless nights in here? Neither Cyril nor Zoltan could measure up to you. We were magnificent—you and I coming together. Cold heat, hot ice. We were the envy of that other lesser brother in blood who always sniveled at your heels like a sad, lost puppy," she whispered. Her hand suddenly cupped him through his jeans, rubbed him insistent and greedy. "Your erection always fascinated me, so delicious against my tongue," she added—with more pressure.

"I'm not feeling it." Two fingers pulled her thin wrist away as if it were an undesirable annoyance. "What a naughty little fox you still are, Veronique. Not thinking about a quick taste or a little nibble, are you?"

Her slender shoulders drifted back...slightly. "Cyril said your blood gave him boundless energy. Is that why you never let me taste you? Maybe the return of a heartbeat has changed the flavor of you yet again." Her body pressed against him as she drew in a deep sniff. "Does the female I smell only like it in a bed and on her back? Is this why you're surly? I could writhe and act human. I'll tug at your hair as you taste me and even whimper when you enter me."

Her eyes flickered amber and then back to their human color. She touched his hip and his leg moved forward to step away, but she mounted his thigh, bucking with the breathy moan, "Oh please, I'll be whatever you want. You'll play hero, and I'll be the demure damsel in distress. I'll hitch my gown and bend over. You can hold my hip and tease me with two long fingers before you thrust your erection into me."

Meeting her wide-eyed gaze, he said evenly, "I'm spoken for."

A feminine peel of laughter filled the room, and her pearly-white fangs appeared. "Spare me the details. Is it that mousy little Guardian again? The one who brought out the beast in you the first time you poked her with this?"

Her hand clamped tight on him again, and his glare slid into a fierce glower. "You have a way with words, Veronique, and you're using all the wrong ones."

Less than an instant later, her other icy hand closed around his neck. "You can't breathe. How ordinary, but a *mere* man must do so." An ungodly shove landed him in the center of her bed, her strength more than expected. She flew at him and held him down, slicing his lip with her fingernail. Blood trickled to his chin, and her cold tongue licked it clean. Her nails carved a path down his chest while her eyes sparked brilliant amber once again. His jeans were suddenly open as her icy hand gripped him. Lips painted the color of wine parted and with ageless anger, she bit into his jugular. His entire body vibrated until she pulled her fangs out to hiss like a snake, "She has *domesticated* you?! What a common wench!"

His vision blurred while his body hummed. Tiny drops of his blood speckled her tongue, and she looked as if she had tasted rare honey. "It's unique, for a domesticated blend." Prying his thighs apart to kneel between them, he had no ability to resist. Veronique's gaze brimmed with unquenchable lust.

Very woozy and a bit slow, he managed to prop himself up on both elbows. A deep inhale didn't force his heart to slow, nor pump steady again. As much as he wanted to touch his neck, he knew better. Instead, he grinned with arrogance to irk her more. But her crafty smile worked like a dark magic spell as she fully pulled him out of his jeans and slid her hand up and down him in a slow, deliberate way.

"You remember the power," sounded like she spoke through an echo chamber. "Put this in me and I'll make you mine again. Together we'll rule a new breed of vampire."

She licked her lips as he hardened. Like a pro, each stroke was pure stimulation, far more than a mortal man could bear. In this altered state, he couldn't fight, couldn't catch a breath to speak. "My lust peaks before somnolence, Michael. I will lace you to my bed and we will fuck and play before I give the gift of undeath back to you. After my legacy seizes your soul, that moral conscience will simply slip away. You are a commanding man. You'll be a commanding creature once again."

Beyond aroused, his hips rocked craving immediate release. Her expertise with his erection hypnotized him. Oh God, he was ready to come. But all he could think about was his sureness that this plan to confuse Veronique's superior senses would work. He had been wrong. The deep draw from his jugular to meet undeath was minutes away. Mustering all of his strength, he managed to get out, "I don't want it back, Veronique. I have what I've always wanted."

Sexual fire lit her eyes as she continued to stroke him. "And what would that be?"

Gasping through his arousal, he couldn't answer. He couldn't think. "He has me," sounded as Leonard was shoved across the room, losing his footing and falling.

Veronique snapped her head back, growled and flew at his Guardian. Alana's rapid punch, overly fierce and right between Veronique's breasts, produced the crunch of cracking ribs.

"Bone knifing through muscle doesn't affect me, foolish girl," she hissed, taking a slight step back to regain her composure.

"But wood through a certain shriveled heart will do the trick, right?" Smiling bright, Alana's trained grip stayed on her short-sword. With a wave of the blade and a catty smirk, she added, "Oh, and silver does the trick, too. I brought a present, and you didn't even say thanks. After almost eight hundred years, a vampire could be a little more gracious. You were a princess, or so I hear. Did you forget your manners, Ronnie?"

The interruption was perfect and just in time. He fixed himself as best he could. He still throbbed as he pulled up his zipper and his legs were weak. Blood trickled down his neck, but he sat up and glared at Gerhardt on the floor beside the bed.

Fixated on Alana, Veronique didn't even bother to look at the old man. "I sent you a case of my finest champagne, Leonard. Did I waste postage as well as the grapes on a loser?"

"With a capital L," Alana replied with a frown. "All Leo managed to do was make his innocent granddaughter very sick. Oops, did I forget to mention she won't be coming? My sweetie saved her life."

Alana glanced his way, and he didn't doubt for an instant that she caught the throat wound. Turning his attention to her, Michael watched those beautiful hazel eyes narrow. "You despicable, jealous, horny creature! You just *had* to use my man as your boy-toy. I'll have to scrub every inch of his gorgeous body in that palatial pool downstairs, after you disintegrate. And since all your minions are air pollution by now, I'll have to fumigate before we move in. Dust and bone may be everywhere, but I adore Florence in springtime. Just think of the shock when all of your undead associates come for a visit, Ronnie."

Fangs flashed. Veronique growled. "You sarcastic bitch, where is *my* demon?"

As his strength returned he sat on the edge of the bed and gave a disgusted snicker. "It's in a box with a super spell, clawing its way toward oblivion for good this time." Then he pulled Leonard off the floor. "As for this blithering bag of wind, maybe you need a closer look." As if the old man weighed nothing, he hurled Leonard her way.

Veronique caught the wizard by the throat. "You promised me, Leonard. You said *nothing* could go wrong."

"Goddess, my dark queen, I have Cyril's journal," he boldly announced.

"Cyril would never be foolish enough to keep such a thing!"

"I swear it is so. Your progeny can be saved. This traitor was to be its last kill—my gift to you."

"Enough," she screamed and forced him to his knees. Contempt swirled in her eyes. "Did you purposely time this devious subterfuge? Did you wait for Michael to reappear in Portofino, mortal? Why, I ask myself."

"*He* destroyed Cyril, who you yourself created. I worshiped Cyril!"

Veronique growled. "I thought you worshiped me?"

"You are my queen. The sire was merely...an idol."

A stifled laugh came from Alana. "That's some fancy footwork. Did you know Leo combed through burnt garbage at Cyril's Vermont estate for some hair or fingernails so he could tap into magic known only to sorcerers? And forget about that journal drivel. I agree with you, Ronnie. Can't see old Cyril stupid enough to actually write down spells, and besides, I know firsthand what this *specific* beast-within is capable of.

You shoved one hell of a demon into a frail, little girl, Leo." Gerhardt glared. Alana paused, and with a dramatic wave of her short-sword stated, "I'm starting to think you wanted this whole soul-invasion thing to fail."

Like an expert, Alana has planted the seed of doubt. Michael watched it blossom in Veronique's devious mind.

Foolishly forgetting about the gutsy, lethal woman standing in her boudoir, the Sire leered at an egotistical wizard. With a swipe of one red nail she opened Leonard's throat. Then, her delicate hand cupped his bearded chin, and with a twist of a wrist, ripped Gerhardt's head from his stout body. It rolled near Michael's foot, and when he looked up, the sire's steamy amber eyes lit on *him—again...* an immediate draw.

The night Cyril turned him into a monster filled his head. And for the second time in his mortal life, he knew he was staring directly at death fully paralyzed by her will.

Veronique flew at him. Alana leapt as well, and with one bold slice of the short-sword, decapitated the sire. Her headless body seemed to hover right above him before black bits of bone and dark dust rained down like icy hail.

"Ding-dong, *now* the witch is dead," she stated.

He staggered off the bed and stared at Leonard's shocked blue eyes. Bitterly, he added, "So is the wizard. Every death is written on his soul, not his granddaughter's."

In Guardian tradition, Alana stood down, rolled her shoulders loose. He heard her heart resume a human pace as her bright hazel eyes swept over him. "Seriously, my love, did she hurt you?"

He went to her, blew out a quick breath and pointed to his neck. "Look! She bit me right here."

She kissed his neck. "Already healed and without a scar."

"And she bruised me right here."

She kissed his chest. "I don't think you're bruised anymore."

"And did you see what that bold hussy did to me right—"

A sassy grin appeared. "Yeah, I'll take care of that later."

He held her in a tight embrace. The short-sword dropped to the carpeted floor. "You saved my life, darlin'. I owe you one."

"I'd walk through the fires of Hell for you."

He could feel her smile against his heart and gave a gentle laugh while kissing her hair. With unending devotion, he replied, "Forever and always."

Not a full minute passed before Petula walked in with a loud "Uh-hem!" They didn't pull apart. "Would this be what Neeb and I can look forward to next year? Kissing and hugging even in the vilest of places when the sacred vow is behind us. Living in the colonies must have softened you, Sir. A true Brit would never be so openly affectionate."

When a charismatic grin reached Petula, Michael heard her heart flutter. "On the night after your vows end, dear Guardian, there will be two plane tickets waiting at the Georgian's Hampton Hill Estate for you and Neeb. And in the heart of Manhattan stands a brownstone, which will be furnished with everything 'colonial' ever imagined... just for the two of you."

Her blush deepened. She bit her lip and looked away.

Alana's arms hooked his waist. "I give them a month before smooching in public."

"I give them a day." Then his smile disappeared. "How far is my son from here?"

"Not very," Alana said as she left him. At the balcony doors, her harsh tugs ripped off every heavy drape. Streaks of morning sun filled the musty room. She turned to Petula. "Do me a favor. Get a local Guardian to call a cleaning service. I want no trace of that bitch left in this place. Bleach everything, top to bottom, but keep her study sealed off to all."

"I'll wager there's some interesting info on her computer," Pet stated.

"Why scrub it down?" he asked. "Simply destroy this house of death...this very minute."

"Let the Georgian Council decide. But that one room has tons to catalog and siphon through. Besides, I'll need to spend some time here and I'd like to look around."

"There are many bedrooms, nooks and crannies."

"And I'm sure you know the exact location of each." The smirk left her lips. "Are you ready to visit Lu?"

"Absolutely." He took her hand.

As they left the room, Petula whispered, "The stride away is just as thrilling."

"I heard that," he called over his shoulder, pulling Alana tight to his side.

Chapter 29

Miles kissed his wife. It was always the first thing he did upon waking. Laura smiled and snuggled close. "You slept in." Her hand came to his cheek. "What happened to that infernal internal alarm clock you insist upon relying on?"

"I suppose crawling into bed well after midnight for months on end has simply screwed it up for good. It also helps to have you beside me."

She smiled. "And well it should. I imagine the sire is history?"

"Thorn would've called if the sun rose and Veronique still walked this earth."

"I imagine Gerhardt's dead or close to it."

"Alana and Michael are quite the team."

"Like none other on the face of God's good earth. Shall I order breakfast?" His next kiss held passion. Laura stared into his eyes. "I love you more each minute, Miles Bookman." His cell phone rang, and after reaching to the nightstand, she handed it to him.

He recognized Deepa's number. "I have to take this, honey."

****

Johnny Baker, Chamberlain's senior scientist, met Alana and Michael as they entered the Medico building. He led them to a private room with a shower, coffee and breakfast as well. Fresh clothes were waiting for them. The one's they'd come in bagged and tagged. Once changed and refreshed, they arrived at Chamberlain's office.

Alana studied him, surely catching his full-on worry. "Medico's doctors are the best and brightest minds in their fields."

Thinking like any parent would, one more issue had his attention. "What do I say when I call Alexa Gerhardt? Your father-in-law is the son of a bitch who did this, and I'm not about to let your daughter out of my sight as long as she lives? Oh, by the way, the good news is a vampire ripped the old man apart, but the terrifying reality is your daughter's barely alive? I'm not great at parenting a teenage boy. What do I do about this girl?" He stopped pacing, stood by the window to observe the spectacular Florentine morning.

Alana came to his side. "Let Dad handle calling her with the news."

"And I want to see my son." Their fingers laced together. He admired the delicacy of his Guardian's hand. "How could something so small end centuries of evil?"

"How could someone so tender be so totally fierce?"

"Did I tell you I love you lately?"

"Yes, many times," she whispered with a smile.

Chamberlain entered, sat at his desk. "No one would ever suspect what you two can do."

Crossing the office, Michael cut to the heart of the matter. "I want my boy."

"Not so fast. He's still sedated. We've placed each shard of bone in alignment, but the Hell-beast did a job on his leg. His right arm is back in its socket, the ribs will take some time to heal." Michael let out a slow breath. "Now take another deep one because pale doesn't become you anymore. So on to the next matter. Everyone who had contact with these mutant creatures will need gamma globulin injections."

"I have a mystical body. I don't like needles," Alana quickly stated.

Chamberlain leveled a grin. "*Everyone* who came in contact with them includes both of you. We haven't seen rabies in Italy for years."

"Rabies?"

"And strains of bacteria not normally found in this area of the world—those animals were made lethal on purpose. Depending on where their saliva entered your bloodstream, symptoms can show up in three weeks or three months. Don't fool around with this, Alana."

Michael shrugged. "Well, if you insist."

"Oh, I insist."

"And Jillian?" he asked with concern. "She was bitten days ago."

"She's already had a dose. And Juniper gave excellent initial care. When someone with her skills is sent to us, no Georgian should question it."

"As I turned the corner she was on Lucy's doorstep." Alana cleared her throat. "But about the injection, I-I don't—"

Leaning into her, Michael whispered, "You absolutely will, my love."

Chamberlain frowned. "You've just destroyed a notorious sire. One pinprick shouldn't make you shake. Baker will meet you both in the examination room."

****

Ten minutes later, Alana felt queasy when they

entered a sealed off ward with connected glass cubicles. Baker said to Michael, "I don't usually work this floor. My brand of science keeps me below ground level in the restricted area. Except when it has to do with Lu. You look damn good, Malone."

"Thanks to you and many others," Michael replied.

She recalled Baker's role in stitching Michael's many wounds last May. Being in the makeshift emergency room aboard Cesar's jet hadn't bothered her. Neither had Lu's monthly checkups with Baker. Only Baker... However, as they passed Jillian's room, she cringed at the smells, the steady beeps from every type of modern medical equipment. Juniper, in white lab coat and green scrubs, gave a confident smile. It didn't relieve her concern for three teenagers in this hospital setting. One by one, inset slats around Jillian's room closed.

When she hesitated, Michael held her arm. "Are you all right?"

"Fine," she replied, not about to reveal her phobia. The adjoining, larger room Baker led them into had two beds. Mick, at Lukas's side, wore two blue hospital gowns, one like a bathrobe.

Michael put a hand on his shoulder. "Get in your bed. That's an order, Guardian."

The quick "Yes, Sir" came with a slow shuffle across the room.

Alana stared at Lukas. Like an anxious mother, the sight of a dull-eyed boy scared her more than any demon she had ever encountered. That he was in a hospital bed jacked up her fear. Lukas's right arm was bandaged, taped to his chest. His face scratched and scraped, and on each side of his leg with the cast lay tightly-rolled white blankets. Steady bleeps of hi-tech monitors for blood pressure and other vital signs certainly didn't lessen her alarm, either. When she brushed those sandy curls off Lu's brow, Michael's tender kiss lingered on his son's forehead.

"Feel weird."

She rubbed his hand. "Gee, ya think? You were way past incredible, Lu."

"Take me home."

Michael's thin grin began, like a burst of relief. "Slow down. Does it hurt?"

"Yeah, but I'll work on it. Can we go now?"

"Forty-eight hours without moving...then we'll see. You are to focus on nothing but healing your leg." He turned to Mick. "No horseplay or heroics, and he does not try to stand. Do you hear me, Guardian?"

"Loud and clear, Sir," Mick heartily called from his bed.

Michael pulled a chair over and kept a casual pose, but Alana's soul quickened. She didn't want the devastating memories that appeared in her mind. *The machines, sour antiseptic smells... It's the same as when my parents died. Just like this, that car accident shouldn't have happened.* It shouldn't have killed them. She studied a boy too old to be her son, yet maternal instincts filled every fiber of her being. *You're a young Champion following in your father's footsteps. Bravery is written in your heart. I'm so proud of you. I'm so worried about you. I'm so sorry.* A soft smile was all she could muster.

"Mom... Hello, earth to Mom? What gives? You're zoning, and I'm the one full of mega-drugs."

His caring shattered her rambling thoughts. His woozy voice forced her into the present.

Chapter 30

For the first time in well over a century, the doors of Veronique's stronghold that faced *Piazza de Michelangelo* stood wide. Everything scrubbed, every window open. Power washers, floor buffers and other cleaning equipment hummed an eclectic symphony. Priceless artwork littered the entry hall. Alana approved of every stripped room, anxious to get to Veronique's study.

Michael frowned on the staircase. "I honestly didn't want to come back to this hellhole."

Alana ignored the possibility of a bickering match while heading straight to the technical lair. He followed, but she wouldn't address more annoyed looks. Throwing her hands up to shush him before he started again, she flopped into the comfy chair behind a carved desk to boot up the computer. "I know what you're going to say, and I don't want to hear it."

"You choose to ignore me, then," he said with another broody frown.

The screen glowed to life. "This place isn't going on the market. Not one innocent soul is buying prime property, only to wake up screaming from nightmares that can't be explained. And it's an historic landmark," she added to stop another protest.

"Why must this be done right now?"

"Because the stench of evil sickens me and every

Guardian who died at that bitch's hand irks me!" Cold rage took her over the edge. "Leonard did it for her! All of it! Killing innocent people, hurting Lu, almost taking you from me again—the thought of living without you... I *hate* her, Michael."

Leaning down his dark eyes captured hers, his perturbed expression softened. "Scrubbing every inch of this place won't lessen your outrage, darlin'." Alana forced her fingers to the keyboard and worked them at an incredible speed. "What are you doing?"

"Sending Dad every file that *demon* had. And if I find her password, I'll do the email thing, too." He came around and touched her shoulder. She slowed down...a little.

"Nigel, Neeb *and* Petula will stay here for as long as you need them. Pet's a wiz with computers. She'll do this. You can monitor everything from our home, my Guardian. You will not stay here."

Tender sternness, he was always good at that, she thought with a breathy sigh. Her eyes began to fill. "I would've had to stake you before the first night of undeath. Lukas would never forgive me; I wouldn't be able to forgive myself."

"Let it go, darlin'. Hate has never been in your heart. We didn't share blood, and I am still all human."

His calm reply deflated only part of her fear. "*Mystically* human," she insisted.

"Mystically human it is." Slipping his hands over hers, Michael guided her out of the chair. "Now we go home."

No goodbyes, no looking back. Her soulmate held her elbow as she walked down the hall. But fear of losing her unique family would never leave. Home didn't mean a luxurious third-floor apartment in Portofino. It meant Michael and Lukas. Forever and always took on a much deeper meaning.

****

Michael drove in silence. On the two-lane road into Portofino, Alana listened to endless voice messages. The way she took in a quick breath of air before placing her cell phone on the console between them, well, he was very aware that her expression changed. She'd become intense, too quiet, and hoping to see her smile, he said, "I'm getting used to driving while thinking. What did Miles have to say?"

"She's dead, Jillian's mother... Alexa," Alana whispered. "Oh God, this girl has nobody. I know how it feels."

He slowed down, realizing the scope of this evil event, and noticed Alana sink silent into the leather seat with her eyes closed. Softly he called her name, but she seemed a great distance away.

"Mom died minutes after Dad died—in the same hospital room. The other driver wasn't even injured. It shouldn't have happened. I went there with the Bookmans... We were there to bring them home... Then they both went into cardiac arrest. Oh God... Jillian is an orphan, Michael. I know how it feels." He reached for her hand, but she drew into herself with a hushed, "I don't want to talk anymore."

He knew Alana had been Jillian's age. *Just a few months older than my son is right now...* Not about to prod someone so raw, someone he loved with all his heart, he spent the rest of the drive thinking about his family, about Alana's sadness as well as her strength, about a very ill child who would have to be told the sordid truth.

When he parked the car in their garage, she whispered, "I so understand Jillian's loss."

"I love you, my Guardian."

Slowly she met his gaze. "I know."

Michael came around the car. Taking her hand, they walked to the elevator door. When it opened, he saw Miles's note taped above the button and pulled it off.

"Dad probably wants your information today."

"It can wait—"

"I'm fine. I just need some time alone."

Only after the elevator's door closed did he turn and walk out of the garage. It wasn't easy to absorb all that happened in the short span of twenty-four hours. Lukas's ability to self-heal would kick in, and Alana's inner strength was still there. He was sure of it. She'd be all right alone.

****

It was a short walk to the rectory, but Michael took his time. Of course, to be grilled by Miles, whether he cooperated or not, didn't sit well. Not one bit. Fresh air, the peaceful sea reflecting warm Amalfi sunshine heightened his desire to forego the necessary encounter with the researcher's questions. By the time he entered the rectory, he accepted the fact that it would be grueling.

Slowing his stride into the office, Michael stared at the man. "Doing the Qualifying Evidence Minuet, Researcher? Good Friday is turning out to be really super." Miles seemed to ignore his obvious sarcasm. Meeting in here, at least he didn't have to see the stone bust or the fictitious mural. Yet it didn't lessen the tension between them.

"I'm sorry to be the bearer of such sad news, Michael. Hopefully, the child will accept the truth when she's fully recuperated."

"You don't pull any punches, Miles; just shoot straight to the heartbreaker."

"She is under our protection for the rest of her natural life. I already have a thought on this."

"I'm open to any help and all suggestions," he replied, and sat near the desk.

"She needs an established family unit, but the details are premature."

"Well make it happen," he stated, knowing the far reaches of Georgian influence. Miles gave a single nod, and then indicated a large stack of folders embossed with the Council's insignia, a dragon with a sword in a circle... all indigo blue. "Is this Mother Anne's report?"

"From every healer as well, while these are the Guardians' reports from Siena and Florence. Now I'll have yours. How's my grandson?"

"Like I'm supposed to believe you haven't already grilled Chamberlain. Give it up, Gramps."

"Somehow that word coming from your mouth has a sardonic tinge."

"I'm really old, but lately I feel really young," he said with a sigh.

"Humanity's ups and downs can be quite humbling. Let's begin." Locking his arms across his chest, Michael gave a loose shrug. Miles narrowed his eyes. "Is there a problem or are you deciding how to dodge the inquisition?"

He braced for more subtle digs. "I've never stared death in the eyes before...well, not in over three centuries, anyway, and in 1690, I didn't survive."

"The account from Mick is accurate, is it not? The knife wound you sustained sealed within seconds, which means the mystical trait to self-heal is still intact. And had you gone after Veronique by yourself, you'd have staked the sire before she could bite, correct?"

"Right on both counts," he mumbled, searching for another excuse to stall. "So now I get to lead a quiet life."

"Come again?" Miles gave a ripe glare before Michael looked away. "We all have doubts. Learn to work through them. Let's continue. I know how much you dread writing tasks. So, start talking and give me details. Now, please—let's begin with the interrogation of Lucy Novak."

Shifting in the chair, he swallowed immediate discomfort. "It's not one of my finer moments. Ask me something else."

With fingers poised over the laptop's keyboard, Miles gave a terse, "Begin."

No. This wouldn't go well at all. He cleared his throat. "We had gotten her back to the student house. I... I pulled Lucy down the basement stairs," sounded more like a confession than a simple statement of fact. He cleared his throat again, didn't continue.

"I won't accept any further procrastination. The Council needs full details. Perhaps we should start with how you found her at her home near the bus depot."

We've just gone from bad to worse, Michael thought, and winced with a groan.

****

Alana's preliminary report for the Georgian Council was complete, yet she couldn't hit the send button. Sadness claimed her head and her heart. Was there anyone like Laura and Miles Bookman in Jillian's life? Did she have a best friend like Celia B? She walked around the room rubbing knots from her neck. Home alone was too quiet. No Michael. No Lukas to snoop around where his nose didn't belong. Her gaze lit on the laptop, then the door.

"The latter wins," she whispered as she walked out and down the stairs.

Celia opened the second-floor door before Alana knocked. Her sister's beaming face and loving hug came with a squeal. Alana didn't pull out of the embrace. "You did it, Ally. I caught it all!"

"And another ancient sire bites the dust." They walked through the small parlor, but upon entering the dining room, Alana froze in total disbelief. Thorn's introduction of Salvatore didn't register. She could only stare at Lucy. "You *flatly* refused my father's offer! Did a vamp make a beeline for your scrawny neck after the walk-away?"

"Hey sis," Celia quickly whispered, "Sal has a cousin who is—"

"Don't tell me. A Guardian… Well doesn't that beat all? Does Monsignor know?"

"He sent them here. She has agreed to Georgian protection. Gabby says if it's okay with you, I mean, can they stay across the hall or… somewhere?"

She wanted to scream, "*Do you know he killed his own daughter too!*" but instead, stated evenly, "No going outside… You hibernate across the hall." While Lucy took her coffee cup to the kitchen, Alana switched to Italian, whispering in a kinder tone the same request of Salvatore.

"*Grazie mille, Signora, mille grazie,*" he replied like a true gentleman.

She inclined her head slowly before looking at Celia. "So where's my nephew? I'm craving cuddly baby time. Come on, sis, wake him for me?"

Celia grabbed her arm and aimed a sympathetic frowned. "No way, let's find Mom to babysit and go for a walk. I'm sensing the need."

Chapter 31

The last two hours had been excruciating. Miles's inquisition was just as bad as what Michael had been put through two weeks ago by the entire Georgian Council—after ten endless months of solitude. Brutal and bumpy didn't even begin to describe *this* grilling.

Unwisely, he had accused the researcher of asking too many questions. The man's terse "Deal with it" made him feel like a criminal. Not one annoying detail was side-stepped and arguing hadn't helped. When he skimmed through pages of detail and signed off on it without careful study, he thought Miles might explode. "Another full Council inquisition is sure to follow, any day now," he muttered as he left the rectory.

After entering the red-brick building, he abruptly stopped on the second landing and honed in on an unexpected scent. He groaned and mumbled, "I'm not even going to ask," before trudging up the last flight of stairs. Once inside his home, emptiness engulfed him. A worried sigh escaped as he stared into Lukas's empty room.

Still miffed at Miles, he walked into the master bedroom. No rest in twenty-four hours and completely done in, the shower he couldn't wait to take turned into a quick one. Then he stretched out on the comfortable sleigh bed to wait for Alana. But as soon as his wet head hit the pillow, he closed his eyes.

****

Hours later, the distant sound of water running penetrated Michael's sleep. He felt refreshed, renewed when Alana walked to the bed. An old black silk shirt of his hung loose on her curvaceous frame. She slipped in beside him barely ruffling the covers. His arm eased around her waist to hold her close. Nuzzling his neck, she rested against his heart, the curve of her matching his like perfection.

"I tried not to wake you."

"I feel you in my soul, my Guardian," he replied. The groan that followed became an erotic, low growl, and the brush of his hand produced a fascinating tremble in the woman he loved. It seemed to take her breath away, as if he drew life out only to replenish her passion with every new gasp. Her sweet, slow kisses ignited desire, and with one strategic swipe, all the covers swooshed to the floor. Their bodies tangled together on soft, silken sheets. Not the cool breeze from the Mediterranean Sea or anything else could lessen the heat she stirred in him.

"Pure ecstasy in your arms," she sighed.

"Every time I love you, it's a new beginning."

"Like no time has passed since last May."

"Since the first moment I touched you, my journey begins and ends in your arms." After ten years, past and present formed a seamless line. "I feel your soul quiver, darlin'."

"It demands connection to you, my love."

A small cry escaped her lips when he positioned his body over hers. Holding her hands he stretched her arms wide across the pillows, throbbing, aching for an intimate bond. There would be no foreplay. She breathed in deeply as he entered her. Tightness intensified around his erection with each thrust to draw the length of him deeper. And joined in love, he held back release for as long as his human body could last until in need, they climaxed together. As living seed gushed forth, her heart raced against his. Alana's soft cries of ecstasy filled his soul...

Afterward, he didn't want to leave her, but slowly, they came apart. Relaxed against his chest, she whispered, "How did we end up by the foot of the bed? This is a really odd perspective. I never saw the headboard from this angle."

Michael folded an arm under his head and not willing to open his eyes, he moaned a satisfied "Umm."

"Maybe we should turn the bed around or move it near the windows."

That's when one eye opened. He grinned at the playful way she sat up, staying close to him. "I like the bed where it is, darlin'."

"*I* like the view of the mountains from the den. We could turn that into the master bedroom and move Lu in here."

He rolled onto his stomach. "I cannot believe you're thinking about this right now. You'd give up the privacy of your *ensuite*?"

"*I* liked that huge tub at the hotel. We could add a bathroom to the new master bedroom with a tub just like it." She massaged his back, and then ran her fingers through his hair. "Am I keeping you up?"

"One could say that," he replied, turning to her with a passionate kiss, once again fully aroused. Tonight felt different, and he couldn't satiate his need for her. Ready to pleasure her throughout the night, he placed the woman he loved sideways across the wide sleigh bed.

****

During their second work session in the Manhattan penthouse, Deepa found Mary as astute as a fellow researcher. She continued to identify the names on the print while Deepa prepared a full profile of Jillian and Alexa Gerhardt's lives for Miles. Late in the day, Deepa heard the elevator come to a stop. Mary quickly whispered, "I'm warning you ahead of time so please don't be offended. She's very wise for seventeen but she's still wild."

Dressed all in black as if she'd just stepped out of a Goth rock video, Martine Kendrick sauntered into the penthouse with a pizza held high in one hand, the other hand clipped to her waist. "I thought since Michael's in Italy this would rate at least one guffaw, Mare." Rolling intense sable eyes like her mother's, an inherited trait, she then flashed a bored grin.

"Is the extra thick purple eye-liner for Deepa's benefit?" A smile teased the young woman's lips as Mary added, "She knows you're strange, so just go do your thing. The art teacher's missing."

In the quiet study, Martine put the oily pizza box on a glass-top side table. The glossy black lipstick she wore accentuated her bright-white teeth as she smiled at Deepa. She strolled over to Mary's laptop and sat down before purple lacquered, long nails clicked away on the keyboard.

Deepa noted Mary's frown. "I know. She's a shocker, but she has incredible form with a spell." They all stared at an unknown woman on the FBI's Ten Most Wanted list on the screen. Martine worked the mouse, and Johanna DeRosa's face suddenly appeared. "What the hell are you doing!?" Mary shouted, "Undo that."

"Your smoky alto voice just hit the range of a coloratura's. Relax, Mare, you'll blow the valve they replaced." The frumpy face reappeared and Johanna's vanished. "I'll tell you what I think."

"Don't you always."

"She either threw herself in front of a train, or she ghosted."

Deepa studied the banter between them with gentle amusement and then returned to her desk with a sigh. Mary handed her a slice of lukewarm pizza on a paper plate that had been plastered on top of the box.

"Look, Deepa, it's only seven p.m. and—"

"Seven-o-three," Martine informed while folding her arms on the table. "I say we retrace DeRosa's steps. Want me to do a Starbucks run for two double-double lattes with triple shots of espresso? I have Gram's credit card because she sprang for the pizza. You're fading fast, Deep. I'd open a window or something."

Mary mouthed, "Cool it, will you?"

"No, don't shush her," Deepa said, "Like this print, every bit of information interlocks."

"Your Guardian said all the faculty left today at 2:40," Mary stated. "Where's that report again?" Both women heard Martine snap her blue bubblegum repeatedly until Valley Township's Board of Education's web site appeared. "What are you doing now?"

"Checking the facts, like you always tell me to do… Okay. Wait… Today was a half-day make up that ended a half-hour before noon. She probably blended in with the kids and has an eight-hour lead. That's piss poor for us. If she's got any dark magic mojo, you'll need a Ouija Board to find her." Martine clicked on Free Cell, totally absorbed within seconds.

Although this new information was frustrating, Deepa found it amazing how the youngest Kendrick witch completed each game—with very few moves. Two minutes later, Martine clicked open the Internet and appearing bothered, Mary said, "Martine, that's personal!"

"Wow. Ninety-one emails, Mare, and here's some from Ally. It's like a day-old already." Instantly, Martine opened it and whistling in awe, she gave a smirk. "Bingo! She sent you the Gerhardt files." Deepa handed her the printer cord over and met Martine's eyes. "It'll be easier if you have a disc, I'll download it and print from your desktop."

Once completed, Martine handed her back the disc. As information appeared on the researcher's computer, Deepa saw the hidden connection. "These names are on the art print from Leonard's office. Now we have meeting dates, aliases, and rendezvous points in Siena and Florence... You are brilliant, my dear."

Mary sank into a chair. "I could kick myself. Why didn't I check?"

Martine rubbed her mother's shoulders. "You're exhausted, Mare. You too, Deep."

****

"This is destiny's call," Johanna De Rosa whispered in reverence. The first Sorcerer of the Second Millennium wanted her with him when the new demon emerged. In somber darkness, she walked the quiet streets of Florence to a rendezvous that would rewrite human history.

As if shielded by dark forces, no Guardian had stopped her. Fate now led her to Leonard's side. His hand-written invitation stayed in hand. The stiff, crème-colored card stock had turned to pliable mush, but it remained a tangible link to him, to his cause. About to enter *Piazza de Michelangelo*, a hand snagged her arm. Momentary shock turned into recognition, and before Johanna could speak, the woman hissed, "He's dead and the dark goddess has been slain."

Immediately, her world fizzled into a vaporous nothing. Sure to collapse right then and there, she breathed out "Nooo…"

"Their deceitful Champion did this, but *every* Georgian is to blame." A heavy object came to Johanna's hand. "Go to Portofino. Take out the head of the snake." The woman's eyes darted feverishly. "It is your charge to avenge his death, to avenge us all." She slithered away.

Sleek steel rubbed cold and smooth against Johanna's hand. Ten months of preparation. All gone… The final touches on the Slovakian forgeries had been brilliant, flawless… and both scenes had precise meaning which were perfect for Leonard's plan. The titles of the murals played on Johanna's mind, and she created a plan.

Chapter 32

On Saturday morning, Deepa's research filled Miles's hands. He sat in the rectory's office barely able to contain his excitement. "Ingenious! Pages of solid dossiers on his cult members are ours. We can put an end to this."

"I agree," Monsignor Scarlatti replied.

"This is indisputable proof. The event is over. Will you call the Council together?"

"On Monday, Miles... Will you have enough time to organize the data?"

"It'll be ready." He studied the priest, who seemed lost in thought.

"Good. We will commence at six in the evening. Would you prefer to work somewhere else today?"

"You've seen enough of me, I presume." He pulled off his glasses, gave a rare grin. "It's rather nice to be kicked out. Laura will be thrilled, you know. Are you all right?"

"Easter's homily will be a special one. I have much to prepare." The monsignor stood, pacing the room straight and tall with a sturdy gait.

To be so spry in one's seventies, Miles thought. Leaning back, his hands ran through his thinning salt and pepper hair. Taking in the serene surroundings, volumes of theological studies, ancient encyclopedias, and scholarly writings by renowned liturgical authors—

a researcher's field day for eleven months, he thought, and far too many hours have been spent in here.

****

Laura beamed when Alana kissed her cheek. "You are a very happy woman, and I dare say, you positively glow. Where's Michael?"

"Probably calling contractors—we're making changes upstairs."

"Then you've decided against moving to England."

She looked around. The bookshop had kept her together during Michael's absence. "Maybe in September…"

"Or perhaps, you'll weekend with us and reside here."

"Neither of us wants to be far away from Lu."

"I understand a mother's love." Laura paused with a nod. "This is a very successful business you've grown. Are you with me today?"

"Totally, Mamma B, are we ready to open?"

Two thumbs went up. "Let's make our Holy Saturday customers happy." Alana switched the sign, unlocked the deadbolt. Cordial grace appeared on her mother's face. "You're a perfect blend of Stefania's strength and Alfonso's serenity."

"But I'd never be the woman I am if you and Daddy B hadn't been there for me," she replied with love in her heart. And when Miles walked in, a bright smile began. "I was just thinking of you."

****

By mid afternoon, too busy and thinking nonstop about Lukas and Michael, Alana wanted to shout for joy when Kayla showed up. And as soon the customer left, she said with respect, "Great job in

Florence at the villa the other night."

The young Guardian beamed. "Thanks to you, it's now the safest city in Italy. Been busy today?" Kayla set a bulging backpack outside the closed office door.

"It's been a marathon. Mom and Dad are working on something. It's off limits for now, so I'm with you. Saturday is always a two-person day."

"I saw Lu before I left. He had lots of company."

"The Brits," she said, smiling. "Pet called."

"He said those mutant Hell-beasts were like playful puppies, but he's homesick, Ally. What time are you going to visit?"

Before she could reply, a loud group of tourists entered. Kayla jumped right in. Without another set of hands in the bookshop, I'll never be able to leave, she thought, unless... "I'm recruiting help. If she gives you a hard time, just use some Guardian strength. She deserves to shake like a leaf."

Not willing to disturb her parents, Alana left through the shop's door and reentered the building from the street. She ran upstairs to the apartment above the store, knocked on the door and waited. When Lucy opened it, she studied the tall blonde. "I don't know how long you'll be here. That's up to Monsignor. But you're going to earn your keep. I need your help."

Lucy twitched, saying, "Just keep Michael far away from me."

"You'd have been dead by now if not for him, so let's call this truth-time because Leonard's plan for you didn't include happily ever after. I know what you didn't have when you were Jillian's age and what you wanted him to be. Innocents at the end of their rope get desperate enough to believe lies."

Lucy's eyes clouded. "I don't need a pep talk from a Guardian."

"You're right. So let's go."

"Michael *killed* Leonard," she hissed in a bitter tone.

Alana slowly shook her head. "Veronique bit Michael's neck, and then *she* killed Leonard."

Lucy swayed and paled, whispering, "He's undead again?"

The remark was too ludicrous for a response. "Just get a grip and go down the stairs."

As Alana stood there, Lucy quickly spoke to Salvatore; then with a defiant huff, rapidly took the stairs. Alana smiled at the silent man before following her. I guess Lucy doesn't remember I understand Italian, she thought. The woman's hushed comment had been, "She needs my help, Sal. It's the least I can do for them all keeping us safe."

****

Thankful that Lucy followed Kayla's lead in the bookstore, Alana went to be with the man she loved. At the dining room table, Michael gave her an immediate grin and held out a sheet of paper. Looking at it, her eyes grew wide. "Oh wow, this is elegant. I like our new bedroom."

"You really want to do this?"

"Of course."

"Why am I not convinced? Something's on your mind."

"Lu has to come home today." Placing the sketch down, she sat on his lap, welcomed his embrace. "Mamma B asked about England."

"This is your home. You've got a business to run."

"This is our home. It's *our* business." He kissed her cheek. She loved him more each minute.

"I'm not dragging my heels or making excuses. I'm back, one hundred percent. When Lukas is home, we'll discuss the move as a family. So what else is on your mind?"

"Our Miss Lucy," she said. He frowned and straightened his shoulders. It didn't stop her from stating what she felt had to be done.

****

On the drive to the Medico facility, Michael refused to talk about Lucy any further. He had enough on his mind. Another terrifying experience for his son to deal with, but Lukas would mend. Jillian might not. Once in Florence, they had gone to the historic piazza and stopped at a quaint stationary store. Now, with gift in hand, he walked Alana down Medico Lab's hospital corridor. Standing by the door, he watched her kiss Lukas's cheek. He'd join them shortly, but first he had to see for himself if Jillian was on the road to recovery.

Walking slowly to her bed, he hoped his gift would have a positive effect. The girl looked frightfully thin and pale. Her eyes were a void … no fear, no emotion. He didn't allow his uneasiness to show, meeting her gaze with calm reserve.

She whispered, "I thought I made you up."

"Nope, I'm real." He sat on the edge of the mattress. "I understand you're quite an artist. I've brought you something." He pulled off the printed Florentine paper, a masterpiece itself. The sketch pad and carved wooden box containing an array of colored pencils didn't even grant him a small smile.

She placed a bruised hand over his. "The doctor

said there was an accident. You saved me."

"And now you have to get better."

Her eyes filled. "Is my mom coming? Can I call her today?"

Lies wouldn't gain trust, nor ease her anxiousness. In a gentle manner, he said, "There's something you need to know." Although, he chose specific words, her tears still ripped at his soul. And as he had done with Lukas, Michael kissed her forehead and held another sobbing child in a careful embrace.

****

The possibility that Jillian might never recover didn't leave Michael when he entered his son's room. He kept a relaxed manner to conceal the sense of injustice in his heart. "You're the most protected kid in the world," he said at Lukas's side.

"Four Guardians as well as super-dad and super-mum," Petula stated with a chuckle.

They each gave a respectful nod as he clasped Mick's shoulder. "You look good."

"Never been better, Sir."

"Ready to go home?"

"Yes, Sir, me and Lu," Mick replied.

Alana pointed to the shopping bag before she followed Petula into the corridor. Neeb closed the door, and Mick pulled clean clothes out of it.

"You'll head home tonight. Your family is chomping at the bit to see for themselves that you're okay." Michael looked at Nigel. "The three of you are off to the states to assist Deepa Chandra. Alana has details." Then he met his son's eager face. "That leaves you."

"I'm going home with you, Dad."

"No testing the leg out and thinking I won't know if you try, little boy. Give me your word or I leave you here."

"I swear I'll stay put."

The earnest expression convinced him, and Michael reached into the bag for a pair of loose sweats and a T-shirt. Already dressed, Mick said his goodbyes before he left with the other Guardians.

Once alone, Michael guided Lukas's good arm into the sleeve. "How lucky you are to have the mystical ability to heal."

"How's Jillian?"

"Not too good. And she doesn't have the ability to self-heal the way you do."

After pulling a tube sock over his son's good foot, he was ready to tackle getting sweatpants over a bulky cast, but outrage still coursed through his soul—over a sobbing child in the other room. *And learning her mother was murdered has fully shattered her…*

Lukas whispered, "Why is she crying?"

"She's… really hurting and facing a slow recovery followed by years of therapy, the talking kind."

"Is her mom coming?"

Michael stopped fiddling with the sock, and said in a low voice, "Her grandfather had her mother killed. She's now an orphan."

Lukas grabbed his arm, searched his eyes. "You *told* her?"

Stay calm. He's just a child himself. Swallow your feelings and ease his mind. "She only knows her mother's dead, I said nothing about how or why her grandfather did this to her." His son flinched and shivered, flopping back down onto the pillows looking ready to cry again. Michael's hands flew off the cast and into the air. "Oh, God what did I do? What hurts?"

****

Like he had jumped into a bottomless pool and was unable to swim, Lukas sucked in a useless breath. *God, she is devastated. Now she has no one. Just blanks instead of memories... strange dreams... no answers.* His eyes welled. He exhaled a harsh, "No... no." Just like him, she'd have never-ending tears and horrible, no, terrifying nightmares. He zeroed in on only her and heard her strangled sobs with her face buried in the pillow. He understood being all alone. Living with something just out of reach. He understood its misery. She'd be scarred inside and out, just like he was.

"Please stop crying. I'm sorry if I hurt you. Look. Forget the sneaker. I'll carry you out." Breathing hard, his father sat close wiping his tears and cupping his cheek.

The nightmares. The terror. He winced and shook his head. His father's heart was racing and instantly, Lukas reached out until he was in powerful arms and cradled for comfort.

"I'm sorry. I... I shouldn't have told you about Jillian."

"I know you love me."

"More than you'll ever know, little boy."

But love didn't begin to describe all he sensed in his commanding father. He did hard things. What had to be done no matter the cost. Lukas held on tight. "I'm so sorry."

"For what?" His father kissed his hair. "What's wrong?"

"I can't leave... I can't go... No. I'm okay, I

swear, but she's alone here, and I can stay. You're the best father in the world and you trust me, right? She'll talk to me, you know she will."

"Where is this coming from?"

He shrugged against his father's chest. His incredible heartbeat was a gift to everyone he loved. And family supported one another. Eased each other's pain. Now, this innocent had no one. "I can help her. We'll talk music, and school things, like all normal stuff, not demons. So she gets stronger, Dad. Please say yes?" He pulled off his father's shoulder and resolve stood in his eyes. He had to do this.

Looking lost for words, his father said, "You don't have to do this. There are people here who can help her—"

"Please, Dad. Please…"

He searched his father's eyes, finally hearing, "Well.. If you think it'll help—"

"Thanks," he quickly said. "But can I ask one favor?"

"I'm listening."

Another truth, he realized. "Don't say little boy around my friends ever again."

"It's an inherited term of endearment… Okay. I concede, but just around your friends."

"You also say it when you're ready to get parental."

"It's an inherited warning as well."

"Yeah, like when you were fifteen… in the 1680's. So, like, your father used it on you."

"When he was proud of me and when he reached for the strap." Lukas rolled his eyes as his father grinned. "Some things never change, no matter how many centuries pass."

After another crushing hug and a few ground rules, Lukas watched the person he loved the most stand and leave. Once alone, he blew out a slow breath and tried to figure out what he would say to Jillian.

Chapter 33

Lucy begged Salvatore *not* to ask Alana if she could leave the building and accompany him to Easter Sunday mass. He did so anyway. Then Alana handed her a short-sleeved lilac sweater and a long, printed skirt. Several inches taller than the Guardian, what should've been ankle length reached a modest, just below the knee on Lucy. *At least the outfit doesn't scream 'hey look at me, I'm religious.'*

When they entered San Giorgio church, Lucy felt for certain she'd burn up. It was packed. Families, old ladies in black, and tourists crammed into every pew. They stood at the back, had missed the entrance hymn because she tried again to back out on the church steps. The doors were wide open as the monsignor said, "Lord, have mercy."

Well, not for me. Fanning her face with the church bulletin, she noticed Thorn's arm around Celia—the way Sal's was around her. The Homily didn't thrill her, either. She turned a deaf ear to words like 'redemption' and 'renewed life.' *I'm going to Hell on a fast-track.*

But Monsignor Scarlatti, a powerful speaker, had eyes full of wisdom and compassion, which even at this distance, she felt on her. Returning to the pews with wafers in their mouths, some worshipers looked pious, some didn't. *That's the thing about religion. It's either heartfelt or for show.*

M. Flagg

Sal suddenly whispered, "It's the final blessing." Her hand didn't move—thinking about all those crosses dipped in blood. Suffocating in sanctity, she couldn't wait to leave. A few minutes later, the monsignor stood outside wishing everyone a Happy Easter.

Sal pulled her over. It was more like an insistent drag. Monsignor Scarlatti took her hand. Lucy stiffened, kept her gaze on anything but him. In a friendly manner, he said, "In tomorrow night's meeting with you, much will be discussed." She faltered before pulling her hand out of his. *You can't save me, nothing can.* He bowed slightly, a gentlemanly gesture. "If you wish to speak privately, you know where I am, *signorina.*"

Lucy began to walk away, but after a huffed breath, she turned to thank him.

He had walked back into the small white church. Sal stood a short distance away talking with Alana. No way do I go near Michael Malone, she thought.

Brushing her hair behind an ear, she suddenly realized she was missing an earring.

****

Alana whispered to him, "You'll apologize today, right?"

"I'd say over my dead body, but that's just too close to home." Michael refused to ruin the day thinking about Lucy. "Didn't you say the Kendricks were flying in?"

"They're helping Deepa with research and will probably take a flight tomorrow, and don't change the subject. Say *something* to her. Be brief but make it right." Turning back to Sal, she continued chatting in Italian.

374

Michael's feet suddenly pointed in the opposite direction, and he studied a nun who had her eyes cast down, her hands tucked in the cuffs. The black scapular matched a short veil, and the brown habit she wore reminded him of the healers in his dream of survival. Odd, he thought, the way her face is cast down to the ground. "The apology can wait a few more hours," he mumbled and turning back to the church, he almost bumped right into her. Swiftly offered, a contrite, "*Mi dispiace, Sorella.*"

She hesitated a moment, didn't look up at him, and then continued to the church. Focused back on Lucy, it came as no surprise that she was still petrified of him. That brought a smirk to his lips, watching her scrutinize the church steps before going back inside.

"Oh what the hell," he moaned with a frown. "Maybe it's meant to be. A quick apology and quicker exit… even though I'm not feeling it." He looked up at the bright sky and then rolled his eyes, doggedly delaying what he had to do. "Okay. It'll be witnessed by the monsignor and a little foreign nun. Alana will stop nagging, and we can put another issue to rest." Signature strides weren't happening. His steps turned halting and slow, dreading the task that waited.

****

Lucy crouched in the corner of the last left pew searching for the teardrop ruby set in yellow gold—the only reminder of her mother who had died a brutal death. With a squint, she shimmied flat against the wooden floor. The earring had wedged between two wide planks, a good reach away. She stretched an arm as the hem of a brown habit and black sandals passed by. But the ruby was still out of reach. She peeked out the isle to see the kind priest at the altar.

"Treaties are to be observed," the nun stated in English, now directly in front of him.

"Do not repay evil with evil," he replied in a calm voice.

"You meddled with a great destiny, old man."

"It is done. Now fulfill yours."

Church bells tolled the noon hour, drowning all sound with twelve loud, long bongs. His white vestment suddenly had a large red splatter, and clutching his chest, he fell to his knees, and then collapsed. Lucy's head snapped back and hit the edge of the pew. She dove for the floor as footsteps came closer. Bright sun poured through a stained-glass window, as if Lucy Novak, soon-to-be-dead witness, had found the follow-spot on a theater's stage.

"I know someone's here. Show yourself," the woman ordered. "Get all the way up!"

Lucy rose, stared speechless at the barrel of a gun. In the aisle, sunbeams glazed her vision, and she couldn't see the face. Her legs wobbled. Her head hurt from the hard crack on the wooden pew.

"I know you. Your picture is in Leonard's study." The woman's voice rose, her words sharp and quick. "You were entrusted with the vessel! *You* let it go! Traitor!"

The impostor took aim. The last bell tolled.

Entering the church, Michael instantly smelled the blood seeping from the compassionate priest's chest. It shocked him—the astounding incongruity of a good man and an evil act. The gun was aimed at Lucy, and with a fast leap, he grabbed for her as the bullet flew. It grazed his right arm, but the hearty push took Lucy out of harm's way.

Then, he faced the assassin, a mere three feet away.

"You," she screamed, "The vampire who moves in daylight! Their twisted champion!"

Beyond furious, he held her crazed stare, barely able to say, "What. Did. You. Do."

The gun went into her mouth. The imposter pulled the trigger.

With both hands covering her ears, Lucy screamed nonstop. Michael pulled her to him as she flailed. "Help him! Do something!"

His eyes teared with the whisper, "There are only two hearts beating right now, yours and mine." Rushing over, Salvatore yelled something in Italian and took Lucy from him.

Then he saw Alana, frozen at the door. With a stunned cry, she ran past the dead woman in a pool of blood. She sank to her knees sobbing beside the monsignor. Steady, with a slow gait, he went to her. A serene expression remained on Monsignor Scarlatti's face. Full of sadness, he pulled out his cell phone and hit a number. Three rings sounded like an endless dirge, tolling the death of a most-honorable human being.

Michael heard Miles's voice but couldn't find his.

****

Lukas considered himself a pro with the sleek wheelchair. He had introduced himself to Jillian. It took a while before she opened up a little, so he did a lot of talking. He kept changing the channel on the TV mounted on the wall as they chatted about the Italian shows. And the fine art of hearing more than one conversation and sensing her feelings had him on top of the world. He did a 360 with the wheelchair. "Neat ride, ya think?"

The giggle hinted how her pretty eyes could sparkle. "Juniper says I can have the IV removed for a while."

"That's mega cool. So, we find some wheels for you and investigate this place." Just like that she started talking about her best friend and art stuff. And when she smiled, his typical shyness around girls was nowhere in mind.

Her bed hummed as it came to a sitting position. "My best friend also broke her leg once, but she didn't even stay in the hospital a whole day."

He wore an impish smile. "I've got complications. My best friend went home yesterday. Lives right outside of London in Hammersmith."

"Paige lives on the other side of town, but we've been friends since kindergarten. You're making me dizzy."

On purpose, he bumped into the bed, let out a loud "ow" and rubbed his good knee. With mischief written across his face, he eyed the sketchpad. "Draw me."

"Portraits take time."

"I promise to sit still." Nose high in the air, he assumed an arrogant pose.

"Your Dad's a hero," she whispered. "He pulled me from a car wreck."

"He's a regular Champion and way cool."

She picked a pencil out of the wooden box and started to draw.

A minute later, he heard a news reporter break into regular programming to say something about Portofino. He shivered. Felt uneasy, thinking about blood and death. "I… I gotta go, but I'll come back," he said. In the corridor, right outside his room, he overheard a conversation many feet away… about something that took away his breath and made him shiver again.

Chapter 34

Johnny Baker had called, and like any worried father, Michael drove like a maniac to the Medico facility. His son was in an ugly mood, an unpredictable sulk that didn't make any sense. When Baker said he had seen Lukas in the hall, Michael knew that Lukas had overheard something he wasn't prepared to hear. It was all over the news already. A murder in a church. On Easter Sunday. And before his son's mood turned into rage, he had to get there.

But Lukas didn't look up when Michael sat on the bed. Lukas pushed the tray of warm risotto away. Michael pushed it back.

"Tell me. Tell me the truth," came at him—right on the ridge of rage.

Just about to swipe the tray off the rolling table, Michael grabbed it as his son's nostrils flared. The tight glare didn't sit well with him because he knew what his son was capable of. Placing the tray down, he handed his son a glass of water. "Unlock your arms and drink it," he ordered. "Don't even think about swiping the tray off again."

"Say it. And tell me the truth." A shaky hand reached for the glass.

After his son drank half the glass, he told Lukas what had happened to Monsignor Scarlatti. When his son turned his face away, he whispered, "Talk to me, son."

"Ever since you came back, I thought it was you who would die. We were flipping channels, and as soon as the news broadcaster said Portofino, I knew there was blood and death." His son paused. "I liked him, Dad. He talked to me and Mom every Sunday. And I wasn't there last week."

Michael handed him the fork. Lukas took it but played with the aromatic rice. "I know he liked you, too. Very much," was all he could manage to say.

Tense minutes passed before his son said, "I'll tell you something else. I think I sense things about people. Jillian won't heal until her best friend is here. I'm positive."

He didn't expect the answer and studied his boy. Pushing straggly curls off his forehead, he caught the lost expression and placed a hand on Lukas's pale cheek. "Tell me how you know."

Those boney shoulders shrugged. "Maybe it's an inherited trait from my mother. You said she was a dark seer."

Stunned, he let out a long sigh. Instinct told him where this was going, not any kind of psychic ability.

Lukas looked at him. "I have a right to know."

He gave a slow nod, still hesitant. "Her name was Deirdre Shepherd. She had delicate features, blond curly hair, and blue eyes but not as dark-blue as yours. Yes, she was powerful, but she wanted more. I assume she had a good grasp of dark magic because nothing else explains how you were conceived."

"Was she as powerful as Auntie Celia?"

"I honestly can't say. I don't know if your ability to sense things is an inherited trait."

"Maybe I just have a touch of it."

Hoping to lighten the mood, Michael grinned. "Maybe. Or maybe you're just smart off the charts and great at deduction."

"Yeah," he whispered.

"Look. We have lots of time now. I'll sit with you and we'll go through all eight days of the dream journal together. I'll answer every question you have."

"You promise?"

"Absolutely. Now eat something."

Lukas took a spoonful of risotto and then another. "What is the middle M in your name?"

"Martin. My father's name. I had Mary Kendrick forge your birth certificate. As it should be, father to son, you are Lukas Michael Malone. I couldn't tell you that day in the basement. You wanted a fight, not an explanation."

"Mystical strength, self-healing, all five senses really sharp come from you, but this sixth-sense thing, is it a gift or a curse?"

"No son of mine is ever cursed," he said with a thin grin.

"I shouldn't leave Jillian yet."

"Lukas—" he narrowed his eyes.

"No. She's not strong enough. Do something. Because nothing's right."

He watched his son take another mouthful of food. Lukas's emotions ran deep. And before his son became distraught, Michael said, "Your... Gramps has a plan. I know it will all work out. Jillian is very sad. But sorrow passes, little boy, and we have to go on. You've got a good heart."

Lukas studied him before saying, "I inherited my

heart from you."

****

Instead of returning to Portofino, Michael drove to Siena. Pulling up to the villa, Mother Anne stood waiting. A serene expression lit her face as he unfolded his long frame out of the car. Without a word, he embraced her. Slowing his stride, they began to walk toward the slope of a hill. "I'm so sorry, Mother."

"Another dearest friend leaves me. Over fifty years ago, I sensed my abilities because of Sebastiano."

"Were you already here... at the villa when you met?"

"Oh, Lord, no. I was a young woman of the world, and a rather tempestuous musicologist who loved knowing questions before they were asked. Oxford sent me to the Vatican for a lecture on Gregorian chant, but I had met Sebastiano as a seminarian at university in Rome, some years before. He was seated in the front row. During the presentation, we locked eyes. And then this calling flooded my heart and my soul."

"My son's birth mother was a dark seer. He's questioning himself."

"Lukas is very special and wanting to know about one's heritage is indeed normal. Share it all with him. About his bloodline, the connection about Helena. No. I highly doubt Deirdre was powerful enough to make herself conceive. That may always be a mystery. As for Jillian, tell him everything. Deepa will assist with Miles's plan for her future. Slow down, young man. There is too much on your mind."

He fully frowned. "I hear you," Michael whispered as she patted his arm.

****

Lukas pulled off the hospital gown and unwrapped his arm. Yards of beige elastic cloth cluttered the bed. He rotated his right shoulder and straightened his elbow with ease. No marks remained on his face and his ribs were completely healed already. Concentrating on muscle and bone, he saw his leg almost healed. He hopped on one foot to the closet, and then sat on the chair to tug on the clothes they had brought yesterday. Wheeling into Jillian's room, he wore a sheepish smile.

"Are you okay?" She put down the pencil.

He sensed intense sadness, like her heart held no more tears but was still crying. "Yeah. Just a lot of things have happened since my accident. Are you drawing?" She held up the pad. After a long, drawn "Wow," he added, "damn, you're good."

"You've got a memorable face. But it needs background, more details."

"Like me standing in a library or something?"

Jillian shook her head. "I think you like action."

"So, is your friend Paige an artist, too?"

"No, she has a great voice..." As Jillian talked about her friend, Lukas sensed some of that sadness lifting. If she kept talking, it would help her heal. He didn't leave when Betts and Sister Phyllis came to visit. The healer smiled at him, and he got the feeling she was telling him he was really helping. And as for Betts, the way she stared at him made him blush. During their visit, he only left her once, to ask Baker for something, and then, he couldn't wait for everyone to leave.

Minutes after everyone left, Jillian reached for a cup of orange gelatin on her tray. Lukas grabbed it first. Grinning, he broke off bits of a chocolate bar and buried them in the orange goop, thrilled to hear her giggles. "My mom says chocolate does a body good. There's a great ice cream place up the coast from Portofino. I went there last May. I had this really bad night."

"What happened?"

"I lost someone I really loved, and I had to trust people I didn't know." Okay, only a small lie, he thought. "Paige is like family, right?" He could feel Jillian's heart beat stronger.

Chapter 35

Celia sat close to Thorn. So much grief made everyone's heart heavy, and her psychic skills weren't all that sharp tonight.

"Sis, are you with us?" Alana asked.

Teary-eyed, she shrugged. "This was supposed to be a happy day. What if evil is on the rise again?"

A cold look came from Michael. "If that's the case, we'll stop it. As soon as the funeral is over, I want you and Thorn back in England, in the safety of the Georgian estate."

"What about the two of you and Lukas," she quietly asked.

"We'll discuss it when he comes home."

"There's no discussion." Alana said, "Do you think he has a refined sixth sense?"

She looked at Thorn, who replied, "He's got something. All guessing aside, the dark seer had incredible skills. This kid is uni—"

"Don't say unique," Michael said. "How the hell do I parent a boy who is so highly sensitive to everything and everyone around him? I'm lost in suddenly having a beating heart and he acts out. It's connected, right Thorn?"

"I'd say so. But how do I parent a boy considered the Fire of God?" Thorn's voice deepened. "You know I can't fight. So maybe you show mine the way a mystical warrior moves, and I teach yours to control those empathic thoughts. See how u-u—" Celia sent a different word quick, "ubiquitous the heavenly help is?"

Michael's glare locked on her. His eyebrows rose, which made her smile. "Ubiquitous? Nice try, Celia B. So we do this together, right?"

"In England," Alana suddenly said.

"The bookshop can't run itself," he replied.

Celia had a thought, felt a familiar sixth-sense tingle, and almost immediately, Michael stood, saying, "I'm beat. No more decisions tonight. Sorry, guys." He kissed Alana's cheek, whispered, "Stay and talk. I'll see you upstairs."

****

In the hallway, Michael noticed the other apartment door wide open and Lucy pacing inside the living room. One foot hit the first step, but with a groan, he stopped and turned back. The horrid scene in the church as well as Alana's request worked on his conscience. He rapped a knuckle on the doorframe.

Lucy startled and then whispered, "You can come in. I… I invite you."

"I'm not a vampire anymore."

"Don't I know it," she mumbled and looked away.

Leaning against the wall, he laced both arms across his chest and casually crossed his ankles. "I apologize for insulting you in Siena. I will not, however, apologize for scaring you. That was necessity."

"Thanks for saving my life."

"You're welcome. Now move on and change." He saw regret in her, something he fully understood. "Don't return to Siena. Start a new life here where you're protected. Vampires play for keeps, Lucy. They have no free will, but you do. A good man died today because of a misguided mind's weird way of worshipping evil. Take what the Georgians offer and do something right for once." He allowed a thin grin. "Above all, don't let Sal down."

She replied with a soft, "I'll try."

"Do more than try or I'll find you. Sleep well," he said with a clear conscience.

"You too," she said.

****

Alana found the curve of Michael's body a soothing place tonight. His arm came around her, and she sighed as he said, "No kiss good night? I apologized to Lucy, as you requested. I even had a brief but kind conversation, which warrants at least a peck on the chin…or maybe the lips."

She snuggled closer. "What a sweet thing for you to do. I'm proud of you, my love."

"Ah, that detestable word brings back a distinct memory."

"I'll just bet it does."

"Did you say it to purposely tease me?"

"Would I dare do such a thing, my sweet?"

"I'll admit it sounds sensual coming from you."

"Really?" She turned into his arms and faced him.

"Truly," he stated before kissing her neck. "Every tease from you is pure torture."

"Really?"

"Truly," he stated in an arrogant way as he unbuttoned the black silk shirt to kiss her breasts.

"I've always admired your long fingers on such sweet, sweet hands."

The shirt slid off her shoulders and sailed through

the air, fluttering across the Queen Anne chair. "You are merciless. I find myself in a certain state every time you're near." The growl of his voice made her quiver and her hand tightened around him. "But I can't do to you what I want unless you let go."

In a sultry way, she sighed, "Really."

"Truly," he whispered.

Kisses traced down her body, teased her until she could hardly breathe. Then his kisses found her core and she sighed as she threw back her head. He was slow and sensual teasing her to that point of no return. And when he slid up her body and entered her, his incredible heart pounded wildly in his chest. Locked in a possessive kiss, he groaned as they raced toward ecstasy.

Equally strong, she sensed their souls join—a sensation that heightened with every heated second. Bathed in his scent, she thought the world spun twice as fast when they climaxed together. Then she stilled in his arms and spooned in the fold of his body.

Minutes passed, maybe hours as she lay there thinking. When she let out a long, slow breath, he kissed her shoulder.

"You're not asleep? It's very late."

"Three-forty-seven, to be exact," he said in a dreamy tone.

"I'll never get up to open tomorrow morning."

"No. No bookshop for you tomorrow. Tourists can do without it for a day."

"About England… Lu needs the Georgian Institute now more than ever. He needs to be with his friends in a normal routine with you there to guide him."

"He'll let us know when he's ready to come

home."

"About England... You'll go back with him and I'll come as soon as I can."

"Under no circumstances will I leave you here alone. He'll have plenty of people around him at the estate. You, however, only have me."

"Can we please talk timeline?"

His eyes shot open with a surprised, "*Now?*"

Pulling out of his embrace, she knelt at his side. "Celia says there's a whole suite of unused rooms in the estate. You could refurbish it and pick the entire décor. I promise to not purchase one frilly pink lamp. I could teach at the institute. You could, too."

"Teach what, I can't teach."

"There's the history of a redeemed vampire, paranormal stealth and strength, not to mention fencing or tracking tactics." Utterly speechless, he turned on his side to face her. "There's also the ever-famous 'I can get anyone to confess anything' strategy that worked with Lucy. You know lots of important things."

"I don't think Miles *or* Headmaster Clarke wants that last one. And what about leaving Portofino?"

"My life is at your side with Lu. I can't say I won't miss this beautiful seaport. It'll be our private getaway."

"Which the whole world knows about... This is not my classification of private, darlin'. Besides, you have many friends here."

"So do you. Two weeks ago, when our neighbors saw you in the piazza, the phone in the shop rang off the hook. Ask Celia. She wouldn't lie. There's been much discussion about the handsome man who has my heart. I think the local girls even captured you on their cell phones. Add to that list little Betts, who visibly melted every time you gave her a grin. Lu has your singular charm, my love." He laughed again as she settled back against him. "I really miss him."

"Our son will be home soon."

"Yes, he will." As his arm came over hers, Alana thought, our son... *We're a loving family of three.*

Chapter 36

Patrice Virelli heard the doorbell. Leaving a pile of unfolded clothes on the dryer, she ran up the basement steps of her townhouse in Valley Township and stared at her brother through the screen door. "I just saw you at Mom's. What's up?"

Dennis came in, sat at the counter. "I got a call." She took a sip of wine, pointed to the open bottle on the bar. "Nah, I'm still on midnights."

"Yeah, but you get to sit at a desk instead of giving tickets to speeders on Hamilton Turnpike. Hey wait... Is this official business? I don't have Mom's need for speed anymore. No encounters of the "my brother's a cop" kind."

"Paige's friend Jillian lives on Castles Road, right?"

"Yeah, and *her* mother doesn't speed, either. You know the old coot sent her to Italy to see Jilly? Paige called without me knowing—can't wait for *that* phone bill."

"I got a call from Ed."

She gave a knowing grin. "Forget it. Alexa is very candid about how her husband went nuts right after Jillian was born. Ed knows they pulled Gunter's body out of the Hudson River. She liked him until he made those comments about her father-in-law, who gives everyone the creeps, but a satanic cult? So what if

Leonard paid off her mortgage and sends checks with loads of zeros every month. Ed should've left well enough alone."

"Look, he followed up on a call from Alexa's nut job of a neighbor about overturned garbage cans. Alexa is dead." Patrice sank down on the tall stool at the counter, couldn't process the words. "This gets worse, Tree. She's been dead a while."

"How," she whispered.

"Stabbed and then raped."

"*Afterward*," she asked.

He took the glass from her hand. "And your phone number was right next to her bed in the picture with the girls. The frame was turned upside down."

She had one too, next to her bed. "There's more. I know there's more."

"Gerhardt reportedly died from a heart attack in Italy. Jillian was in a bad car accident. She's in a private hospital, pretty banged up. Ed's gonna call when he has the facts together. We put an unmarked car on this street. Make sure the alarm's on." Tears flooded her eyes. She pulled herself out of the questions racing in her head, as he walked to the door. "I don't want anything to happen to you, so check every lock and maybe rent a big dog."

After he kissed her cheek, Patrice locked the screen door and the wooden door before turning the deadbolt. Did the murderer have her phone number? Could he find out where she lives? Fear felt like an adrenaline rush. She couldn't get to Jillian in some private Italian hospital with no other information. And thinking about Alexa brought fresh tears to her eyes. Luckily, her mother's promise of an entire day shopping at the

Garden State Plaza mall enticed Paige to sleep there one more night.

The townhouse attached to hers was empty. She felt paralyzed with fear.

****

Deepa Chandra sat with two friends from England in the living room of the Manhattan penthouse. "Nigel is in place, watching the Virelli townhouse. Miles knows the Georgian who will meet with me tomorrow morning. Another interesting connection, however, he is not a Guardian."

"When's the monsignor's funeral?" Petula asked.

"Wednesday, which means all must be in place by Tuesday evening."

Neeb asked softly, "And what can we do to help?"

"Alexa Gerhardt's body will have a set of fingerprints that match the ones by the shattered window."

"If they belong to one of Gerhardt's followers, consider it done," Petula said with a nod.

"What about the girl?" Neeb asked.

"Jillian is already under our protection."

"She needs something to make her want to live," he whispered.

Deepa smiled. "You have a tender soul."

He gave a shy nod as Petula said, "And that's why I adore him."

"If the Georgian accepts this mission, Jillian will be fine. For now, you are to focus on the safety of Patrice and Paige Virelli without making contact. Tuesday evening, both of them must be on that plane to Italy. Neeb joins Nigel at the townhouse and a local Guardian will take you to the block where Patrice's parents live, Pet."

"Is there a chance the Georgian won't accept the mission, Deepa?" Petula asked.

"Tomorrow, I'll have the answer."

She walked with them to the penthouse elevator. When the door closed, sadness descended like a black shroud. Monsignor Scarlatti had given her this post less than a year ago. Returning to Portofino would not be a joyous occasion.

Chapter 37

The next morning, Deepa Chandra sat across from a dapper man in his forties. When Robert Majors extended his arm, the handshake was firm and forthright, his warm blue eyes full of genuine kindness. He placed the order at a quaint coffee house in Valley Township, and they sat in a quiet corner.

"I understand you have a lucrative business with multiple facilities in Passaic County. Miles Bookman speaks very highly of you."

"We go way back. I've worked on his cars since 1982."

"You were part of the event last May?"

"I burned Philip's pick-up on Rte. 80 and made it one terrific crash."

"It got him out of Manhattan and to safety, a testament to your talent."

"You've read my file, Miss Chandra. I'm good to go."

She preferred conversation, simply stating, "Mister Majors, you must be sure."

"Call me Bob, and I'm positive on this one."

The girl from the counter had a bright smile as she placed two coffees on their table. Bob smiled back with a soft "thanks" and handed Deepa the cup. "I take it we both like it black?"

She nodded. "I'm sorry for the loss of your wife."

"Cancer is a killer...like a demon, just more merciless. She was a good woman."

"How long were you married?"

"Twenty years. No kids... I built a business, and she had a career. It's only recently that I feel like a human being again, not one of the walking dead, no pun intended." His eyes held sadness, but a sincere smile remained.

She knew instantly that Miles had picked the right person. "You're aware this assignment will last a lifetime."

"I have no ties that bind, Ms. Chandra, and I believe in what we do." His arm stretched across the table, and she noticed the Georgian symbol of a dragon with a sword in a circle on his wrist. The tattoo was indigo blue. "I wear it with pride. Whatever you need," he added. As he tilted his head, soft brown hair touched the collar of his leather jacket.

She slid an envelope embossed with the official Georgian Seal across the table. The same dragon in a circle could be seen. He took it and leaned back in a confident fashion. "Your Clifton home will be sold. 519 Orchard is on a quiet cul-de-sac. You will move in later on today. It's all in here." He tucked it into the inside pocket of his jacket. "No questions, then? Even one little one?"

His hands came to rest upon hers. "Whatever the Council needs, I'm prepared."

"We'll see to everything."

"I trust you."

Deep morals and innate goodness—a Georgian trait and a winning combination. "Miles suggests we see your new home before you enter this agreement with us."

"Today I have the Porsche. So that means I drive."

Bob stood, held her elbow in a gentlemanly fashion. His grip was sturdy, and Deepa sensed him the perfect choice. Once outside the coffee shop, her eyes feasted on a most stunning silver-blue car. In sunlight, its color matched his eyes. With a charismatic smile, he opened the passenger door. They drove down Hamilton Turnpike. At the third light, he turned right. Narrow streets gave the complex a cozy village feeling.

Pulling into the attached driveway, he asked, "Why is there no For Sale sign?"

"The association doesn't allow one."

"So much for finesse, or lack thereof, I guess. I've lived in three apartments and one house. Never had to deal with 'the association', but I guess I'll learn."

As he pulled the key out of the ignition, Deepa said, "I prefer to remain here. Please take your time. Have a look around. By all means, check the lovely backyard as well."

****

Canvassing the deck off the back of her home, Patrice said into the phone, "All right, well, have a good time at the mall and don't bug Grandma too much. Promise me." After a typical teenage response from her daughter, she laid the phone on the counter, grabbed an oversized mug and the latest best-seller. Relaxation and a good read were waiting. She'd been on the computer since dawn working on client's tax returns and really needed a break.

On the deck, she settled into a chair. Thinking about Alexa and Jillian last night, sleep had never come. She placed the mug on the arm of the chaise lounge and opened the book.

Twigs suddenly crunched. Her heart jumped to her throat. Losing her place, Patrice scanned the page. Someone whistled the melody of her favorite song by Bon Jovi. She shook her head, positive a murderer wouldn't announce himself with *we're gonna make a memory.* More twigs snapped. Or would he, she thought. Words swam on the page as she whispered, "Oh God, please. No one will find me for days, just like Alexa."

The tall hedges at the side of her property began to shake, and jumping up, the mug teetered before toppling off the chaise's wide arm. Hot liquid splashed down her legs. The book flew into the air, and she screamed before feeling the coffee sear her skin.

A brown leather arm punched through the hedges, and then the murderer charged. Too numb to move, his brutal grip crushed her arms. The burning sensation on her legs didn't matter; she was about to die.

"Are you okay, oh God—Patrice?"

She gasped for breath, slowly opened her eyes. Very tentative, she whispered, "Bob?" and stared into soft blue eyes carved into her memory. You don't have your first serious crush on a new boy in the neighborhood at fifteen, and you definitely don't find him in your backyard thirty years later, she thought.

His gaze drifted to her drenched legs. "Jeez, are you burned?"

A crisp white handkerchief came out of his leather jacket, a quirky habit. That he still carried one, neatly pressed into a square, drew her back to those innocent years. The starched rectangle brought to mind a white flag of surrender. And when he crouched down to dry her legs, Patrice's eyes stayed focused on his mop of brown hair, very soft and still a bit too long.

"What on earth are you doing *here*? I-I'm sorry, I mean, how, why—"

He stood and stared directly into her eyes in a curious way—for a full minute before collecting the broken pieces of a pink mug, placing each one carefully on the white resin table. "I'm your new neighbor. My townhouse is attached to…yours?"

"Yes. Mine. All mine," she whispered.

"Are you okay now?"

"What? Oh. Yes. So how are you?"

Picking up the book, he placed it in her hand—with a charming grin. "I'm actually much better now. Are you always this jumpy?"

"Oh. No. It's a long story."

"I'm moving in later on today. I'll have all the time in the world to hear it."

"Did you say moving in?"

"Let's have dinner together. Will you be home?"

"Yes," she whispered, "I'm working from here— for a while."

"Then I'll order. See you at seven."

Her heart skipped a beat when he disappeared through the thick bushes. She clutched his sopping wet handkerchief, not willing to let it go.

****

Later that day, Patrice breathed a sigh of relief when her brother pulled up in a police car. Dennis always looked like hell after a twelve-hour shift, but more than a little shocked, he came up the front stairs and continued to stare at her new neighbor. "Isn't that Bobby Majors from the old neighborhood?"

Patrice nodded with wide eyes. Dennis introduced a stately Indian woman, and then walked across the patch of lawn. She saw them shake hands before turning back to her guest. "I'm sorry, Miss Chandra, I'm having a, well, a strange day today."

The woman's expression was warm and friendly. She ushered her into the living room and settled on the sofa. "My brother said you have information about Jillian."

"I believe your daughter will be hearing from Jillian shortly, Miss Virelli."

"Oh, thank God, but how do you know?" Could this day get any stranger, she thought as the visitor handed her a business card with a silver dragon embossed on a circle of gold.

"The organization I represent works closely with Medico Research Laboratories in Florence. Jillian is at their private hospital."

"Why is Jilly there? I mean, they're known for great work on infectious diseases, cutting edge and then some."

"The person who pulled her from the highway wreckage is indeed a special man. He insists she have the best of care. That's why the child was taken to their exclusive facility. However, her ability to heal is slow, and she is despondent over the loss of her mother."

"She has no one, Miss Chandra. Alexa and I, well, we were close, just like our girls, for over ten years." Two thick envelopes came to her hand.

"The gentleman requests you and your daughter go to Jillian immediately. Private transport is arranged. These papers serve as your passports for customs officials." Patrice studied the bottom of the letter somewhat surprised. "I see you've noticed the Papal Seal."

She looked up. "Who rescued Jilly, a cardinal or something? I didn't think you could travel without a passport."

"This is a most special case which requires immediacy, but no, he's not a member of any clergy. The girl's welfare is his only concern."

"She'll never be alone, not if I can help it, Miss Chandra. Thank you. I'll reimburse him for everything."

"Oh no, Miss Virelli, reimbursement would offend this gentleman immensely. Your suite in Florence is booked until Jillian is well enough to travel home. He *insists,* and he'll not allow you, at any time, to pay for a blessed thing."

"Blessed is right," Patrice said with grateful heart, "Thank you, once again."

"Will someone look after this lovely home for a while, perhaps a neighbor?"

Patrice thought about Bob, about the moving van outside and her brother shaking his hand. With a small smile, she nodded "Yes, I'll ask."

****

"Is this a private party," Michael asked as he strode into Jillian's room. The strong desire to hug Lukas intensified, but he had the definite impression it'd be an embarrassment. Keeping an easy smile, he added, "You look much better today, Jillian."

"Hey, show my dad."

Reluctantly, she gave him the sketch. He studied the quality of her work, which astonished him. "This is a masterpiece, young lady. Name your price."

"It's not finished. The blue in his eyes isn't dark enough."

"You've captured the essence of Lukas Malone. Name your price. I insist."

"Does your phone make international calls?"

"You're selling me for a cell? I'm insulted, Jilly." Lukas snapped his fingers with authority, held out a palm, and Michael handed him the phone. Maneuvering the wheelchair to the door, he heard a small giggle.

"Wait. Do you have texting?"

Instantly dumbfounded, Michael said, "I don't…" Lukas just nodded. "I do," he proudly stated. "It takes pictures as well."

As they left the room, his son whispered, "She's calling Paige."

Chapter 38

Three different shades of lipstick were stamped on Lukas's cheek, each one smudged by well-meaning, maternal hands. He fidgeted in the wheelchair until Thorn placed Uriel in his arms. Chubby fingers locked around tangled strands of his sandy-blond curls and pulled.

Everyone laughed—except his father. Lukas knew exactly what he was doing—listening through the wall to Jillian's conversation with Paige.

Alana pushed the wild blond locks behind his ears. "I told you to get a haircut days ago, Lu, and I miss you. Please come home."

"Soon, Mom," and before Miles could ask, he added, "The leg's fine, Gramps. I'm ready to walk on it."

"Not yet. Let Arthur Chamberlain agree first."

"I second that," his father sternly added.

As Celia took the baby from his arms, Lukas thought a question, and she replied aloud, "Yes. Everything's set in Valley Township. Of course she'll be safe, sweetie."

His father gave a bothered glare. "Am I the only one who feels out of the loop?"

Full of mischief, Lukas grinned. "I'm sensing you're in the minority."

"You're not sensing anything that solely belongs to

me and Dad," Alana quickly said.

Words suddenly echoed around his brain. "Totally no, Mom! It'd be, uh, a-an egregious error *ever* to eavesdrop."

His father's dark eyes fixed on Thorn before he left, and then, sheepishly, Lukas glanced down and to the side.

Alana hugged him from behind. "Wow, that's some fancy term, Lu."

There was something different about her, Lukas thought, just as Celia let out a shriek and then a shrill, "Oh my!"

"What's the matter, sis? Why are you staring at me?"

"I…I was staring? Ooh, there's a baby spot on your blouse," Celia replied.

"No, that's part of the print. Are you okay?"

Lukas narrowed his eyes and suddenly Thorn's hand was on his shoulder. "I caught it too, honey. I saw his thought right there in my mind as clear as day. Shame on you, kid, wanting to stand up right now and put full weight on that leg!"

"Wait. What? No… no!" An audible group gasp rolled through the room. Everyone looked his way—with stern disbelief. He still didn't get why Auntie Celia let out that shriek.

****

Michael held out his arm. And it happened as soon as their hands touched each other's. Jillian placed the phone in it and she lost all color yet didn't pull away. He saw what he had hoped *not* to see in her face, in her watering eyes.

Her head met the pillow with a sigh. "There wasn't

any car accident, but you did save my life." She locked his gaze. Her hand stayed in his. "Something evil was in me. My grandfather knew. So do you." She let go of his hand and curled on her side.

"Jillian, this conversation is premature."

"She was mesmerizing. There was no heartbeat and she bit my wrist."

"The puncture wounds will look like two tiny freckles."

"Will she come for me?"

"She no longer walks this earth."

"I know Lucy tried to trick it, getting things it wanted without..." Now trembling, she searched his eyes. "It saw you... *I* saw you. Please tell me how?"

"What was put inside your soul once swallowed mine as well—for over three centuries."

"But you're not evil."

Too many disjointed facts put together too quickly—he could relate to that. "No. I'm not. Now you must let this rest."

Ribbons of tears dripped down her cheeks. "I swear I fought it."

The sincere declaration melted his heart. "I understand what you feel, believe me, more than you will ever know."

She began to cry softly. Still bruised and cut, the purple patches of skin where muscle strained against the ungodly beast-within were slow to heal. *Fang marks, unseen scars—all because of a sinister man. A child lost in nightmares, just as Lukas had once been.* Then brittle sobs began. In a gentle way, Michael smoothed her short brown hair. Pulling the white blanket up, he tucked it around her.

****

When Michael returned to his son's room, the conversation sounded animated. All Lukas had to do was look up at him from the wheelchair, and he shook his head. His father came over and whispered in his ear, "She knows."

The room went silent. "Can I answer her questions, Dad?" Lukas asked.

"Very discretely. You'll sense how much she can handle."

Thorn and Celia both shook their heads. "She's sleeping now. When you go to her room, let her talk, kid. Trust yourself."

"I will, Uncle T. I promise," he said and sensed tension ease around the room.

One by one, everyone said goodbye, but his father stayed behind. And when Lukas started to get up from the chair, he was at his side to help him back into bed.

His father cleared his throat. "Have I told you how proud I am of you?"

"Yep."

"Have I told you how much I love you?"

"Yep."

"You need a haircut."

"I think girls like it long."

"Oh fantastic… One more thing I have to worry about now," his father said with a frown.

Once alone, a mischievous grin slid across his face. He could just imagine how far that put his father over the edge. He had a way with girls and also with all the women who came into the bookshop. He'd give a dimpled grin, and they'd buy another book. Yep, he thought, I'm my father's son, all right.

Chapter 39

Four Weeks Later, May 19, 2006

Lukas hung up the phone on the antique secretary and walked over to his parents who sat close together on the leather couch. He sank into an armchair. "They're on the ground at Gatwick and heading for the estate." He met his father's smirk with one of his own.

"Everyone's okay?"

"Yep."

"Including the baby?"

"Yep."

"Can we have something other than one-word answers?"

He offered a shrug and blew out a long breath. "Dad, I've got an hour until the official end of my first day of being sixteen."

His mother shook her head. "Come midnight, your decision is strictly personal, Lu."

"I know, Mom. So tell him to stop with the worry." His father raised an eyebrow. "Dad, I'm not doing *nuts* over something that may or may not happen in sixty minutes."

"It will mean ten years of your life."

"Stop meddling, my love," she whispered in his father's ear.

Lukas sensed nothing about whether or not he'd be

called to the mystical mission. To him, fighting evil seemed more like a forever one—not just ten years as a Guardian of Souls. *Hell, I'm already mystical and a warrior. I can walk my own path.*

"You're lost in thought," his father stated.

That forced another shrug, and he changed the subject. "Jillian says hello."

"You text her every hour, it seems. Of course, I'm assuming emails, calls... How else do teenagers communicate these days?"

"She's good people, Dad. Miss Virelli said they'll be at the estate this summer. Did you invite them?"

"Absolutely, and that means two weeks of escapades in England, no doubt. Then Martine's coming to visit Celia right after they leave."

"Cool," Lukas said with a smirk. He paused before asking, "You okay, Mom?"

She smiled with a tilt of her head. "Yeah... Just a little tired lately."

"That was a great dinner. Thanks."

"It was my pleasure, Lu."

Everything's really good, he thought, a great family, super friends, and lots of love in this place. *But Mom looks off, and I don't want to say what I sense. She should go see Sister Maggie.* But his intuition told him that wasn't the kind of doctor she needed to see. She was throwing up a lot, and he totally knew how horrible it was to puke. The move to England was only a week away, but having Lucy and Sal take over the bookshop had relaxed her, at least a little. He smiled and kissed both of them good night, a ritual that came as natural as breathing.

No fears remained about his father's heartbeat

suddenly disappearing; no question about how much he was loved by two terrific parents, either. Whenever that old rage rumbled through him, his father addressed it immediately. Someday he'd learn to control it, at least he hoped.

Lukas Malone walked into his room confident his future held many possibilities…all of them good.

****

In the master bedroom, Michael kissed her. Alana sat entrenched in his embrace as he rested his head back against the Queen Anne chair with her on his lap.

"That was the most magnificent birthday dinner I have ever seen."

"It has a history."

"I want to hear every detail." He sealed her to his heart, their fingers laced together.

"Let me take you back to a certain September evening. I came home from school with Celia B., and Philip arrived after the Fordham football game. He was a college *senior*, you know."

"Um-hum," he sighed, resting his chin on top of her head.

"Mom and Dad had the living room decorated in pink and purple for my Sweet Sixteen. Tiny sweetheart roses everywhere… they even covered the old baby grand. Dad bought sixteen dozen from the florist wholesaler."

"And in the dining room, what awaited you, darlin'?"

"*More*," she stated full of drama. "Long-stem pink roses surrounded by tiny white orchids and gardenias, the most stunning centerpiece I have ever seen. Dad designed it himself. He had an artistic flare. At 5:47

p.m. *precisely,* Mom sat at the piano and played—"

"Blue Moon."

She kissed his cheek. "No. Happy Birthday."

"And then?"

"Celia B's parents arrived, plus more family friends. We had a fabulous dinner of—"

"Homemade Fettuccine Alfredo—and the birthday cake your mother baked just happened to be chocolate with raspberry mousse in the center."

"How *did* you know?" He hooked her chin and kissed her deeply, full of passionate devotion. "Lu deserves total happiness, Michael. Taking care of Jillian with a Guardian's tenacity, and in the kitchen, he said he couldn't wait for Martine to visit, after meeting her last month."

"Ah... the wild-child caught his eye. But will she tempt a young Guardian to test his sacred vow? I know what's on your mind, darlin'."

She left him, sat across from him and on the edge of the sleigh bed. "I *so* want to share my experience with him. He'll be—" She stopped talking, let out a sigh. "Who am I kidding? He's already a fearless mystical warrior. Celia said it before all this madness started. As he matures, he'll be one-of-a-kind."

"That's our boy." He added with unequivocal admiration, "Born in a deserted midtown alleyway at three seconds after midnight." Moving to the bed, he kissed her again and her hazel eyes glistened. "I'm worried about you, darlin'."

"So many years of fighting unnatural things... So much has happened this past year. All the worry. All the changes. I'm just tired."

"Shhh, Alana—"

"What if he *does* accept the mission and some unforeseen evil takes him from us? We have to be prepared if he says yes, Michael." She swiped her eyes. When they curled on the bed together, he tucked her to his chest.

"I'm sorry," she whispered, "I'm just tired, really like exhausted."

Her insecurity, very unusual for the woman she had become, took hold so quickly that he continued to study her. Alana's strength had never wavered. *Tomorrow, I'll insist she see Arthur Chamberlain. Without a doubt, whether she bickers or not, I will get her there.*

He pulled her close. She cleaved to the curve of his body, a perfect fit. "A kiss for your thoughts, darlin'… Where are you?"

"Right here at your side, forever and always."

Michael unfastened the buttons of his black silk shirt, the one Alana wore every night. Running his hand down her supple curves, he called her to life, called her to him.

"I'd walk through the fires of Hell for you," he vowed. And holding his soulmate in a fierce embrace, he added with devotion, "My Guardian, my love."

A word about the author...

Always an avid reader, the realm of paranormal fiction continues to be the perfect landing point for M. Flagg. After a successful career as a music teacher and an urban school administrator, she continues to spin stories of passion, love and redemption. Besides being published in the genre of paranormal fiction, she has been a contributor in a book on urban music education and has also authored an article for Still Standing, a web-magazine about loss and healing. Her Action Research Project was recognized for Outstanding Writing in 2006 and she was named a Distinguished Music Educator at the Yale Music Symposium in 2010. A life-long New Jersey resident, M. Flagg is a member of Liberty States Fiction Writers and serves as a Professor in Residence at a local university.

www.ingramcontent.com/pod-product-compliance
Lightning Source LLC
Chambersburg PA
CBHW072256020726
47501CB00002B/290